The Embrace

A Living Art Series

Cara Anglin

C & J Garcia Publishing

Cover Illustration by Leslie Allen Fine Art

Cover formatting by Michi L Turner

ISBN-13: 978-0692478363 (Custom)

ISBN-10: 0692478361

I dedicate this with heartfelt thanks to amazing

friends from RCH, my wonderful family, and most

of all, to my husband Jerry. Your love makes

everything possible and I'm grateful for every

moment that we're together.

Chapter 1

Noon threatened another small victory for Miranda Cova, who battled an invisible affliction as she tried to focus on the sounds of the distant surf. Unable to will her fingers to release their grasp of the door's heavy frame, she stood at her entryway and once again suffered through heart-pounding anxiety. In the last week alone she had managed to successfully breach the safety of her bungalow three times. It had been a personal best; she had only made it four times in the whole of last month.

Opening the front door was always the hardest part; first came the rapid pulse followed quickly thereafter by the complete absence of any moisture in her mouth. A diffuse rigidity found her muscles and every aspect of her body seemed to detach from the rest somehow. Miranda imagined that it must be how death feels, if one could actually feel being dead. It was a thought that brought both comfort and distress. Death would mean that it was finally over. The loneliness, the anger, and the gut-wrenching fear would all be gone.

And while Miranda did not want to die, she didn't want to feel only partially alive anymore either. Perhaps, she imagined, that was why her journeys always led her to the sea. She could see herself sitting in front of the ocean, every sense captivated by the power of its energy. Using that memory she once again she relied on the weapon she had wielded since her childhood.

Miranda wrapped her trembling fingers around the frigid door handle, aware of the fact that soon a terrible cascade of symptoms would begin. Closing her eyes tightly she conjured memories of her favorite cove… the smells, the fickle breeze that would briefly visit then hastily retreat, the rush of the tide. She let the images wash over her, filling her. The goal was to detach; to use the strength of nature to make herself temporarily powerful enough to turn the handle. When she opened her eyes she realized that the warmth on her face was not imagined. She was out.

Miranda forced her eyes to the ground. Once, she had made the mistake of glancing out over her surroundings and found herself back in her room before she knew what had happened. Setting a moderate pace she began the short walk to the beach. Delicious smells emanating from a local bistro invaded her nostrils, making her stomach dance. Keeping her gaze limited to her footsteps she imagined dining there. She could see herself happy and healthy; maybe even with someone. That was a good sign apparently.

Dr. Bales had told her that it meant she was progressing, if at times merely subconsciously, toward a real life. Of course he had called it a "harmonious existence" but that was how every therapist spoke. It was as if they had all taken the same yoga class. Childishly encouraging as his words may have been, they did bring her comfort. He had asked her about the nightmares. Though they were still in full force, she couldn't help but focus on her first pleasant dream in... she refused to continue the calculation. It had been a long time.

During their session she described her future smile and the heaviness no longer present in her eyes. She could hear her own laugh. It was beyond surreal. She decided it was not a memory of laughing because she hadn't done that since she was in elementary school. This was a grown up laugh and it sounded good. That was when the doctor made the "harmonious existence" comment.

His prediction gave her a considerable amount of hope. She had been through nearly ten years of therapy and though he often told her he believed in her recovery, he had never actually said anything like that before. The next day she made her first self-directed journey out of the house in more than a decade. That was six months ago and her progress, while discouragingly slow at times, was still remarkable according to the good doctor.

As the aromas of the bistro gradually evaporated Miranda decided that while she may not be ready to dine there, she could order lunch to go soon. Maybe in a month. No, that would be too soon; perhaps three. She realized that a goal needed to be set. Three months... final decision. She would call from home and place the order. She could pick it up and pay without looking at anyone. They would see her but as long as she didn't look directly at them she should be alright.

Imagining the interaction she felt her heart rate quicken, and considered adding a clause to the goal just in case she wasn't ready. The deliberation brought with it internal admonishment and she cursed herself for being so cowardly. Her own vision of her happy, healthy future-self was not of a forty-year-old and Miranda knew that if she didn't pick up the pace of her recovery she would never see the woman as she imagined in her good dream; a woman only slightly older than her current age of twenty seven.

The beginning of a smile toyed with the corners of her lips, rescuing her doleful expression. She could see her future-self; wavy blonde hair brushing against tanned shoulders. It occurred to her that her shoulders were actually showing in the fantasy. The idea was intimidating, though her future-self seemed completely at ease. She relaxed, her thoughts returning to the image. Her 5'10" frame was no longer anorexic, but strong and balanced. The gaunt, petrified, reclusive body that she had been trapped inside was a thing of the past. Thick garments did not drape over her, masking her from the world. Her hands did not tremble. She was beautiful.

Miranda stopped, taken by her own persona until the honk of a car horn propelled her awareness back to the reality of her pallid frame. She looked down at her fingers and noted their unintentional vibrations. The thought of still hands was enviable as hers always shook; except for when she was painting. She was different when she painted. It may not seem the case to someone watching, but it was true. It was the only activity which made her feel a hint of the confidence and peace her future-self seemed to experience perpetually.

She decided that when she returned home she would go about giving life to the woman inside her mind; she would create a portrait of her future-self. The decision gave her strength; that and the tantalizing, misty beach air signaling the proximity of her favorite spot. She crossed the busy street, concentrating on the now sandy concrete below her feet, instead of perseverating on the intimidating crowd.

Miranda felt the road dissolve into soft granules; she was almost there. A surge of relief came over her just in time to be inexplicably displaced by uneasiness. In what was becoming a common occurrence, Miranda suddenly had the unmistakable and seemingly random sensation that someone was watching. Standing still she focused on her breathing. Her impulse was to search the throngs of beachgoers with her eyes, but she knew that such a decision would end poorly. The anxiety would surely warp her perceptions and could easily lead to a fierce panic attack, ultimately negating weeks of progress.

She turned toward the ocean, forcing her eyes to lock onto the glistening water. How many times had she felt the same eerie sensation? Too many to count, she reminded herself. It was an "unfortunate side effect of the trauma" according to Dr. Bales. It didn't have to control her life and she didn't need to give it her attention. No one was watching. Miranda closed her eyes and took a deep breath before heading to the cove.

Having lost sight of her, the figure across the street seemed to contemplate closing the gap between them. After a moment of hesitation the figure dissolved into the crowd.

Maxwell Turner inhaled happily as he stepped out onto Pacific Coast Highway from his nearby home. He realized how prosaic it seemed; indulging in a lungful of ocean air while forming a content smile. Still, he didn't let it hamper the moment. He lived in Laguna Beach, California. The physical beauty of the city was comparable to the Amalfi Coast. Impossibly charming coastal homes dressed sloped hillsides. Along the highway which was little more than a large main street, a plethora of wonderful shops nested. While it possessed all of the predictable components of a Southern California beach city, Laguna was uniquely "artsy." Max hated that word, but found it the most succinct description.

Laguna was truly an artist's town; both for those who created it and for those who appreciated it. And though he was native to this place, a real rarity, he did his best to avoid taking it for granted. Every morning he maneuvered his car down the windy road leading from his clifftop home, only to park in a public garage, foregoing a tram and walking the remaining ten blocks to work. This ritual originated from a commitment to appreciate every enchanting detail of the city, but quickly proved practical, especially during tourist season when traffic was at its worst. His employees often asked him if he walked for health reasons. Tempting as it was to be perceived as athletic, he always admitted that it was simply gratifying.

While the entire walk was ripe with beauty, his favorite stretch allowed him to peruse a row of art galleries. He loved watching proud owners nervously overseeing the delivery of new pieces; loved peering into the dark studios only to fall for a fresh perspective or classic interpretation. His strolls were at times inspiring, and at other times cleansing. Once in a while they led to uncomfortable reflection. There were mornings when seeing a couple kissing on the street seemed so uncomplicated and pure that Max wondered how long his relationship with Christy might last.

Christy was strikingly attractive, quite intelligent, and certainly a good person. There was nothing tangible about the disconnect he felt when regarding their future. She did have some erratic emotions regarding her father, but Max tried not to count that against her. His best intentions aside, he couldn't help the fact that that "Daddy issues" popped into his head when weighing their relationship's pros against cons. Max noticed that a pang of guilt always followed the tally.

Arriving to work Max looked upon the entrance of the amphitheater and fairgrounds with youthful wonderment. The Exhibition of Living Arts, an off-shoot of the legendary Pageant of the Masters, was now in its twenty-first year. Creative excitement fused with the comforts of home each time he gazed upon the structures which housed the summer show modeled after the very one he'd watched throughout his childhood. Max often smiled as he reminded himself that he was now the director. He had been fascinated by art since before he could speak. His parents routinely chronicled stories of his youth, boasting about their one-year-old who couldn't take his eyes off a painting by Henry Darger, a relatively unappreciated Dutch neo-classicist. Max dreamed of his own future creations. He would lose hours imagining how fulfilling it would be to share his visions with the world. His parents, happy to encourage his artistic tendencies, eagerly enrolled him in a variety of classes.

Years passed and dozens of courses left Max angry and confused. By the time he was a teenager he had grown very aware that his desire far exceeded his abilities. It seemed that no amount of training could connect his eyes to his hands. The first time he saw the movie Amadeus he cried himself to sleep. He spent the better part of a year working through the disappointment, knowing that he was vastly more similar to Salieri than to Mozart. To his credit, his parents reminded him, he did not let jealousy and bitterness dictate his fate. An art major he would still be, if sadly academic as opposed to practical.

Max squelched vestigial lament as he entered the festival grounds. He let his eyes fall along the barren exhibit areas that, in a few short months, would display works from well over a hundred California artists. The excitement of thousands of patrons eagerly examining sculptures, paintings and even jewelry filled him with delight. Invigorated, he made his way toward the exhibition's office area. Entering the research suites Max pretended not to notice the attention he received from women. He was once told he had the build of a robust man with the complexion of a young girl. That seemed like an oxymoron to him, but it was suggested that he take it as a compliment and Max decided not to argue. A secretary straightened her pony tail as she noticed his approach.

"Good morning Mister Turner. Katherine and Marcia are ready for you in the conference room."

Max huffed at the young woman, stopping in front of her desk. "It's nice that they warrant a first name basis though it hardly seems fair," he said with a grin.

The secretary smiled back, blushing with her eyes. "Sorry Max," she squirmed, as if still not comfortable with the informality.

"We'll get there… Noreen," Max emphasized before heading toward the conference room.

Inside the large space Katherine and Marcia sprang from casual to professional as their boss entered. Katherine put her coffee mug on the round table and grabbed her cell phone, reviewing her electronic notes as if for one final time.

"Morning Max," she offered matter-of-factly as Marcia opened her laptop.

"Ladies," Max greeted. "How's the new kitchen?"

Marcia seemed to ease slightly. "It's so posh. You'll have to come by next week."

"Definitely," Max agreed as he removed his brown-framed eye glasses, cleaning the lenses. As he repositioned them Katherine noticed how his eye color seemed to change depending on the hues surrounding them. Without the frames his eyes were a marbled brown, but against them, flecks of green stood out. His commanding features were cushioned by an unusually creamy complexion for a man, partnered by florid cheeks. His wavy brown hair, streaked with caramel highlights, was just long enough to allow for an occasional loose strand to brush against his lenses. Watching him for a few seconds made Katherine imagine what a beautiful woman he would have made.

Marcia appeared impatient when she cleared her throat though, to Katherine's relief, she appeared unaware of her partner's momentary fascination with their boss and friend. She clicked the mouse and looked up at the 42 inch flat screen mounted on the wall. A photograph of a painting appeared; a couple on a rooftop terrace, backlit against the amber city beyond. Max studied the piece as Katherine read from her notes.

"Le Soleil De Mes Nuits. Offset lithograph from Canadian artist Denis Nolet."

Marcia glanced at Katherine whose concentrated tone and consummate professionalism unfairly concealed her affection for the piece.

"He specializes in urban scenes, many of them inspired by the landscape of his hometown, Quebec. I thought it might be good for one of the nook pieces."

"Nice, let's definitely consider it," Max agreed with a polite smile.

The image on the screen changed. The next photograph featured a well-dressed couple enjoying the beauty of nature as they gazed amorously toward each other. Marcia, emotional and earthy, described her pick with contagious enthusiasm.

"The Pride of Dijon; one of many classical, romantic oils by Irish painter and noted pre-Raphaelite, William John Hennessey. The scene portrays a discussion between lovers in an exquisite garden setting."

Marcia took on a gracious smile as Max offered her a boyish grin.

"I love this one. Add it to the list," he instructed.

Marcia shot her partner a playful *I told you so* forcing Katherine to cover her lips with the back of her hand to avoid breaking character with laughter.

The screen changed to reveal a scene illustrating a group of children in period dress, partnered and dancing in a large ballroom. Katherine reclaimed her focus.

"May I Have This Dance; an Oil-on-canvas from late Victorian master Alexander M. Rossi. It's a beautiful piece featuring one of the more popular subjects of the era."

Katherine studied Max as he examined her submission.

"The casting may be too ambitious. So many kids… Let's keep it as a maybe."

Both women seemed to know instantly that Max was not interested though they were clearly appreciative of his genteel pass.

The screen changed to the photograph of a gold statue featuring a nude man and woman. The female subject stood with her back against her partner's chest. His arms were wrapped around her, his hands partially covering the woman's breasts and the apex of her thighs. Max could barely hear Marcia's description as he focused on the image.

"The Embrace; a solid gold sculpture from the late Hellenistic Period by an unknown Greek artist. The couple is thought to be Galen and Isaura," Marcia continued, her gift for storytelling evident. "Not much is known about them, but some legends refer to a tragedy that struck Isaura at a young age, something that left her unable to have, well... sex. Apparently Galen refused to leave her, and his embrace is supposed to represent his love, protection and loyalty despite her handicap."

Max, totally riveted, was unable to take his eyes off the piece. Marcia again toyed with Katherine, smiling subtly at her as if confident she was winning a covert contest between them.

"You just found our finale," he replied. Max paused as he let the story sink in, his good looks enhanced by an optimistic stare. "I can't wait to show Christy."

Chapter 2

The next evening, outside a modest Orange County home, Max struggled to unlock his car door while holding up his inebriated girlfriend. Just as he opened the passenger side he heard Christy wretch, her body lunging forward. He reflexively supported her at the waist, vomit splashing all over his shoes.

"Oh God," Christy lamented.

"Yeah," Max replied as he closed his eyes, disappointment depleting his expression. He looked up, hoping for her sake that her father wasn't still watching from the front door. The older man, back lit by his porch light, offered an apathetic wave before retreating into his home. Max winced as the front door closed and the porch light snapped off, signaling a frosty goodbye. Emotionally exhausted, Max helped Christy into the car. He stared at her for a moment, pity not outweighing his sense of resignation. There were things that he would miss about Christy. Daddy issues, however, would not be making the increasingly short list.

Max drove in silence and earnestly hoped she would remain asleep until they reached her home. He internally cursed at each street light that interrupted the cabin's darkness, shooting strobes of illumination into the vehicle just long intermittently enough to disturb his passenger's fragile slumber. He was tempted to breach the speed limit, but forced himself to be patient.

Once inside her home Max dispassionately tucked Christy into bed. Though he had contemplated undressing her first, and would have on any prior night, he feared the gesture may confuse the situation. *Situation*; he mused at the benign word he had assigned. Breakup; that's what this really was. As if reading his thoughts, Christy stirred. Max, his steps as delicate as he could make them, ambled toward the door leading out of her room. Christy opened her eyes, sadness filling them as she examined his posturing.

"I'm sorry," her voice slurred. "Really sorry," she pushed, her voice growing louder. Obviously aware of his skepticism, a twinge of anger clouded her expression. "It's not like I did this on purpose."

"Get some sleep," he droned, staring at her night stand in an effort to avoid eye contact.

Christy jolted out of bed, her eyes narrowing as she looked at him.

"I apologized. I feel like an idiot, okay? What more do you want me to say?"

Max shook his head, unwilling to entertain an argument. "You don't have to say anything."

He again headed toward the door.

"So that's it? We're done, aren't we?"

Max turned, searching for a pain-free resolution.

"It was a mistake. People make them," Christy hissed and tried to avoid stumbling over her own feet.

Max studied the floorboards as he waited for the fight to end. "I'm aware of that."

"Are you? Because it seems to me you have a real problem with mistakes of any kind."

He looked up at her, wounded by the harsh comment. "That's not true."

"Oh spare me, Max. We both know that this was destined to end. I'm human, after all," she lashed out, her tone reeking of sarcasm.

"Stop."

"Why, because I'm wrong?"

Max contemplated the accusation before turning and walking down the hall toward the front door.

Christy shouted as she ran to catch up with him.

"God luck, Max! Let me know when you've found the ideal combination of flawless and perfect! I can't wait to meet her!"

She slammed the front door, bracing her back against it before bursting into tears.

Outside, Max entered his vehicle and closed the car door. He glanced at Christy's home, his eyes revealing uncertainty. He reached into his glove box and pulled out a photograph of The Embrace statue, disappointed that he never got the opportunity to show it to her. Examining the image he wondered if Christy was right. Maybe he was being too hard on her and his expectations were unrealistic. No, he thought. After all, he wasn't looking for perfection... not actual perfection.

On the drive home Max's thoughts jumped from Christy's hurtful words to his internal defense of them. He'd been accused of this before, yet he still didn't find it fair. Once he had taken a woman to a museum. They had been dating for two years and Max knew that he should have felt rather endeared to her after so much time. As they strolled through the gallery Max's eyes came to rest on a portrait of a woman staring into her lover's eyes. He was immediately taken by the piece, his enjoyment interrupted by his perturbed date. She had interjected an unexpected barb about his alleged need for perfection; something about the way he looked at art. She had angrily admitted that he'd never looked at her in such a fashion, and was sorry that she was a 'real person rather than some six hundred year old dried paint'. The blast had ended what Max considered a mediocre relationship at best.

Making his way up the winding road leading to his home, a feeling of loneliness crept over Max. At first he was annoyed by the unwelcome and highly unusual emotion. Annoyance turned to curiosity as he glanced at the image of his now favorite gold sculpture, the photo innocently gracing the passenger seat. Max pulled into his driveway and turned off the motor. Sitting in silence he picked up the photograph, analyzing it again. Why on earth was it so mesmerizing? And why did looking upon it fill him with a hybrid of sadness and warmth? It didn't make any sense. Max dropped the photograph back onto the passenger seat before getting out of the car.

Having totally captured the encouraging smile of her future-self, Miranda examined her portrait and made an awkward face as she tried to mimic the grin. Placing her palette on the ground Miranda slowly surveyed her home. She looked at the large velvet curtains protecting her from the world just beyond the glass. It always distressed her to imagine what would happen if all the curtains were gone. So many windows… and so large. She had argued fiercely with Claire when they were contemplating the home's purchase. It turns out, however, that finding a home in Laguna Beach without breathtakingly expansive views was next to impossible.

In the end the home's location was the lesser of several evils. It was close to Claire's gallery, so strange men showing up to gather completed pieces wouldn't be necessary. Claire had promised that she would pick them up every time. Alone. It was much easier for Claire to stop in during lunch and check on her friend as well. The home was also was close to

Dr. Bale's office and residence. That too was a necessity. Happily, a grocery store that delivered was well within range. And of course the entire neighborhood was privy to a profound ocean breeze, which was supposed to reduce anxiety, however negligible the effects during the first several years of home ownership had been.

Miranda looked at one of the curtains toward the back of the den-turned art studio. She concentrated on remembering what was on the opposing side. Was it exposed? Could someone just stand there looking in? She recalled the barren back yard as it was when she purchased the home, her nervousness growing. Cautiously she peeled back a small section of the fabric and peered at the comforting foliage beyond the glass. Oversized leaves provided assurance that her refusal to hire gardeners had served several purposes. Inhaling slowly, she eased open a breach between the pair of curtains before nervously parting them. She created a foot-length gap, forcing her breathing to remain unlabored as she slid the lower sash upward, opening the window.

A sudden gust of coastal wind bent the leaves toward her dramatically, causing Miranda to jump. She grunted in frustration at her overreaction, pulling hard on the curtains. The massive drapes spiraled to the floor, taking down the curtain rod with them. Miranda leapt out of the way as the metal struck the ground with thunderous force. *There, you see? That's what you get if you can't keep it together.* Startled by the voice that had scolded her, Miranda quickly scanned the room to find no one. She hadn't heard the voice of the angry one in years. Certain that she was alone her memory flashed to her twelve-year-old reflection; hair cropped at the ears, her cadaverous eyes peering back at her from the mirror in her friend's bathroom. *That's what you get!*

Inside the reassuring office of Dr. Marcus Bales, Miranda shared her concerns. Dr. Bales, now more a friend than a clinician, smiled at her.

"No, you do not have multiple personality disorder," he gently chuckled.

Miranda struggled to speak out loud; something that she so seldom attempted, her own voice sounded foreign. "I don't?"

"Absolutely not. We all have internal dialogue. Yours has simply undergone a bit of a metamorphosis."

"Why?"

"I think you know. Your recent progress of venturing out, your images of the future you, the self-portrait."

Dr. Bales leaned in toward the uncertain woman. "You are actively evolving into the person you are going to become. And yesterday you heard the voice of your own frustration; the one that drives you to push yourself."

"She pulled the curtain down," Miranda offered.

"You pulled the curtain down. You remember doing it, don't you?"

Miranda nodded as she recalled the feeling of velvet inside her tremulous grasp. "It was a punishment," she admitted.

Dr. Bales shook his head. "This was not a penalty, it was a challenge. Obviously you have two personas right now, one that is fearful and one that is brave, to put it simply. But they are both you, and they are not independent of one another."

Trying to get her mind around the explanation, Miranda looked at her misshapen image, which was reflected against the glass side table.

Sitting at his desk, Max finished recounting the painful events of the prior night as Marcia and Katherine listened.

"Way to meet the parents," Marcia quipped.

Max shook his head. "Yeah, lots of fun," he answered ironically as Sally, the show's frenetic costume designer, exploded into the office.

"Max, do I have to buy stock in acid reflux manufacturers? Where are my photographs?" she demanded.

"Relax, Sally. I have them right here as promised." He handed her a large envelope.

"As promised two days ago," she jabbed before hurrying out of the office.

Katherine smirked as Max closed his eyes and smiled. "Hell hath no fury," she concluded, making him chuckle.

Though directing a project as monumental as the Exhibition of Living Arts always made weeks seem like days, the last three months had elapsed even more quickly than they typically did for Max. Perhaps it was the relief he felt after his relationship with Christy had ended. Whatever it was, it was as unnerving as it was exhilarating. Max adored this time of year. The research was finished and the sets were nearly constructed. Soon, casting calls would go out over local radio stations. Winter had given way to spring, though the city had barely changed as a result. It was still bright and sunny; still awash with activity.

The exterior of the exhibition appeared modest in the early morning hours. Already blissful from his walk to work, Max felt somewhat euphoric as he passed through the theater entrance and emerged inside the amphitheater. Behind him, as if aware of its own potential, the stage and orchestra pit seemed to yearn for opening night. Max forced away just enough excitement to allow for his own productivity. *Best job ever,* he reminded himself.

Max watched in delight as one of the set artists, his clothes and hands sullied with plaster, approached from behind the stage.

"Hey Max, just finished the Cupid and Psyche piece. We're starting on The Embrace platform next."

Max beamed at the thought, and realized they were close to completing the sets. What a finale The Embrace would be, he imagined.

"Fantastic. I'll check on Sal." Before Max could turn, Sally hurried out from the stage's wings and bolted toward him.

"I heard that," she exclaimed.

Max cringed, realizing his mistake as Sally frantically measured a six-by-six reproduction of Psyche Revived by Cupid's Kiss, a stark white statue of a winged cupid enveloping his lover.

"Don't rush me, Maxwell. I'm working as fast as I can," she rebuked.

Max marveled at the reproduction as Sally, without looking at him, went about her work.

"I'm not rushing you, I was just hoping to put out the casting call," Max said, his eyes glued to the statue.

While he was used to being impressed by his artists, occasionally their accomplishments exceeded even his high expectations. This was one of those moments. He ran his hand along the crest of Cupid's wings, noting with astonishment how true to life it seemed. The surface was as smooth as skin, and he could almost swear it was carved out of the same marble used in the original piece. Sally looked over, smacking him away from the reproduction.

"Hands off, Mister," she snapped.

"Sorry," Max half whispered as he continued to peer at the piece in wonder.

"You can speak to my assistant about the ones that are finished, but I won't have final measurements until Friday. Got that? Friday," she warned.

A smile played across his face. "Friday's perfect."

"You're a real slave driver, Max."

He laughed at the agitated designer as Katherine approached. She looked pleased to see his lively expression.

"I take it everything's on track?"

Max nodded. "Air the ad," he instructed happily before walking off stage.

Katherine grinned as she watched Sally shaking her head, obviously exasperated by Max's child-like persistence.

Sitting at her desk, Claire Simmons listened to classical music while typing at her computer. Having spent her youth being described as lanky, Claire had grown quite comfortable being tall and thin. She was an elegant late-thirties, the owner of a popular art gallery and had an excellent reputation in the community. She sometimes wondered how it was that she was still single, eager as she was to share her rather enviable life.

Her mother, a jewelry maker, always reminded her that she was too serious. She would go on and on about how "you have to take risks if you want great experiences". Claire sometimes had to physically cover her own mouth with her index finger to avoid snapping back about her disinterest in smoking ten bowls of pot a day out of assorted, albeit creative, bongs. She swore if it wasn't integral to her jewelry making she would shatter the free-spirited senior's glass blowing tubes. Still, the older woman had a point. Claire did tend to play it safe in life. As if cosmically preordained, she froze as she heard the radio announcing an opportunity she had long considered.

"The famed Exhibition of Living Arts has once again opened its doors for volunteers who are interested in being a part of the magical beauty that is the yearly show. Anyone interested in becoming a part of the Living Arts cast for this season is encouraged to call 1-800-L-I-V-A-R-T-S for more information. The Exhibition of Living Arts; see the show, be the show." The announcement ended as Claire jotted down the number.

Chapter 3

The exhibition, thriving in its third decade, was more than a city treasure. It had gained international notoriety and was one of the only Tableau Vivant, or living picture, performances of its size, boasting twenty different tableaus. The show ran from eight to ten thirty each evening for eight weeks straight. During those weeks Max's research team worked by day in their offices, made it home by four pm, enjoyed a three-hour rest, then headed back to the festival grounds to oversee the show. And while it made for a hectic summer, it was well worth the effort.

Max nervously started his car. Opening night was always emotional whiplash for his team. Soon his quiet amphitheater would be packed with art patrons from around the country. Katherine and Marcia would do their part to assure the show would run as smoothly as possible, but ultimately it would be his burden. He parked and walked quickly toward the main entrance.

Max hurried past the festival grounds and through an inconspicuous door leading to a serene outdoor space, an area commonly referred to as the talent garden. Models of various ages and sizes were arriving and checking in with Frankie, the casting coordinator who sat at a small desk at the mouth of the doorway. Max waved upon seeing her, comforted by her presence. Having been with the show since its doors first opened, Frankie was exuberant and eclectic in addition to being unusually dedicated. With wild hair and an unforgettable laugh, she made sixty look like a pretty great time. Max approached and gave her a jittery smile.

She met his eyes with a maternal gaze. "Pins and needles?"

"I've been worse," he confessed, doing his best to charm away his nerves.

"Oh Maxy, when are you going to learn that opening night is something to enjoy, not something to fret?"

"Once I find a way to conjure even a tenth of your spirit, I suppose. Any no-shows?"

"Nope, casting is a go," she proudly reported.

Max nodded, grateful for one less concern. He hurried to the sliding glass doors leading to the casting design suites. Once inside, he weaved his way through a current of performers, stage hands, and musicians, all eager to reach their various destinations. Passing the makeup room he waved to his lead artist Annie, as she coated a young face in beige foundation. Seeing her smiling back it occurred to Max that this show, this entire enterprise, would be a hundred times more difficult and a thousand times less enjoyable if not for the happy faces of that staff that had become like family. He smiled to himself before dashing onto the stage, the audience beyond it concealed by a large curtain.

Wasting no time a designer dressed in all black handed him a photograph of a painting, then pointed to the life-sized version of the same piece. Max approached the reproduction, studying the massive backdrop while comparing it to the photograph. While amazingly accurate, the facsimile seemed rather unimpressive in the dim stage corner, the ten-by-ten-foot canvas featuring nothing more than a quaint beach backdrop.

Two young children, their hair, makeup and clothing carefully designed to replicate the subjects of Pino's Golden Afternoon, were assisted into place against the canvas. Sally performed last minute touchups on the children's makeup. Katherine joined the group, examining the piece as a woman, also in full dress, completed the ensemble. The well-rehearsed children reached for her hand and the three subjects froze, demonstrating their final pose against the backdrop.

"I think her left hand needs to be a little lower," Max whispered.

Another designer adjusted the woman's arm as Max gave a thumbs up, his concentration broken as Marcia hurried toward him, her haggard face overcome with concern.

"Our female nude for The Embrace piece broke her arm. She tripped in the talent garden just before the show started."

Max pulled her aside and spoke in a hushed voice. "Is she alright?"

"She's out for the whole summer."

Max closed his eyes, running his hand through his hair. "We've got two hours until the finale. Call her stand in."

"She didn't have one."

"How is that possible?" he questioned, unable to combat the annoyance from his tone.

"Max, the woman's nearly six feet tall and weighs one-hundred-and-thirty pounds. Not the easiest measurements to come by, even in this city."

"What are we…" Max lost his train of thought as he studied Katherine, cognizant of her exceptional frame for the first time.

Katherine's eyes darted around and she swatted Max.

"Don't you look at me," she warned.

Max turned, doing his best to keep remain calm. "Find someone... anyone. Just make sure she's tall."

Marcia and Katherine glanced skeptically at one another as they descended the backstage staircase.

Gentle Laguna winds skimmed the occupants of the open-air amphitheater. Less than a handful of seats remained vacant, which was remarkable given the nearly three-thousand person capacity. At his backstage post, Max observed one of several video screens. While it magnified his nerves, he could never resist observing the behavior of the audience, especially on the first night of the season. He watched as art patrons of all ages and backgrounds chatted with each other, clearly eager for the show to begin. He let his eyes close, taking in the familiar sounds of instruments being tuned against the collective hum of his guests' banter.

Three bell tolls, along with the flickering of even the scant back stage lights, boded the show's commencement. From the auditorium a sea of voices intensified for a fraction of a second, only to rapidly diminish. Max took an anxious breath as orchestra members positioned their instruments. The conductor swiftly situated himself at his podium. Max glanced at the video screen featuring the Master of Ceremonies. As if the older man could sense Max's watchful eye, he nodded before adjusting his headphone and speaking into a large microphone.

"Ladies and gentlemen, thank you all for joining us this evening. The Exhibition of Living Arts proudly presents tonight's celebration: A History of Romance."

Applause swept over the auditorium as cheerful orchestral music competed for perceptibility. A wide smile came over Max and he was certain his heart beat danced in rhythm with the orchestra for at least a few measures. As the clapping slowed and the music grew faint, the MC's voice boomed over the arena.

"Love; an emotion so powerful, lives have been sacrificed on its behalf. A feeling so universal, there exists no culture on the Earth which has failed to give it a name. A need so undeniable, people have perished due merely to its absence."

Inside a sound booth situated at the back of the auditorium, the MC continued to read from his script.

"Tonight, you will be taken on a magical journey through some of the art born of this timeless phenomenon."

From the orchestra pit housed just below the stage, musicians performed a spirited overture. Backstage, Max watched as three cast members, a man, woman and child, posed against a dark canvas. Stage hands, all dressed in black, rushed to frame the piece with a massive wooden border. In the darkness the living pictures were creepy and almost cartoonish, Max noted. There was something disturbing about coarsely painted models sitting motionless against obscure backdrops.

Amazing what lighting can do, Max said to himself. As if on mental cue from the director, the large curtains parted and stage lamps burned, revealing a stunning recreation. Gasps from the audience drowned out the MC's oration.

"French Neoclassicism painter Jacques-Louis David brilliantly captured the reverie of love in his magnificent piece, Sappho and Phaon. Greek mythology tells the story of Sappho, the love-struck poetess, and of her adoration for the breathtaking Phaon. The renowned oil on canvas was originally commissioned by Count Nikolai Yusupov, and it's easy to see why. This masterpiece begins our look at lovers throughout the ages, and how the magnificence of love has forever touched art."

The formerly drab depiction seemed to animate under the glow of the stage lamps. The models, their makeup once vulgar, had been transformed into stupefying replications of the painting's original subjects. Max gazed at the audience, energized by their reactions. Most guests exhibited a homogeny of disbelief and fascination. Max enjoyed watching them, aware of their tendency to study his models for signs of life. He knew from personal experience that even the smallest of movements would delight viewers greatly, and remembered watching the show as a child, praying that a model would sneeze or cough.

Without warning his thoughts went to Christy's painful criticisms. She assumed that he considered art to be flawless. Not so, he thought to himself now. It is inanimate and therefore imperfect. His contribution to the world was to assist in bringing art to life; giving it shape and dimension. And nothing brought him as much joy as seeing his contribution come to life each season.

Miranda paced in her living room, agitation dictating her movements. Everything had been fine… she had met her goal of getting lunch to go. She had interacted with the waiter sufficiently, avoiding eye contact and unnecessary communication of course, and had even removed another curtain from one of her windows. It was unfair that some stranger, some completely inconsequential person who just happened to look like *him* could rob her of her progress. It wasn't right. She had lost nearly three weeks due to the latest relapse.

The child with the cropped hair and dead eyes was angry. Very angry. Miranda tried to think of a gesture she could offer, some fitting punishment that would satisfy the scorned girl. Though she tried hard the only thing that came to mind was... She jumped when the phone rang, wondering if it was Claire again. She forced the thought from her consciousness, hopeful that if she stopped thinking about her friend, the angry one would not consider the potential punishment; the one that made Miranda shudder. Letting the call go to her answering machine she listened to the generic electronic greeting followed by an unwelcome voice.

"Miranda, it's Mom. I just wanted to wish you a happy birthday. You're a special, talented, beautiful person. I love you very much. Please call me. I want to be here for you. I want to be a part of your life." A choked sob and dial tone followed.

Miranda could feel a stinging in her eyes and fought the impulse to cry. Her fleeting sadness was expelled by anger which arose from a now familiar place. The cold child's eyes stared at her inside her mind. She trembled, no longer able to deny the penalty she feared was now unavoidable.

Backstage, Katherine and Marcia faced their troubled boss.

"We have to make a decision," Katherine admitted, unable to look at Max.

"Cancelling The Embrace is not an option. Okay, find the script writer. Have him exclude the heroine. He can make up something existential, or rename the statue Narcissus: An Image of Self-Love. That still works," Max stammered.

28

Before he could respond to Marcia's uncertain expression, Sally ran up to them.

"Max, we have a five-year-old with a makeup allergy."

Sally hurried toward the makeup room, Max urgently following.

An hour had passed since they'd learned of the accident. Katherine chewed her lip and looked at her watch as Jonah emerged from the makeup room. The six-foot-four, muscle-clad Adonis, wearing only a loin cloth and a layer of gold spray paint, seemed to add to her nerves. She quickly explained the feeble new plan. Max approached as Jonah made his first objection.

"So, I'm supposed just stand there holding nothing?"

Max reached out to put his hand on Jonah's shoulder, rethinking the idea as he saw the gold body spray.

"There isn't anything I can do on such short notice. We've already amended the script. Everything's going to be fine."

"But I'm going to look like an idiot."

"Are you kidding? Jonah, you'll look fantastic. Herculean."

Jonah studied him with uncertainty, but seemed to accept the compliment when Marcia, her timing impeccable, approached and nodded in agreement. Jonah walked away with an apparently healed self-concept, following two designers toward the stage door.

"Way to a man's heart?" Marcia questioned.

Max laughed. "Ego is a beautiful thing."

Katherine appeared impressed as she looked at her boss. "You seem to be handling this well."

"I'm actually quite petrified at the moment, but I'm glad it's not obvious."

"I'm sure everything will work out."

"Oh, yeah. The audience, under the impression that we're celebrating the rapture of love and seeing a naked Swede on a lone platform, will probably just think masturbation. Exactly the kind of subliminal thoughts I was hoping to conjure for our first show of the season," Max replied with feigned optimism.

Marcia frowned as if disturbed by an unwelcome image.

The stage lamps dimmed. Max, very aware that the finale was imminent, clenched his jaw.

Soft orchestral music played as the MC's voiced echoed over the amphitheater.

"One of the most compelling love stories in all of the world must be that of the romance between Isaura and her faithful partner Galen."

Max, Katherine and Marcia anxiously watched the monitor.

"He's going to look like an idiot," Max admitted.

The MC's voice continued. "Greek folklore describes a tragedy which befell the beautiful Isaura at a tender age; an event which, according to the legend, left her irrevocably tormented and unable to give herself to a man physically. Galen, smitten and unwilling to forsake his feelings for Isaura, tried for one hundred years to heal her invisible scars, but was unsuccessful. All that her injured spirit could allow, and therefore all that Galen could offer her was his promise of undying constancy and his eternal... embrace."

Max looked at his team in horror. "He didn't read the changes!"

"Oh God," Katherine uttered.

Max turned toward the monitors, scanning for the screen which he imagined would soon feature his

30

ruined finale piece and simultaneously end his tenure as director.

"Can you see anything?" Marcia inquired frantically.

"Just the forested platform. It's black as pitch without stage lighting." Max forced himself to take a few deep breaths as he studied the monitor.

A lone clearing on the forest bank above the theater seats seemed to ignite as a dozen lights focused their energy on the platform. Two motionless models stood atop the platform. Nude and painted in gold from head to toe, the virtually inanimate couple posed, replicating The Embrace statue perfectly. Gasps again filled the auditorium as audience members experienced the piece.

Dismayed, Max and his team stared at the monitor. Max dropped some of the tension in his shoulders.

"What the hell is going on? I thought our Isaura broke her arm."

"She did," Katherine confirmed. "I don't understand. Maybe Frankie got a last minute replacement."

Max again peered at the monitor, looking as closely as he could at the Isaura subject's face. A dulcet melody drifted from the orchestra pit, stretching out over amphitheater. His attention on the Isaura subject, Max nearly forgot the second portion of the finale. The Embrace lights dimmed as the MC spoke again, his balmy voice complimentary to the music.

"Ah, the utter exhilaration of finding true love. In Plato's Symposium, Aristophanes describes love as the search for the other half of one's soul. Perhaps it was this belief which inspired Italian sculptor Antonio Canova to immortalize the tenderness and passion of Cupid and his beloved Psyche."

Another platform on the opposite forest bank slowly illuminated revealing a second motionless couple, their dress, makeup, and positioning perfectly mimicking the famous piece. The amphitheater erupted in applause and whistles.

Backstage the three watched the Isaura model via the monitors, their relief overt.

"I wonder who she is. The original cast member? Maybe her arm was just sprained," Marcia said.

"Whoever she is, she saved tonight. Don't let me forget to thank her." Katherine mentioned, studying the still Embrace subjects atop the dark platform.

"Thank her? I'm putting her in my will," Max joked.

Both platforms exploded with illumination, allowing the audience to view both The Embrace and the Cupid and Psyche pieces in unison as the orchestra played triumphantly.

Backstage the team celebrated as they heard the sounds of audience approval.

Staring at The Embrace, his fears allayed, Max smiled. "It really is a gorgeous sculpture."

"You've outdone yourself again," Katherine praised.

Their gaze on the monitors, they watched as the platform lights faded to black. Max stared at the darkened image of Jonah and the Isaura subject. Something was wrong. His eyes remained fixed on the mysterious woman when, to his shock, she leapt from the platform and scampered off into the forested hillside. Max jumped involuntarily, a genetic overreaction he hoped would go unnoticed by his friends.

"That's kind of odd," Katherine said. "Why didn't she wait for a designer to escort her down?"

They continued to watch as Jonah was guided off the platform by two set designers.

Max shook his head as he eyed the platform suspiciously. "I don't know."

The exhibition offices bustled with an energy that was impervious to the Mondays of the typical world, a benefit Max acknowledged with his quiet, nearly perpetual smile. Having thanked a generous benefactor profusely, he escorted the gentleman to the door and shook his hand.

"Thanks for all your help. Everything went very well."

As if fearful she might miss the chance, Katherine took the vacant spot at Max's side once the older man stepped outside.

"Max, I couldn't get a hold of Claire Simmons," she said, her face tense.

"Who?" he asked, trying to appear attentive despite his first care-free mood in weeks.

"The woman who was supposed to be our Isaura subject... Broken arm?" she reminded.

"Don't worry about it. I'm sure we can get this straightened out tonight." Seeing Marcia walking down the hall, Max yelled out to her as if unconcerned that she was in the middle of a phone call. "How's the kid with the hives?"

Covering the phone, Marcia answered before heading down the hall. "Milking it, but fine."

Max laughed as he stopped her, still reveling in post-opening-night afterglow. "I have a few notes for this evening's show. Let our tech crew know that someone's sporting tennies with fluorescent logos. And introduce our Cleopatra to some non-drowsy allergy tablets. Art isn't supposed to have a runny nose, especially two-thousand-year-old art."

"Will do." Marcia quelled, uncapping the phone and escaping into another office.

Max put his arm around Katherine. "Ready for another night of nail-biting uncertainty and nauseating adrenaline surges?"

"One show down," Katherine teased.

"And only fifty-nine more to go. It's very exciting," he added dryly.

Chapter 4

The second show of the season was already well underway when Katherine joined Max at the backstage monitors. Max concentrated on the screens, suppressing nerves born of anticipation. Next to The Embrace, this was his favorite piece. The Reveal Scene, the tableau's nickname, was as old as the show. Max and Marcia watched as faint outlines of the scene's frame came into view across the dark stage. Nondescript forms moved about the frame as the MC began his monologue.

"Have you ever wondered how the exhibition makes each recreation seem so realistic? Ladies and Gentlemen, it's time for our famous Reveal Scene. Using specialized red stage lights we will demonstrate all that goes in to making art come to life, so to speak."

The image of The Embrace cutting into Max's consciousness, Max turned to Marcia suddenly. "What ever happened with the Isaura subject?"

"Katherine's working on it. Everything will be fine," she reassured sheepishly, as if not so certain.

"Working on it?" he probed with his eyes.

Unsuccessfully dodging his stare Marcia bent her neck to the side and closed her eyes. "She didn't check in tonight."

"Again? We've got less than fifteen minutes," Max barked.

Marcia grabbed his arm before he could hurry away. "Please, stay here, Max. There's nothing you can do that Katherine can't handle."

"Maybe not but I'd handle it with a lot more spasticity," he half joked, hoping the weak stab at humor would be enough to ease his own tension.

"Exactly," Marcia nodded. "You're an amazing director; you're so passionate. But right now we need calm. Trust me?"

Max reluctantly accepted, forcing another deep breath. "I'm just going to look at this monitor." He focused on the screen, doing his best to maintain composure.

Marcia rubbed the back of her neck, her relief obvious. They watched the screen and saw two members of the technical crew, under a red glow, rolling out The Reveal backdrop and helping cast members into position. The red lights, barely illuminating the stage, casted a dullness over the three-dimensional scene. The audience watched in fascination as final adjustments were made to the scene and the MC narrated.

"Our crew begins by rolling the backdrop onto the stage. Next, our designers help position the cast members. A frame is snapped into place in front of the piece."

Studying the screen Max objected, "The second kid…"

"I see him," Marcia declared before hurrying toward the scene.

On the monitor, Max watched as she approached the frame and adjusted a child's leg.

She returned to Max's side as the MC continued. "Final places are confirmed by the backstage talent, and Voila!"

The red panorama was suddenly snuffed out by a lustrous bath of main lamps, their candescent reach once again reducing three dimensions to only two. Max had to stifle a sigh as he gazed upon the awesome transformation and listened to the wild applause which echoed over the amphitheater.

"I'll never get over that part," Marcia smiled.

Max returned the grin. *Neither will I,* he agreed internally.

Katherine approached clutching a clipboard, her face heavy.

"Time flies when you're holding your breath," he ribbed, his smile uneasy.

As if admitting defeat, Katherine nodded. "I don't know what to say. It's like last night all over again. Isaura hasn't checked in, no one knows anything, and Claire's not answering."

Max reached out his hands. "What about Frankie?"

"Threatening retirement," Katherine replied.

"Perfect," Max uttered under his breath.

Marcia pointed to the monitor. "They're positioning Jonah."

The muscular model, again coated in gold paint, stood in darkness on the platform. Noting the Isaura subject's absence, Max yelled to Marcia.

"Call the sound booth and have the MC do the alternate script. Remind them that they need to actually read it this time."

Marcia dialed a number as Max examined the platform.

"Wait," Max exclaimed. On the monitor, faint movement could be detected in the forest's clearing just behind the platform.

As orchestral music signaled impending illumination, the Isaura subject emerged from the forested hillside and slipped into Jonah's arms.

"She's back," Marcia announced, disconnecting the call.

"Why does she keep waiting until the last minute?" Max questioned, his eyes committed to the screen.

Katherine shook her head. "The designers are supposed to escort them to the platforms and confirm the final position."

Marcia watched the screen. "Weird."

Katherine thumbed through pages of her clipboard. "Something's wrong. The makeup log doesn't even…"

Max waved, cutting her off.

The three watched as The Embrace's sequence ended. As darkness fell over the platform, the mysterious woman again leapt from Jonah's arms, disappearing into the surrounding forested hillside.

"She did it again," Max shouted, running his hand through his hair in unveiled agitation. Katherine seemed unable to hide her bewilderment. "I'm going to go talk to Annie. Maybe there's some arrangement that we don't know about."

Max followed Katherine toward the backstage steps. "I'm coming with you." He descended the decaying backstage staircase, cursing as its faint sway reminded him that it had yet to be repaired. Making what would likely be another futile mental note, he maneuvered past the wardrobe and headdress rooms before he and Katherine finally arrived at their destination.

Once inside the brightly lit makeup room, Katherine carefully explained the mysterious cast member, and her bizarre visits, to the lead makeup artist. Distracted by a dozen large mirrors, and by the noise of his overwhelmed mind, Max only half-heard Katherine's account of the recent events. Max did his best to avoid taking on an interrogative tone as Annie denied any knowledge of the Embrace subject.

"I don't understand. So, no one from your group worked on the Isaura nude? That's kind of impossible," Max insisted.

Annie looked around the room as her team packed up their kits. Catching her silent question, their responses ranged from shrugged shoulders, to verbal no's, to head shakes.

"I don't know what to tell you, Max. We thought she was written out of the piece," Annie explained.

"Well, how is she appearing in proper dress each night?" Katherine argued.

"We're as confused as you are," she said apologetically.

Max glanced helplessly at Katherine as she walked out into the hall. He joined her as she left the makeup area, exiting through the sliding glass door and entering the talent garden. A tranquil outdoor courtyard of red bricks and lush greenery, the garden was the perfect conclusion to the hectic backstage compartments. As inviting as the haven was, it emptied quickly each night. Max watched as musicians lugged away large instrument cases and models poured out of changing areas, all headed toward the exit.

Seeing Jonah emerge from the design suites, Katherine motioned him toward them. Taking a seat next to them, Jonah lifted and squeezed his water bottle, squirting liquid into his mouth. Katherine gently questioned Jonah while Max, scarcely listening, contemplated the beauty of the space. The verdant garden would have been completely dark were in not for the handful of delicate paper-mache lamps which hung from the plants and tree, and from the ambient light which spilled out from the adjacent backstage area. It was a supernal space; yet another hidden treasure within the festival grounds.

Jonah towel dried his hair. The gold body paint no longer hiding his rugged complexion, Jonah's big turquoise eyes seemed to gleam as if happy to again be the center of attention. He continued to squirt water into his mouth as he spoke with Katherine. Max briefly wondered if Jonah's unusually good looks affected her at all, but quickly chastised himself for the ridiculous thought. She was no more attracted to Jonah than Max was. She and Marcia had been together for six years. No longer able to mask his impatience he cleared his throat.

"So, she hasn't spoken to you at all?"

"No, she never says a word. She just silently appears naked in my arms every night; kind of the perfect woman now that I think about it," Jonah laughed.

Max ignored the joke, his mind consumed with countless questions. "And she doesn't walk up the hill with you and the designers?"

"I'm telling you, she just appears suddenly and then takes off as soon as the lights go out," Jonah asserted. "You guys don't know who she is?" he asked, alarm biting through his tone.

"Yes, well, we think so," Max stammered. "Don't worry about it. We'll take care of everything."

Jonah stood, finishing the rest of his water before crumpling the plastic bottle into a ball with his left hand. "Okay. I've got to jet."

"Yes, you do that," Max replied.

Jonah headed toward the exit, waving flirtatiously at a group of pretty cast members before disappearing through the door.

"Don't tell me we have a mystery on our hands. And at a theater? It's way too Scooby Do," said Katherine.

Max laughed. "Please. It has to be the original volunteer," he decided. "I'll call her myself in the morning."

Max sat at his desk, vaguely aware of an anxiety that had come over him upon entering the building. Though he had outlined his day well, a habit which usually helped calm his nerves, the idea of actually having to investigate a cast member was distressing. He cleared his throat and dialed a number on his phone, elongating his posture as a secretary answered the call.

"Yes, I'd like to speak to a Claire Simmons please. This is Maxwell Turner, Director of the Exhibition of Living Arts."

"Just one moment," Max heard the secretary reply. Switching the call to speaker, he piqued when an elegant voice cut through the silence.

"Mr. Turner? Hi, Claire Simmons. I do apologize for my sudden cancellation."

Max frowned, realizing that his original-cast-member theory was now officially blown.

"Please, don't worry yourself. I was sorry to hear of the accident." Max fought against his racing mind, struggling to keep his concentration on Claire as she continued.

"I feel so ridiculous; slipping on a stupid piece of ice."

"I am sorry," Max offered abruptly. "Do you happen to know the woman who took your place?"

"No, I'm afraid I don't," Claire replied, her tone reflecting genuine confusion.

Max stood, pacing as he searched his mind for a new theory.

"Mr. Turner?" Claire nudged.

Her voice reminded Max she was still on the line. "I see. Well, I do hope you have a speedy recovery, and that you'll consider the show again next year," Max said, doing his best to sound light.

"I will. I was really looking forward to it."

"Thank you for your time." Max disconnected the call, slumping into his chair.

Marcia approached and tapped gently on the door frame. "You look sullen."

"Our original Isaura knows nothing about her replacement," Max replied, creases in his forehead giving away his concern. "No one from the makeup artists, to the designers, to the other cast members knows who she is," he confessed aloud for the first time.

"That's kind of freaky," she said. "I'll have security monitor the platform this evening."

"No way. I definitely don't want to scare her off now. Let's talk to Jonah again. Maybe he can get some information out of her tonight.

"Okay. I'll be in my office if you need me."

Just as Marcia turned, Katherine entered and approached Max, handing him a medium-sized cardboard box. Marcia inquisitively returned her attention to Max.

"Special delivery from Athens," Katherine smiled.

Max hopped to his feet, grabbing the box. "Finally. I've been waiting for this for six months."

"What is it?" Marcia asked.

Marcia and Katherine watched as he opened the package and searched through padding. He carefully lifted a small replica of The Embrace statue out of the box. He turned it in his hands, his face alive again.

"It's magnificent," Max lauded.

"There's something about the piece. I can't describe it." Katherine said before glancing at her watch. "Oh, we're almost late for lunch."

"Yeah, I'll be right there." Max carefully placed the replica on a shelf above his chair. Rethinking the decision, he moved the piece to his desk.

Inside the makeup room, a nearly nude Jonah stood in the middle of the space as his entire body was sprayed with a metallic, gold-colored body paint. Max watched from the doorway, their conversation already underway.

"I know, but I'd like you to try."

"What do you want me to say to her?" Jonah asked, his uncertainty apparent.

"Just a minute, Jonah. I don't want you ingesting the paint," Annie warned as she scolded Max with her eyes.

Instantly aware of his mistake, Max stepped back. "Sorry, I'll wait outside."

Minutes later Jonah walked out of the makeup room, his arms and legs dutifully extended. Max stood from his nearby folding chair and approached.

"Do you know how long this stuff stays in your pores?" Jonah asked, glancing over his own frame as if to indicate the gold paint coating his body.

"No, I can't say that I do," Max admitted.

"I sweat glitter every time I work out. It's making me a little self-conscious." Jonah griped.

"I'm sure it's only adding to your popularity at the gym," Max said, offering an encouraging smile despite his desperation to get to the point. "Anyway, we'd like you to try to make some friendly conversation tonight. Maybe even find out her name."

"I'll give it a shot but like I said, she never makes a sound. I can't even hear bushes rustling or footsteps. It's creeping me out a little."

No sound? Intrigued, Max persisted. "Just the same, we'd appreciate any attempt you could make."

"I'll see what I can do," Jonah agreed.

"Thanks, Jonah. Good luck tonight," Max said before hurrying to the backstage area. Once there, Max approached Marcia and Katherine where they stood watching the monitors.

"Jonah's on board?" Katherine asked.

Max gave her a skeptical look. "He didn't sound very optimistic."

On the stage, The Reveal scene concluded with wild applause and dimming stage lights. Max and his team watched the hillside platform on the screen. Seeing movement, they noted Jonah as he was helped onto the platform by designers dressed in black. He furled his arms into the designated pose as the designers made minor adjustments to his stance. The MC began the Embrace monologue, and sweet, symphonic music flowed from the orchestra pit.

"He's in position," Max said.

Katherine looked on, her face firm with tension. "Let's hope she talks."

Max watched, a prisoner of futility. "Let's hope she shows."

On the screen, Jonah maintained his posturing as more movement just beyond the platform caught Max's eye. "Is that…"

The team watched as the faint outline of a woman with long, curly hair emerged from behind a bush and disappeared into the forested hillside.

Katherine's face took on a look of unbridled dismay. "Was that her? She's not in costume."

The team watched, startled to finally see the Isaura subject, in full Embrace ensemble, leap from the hillside and assume her position in Jonah's arms. Romantic music played and stage lamps illuminated the platform.

The confusing event seemed to upset Marcia more than the others and she looked a little panicked when she spoke to Max. "What's going on?"

Max glanced at her, feeling just as distressed as she looked. "This doesn't make any sense. She couldn't have put on the headdress that fast."

"Was her skin gold? I saw the long hair, but..?" Marcia's voice quivered.

"I couldn't see. I just saw a shadow and then her hair," he answered.

On the platform, an oblivious Jonah began whispering to his strange partner.

"Hey, it's me, Jonah. Are you from around here?"

The Isaura subject stared blindly over the audience, her body completely still.

"I've been a nude for the exhibition for about three years. Is this your first time?" he asked. Again, the mysterious woman ignored his question. "Hey, you know my name but I don't know yours." Jonah offered, as if attempting to up his appeal.

The finale continued as Max and his team watched from the monitors. Stage lamps blazed over both platforms, causing the audience to clap and cheer. Just as the lamps went dark, the Isaura subject retreated into the dark foliage of the hillside.

Max pointed to the screen. "Okay she just veered left into the forest. Let's keep watching."

The team stared at the screen, noting Jonah's assisted departure from the platform.

"There goes Jonah," Max continued.

On the screen, the deserted platform was little more than a dark green mass against the surrounding black forest. The image was completely still. Max maintained his scrutiny until the moonless grounds began to sway and pulse.

Max closed his eyes, turning from the screen. "There's nothing there but my eyes are starting to play tricks on me."

Marcia jerked in fear and pointed at the monitor. "Did you see that?"

Katherine and Max whipped their attention back to the screen.

"What?" Max urged. "What did you see?"

Marcia trembled. "The woman, just a silhouette, but she had the same hair; long and wavy, maybe blonde."

Katherine looked at the motionless screen with frustration. "Where?"

Marcia pointed to the upper left portion of the screen. "Right here, just where she was before she went out of frame last time. She cut across and headed to the left."

Marcia moved her unsteady finger across the monitor.

Max appeared even more disturbed. "She was going in the same direction as our Isaura?"

Marcia nodded. "It's like she was following her."

For the first time in as long as he could remember, Max felt a shudder of fear.

Chapter 5

Miranda walked along a moderately populated Laguna Beach street. Her stride had grown sure enough to where she seemed almost normal, though clothing still concealed most of her body. She entered a restaurant, her gaze downward despite the dark sunglasses that shielded her eyes. She glanced up just enough to guide her approach to the young waiter who smiled and handed her a bag.

"Good afternoon, Ms. Cova. Here's your order," he said cheerfully.

Miranda passed him a twenty-dollar bill as she took the bag and headed toward the street.

"Thank you very much, Ma'am. See you next week."

Miranda walked several blocks before arriving at the cove. Her feet sunk into the velvety sand as a salty gust of air welcomed her to an area sheltered by the base of a cliff. She removed her jacket and scarf, carefully forming them into a make-shift blanket. Sitting on the clothing and unpacking her food, she took a tiny bite of her lunch and allowed her eyes to take in the cadence of the waves. Claire energetically approached, plopping next to Miranda. Helping herself, she fished through the bag and pulled out a sandwich.

"Sorry I'm late; one of the shipments was missing this morning and I've been running around like a mad woman. You're looking well. I've got so

47

much going on. Can you believe the next opening is in one week? How's your hot dog?" Claire rambled.

Miranda nodded.

Claire placed her hand on Miranda's shoulder. "How's therapy?"

"Good," Miranda supposed aloud.

"I think you're doing really well. This has been an amazing year for you. And your skin is practically glowing," Claire praised.

Immediately worried, Miranda looked down at her glittery arm, then conspicuously concealed it. She closed her eyes, intensely relieved when Claire prattled onto the next topic, failing to notice the particles of gold body paint still holding onto Miranda's flesh.

In the talent garden, Katherine and Max sat with Jonah as he dabbed his wet locks with a gym towel.

"I told you she wouldn't talk. I've tried everything. I'm not even sure she was breathing," Jonah reported nervously.

"Well, obviously…" Katherine argued before Max interjected.

"What did you say to her exactly?"

"I don't know. I asked her if she had ever been in the show, if she was from around here; small talk, just like you said," Jonah replied.

Katherine looked at Max as if suddenly aware of a possible explanation. "Maybe she doesn't speak English."

Jonah gave Katherine an incredulous look. "Or maybe she's a nut case. Either way, she's giving me the heebs."

"Thank you for trying, Jonah," Max said, disappointed by the news.

Jonah grabbed his duffle bag and walked toward the exit as Sally approached Max and Katherine.

"Any luck getting the identity of our mystery lady?" Sally asked.

"I'm afraid not," Max admitted quietly.

"I don't want to alarm you, Max, but the word is spreading among the cast and crew members. Even the musicians are talking about her. People are getting nervous."

Max held his face with his hand before offering her a pleading look. "Make up something, will you? I need a little more time."

"I'll do my best, but we should probably think of a plan," she insisted.

As Sally walked away Katherine turned toward Max. "Now what?"

Max rubbed his temples, squinting away tension. He shot up as an idea came to him.

The next evening Max and his team stood outside the makeup room with a freshly painted Jonah. The Reveal scene's monologue and spirited orchestral music could be heard in the distance.

"So, what do I do this time? I've already tried everything. I can grab her as soon as the lights go out?" Jonah proposed with a salacious grin.

Max smiled at the thought, an impulse he couldn't blame the guy for having. "Thanks for your generous offer, but that won't be necessary. We have surveillance equipment ready to capture her appearance tonight."

"Good, cause I'm getting tired of this mystery B.S." Jonah said. Seeing his designers, Jonah followed them to the side door of the theatre.

"What kind of equipment are we talking about?" Marcia asked as Katherine studied Max with curious eyes.

He smiled proudly. "Two video cameras. We'll capture anything that approaches the platform from either hillside staircase."

"What if she's not using the staircases?" Katherine pointed out toward Laguna Canyon which ran just beyond the clearing, its miles of darkness dispiriting.

"The bushes would scratch the gold paint off, right? So she has to be." Max contemplated the comment, unsure of his own theory.

"Both of them?" Marcia asked Max. "I saw two different women last night. You said so yourself, there's no way she could have changed that quickly," she insisted, shifting her gaze to Katherine. "Come on, back me up."

Katherine gave her partner a culpable glance. "I'm not sure about last night. It was so dark."

"How could you say that? We all saw her."

Max put his hand on Marcia's shoulder. "I know we saw something. That's why I got the cameras. And these."

Katherine looked at Marcia with uncertainty as Max eagerly removed a pair of binoculars from a box on the ground, having fully recovered from his apprehension.

"I managed to get the sporting goods store to loan them to us. Let's go," he directed.

The two followed him to the side door of the theatre.

The Embrace monologue began. Max and his team, careful to avoiding the audiences' field of vision, crouched outside between a side door exit and the hillside platform. Max brought the binoculars to the orbits of his eyes.

"Are those night vision goggles?" Katherine whispered?

"That's right, my dear. Tonight we're getting to the bottom of Isaura."

Katherine cleared her throat as if offended by the unintentional pun.

"You know I didn't mean it like that," he smiled. "We're going to find out the truth."

Marcia responded with more than a trace of anxiety. "I hope so. The M.C. has been referring to her as the exhibition apparition."

"Cute," Max commented sarcastically as he scanned the forested hillside with the binoculars.

The Embrace monologue ended and romantic music played. Katherine motioned to Max who quickly pointed the binoculars toward the platform.

"Can you see anything?" Marcia urged in a hushed tone.

"Just more of Jonah than I was hoping for in peace time."

Katherine let out a girlish giggle; one that seemed out of character.

Against the dark green glow of the goggles, Max watched as Jonah took his final position. Max surveyed the dark forest for any sign of movement. He focused the binoculars on the tree that the shadowy woman would have been hiding behind the night before.

"She should be showing up at any second," Katherine said.

Max directed his gaze to the stairs on the right and left, shocked to find them empty. He focused on the platform area. A branch on the outskirts of the clearing swayed gently.

"I see something," Max whispered.

"Which one is it?"

"It's Isaura."

The female subject seemed to glide from the clearing before slipping into Jonah's arms and posing perfectly.

Max stared, dumbfounded as the stage lamps illuminated the platform, and the audience reacted with awe.

"What direction did she come from?" Katherine asked?

"The canyon," Max admitted in disbelief.

"Not the stairs?" Katherine asked.

Max ripped the binoculars away from his face. "Damn! We still have nothing."

Katherine placed her hand on his arm. "Maybe we should go up there."

"The audience would see us. We'd have to be in black. Tomorrow night." Max shook his head in frustration.

"Max," Katherine stammered.

"What is it?"

Katherine's voice quaked. "I just saw a shadow. It was moving up the stairs on the left."

Max repositioned the binoculars and focused his gaze on the stairs. He wracked his brain for any possible explanation. "This forest leads directly to the canyon. It could have been anything. A deer…"

Her voice quivered. "It was a woman."

The seriousness of her tone made Max lower the binoculars.

Marcia looked fretfully at her partner. "Oh God. And Isaura's still on stage. So, there are definitely two of them."

Max peered through the lenses and scanned the forested hillside.

Marcia took off the last of her makeup before joining Katherine in the master bedroom.

"What are you watching?" Marcia asked.

Katherine, already tucked into bed, pulled back her partner's covers. "Some ghost investigators," she replied quietly.

Marcia grinned at Katherine. "Really? You?"

Katherine shifted and readjusted her pillow. "It was just on. I'm not really paying attention."

"Oh, I'm sure," Marcia teased.

"I mean it."

Marcia climbed into bed and nestled herself into the covers as they watched the television. On the screen, two men in their early thirties crept around a dark cave with night vision cameras.

"Is this the show with the really cute guy… paranormal something?"

"Who knows?" Katherine yawned.

"Where are they?" Marcia asked.

"Some old beach town in Northern California, I think." Katherine's eyes widened. "Oh my gosh."

"What is it?"

Katherine chuckled. "I went to high school with that guy."

"The bald one?"

Katherine waited until the camera switched from its angle on a short surfer with a shaved head. She pointed to a tall, well-built man wearing deliberately grungy beach wear. His sandy blond hair was fashioned into dreadlocks and pulled into a loose ponytail.

"No, the muscular one with the crystal-blue eyes. He sure filled out."

Marcia eyed her partner for a hint of intrigue. Sensing her jealousy, Katherine rolled her eyes.

"Please. He looks like he hasn't bathed in a month. Oh, and he's not a girl. Don't know if you caught that part."

Marcia smiled as if suddenly feeling foolish. "Okay, I get it." They continued to watch the show.

Katherine sat up a bit. "Jeez, they have a lot of gadgets."

"Yeah. And at least ten cameras. Bet they'd have fun at the exhibition," Marcia quipped. "Hey, you should call him."

"Give me a break."

"I'm serious! Something is definitely going on in that forest. I bet he could figure it out."

"I'm not calling him," Katherine decided.

"Whatever." Marcia said before turning off her headboard lamp and pulling the covers over her shoulders.

Katherine eyed her suspiciously. That was too easy.

Miranda sat before her easel and stared at the blank canvas. The gallery opening at Claire's was just a few days away and though she had several new pieces to choose from, she found herself feeling uninspired with regard to showcasing them. Her mind went to the exhibition; to the platform and the voice that spoke to her each night. Why did he insist on a conversation? He was clearly simple and didn't seem like he'd have any trouble finding company. Miranda wished he would just stop talking and let her concentrate on staying in control. After all, this was no longer just a punishment. She'd come to appreciate it as more as an exercise for her; a way to be seen without being seen. And though she had dreaded darkness for years, she was starting to grow rather fond of the solitude if afforded.

The snap of a branch just outside her window made her gasp, her heart pounding in her chest. Her eyes made it to the window in time to see a shadowy outline fleeing past and heading toward her back yard. Panic set in but was undermined by a powerful command. *Get up*, she heard the angry one yell. Hurrying to her feet she ran through the house and into the kitchen, the shadow cutting though the moonlight which was reflected off the tiled floor. Miranda crumpled to the ground in fear. Inside her mind she was in a child's bedroom, its walls blanketed in a red glow. She could hear approaching footsteps followed by the creak of the door hinges. Against the wall, dolls with fixed eyes lay motionless as the door opened. Though she sat on her kitchen floor, in her mind she was in the tiny bedroom of her childhood home. Miranda sobbed as she tried to forget what happened next.

Backstage Katherine chewed on her lip as Max paced. He glanced at his watch.

"Isn't he supposed to be in makeup by now?" Max asked, though fully aware of the answer.

Marcia ran up to them, handing Max a slip of paper. "Max, I just got a call from Jonah. He's quit the show."

"What?" Max asked frantically.

"He said things are getting too weird and he's not coming back," she explained, her nerves making her voice shake.

Max ripped his cell phone from his pocket. "What's his home number?"

Marcia pointed to the bottom of the slip as Max dialed.

"Jonah, this is Max Turner," he announced, attempting to sound calm.

Inside his home, Jonah sat in an oversized bathtub as he spoke into his cell. "I'm not coming back, so don't even bother."

"But why? We're so close to finding out…" Max persisted before Jonah interrupted.

"Who she is? I'll tell you who she is. She's a creepy old Greek ghost who's haunting the show, and I'm not wrapping my arms around her anymore," Jonah declared, his voice filled with concern.

"Jonah, don't be absurd," Max uttered in annoyance.

"Forget it, Max. I'm sorry, but I signed up to pose with a woman, not to stand in the dark groping some pissed off banshee all summer long."

"Jonah, just," Max looked at his phone, noting that the call had ended. "We're screwed."

Marcia pulled her phone from her pocket, dialing fast. "I'll have casting look for a replacement. Maybe one of the valet boys?"

"There's no time," Max responded quietly, his despondent tone turning to one of desperation. "Damn it, I can't cancel the finale."

Max paced as Katherine and Marcia look on helplessly. Marcia smirked, eyeballing Max strangely.

Instantly worried, Max was all too aware that he was being sized by a skilled art researcher.

"What?" he responded defensively.

Katherine and Marcia positioned themselves at his sides and wrapped their arms around his, walking him to the makeup room.

"No, no. Absolutely not!" Max yelled.

"You'll be alright, Max. No one will even know it's you," Marcia assured.

They entered the room, pulling Max behind them.

"I can't do this," Max begged.

"Sure you can. It's for the good of the show. Any director worth his weight in gold spray paint would sacrifice his own comfort for two measly minutes a night," Marcia said, pushing him toward Annie.

Annie took his hand and guided him into a changing room before holding up a nude-colored thong. Max examined it in horror.

"The big part goes in front," she explained nonchalantly.

"Oh, Jesus..." Max muttered, his eyes wide as he leapt out of the changing room.

Annie yelled to another makeup artist as she shoved Max back into the changing room.

"Miguel, I'm going to need the electric razor," she said, jamming the thong into his Max's hands.

"I changed my mind. We're cancelling the finale. I have a natural tremor," Max pleaded, trying to escape only to be pushed back into the changing room again, Annie forcing the curtain closed.

"I resign my position as director. Annie, you're fired. Show's over," Max wailed.

Outside the makeup room Marcia and Katherine waited for Max. They stifled smiles as the door slowly opened, revealing their humiliated boss, who shuffled apprehensively out of the makeup room. Covered in gold body paint, and wearing only a loin cloth and head piece, he awkwardly held his arms outstretched as he approached them.

Katherine and Marcia pursed away grins as he sauntered closer. Miguel, a flamboyantly gay makeup artist, popped his head out of the room. "See you tomorrow night, Tiger," he teased.

"Miguel!" Annie snapped from inside the makeup room. Miguel closed the door, leaving Katherine and Marcia to their now uncontrollable laughter.

"Maxwell, I had no idea," Marcia said provocatively.

"Shut up," he grumbled.

"Just remember, you're doing it for the show," Katherine giggled.

"We won't tell a soul," Marcia promised, wiping tears from her face as the last of her laughter sputtered to an end.

"I had them only send one designer since Isaura is certainly not going to be changing her ways." Katherine said. "At least you won't have to deal with two of them."

"And we told your designer that Jonah has laryngitis, so try not to talk to him," Marcia instructed.

"I won't even be making eye contact with them. This is so humiliating."

The designer opened the side door, calling out to Max. "Jonah, you're up."

Marcia reacted to the unfortunate word choice, lifting her eyebrows as Max sighed in disgust.

"Good luck, Jonah," Katherine smiled.

"Yeah. Break a ... leg," Marcia yelled.

Max looked back in irritation as he and the designer exited the side stage. Seeing it close, Katherine and Marcia were consumed by laughter.

The Embrace monologue and music in progress, Max awkwardly stepped onto the platform in almost total darkness as the designer helped him pose. Max lifted his arms to mimic The Embrace stance, elevating the wrong arm.

"Switch hands, buddy. You feeling okay tonight?" the designer asked.

Max nodded vigorously, trying to switch arms without appearing as flustered as he felt.

"Oh, right. Laryngitis. Another all-nighter with the ladies?" the designer joked.

Max again nodded, performing a diminutive gesture of manhood by mock-thumping his chest. The designer guided his arms into the proper position.

"Okay, perfect. Fifteen seconds. Say hello to that sexy mystery lady for me."

The designer smiled before descending the steps back to the theater. The MC's monologue came to a completion as the romantic music began. Max struggled to control his breathing, his heart pounding heavily against his chest. *Please come,* he silently prayed. An intoxicating herbal bouquet wafted through the air as the Isaura subject emerged from the forested hillside, effortlessly breezing into his arms just as stage lamps illuminated them.

Max swallowed hard as the audience gasped and applauded, their sounds of approval strangely hollow from his new vantage point. Max couldn't decide if a structural phenomenon was causing the echo, or if he was hallucinating. He let his eyes drift downward without moving his head. Was she actually in his arms? Had he imagined it? His eyes skimmed over his partner's shoulders. She was really there and she was perfect. Max silently endured the minute of illumination, feeling that it was the longest sixty seconds of his existence.

To his relief the Cupid and Psyche monologue began, foreshadowing a change in music and a maddeningly welcome fade out of the platform stage lamps. Max and the Isaura subject stood in darkness as the show continued. Aware that he had only ninety seconds, Max fought to speak while keeping his lips as still as possible. He chose his words carefully.

"Hello, my name is Max. Jonah isn't doing the show anymore. I'm not a model. I'm an art director," he paused, her beauty making it hard to focus. "Thank you for coming every night. Our first Isaura broke her arm. You saved the piece."

The woman remained motionless.

"I've never done anything like this before. It's a little scary, isn't it? But you seem very calm." Max whispered through still lips. Waiting a moment, and noting her silence, Max reconciled that his time was nearing an end. "I'll see you tomorrow night. Thank you again."

The lights came up to reveal both platforms, compelling the audience to cheer and applaud. Max breathed hard while the finale music played. As the platform lights again faded to black, the strange woman dashed into the forested hillside, absconding into the woods as the rousing fragrance disappeared with her.

Chapter 6

Inside the talent garden Katherine waited on the large planter bench. Max exited the wardrobe door and slowly approached her, scanning the eyes of everyone he passed. To his relief, no one seemed to take any special interest in him, a sign he assumed meant his secret was safe. Back in his regular clothes with neatly styled hair and a boyish smile, Katherine couldn't deny Max's natural appeal.

"You blow-dried your hair?" she teased.

"I didn't want anyone to figure it out."

"Oh, don't be silly. That's not going to happen. So, how did it go?"

Max continued to search the faces of exiting cast member. "It was completely horrifying, thanks for asking." Noting consistent apathy in the passersby, Max relaxed.

"But you got a better look at Isaura, right?"

Max was unable to hold back a tender expression. "That's very true," he said, his unusual smile not lost on his friend.

"Did she say anything?" Katherine asked.

The question robbed Max of his happy expression as he contemplated the answer. "Jonah was right. She didn't make a sound," he answered.

"How did she feel? Human?" Katherine joked.

"She felt... scared," Max replied, a strange sadness coming over him.

Marcia hurried toward them. "Did you tell him?" she demanded.

Katherine eyed her partner in irritation. "I was getting to it."

"Tell me what?"

Marcia opened her mouth and was immediately shushed by Katherine.

"We saw something on the monitor. It looked like the same woman from the night before."

The news seemed impossible as he hadn't heard anything unusual while on the platform.

"Where was she?"

Katherine glanced down as if reticent to elaborate. "She was right behind you."

Max was blown away. Once again, fear invaded his senses. "Are you serious?"

"I'm scared Max," Marcia said.

Katherine nodded as she looked at Marcia. "So am I."

"Great, so can we call your friend? Please?" Marcia asked.

Katherine studied Max. The concern on his face seemed to melt away the last of her resistance. "First thing in the morning."

Max walked along the early morning streets enjoying the mild fog layer that rested over Laguna Beach. He basked in the beauty of the temporarily sleepy city, his warm latte the perfect accompaniment to the nippy morning. His thoughts, as they almost always did these days, returned to Isaura. As filtered sunlight breached the clouds, Max arrived at the exhibition. He entered the festival grounds to find Marcia and Katherine sitting on a rocky plantar. They hurried toward him.

"What's the matter?"

Katherine looked bare of expression, a stark contrast to her effervescent partner.

Marcia almost squealed as she told Max the big news. "They hopped on a plane last night and will be here by lunch!"

Max searched for anything that might help him understand what Marcia was talking about. "Who?"

"Katherine's friend from high school; he's one of the Paranormal Knights on television. The one with the dreadlocks and the guns," Marcia flexed her muscles as a demonstration.

Max looked at Katherine. "You went to high school with that guy?"

"You've seen the show?" Katherine asked, as if embarrassed.

"I've seen the commercials, sorry, why is he coming?"

Marcia seemed confused by his naivety. "They're going to investigate the lady in the forest. Did you forget about what happened last night?"

"No, but I guess I didn't realize that this was the next step," Max looked at Katherine for support.

Katherine motioned toward Marcia as she explained. "I thought they'd blow us off but then this one started talking about all of the peculiarities and they got excited. I told them to meet us at that place that serves free pie with any lunch."

"Eww, no. Why would you pick that place?" Max complained.

"Cause no one that we know goes there."

"Good thinking," Max said. "Okay, well I guess there's no harm in meeting them." He gave Katherine a nervous smile as the three headed toward the amphitheater.

On the stage, Max watched as Marcia and Katherine worked with painters to touch up some of the backdrops and reproduction facades.

"Looks like one of the kids has been chipping away at that spot," Max said as he pointed toward one of the backdrops. The team, comparing the reproductions against photos of the original pieces, painstakingly returned the backdrops to their prior condition. Max hopped down from the stage and walked toward the middle of the amphitheater. "Bring up the house," he ordered. Intense white lights hit the stage. "Ambers," he continued, a golden glow washing over the proscenium. "Reds," he yelled, the stage suddenly blanketed in a deep burgundy as if submerged at the bottom of a wine bottle.

"It looks like we found the right place."

A booming male voice cut through the team's concentration as three men, sporting casual beach wear and a multitude of recording devices, walked toward them.

"Oh my gosh it's them!" Marcia jumped.

Shocked, Max looked at Katherine. "What happened to the gross pie cafe?"

"Sorry about that," the dreadlocked leader approached Max. "We didn't think we'd get here this early but hey, we made it. I'm Jace Benson. That's Jake with a "C." I'm the host of Paranormal Knights." He reached for Max's hand, shaking it forcefully.

"Max Turner, director of the exhibition," he replied, his eyes wide.

"Great to meet you, man. These are my bro's Cain and Thai."

"What up," Thai smiled, offering an alternative hand shake that left Max fumbling.

Cain lifted a video camera from his bag and began recording.

Jace turned to Max. "Dude, so you have a living arts show, is that right?

"Whoa, can we talk about this?" Max tensed, waving his hand. "Katherine?"

Katherine, clearly mortified, nodded from the stage before making her way toward them.

"Kat, is that you? Wow, man, you haven't changed," he smiled, hugging her into his side. "Still into chicks?"

Katherine nodded, indicating toward Marcia who cheerfully shook his hand.

"Yeah? Me too, right?" Jace laughed at his joke and slapped hands with his buddies. He seemed to notice Max's apprehensive face before returning his attention to Katherine.

"So you told him that we're filming, yes? He looks a little freaked out."

Max stuttered despite doing his best to appear relaxed. "I am, Jace, just a little freaked out. What exactly are we filming?"

"The haunted theater, man. It's gonna be awesome!"

Marcia chimed in before Max could object. "It's the forested hillside that's been getting the most activity," she said as she gestured toward the platform.

"Oh, that's cool. We brought an arsenal," Jace said.

Max's alarm grew. "Sorry, an arsenal?"

"Relax bro, I meant all of our investigation equipment. We would never hurt a spirit, man. No disrespect, you know. We have nothing but respect. We just want to help get their stories heard so they can find peace."

"We can't have a film crew here. Our show runs every night of the summer. Actually, can we talk about this somewhere a little more private?" Max looked around at the exhibition crew members who listened to the conversation with obvious intrigue.

"No, of course. That's totally cool, man. Do you have an office?"

Max closed his eyes in frustration, giving himself a quick timeout before answering. "Yes, but there are people there too. Follow me."

He nervously walked the group out of the amphitheater. Veering to the right, he led them from the festival grounds and guided them down a narrow path toward an empty parking lot. The group situated themselves in white plastic chairs under a tree at the mouth of the lot's street entrance.

"Cool parking lot. You've got chairs and everything."

"We have several parking attendants and they must stay here during the entire show. The lot is for the musicians. Sometimes they need assistance lifting and transporting their instruments."

"Gotcha. So, why don't you tell me what's been going on," Jace said, motioning to Cain. His friend responded by leaving his seat and setting up a video camera. Aiming it at the group, he gave Jace a nod.

"It all started…" Marcia was immediately cut off by Max.

"I'll just give you the fast version. Our show portrays reproductions of famous art, mostly paintings, using massive backdrops and live people as the subjects."

"Very cool," Jace bobbed his head.

Max carefully phrased each sentence, doing is best to downplay the season's bizarre turn of events. "This year one of the models has chosen to appear each night in an unorthodox manner."

"What do you mean by that?"

"Instead of being escorted from makeup to the platform where she poses, she kind of comes in

66

through, ah… well from the forest behind the platform."

"Okay, that is pretty weird. Why does she do that?"

Max shifted uncomfortably. "We don't actually know."

"Well, when you asked her…"

"She doesn't talk much. She rarely responds. Verbally, that is."

"So, we just go up to her while she's getting her makeup done and totally demand to know what's going on."

Max could no longer find a decent explanation for the oddity. Marcia seemed to note his floundering and chimed in.

"She doesn't use the makeup room. We don't even know how she gets painted or anything."

"Painted?" Jace repeated.

"She's a nude," Marcia replied simply.

"Oh man, bonus," Thai interjected, high-fiving his friends.

"The talent is starting to get creeped out of course. Some of them even think she's the ghost of Isaura," Marcia smiled, clearly loving the attention.

Jace looked lost. "Who's Isaura?"

Marcia seemed unable to suppress her delight. "She's a character in an ancient Greek love story…"

As Marcia filled in the crew, Max stood and walked toward the festival entrance, stopping and rubbing his temples.

An apologetic Katherine joined him. "I'm sorry. You know she lives for this."

Max closed his eyes and exhaled slowly. He glanced at Katherine, softening upon seeing her concerned expression. He put his arm around her, provoking a subtle smile which he quickly returned.

"It really does sound kind of spooky when you hear the whole story," he laughed.

"I guess. We don't have to film anything, you know," she assured, as if guilty that the crew was causing Max any distress. The two walked back to the group just as Marcia's story concluded.

Jace stood, smiling at his crew. "This is awesome. I'm super pumped. Are you guys ready?"

Cain maintained his angle on Jace while Thai nodded and removed his camera, focusing on Max.

Jace peered into Cain's lens. "How's the hair, man?"

"Dude it rocks. Let's do this thing," Cain replied.

Jace perfected his posture, took a death breath and looked directly at Cain's camera. "The Exhibition of Living Arts team was shocked when a mysterious woman enigmatically joined the show after their lead canceled at the last minute. But that's not all. This evening Paranormal Knights takes you on a wild adventure to find this haunted theater's Exhibition Apparition." Jace turned to the others, his excitement visible.

He dropped the on-camera persona as he polled the group for feedback. "How was that, was that chill?"

Max bowed his head into his hands as Katherine rubbed his back. "Oh yes, very much so," he muttered.

Jace approached him. Cain and Thai followed, their camera's pointed at Max. Jace spoke to Max as if recapping for his viewers. "Dude, we just got done hearing the story of Isaura, the lady in gold. Then Marcia here, one of your art researchers, tells me that there isn't one mysterious spirit but two."

"We don't really believe that there's anything paranormal going on here. Our model may have personal reasons why she doesn't wish to follow the customary trail toward the platform."

"Sure bro, but let me ask you something. What's beyond the platform?"

"A clearing which leads to the canyon," Max said.

Jace continued his viewer-driven performance. "Laguna Canyon... a seven mile chasm which is home to mountain lions, bobcats, coyotes, and like tons of coastal sage brush. You're telling me that the lady in gold emerges from this super deadly forest every night, basically in the nude, just to perform in your show for two minutes. And no one knows who she is or why she's doing this? Am I right on so far?"

Max squirmed, his eyes avoiding the camera. "Well, I don't know that I'd call the forest deadly."

"The show runs from about eight to ten thirty each night, so we're going to go set up. We need to capture any paranormal audio, video, electromagnetic or thermal signatures during the performance. After the show is over we'll spend the night in the canyon."

"Seriously? You're very committed." Despite being momentarily impressed, Max couldn't help but imagine frightened cast and crew members. "You will stay out of sight though? If anyone saw you it... look, no one can see you," Max gently warned.

"Don't worry bra. We're going to solve this mystery and bring peace back to this place. Bring on the Knights!" Jace exclaimed while launching his face toward the camera.

The group followed Max out of the parking area and onto the festival grounds which already teemed with art patrons. Jace ostentatiously took the lead and headed toward the amphitheater. Unfazed by looks from several guests, he maintained an overly intense stare straight ahead.

"There's nothing to see dudes, just investigating some ghostly activities," Jace shouted, clearly thriving on his own melodrama.

Max hurried to catch up to Jace. "Can you keep it down please?"

"I know man, I just told them there was nothing to see."

The group passed through the amphitheater entrance. Thai immediately set a primary camera on the entire group while Cain filmed Jace's survey of his surroundings.

"This is pretty creepy. I mean the forest bank is only about ten feet from the audience. You've never had like an animal attack jump down and attack?"

Max willed away a sarcastic tone. "No, sane animals generally fear huge crowds."

Jace seemed impervious to the barb. He again straightened his back as he looked directly into Cain's camera. "In just a few hours the Exhibition of Living Arts will begin its nightly performance." Jace approached the bottom of the platform as he spoke to the camera. "While we can't actually record the show itself, we will have plenty of surveillance around the platform here and in the forested areas around the theater. And when the lady in gold emerges, infrared cameras will solve the first of many mysteries surrounding this season's show; is she human?"

Max's face was strained with uncertainty. He approached Jace with as much restraint as he could garner. "Sounds like you have quite a bit to set up. The cast and crew will be here in a couple of hours."

Jace looked at his team. "You heard the dude, let's get going. I want an infra on the platform, and five in the forest and clearing. We have to see her from every possible direction. Get at least four cameras on the auditorium and aim two of them at the stage, just in case any spirits visit the cast members.

We need digital recorders backstage, on the platform, and throughout the forest. Of course all the night-vision cams will cover the forest."

Jace and the others quickly assembled their gear and positioned the equipment. Marcia's colossal smile proved she hadn't noticed Max's grim expression. "Isn't this exciting?"

Max stared at her, his face flat as he turned to Katherine. "We should seriously consider updating our resumes."

Katherine pulled Marcia aside and guided her a few feet away from Max. "Why don't you go have a talk with Frankie? We need her to keep the talent contained in the garden tonight; no walking around the amphitheater while they set up. I'll handle the tech crew; I'll make up something about grad students working on an aphid thesis," she whispered.

"Aphid thesis?" Marcia smirked.

"Whatever. Just go talk to Frankie."

Marcia left the auditorium as Katherine rejoined Max.

"Nobody's going to know they're here."

Max flashed her a judgmental look. "Everyone's going to know they're here."

"I'll handle it. You just," she seemed to search for the right word. "Relax," she added as if more worried about Max than the ghost crew. She headed to the stage and beckoned one of the stage hands to approach. Watching as she whispered into the gruff man's ear, Max felt certain he didn't want to know what she was saying. He turned his attention to the ghost team working around the forested hillside. *At least they'd know definitively if...* he shook his head, amazed that he was once again consider something as ludicrous as a supernatural explanation.

As his team finished, Jace postured for the cameras which Thai and Cain trained on him. "Okay, we've surrounded the grounds with monitoring equipment. When the lady in gold visits tonight we'll be there to capture every move she makes. Now all we have to do is wait for nightfall."

Chapter 7

The show well underway, Max and his team gathered around the backstage monitors while Jace and his crew vied for space.

Jace wiped his hand across the screen as if expecting to find dust. He looked surprised to find none. "Dude, you seriously need to upgrade this stuff. The monitor is so grainy."

"We've never needed the clarity before," Max realized.

Jace shook his head. "Yeah, this is terrible. Let's just go to the swell."

"The what?" Max asked as if reluctant to understand the answer.

Despite being precarious, Max and his team followed the ghost crew down the steps and into a cavernous storage area along the side of the theater. Two men sat at a long desk watching a dozen monitors. With their Rasta hairstyles and multiple tattoos, their headphones and unwavering focus on the screens served as the only evidence of their professionalism.

"We totally upgraded your old storage room. This is now officially 'the swell'. It's decked with the latest in paranormal surveillance. Max, Katherine and Marcia, meet CJ and Sunny, my audiovisual guys."

Only when Max's team approached did the two men look away from their work. They exchanged handshakes with Max and with the women before resuming their vigilant monitor scrutiny.

Max frowned as he inspected the screens. "Well, you were right. This is far superior to anything we have. The detail is remarkable."

"It has to be," Jace bragged. "How can we show people the truth if we can't see?"

Max ignored the self-indulgent comment, his concentration absolute as he gazed at the monitor featuring the platform. Noting a dark area he pointed to the screen.

"What if she comes in from this angle?"

Jace tapped on a different monitor. "See this? It's the area behind and to the right of the platform." He tapped another monitor. "And this one? Same but it's the left side. Right now it looks like nothing because it is nothing; just a shot of the forest. But when she enters the frame, you'll know it."

Katherine whispered discretely in Max's ear. "Shouldn't you be going?"

Max felt a little nauseous as he appreciated the meaning behind her question. "Oh yes, I have to check in on the makeup room. I'll probably be there for at least a half hour," he announced to the group, hoping his nerves hadn't sabotaged the weak fib.

Jace waved. "No worries bro, we got this." He glanced at Katherine. "How are we doing on time?"

Katherine checked her watch. "The finale is twenty minutes away."

"Perfect." Jace looked at Thai and Cain. "Obviously we can't go down there with cameras but I do want us to be in the auditorium during the finale. Stay out of sight but keep your eyes open. Once it's over we'll meet back here, wait for the audience to bail, then head back down for the real investigation."

"Sounds good, bro," Thai said.

Jace reached into his pocket and pulled out three behind-the-ear security headsets. "Almost forgot," he remarked as he passed them to Thai and Cain. The three donned the equipment before following Jace out of the storage room, leaving Katherine and Marcia with the deadpan audiovisual team.

The ghost crew discreetly entered the dark amphitheater and headed in different directions, each searching the packed area for an empty seat. Jace positioned himself close to the platform. Sinking into an aisle seat, he waited for the MC's narration to end. He pushed a button on his earpiece.

"Can you guys hear me?" he whispered.

Cain responded first. "Loud and clear, bro."

"How about you, Thai?"

"I'm with you," he replied.

"Okay good. Let's lay low but I do want to be told if anyone sees anything strange. Over and out."

Jace depressed the button again and glanced at the woman sitting next to him. Seeing her disapproving face he stared back at her until she relented. Cutting through the darkness, a giant reproduction of a painting glowed on the stage. The life-sized Last Supper tableaux earned gasps as Massenet's sacred Meditation accompanied the piece in glorious symphonic mastery.

"Whoa," Jace let slip, either unaware of or unconcerned by his dumbfounded reaction.

Cain's voice rang out from the earpiece. "Dude, is this for real?"

Thai's voice followed. "Totally. Some guy let me borrow his binoculars and I saw Jesus blink."

Jace pushed the button on his earpiece. "Those are actual people. This place is sick," he remarked in wonder.

The woman next to him again glared, pushing her finger against her lips. Jace huffed in irritation. The lights faded as applause filled the amphitheater. The MC's voice heralded the finale. Jace sat up as he listened to the story of Galen and Isaura. He stared at the platform as if readying himself. In the darkness, two faint outlines approached the platform, the figures moving about before one departed. Jace squinted as his eyes made sense of the lone figure standing still on the platform.

Jace depressed the talk button. "Okay, the Galen dude is in position and the designer guy took off," he whispered, his voice finally quiet enough to be pardoned by the dictatorial woman next to him.

"Copy that," Cain answered.

The MC's monologue concluded as a slender outline slipped into the darkened Galen figure's arms. Jace stared as the lights came up and the powerfully beautiful finale music completed the wondrous scene.

"Oh my God, did you see that, bro?" Cain's voice broadcasted.

Jace drew his shoulder inward as he whispered his response. "Dude, she came out of nowhere. That was crazy."

Thai's voice revealed that he had jumped on the ghost bandwagon. "She looks fake, dude."

"I think I can see her breathing but I'm not sure," Jace admitted, his eyes moving up and down the couple. Noting their motionless frames, their impressively fit bodies, lustrous from the metallic gold paint, a provocative smile played across Jace's face.

"It's kind of hot. A little freaky, but hot."

"Dude, can you see her box?" he heard Thai ask.

"That's enough, man. Watch the forest," Jace commanded.

The platform lights diminished as the MC explained the next piece.

From the platform, Max looked out over the audience. An uneasy feeling had plagued him ever since the Isaura subject took her place in his arms. It was a sensation he wasn't accustomed to and its origin was unclear. *The ghost crew; maybe she knows about them.* His fret over the thought was harshly interrupted as a twig broke behind him, sending chills across his back. He jolted slightly, a mistake he immediately regretted. Before he could internally scold himself, another twig snapped. His now sentient skin felt cold as the hairs on his arms became erect. Something was behind him. He gazed at the beauty in his arms. Her breathing hadn't changed. She appeared perfectly composed; almost lifeless. He forced the fear from his awareness.

The lights illuminated the platform once more and applause drowned out all other sounds. Max concentrated on controlling his breathing. From his seat, Jace peered at the couple before hurrying out of the amphitheater and to the side of the stage. Thai and Cain followed his lead as both platform lights faded.

The crew bolted into the storage room, their eyes wild with excitement.

Jace shouted to his audiovisual team. "Something is definitely going on. Did you guys see the Galen dude jump like he was startled?"

One of the audiovisual robots responded in a dull voice. "It was barely noticeable but yeah, we got it."

"That was insane," Jace continued.

"And what about the chick just chucking herself off the platform like that?" Cain added.

Jace winced. "Man, I missed it. I took off before the lights dimmed. How fast can we review footage?"

"Shouldn't we wait for Max?" Katherine asked.

"Yeah, where is he?"

Her right hand fidgeted with her lapel of her jacket. "Oh, he'll be along shortly. He's got to, uh…"

"He's giving tours backstage tonight," Marcia interjected, causing her grateful partner to relax her grip on her clothing.

In the shower room Max frantically lathered his skin as sheets of gold rolled down his defined, freshly shaved calves. Scrubbing hard, he searched for a way to logically explain having wet hair. *What about an errant pigeon accident? Not at night. A spill of some sort? The clothes would have been affected as well. Damn.*

Dashing out of the shower he threw on his clothes and blotted his hair with a towel. He made his way to the makeup room and grabbed an industrial-sized bottle of grey face paint. Looking at his suit, he grimaced as he drizzled some of the paint down his shoulder; it was better than having his identity known by Jace. The guy was as delicate as a bulldozer. It would be awful enough if the cast and crew found out, but Max certainly couldn't risk Jace's entire viewing-audience finding out. He smeared the paint into his jacket as if he had tried to clean it. He looked at his work in the mirror. *Not too bad*, he smiled.

Max arrived at the storage room-turned ghost headquarters to his friends' relief.

Jace peered at him strangely. "What happened to you?"

Max pointed to the stain on his jacket. "I had a small collision with one of the makeup artists. It even got in my hair; had to wash it in the sink."

"Bummer," Jace responded.

Katherine seemed impressed by the quality of the lie.

Jace approached the monitors. "Okay, let's review this footage. What have we got, starting with the infrared?"

CJ, his voice monotone, spoke for the first time. "We picked up two figures coming toward the platform at ten twenty pm."

He pointed at a monitor which displayed two, deep-yellow figures walking against a black background. Marcia impulsively responded. "There's Max… Max's designer and the Galen subject." She swallowed hard, clearly aware that she had nearly exposed Max. Katherine looked at her rigid boss who did not return her gaze.

"What about the lady in gold?" Jace asked.

CJ scrolled to a later portion of the video's timeline and hit play. The monitor revealed a yellow figure approaching the platform from the left of the forest, then darting in front of the Galen figure.

"She's using the trail from the sound booth," Katherine explained.

Jace studied the footage. "Well now we know she's not a ghost. You see how warm this is? It means we're looking at a human temperature."

Max poorly suppressed a smile as he watched, finding it amusing that even her outline delighted him. Seeing his reaction Katherine watched him suspiciously. When their eyes met he attempted to play off the response. They continued to watch the monitor, as the yellow form indicative of the Isaura figure, slipped back into the forest and fled toward the left.

"She's using the same path each time," Jace said.

Max watched closely, surprised by the conclusion of the footage. "That was it? There was nothing else out there?"

"Should there be?" Katherine asked.

Max peered at the screen. "A twig broke. Two actually."

Katherine cleared her throat.

Max quickly understood her message and his face flushed red. "One of the designers mentioned that they heard the snap of a branch. He said it sounded like something was out there with them."

"Replay that sequence," Jace ordered.

CJ adjusted the timeline and they watched the scene again. "Yeah the guy flinches, but I don't see any cause, man."

Max searched his memory, unable to deny the intensity of the cracking branches. *Strange.*

"This was just a peek-a-boo though. The lady in gold is clearly human, so that we've established. The rest of this footage will be totally scrutinized, including the audio. CJ could catch a moth fart, but it's going to take some time. And we haven't even done our night set," Jace replied.

"Please, don't let us stop you. Surf away."

Jace looked slightly embarrassed. "Oh no, dude... Sorry. We're not catching any waves on the job. Night sets are what we call it when we spend the whole night doing an investigation. You know what I mean."

"Sure," Max said.

Jace looked at his crew. "Let's get going."

The crew followed him outside.

"See you in the morning?" Max hinted to Katherine.

"Yeah, I'm exhausted." She and Max left the swell with Marcia in tow.

Catching up to them, Marcia begged her partner with her eyes. "You don't want to watch them?"

"No."

"Not even for a little bit?"

"No."

Max chuckled as the three headed toward the parking lot.

"You're tons of fun," Marcia complained.

Chapter 8

Another stunning morning pulled a smile from Max as he locked his front door. Patting himself down, he realized that he didn't have his cell. He depressed a button on his car remote and opened the passenger door find his phone still on the seat. *Twelve missed calls; so much for a leisurely walk to work.* He suppressed a curse as he walked around the car, slipped into the driver's seat and started the car. Maneuvering down the hillside he played the first message.

"Hey man this is Jace. You might want to come back here. We got some alarming EVPs. Call me back."

Max frowned. *And an EVP is what exactly?*

He played the second message. "Dude, it's Jace. We are picking up some serious paranormal evidence. You should get down here."

Max shook his head, choosing to ignore the rest of the messages. As he made his way passed his parking garage and toward the exhibition, his thoughts found Isaura. He remembered the footage from the night before; how the fiery outline against the black forest proclaimed her existence, as if that was ever in question. He realized how absurd it was that he was now reflecting on an infrared image with fondness. He pulled into his parking space as his phone rang.

"This is Max," he answered. He listened for a moment before objecting, his annoyance coming through.

"Jace. I was not ignoring your call, I was sleeping. Weird, I know. I'll be there in thirty seconds."

He disconnected the call and headed toward the storage room. Once inside he was met by a very nervous ghost crew. Marcia and Katherine appeared concerned as well.

"Are you guys alright?"

Jace's dour expression only contributed to Max's uneasiness. Cain and Thai readied their cameras and began recording the meeting. "Dude, you might want to sit down, seriously."

Max's instinct to protest was squelched by Jace's foreboding tone. He took the seat reserved for him in between the audiovisual team members. Glancing at CJ's computer he noted the graphic representation of a sound wave.

"Did you find an explanation for the branches that snapped behind the platform?"

"No dude, may have just been an animal."

Max wondered if he had imagined the sound.

"I'm going to go in order of events. This sound bite was collected on the trail from the MC's booth. We've merged it with the time Isaura is first seen by our cameras, so we know this is the rustling of leaves as she walks toward the clearing just behind the platform," CJ explained before clicking the mouse.

The rhythmic crackling of dried foliage filled the room, the timing consistent with footsteps.

Max hoped this was not what all the fuss had been about. "Okay, you mentioned something about supernatural activity?" he directed at Jace.

"Patience, man. We're just trying to show you our methods."

CJ reduced the sound bite window and maximized the window of a movie file. "Here is Isaura walking toward the forested area." Clicking the file, a dark image could be seen moving across the screen.

Unimpressed, Max tried to mask his growing impatience. "I'm with you so far."

CJ clicked open another movie file. "This camera is the one capturing the area from the taper of the hillside to the clearing just behind the platform. It's facing the audience." He pointed at the screen. "Galen would be right here if he were in frame."

Max appeared confused.

CJ turned to Jace. "Hey man, can you show him on your phone?"

"Oh, good idea." Jace pulled out his phone and entered his passcode. He brought up his photo album and selected a daytime panoramic photo of the forested area, which included the platform. He pointed to an area to the right of the platform from the audience's perspective. "The camera was right here. We had another one on the opposite side that would have captured her if she was coming from the right."

"Okay," Max nodded his understanding.

CJ played the movie clip. For several seconds the darkened clearing was barely visible. Max inhaled as the Isaura figure entered the back of the clearing and stopped.

"What time was this? I mean in relation to the finale?"

"Galen is already on stage so this is like 60 seconds before the platform lights come up for the first time," Jace said.

"She's just standing there."

Jace's expression seemed cautious. "Well, not exactly."

CJ pointed to a time at the bottom of the video window. "Ten fifteen." He opened another sound bite and scrolled until the playback bar hit a small flag at the bottom of the timeline. "Same thing right? Ten fifteen. Now listen to this."

The softness of a young woman's voice was heard, though Max couldn't understand what she was saying. Marcia and Katherine seemed fearful as they looked at each other.

Max shook his head. "What was that?"

Jace referred back to the image on his phone. "We had digital recorders all over the place. This EVP came from the recorder next to the tree; right where she's standing," he explained as he pointed to the corresponding spot on his phone.

Max looked at him dubiously. "An EV..."

"Dude, my bad. An EVP. It stands for electronic voice phenomenon. It just means that the recorder picked up a sound we couldn't hear with the naked ear, which is pretty typical of the paranormal. It's hard for spirits to make vocalizations so using the recorders gives us an advantage. Although, in this case we couldn't really call it an EVP."

"Why is that?" Marcia asked almost defensively.

"Because she's not a ghost. The infrared indicated a human temp, not to mention the quality of the voice. Definitely doesn't sound disembodied, not that it's impossible. We've gotten Class A's that are this good, but given the infrared evidence, and the fact that it was from the recorder next to her it seems pretty likely that it's her voice."

CJ replayed the sound bite, the foreign phrase confounding Max. "You think she said that? It sounded like another language."

"Good ear. That's kind of what we thought," Jace emphasized.

CJ pulled up a window to reveal another sound program. "I clarified the wave, cleaned out the background noise which was pretty easy since the only other sound is the MC's low-pitched voice, and ran the wave through this translation software." He played the sound bite again as the software processed the wave.

Max watched as foreign letters appeared. He turned toward Katherine, unable to hide his disbelief. "It's Greek."

Katherine's and Marcia's eyes widened.

Jace smiled as Thai captured their reactions with his camera. "It gets better." He put his hand on CJ's shoulder. "Why don't you translate that for us, buddy?"

CJ used his mouse to copy the letters and then pasted them into another program, which translated Greek to English.

The rendered transcription rattled Max to his core. He shot out of his seat, running his hands through his hair.

Katherine hurried over and peered at the screen. Reading the short sentence she stifled a gasp.

"What is it?" Marcia insisted.

Katherine stared at Max. "My only love; never leave me."

Marcia covered her mouth with her palm. Cain documented the reactions with his camera as Jace approached Max.

"Paranormal enough for you?"

"We've already established that she's not a ghost," Max said, more for his own pacification.

Jace looked to the camera. "Yeah, which means we may be dealing with possession, or at least a reincarnation."

"Oh, come on," Max balked.

Jace looked at him as if he could pin him down with little more than a potent glance. "Do you have a better explanation?"

Max stared at the wall as Jace walked toward Katherine and Marcia. "I think we need to stay here for a few more days. This is pretty serious."

"Definitely," Marcia said without hesitation.

Max hoped his words wouldn't come out as adamantly as he felt about them. "I'm sure that's not necessary."

Katherine spoke gently. "I think it may be a good idea, Max. This is... we don't really know what this is."

Seeing the worry on her face Max conceded. "Two days."

"Awesome." Jace smiled. "Let's get some sleep, boys. We've got another long night to look forward to."

Marcia clapped giddily as Katherine gave Max a comforting smile.

Max sat at his desk unable to rid his mind of the voice he had heard. After leaving the swell he had spent over two hours scouring the internet for information on Galen and Isaura. The book, having not been a tremendous success and now out of print, seemed unattainable. Max reminded himself that the statue had taken him months to locate. He would eventually find the book, though doing so in the next four weeks was rather unlikely.

Max headed toward the door and stepped out of his office just as Katherine arrived in front of him. She looked at him with surprise.

"Are you leaving? Should I cancel our lunch meeting?"

"I need to see Claire Simmons. She must know something about our Isaura. Maybe she just didn't want to tell me over the phone," Max rationalized, sliding his arm into the sleeve of his coat.

"I'll come with you," Katherine said.

"I'd rather go by myself. Besides, if we keep spending all this time together Marcia will think you've switched sides," he winked adorably.

"I doubt that. Keep me posted?" Katherine made him promise.

He hurried out of the building, yelling back to her. "Yep."

Max arrived at Claire's shop, instantly recognizing the gallery as one he had strolled past many times. In any other business an overworked entrepreneur would despise the idea of an impromptu chat, but gallery owners, to Max's good fortune, always made time for guests. He entered and approached the secretary.

"Hello, I'm Maxwell Turner. We spoke earlier in the week. I was hoping that I might see Miss Simmons for a moment."

The cordial woman glanced up at Max. Taking pause to study his pristine features, she flushed before answering.

"She's in a meeting right now, but she should be finished shortly. Would you like to have a look around the gallery while you wait?"

"Thank you," Max agreed. He walked toward an exhibit, perusing it with polite interest. He made his way through two more artists' works, his eyes finally coming to rest on a beautiful, avant-garde collection of oil on canvas pieces detailing people as they experienced various emotions. Max was mesmerized by the display. The secretary watched from her desk, rising to refill her coffee. She eyed Max before joining him.

"Lovely, isn't it?"

"Very."

"One of our brightest stars," she smiled.

Continuing his examination of the collection, Max focused on a painting of a young woman whose neck branched into two heads with very dissimilar facial expressions; one exhibiting confident independence and the other gnarled as if from hellacious despair. "I can see why. This is incredible."

"That's the Vie Diabolique. Certainly a crowd stopper."

Max glanced at the artist's name plate. *Miranda Cova*. "Does she come in often?"

The secretary shook her head. "I'm afraid not. Miss Cova keeps to herself, mostly. It's all Claire can do to get her to attend her own openings. I understand she had a difficult upbringing though I'm not familiar with the details," she admitted.

"When is her next opening?"

"It happens to be this weekend." She picked up a tri-folded brochure, handing it to him. "Here's a program. We'd be delighted to have someone of your reputation in attendance."

"I'd love to," Max agreed before remembering his recent transition from director to model. "But I'm a bit more, ah... well I'm unusually involved with the art this season," he said nervously. "I'll do my best."

Max looked across the room to see Claire, a tall and slender woman with an almost sculpted complexion. He watched as she exited her office with three other individuals. The group shook hands awkwardly, Claire's right wrist in a cast. She escorted her guests out before heading toward her office entrance. As if sensing his presence, she turned to see Max standing next to Miranda's display.

"Hello. Can I help you find something?" Claire asked.

"No, actually, I was hoping to speak with you. I'm Max Turner."

Claire slid her left hand into his right, squeezing it gently.

"You're the art director?" she asked as if his looks were a pleasant surprise. "I pictured you a bit differently," she smiled. The innuendo made Max look away shyly. "Is everything alright at the exhibition?" she continued.

"Well, not really, no. I'm having a rather difficult time with the finale."

Claire's eyes dropped and she seemed to question her own relevance in the matter. "Is there something you think I may be able to help you with?"

Max felt a twitch of disappointment, her reaction convincing him that she was ignorant as to the show's odd happenings. "I know I already asked you about the woman who replaced you. You said you don't know her?"

"Not at all. I called your casting director, Frankie I think, as soon as the x-rays confirmed the fracture. I hadn't heard from anyone at the exhibition since your phone call." She seemed to realize that her words may have been misleading. "Not that I expected... I mean I would never expect the exhibition to take any responsibility for my accident, it wasn't anyone's fault," she stammered.

Max gave her a reassuring nod. "Of course. It's just that... ah, we're a little perplexed about the identity of the woman who took your place."

"I don't understand," she replied.

"That's the sentiment of the month. You see, when we heard of your injury we had no time to replace you. Apparently there was a height and weight requirement that was somewhat difficult to match."

Claire smiled at the unintentional compliment. "Yes, I know. When I signed up to join the cast I had no interest in being one of the nudes, but Frankie is quite a persuasive person," she grinned.

"I very much agree with you. Anyway, you can imagine our surprise when a woman with your proportions, appeared on the platform in full... dress, you might say."

"Wait, what do you mean, appeared on the platform?"

As much as he hated it, Max knew that this was not the time for ambiguity. "On the night of your injury she emerged from the forested area just before the lights went on, assumed the appropriate pose, and then slipped back into the woods as the lights went out."

Claire studied him, clearly shocked. "You're kidding."

"And every night since then she's been doing the same thing. We're more than a little concerned."

Claire shook her head. "Can't you talk to her?" she asked.

"She won't respond to us, and we can't exactly pin her down, considering her attire for the show."

Claire's looked away as if embarrassed by an uninvited mental image. "No, I wouldn't recommend that."

"Do you know anything that could be of help to us? Is there someone that may have been aware of your cancellation? I mean, whoever she is she had to have known of your situation in plenty of time to get someone to spray her with gold paint and teach her the pose."

"No, unless someone from the emergency room overheard me talking about it," she assured him.

"So, you didn't discuss it with anyone else?" Max fished.

"Just one of my closer friends, but she's an agoraphobic. She barely leaves her home and spends most her time painting," Claire smiled with pride, indicating toward Miranda's work.

Max's eyes grew bright as he contemplated the unlikely yet gripping possibility. "You don't mean the same woman who painted these?"

"Yes, Miranda Cova." Max returned his gaze to the painting as Claire continued. "She's an intensely talented person but has been battling emotional problems for most of her life."

"I'd love to meet her," Max heard his eager voice announce.

"That would be very difficult. Her condition is quite severe."

Max tried to sound impartial as his mind frolicked. "Will she be at the opening?"

Claire offered a weak smile, the subject clearly disheartening. "I can't say for sure but I always try to convince her. We're holding it at six thirty in the hopes that she'll make a quick appearance. It should give us an hour or more of sunlight. She's grown terrified of the night. It's always been a challenge for her but these days she won't even pick up her phone after seven pm."

Max pondered the comment, vaguely aware of his subconscious as it indulged in an audacious theory. *Maybe she won't pick up after seven because she's not home.* "I see. Well, thanks again for your time, Miss Simmons. I'm sorry to have bothered you twice this week."

"Not at all," she said, almost caressing his hand as he again shook hers. "I certainly hope to see you at the opening."

Six thirty, Max thought. It would be tight but he knew he couldn't miss the opportunity to see Miranda

Cova, if only for a few moments. Max nodded as he reached for the door. "I believe you will."

An odd feeling crept over him, drawing his attention to the window. Just outside the gallery an older woman peered at him, the look on her face filling him with a sense of doom. He stopped, alarmed to see her slink away. He looked back at Claire who didn't seem to share his concern, a fact that made him feel foolish. He said goodbye as he left the gallery.

Grateful to start a morning with no calls from Jace, Max looked forward to the walk he'd been deprived of the day prior. He parked his car, waving at the shuttle filled with Laguna Beach business professionals. Max glanced around the captivating city as he considered which route to take to work and smiled, swiftly aware that he knew exactly which route to take today and every other for the remainder of the week. Locking his car door, Max headed toward Claire's gallery. Sauntering down a sloped cobblestone road, the vast sea holding up the horizon ahead, Max's thoughts were consumed by his mysterious Isaura. *Or is it Miranda?*

He shook his head. It didn't make any sense. *What had Claire said? Her condition is quite severe,* he remembered. Max chastised himself for entertaining the possibility that Miranda Cova was his Isaura, the enigmatic beauty who now so easily commanded every spare moment inside his mind. The woman who, for reasons which Max could not reconcile, found a way to shed her clothing, coat herself in gold spray paint, and struggle through the brush of the amphitheater each evening, only to arrive in his arms as the motionless, silent embodiment of a Greek tragedy.

We may be dealing with a possession or at least a reincarnation. Max laughed as he recalled Jace's words, surprised that any part of him could consider such a theory. Still, how she was pulling this off was inexplicable. And Miranda Cova, no matter how ill, was the only person aware of Claire's broken arm. Why would someone so frightened of others be inclined to participate in something so bold? And why do so in secret?

A few feet away a local artist practiced her craft on the small section of sidewalk she had claimed. Her focus steadfast on her work, she scoured a thin, three-by-five foot piece of sheet metal which she had propped against an easel. Max looked at the bottles of acrylic spray paint around her, curious as to her goal. Slowing his pace he noted several finished pieces and worked fast to discern what he was seeing. One of the pieces was a luminescent depiction of the ocean against a crisp sky. As Max moved in closer, the waves making up the lower half of the piece seemed to move with him. Dazzling hues of blues and greens appeared to undulate despite their dimensional constraints.

"These are amazing. I've not seen this technique before," he divulged, intentionally swaying as the waters danced back at him.

The silent artist continued to scrub the sheet, creating semicircular abrasions in the metal.

Max watched carefully. "These are the waves. You'll apply color next? How do you get them to be so glossy?"

She answered plainly without looking up from her work. "When they're finished I take them to an auto body shop. They glaze them in a clear topcoat." The woman lifted her hat and blotted her forehead with the scarf, which also served as her hair tie. Her blousy, bohemian style of dress was consistent with that of an idiosyncratic Lagunaphile. Max spotted another piece which was tucked in the corner of her sprawl, hiding behind some paint cans and bags of scouring pads. He carefully lifted it, amazed by its weight.

"It's so light." Max studied the piece, its intensity overwhelming his senses. The image portrayed a woman in apparent agony. Her contorted face seemed to scream at the heavens; her long, creamy neck extended toward the sky. It offered brilliant contrast to her fiery red hair, which also flowed upward and whirled around her face like flames. A strange feeling of sorrow penetrated Max. "What is the title?"

"It's unnamed,"

"I'll take it."

The woman looked at the ground as if sad to part with it. "Two thousand."

"I'll take it," Max repeated.

Chapter 9

Max arrived at the exhibition entrance in time to enter with Marcia and Katherine. He quickly described his encounter with Claire.

"So, you honestly think our Isaura is this artist woman; the one with all of the anxiety problems?" Katherine asked.

"I realize it sounds a little outrageous, but no one else knew about Claire's cancellation. I can't rule her out until I see her in person."

Katherine glanced down at the wrapped, rectangular object tucked under Max's arm and seemed to fight to keep her eyes from rolling. "Not another local artist."

Max smiled as he turned away.

Katherine groaned. "Come on, Max. You're like a crazy cat lady."

"Except for the fact that I'm not a lady. Oh, and this isn't a cat," he said as he lifted the rectangular object and walked toward his office. Katherine followed quickly behind him.

"The metaphor was in reference to your commitment to purchase, at ungodly prices I might add, every visceral creation from the 133 to Corona Del Mar."

"I hope you're ready to apologize," he predicted playfully, unwrapping the piece. "By the way that was a simile."

"What?"

"The cat thing. Not a true metaphor."

"Thank you very much. I'm super embarrassed," she replied wryly.

Max smiled, thoroughly amused by their back and forth. "You should be."

"Hurry up," Marcia urged, clearly a fan of his impulse buying.

"At least someone enjoys my spontaneity." He turned the piece over, eliciting an unreadable look from Katherine and a sigh from Marcia.

Max beamed. "I know. You love it, don't you?"

"Oh my God, it's incredible," Marcia said.

Max kept a cocky stare on Katherine as he waited for her verdict.

"It's amazing," she muttered.

Max bowed his head, accepting her apology.

"What's it called?" Marcia asked.

A hint of frustration accompanied Max's reply. "Unfortunately it's untitled."

"Is she victim or villain?" Marcia asked, as if uncertain if the piece portrayed pain or anger.

Max nodded. "Maybe that's why it's untitled."

Katherine shot Max a knowing smile. "It's going on the wall just outside your bedroom, right?"

Max slapped his palm against hers.

Miranda sat on her living room floor eating Chinese food straight out of the box while Claire effervesced.

"Of course I thanked them until I was hoarse; I just can't believe they bought the entire series."

Miranda nodded supportively.

"But why am I bothering you with business stories, when I could be telling you about the very interested patron that couldn't stop asking about you today." She grinned as she studied her friend for a reaction. "Tall, handsome, and totally intrigued by your work."

"Liar," Miranda said softly, her eyes on her food.

Claire continued. "Sorry, Darling, but it's all true."

Miranda regarded her with uncertainty. "Who?" she asked before guiding a bite of fried rice into her mouth.

"Oh, just Max Turner, the director of the Exhibition of Living Arts." Miranda choked and coughed, Claire instinctively patting her back. "He's unbelievably good looking. I'm going to the show next week." Miranda's eyes widened as Claire spoke. "I guess they're having some drama with my replacement." Miranda turned her face from her friend, desperate to hide her sudden distress. "Are you alright? You look a little pale," Claire said.

"I'm fine," Miranda lied, grateful for Claire's lapse in intuition.

"Anyway, what a babe. I'm not kidding, Rand. Maybe you should come with me."

"Ah... I don't think so," Miranda replied, her hands starting to tremble.

"Okay, we'll take it slow. But I hope you're doing your exercises, because the opening is only three days away and I need you to come; even if it's just for an hour." Miranda recoiled.

"Have you been taking your new medication?" Claire asked.

"No."

"Why not?"

Miranda's eyes grew damp as she looked up at Claire. "I can't paint when I take them."

Claire hugged her hard. "Miranda, I think it's time for you to start pushing yourself a little more."

Exactly, an all too familiar voiced echoed in Miranda's mind.

"I know you're scared, sweetie, but you're safe now. You have a city of admirers, an amazing gift, and a fabulous best friend."

Miranda laughed, wiping her eyes before taking another bite.

Max stood on the dark platform overlooking the infinitude of patrons. In a few moments his strange beauty would emerge. He wondered if she would speak. The thought reminded him of the eerie EVP, and Jace's words once again invaded his thoughts. Before he could replay them, the crack of a branch redirected his attention. *Isaura?* The herbaceous sweetness of fig leaf and cassis filled the night as the female subject slipped into Max's arms, the fragrance proving that he had correctly attributed it to her on their first night together. While it was difficult to avoid speaking, he reminded himself that cameras and audio recorders surrounded them, and he certainly didn't want to give the ghost crew any clues as to his identity.

The stage lights came up, bathing the couple in a warmth which momentarily caused Max to forget the world around him. There she was, whoever she was, nestled in his arms as if she belonged to him. Gilded and transfixed, showered in lights that may as well have been from the heavens, Max couldn't imagine a more perfect feeling. It was as if God himself had willed their union, however unconventional.

The lights dimmed and Max and his partner were once again consumed by the night. It was amazing how quickly a feeling of rapture could be replaced by one of frigid darkness. The snap of a large twig once again startled Max. This time it was followed by distinct footsteps. His heart raced as the footsteps approached from behind. Isaura had clearly heard something as well, her smooth shoulders now subtly pulsing with each breath. The footsteps stopped and Max froze, refusing to breathe. A hissing sound arose from behind them, filling him with a dread he had never experienced. Something was whispering, of that he was certain. It took all of his willpower to remain still. The footsteps picked back up, then tapered off until he could no longer hear them. The platform lights came up and music triumphantly played, ending the terror.

Ten minutes later Max burst into the storage room, his wet hair dripping onto his shirt. His face still tight from the frightening sounds he had heard on the platform, he made no effort to conceal the fear in his voice. "There was something with us in the forest."

Jace barely looked up from the monitor. It was then that Max realized everyone in the room was focused on the screens. Katherine looked sick.

"Yeah, we know man. Come over here."

Max joined him at the monitor as CJ cued up the footage.

"You know you could have just told me about being the Galen dude. It's not like I'd frown on it."

Max looked down. "It's not something that I wished to discuss."

"I got it. Just saying, it's not a big deal." He refocused his attention on the screen. "This… is a big deal. Tell him, CJ."

CJ clicked his mouse and surveillance footage began to play. "This is the angle on the actual platform. Everything looks normal until the lights go out," he explained.

Max nodded. "That's when I heard the branch snapping, then the footsteps. Can't you get an angle on what's behind us?" CJ looked reluctant to share the next clip. He opened the file and cued the footage to ten fifteen. "That's the same time I heard the branches snapping last night."

"Yep. We're thinking she might have been behind the tree; that's why we didn't see her when we reviewed the footage."

"What do you mean by she?" Max asked.

"After you heard the branches last night, we decided to expand the angle to include the clearing and the platform in the same shot. We figured whatever you heard had to be close by."

CJ played the video. Max watched as the image of the platform and adjacent clearing was displayed; he could see himself and Isaura in position. His eyes flickering as movement entered the frame. Panic set in as the outline of a woman slowly approached the platform.

"Who the hell is that?"

Jace shook his head. "We don't know but she sure hates your partner."

The image grew more disturbing as the woman stopped less than an arm's length from Max, leaning toward him and appearing to speak.

Katherine and Marcia watched as the terrifying footage unfolded.

Max fought to get his words out. "What's she doing?"

"Cue up the audio recording," said Jace.

CJ brought up a sound bite and matched it to the exact time on the video. Playing both sound and video together, an insidious whisper filled the room.

Max looked at his friends, their fear potentiating his own. He shook his head. "What did she say? Play it again."

CJ hesitated before cuing up the tracks and hitting play. Max was again assaulted by the haunting image of the dark female figure as she hovered behind his exposed back, her mouth moving in alignment with a hiss of vowels. An A, another A, an E, and an extended I. The stream was indiscernible until Jace gave his interpretation of the phrase.

"St-a-a-a-ay aw-a-a-a-ay, he-e-e-e's mi-i-i-i-ine." Jace whispered forcefully, over-emphasizing the explicit vowels.

Max couldn't argue; Jace's assessment was spot on.

Katherine put her hand on Max's shoulder. "We have to cancel this piece."

"No," Max insisted. "I won't do it."

"Did you see how close she came to you?" she argued.

"Can we look at her on infras? Maybe the chick behind you is the real Isaura and she's pissed at the gold imposter. 'Stay away, he's mine'," Thai hypothesized.

Jace wagged his finger as he seemed to contemplate the thought. "That's a very good point. Hit it."

CJ complied by isolating the infrared footage and cuing it to ten fifteen. He clicked the mouse, and the video displayed a yellow figure which stood behind the similarly-colored couple on the platform.

"Human," Jace said.

For Max, the words brought some relief.

Katherine looked at Jace with disbelief. "I'm sorry, but does that really matter?" she asked, turning to Max. Your obviously not safe, either of you. It's not worth it. If you can't be protective of yourself then think about her well-being."

Max looked down, no longer able to disagree. "I can't secure the trails. If I do Isaura, won't be able to get in. I guess we don't have a choice."

Marcia seemed contemplative as she approached the monitors. She turned to look at Jace. "Where did the other one come from?"

"That's the big question," he replied.

"No, I mean from which area. Right, left…"

Jace pointed to the screen. "It's got to be from the canyon. The side cameras only show the lady in gold entering and exiting."

"So, is she living there?"

Jace shook his head. "Impossible. Like I said, there's some serious wildlife in that canyon."

Marcia countered. "Yes, and a seriously monstrous gorge just beyond the trees. She has to be using our trails to even get back there. The only question is *when* is she coming, since the cameras you set up just before the show aren't picking her up."

The explanation finally clicking, Max nodded. "She must be coming before we set up the cameras. She's probably using the same path as Isaura to get to the clearing, then hiding behind the trees until the finale. It just looks like she's entering from the canyon."

Jace frowned as he considered the idea. "What in the hell would make someone want to go to that much trouble?"

"You already said it, bro. Maybe she's possessed," Cain replied.

Katherine glanced warily at her boss. "Or obsessed, Max. It's not safe. Cancel it before something bad happens."

"No, dude; check it out. We'll just beat her to the spot. The guys and I can wait behind the trees. If you're right, she'll come early and we can grab her before anyone even arrives. If that doesn't work then go ahead and cancel it."

Max looked at Katherine, then at Marcia. Neither of them seemed to have an opposing viewpoint.

"Okay. Either way this ends tomorrow night," he said.

Lying on his bed in darkness, Max stared as his ceiling, his mind too overwhelmed for a night of rest. The thought that the mystery of the second woman could finally be solved was of little comfort given the fact that Isaura's identity was still unknown. Accepting the futility of sleep, he hopped out of bed and grabbed his glasses from the nightstand, climbing out of bed. Heading to his desk, he put on his glasses and took a seat as he fired up the computer. Max opened his page of computerized bookmarks and systematically revisited each site pertaining to his search for the Galen and Isaura novel. Just as before, the book proved unattainable. He continued his efforts for another three hours, fatigue ending the pursuit. When sleep finally found him, it came with dreams of his Isaura.

Fractured memories, one after another, streamed together as if longing for meaning. *My only love; never leave me,* her heard her voice beg both in English and overlapping in Greek. The phrase jolted him from his dream, the voice that whispered it still fresh in his mind. Max glanced around the room to find it empty, save the brisk morning breeze that whipped through his open windows. He didn't recall leaving them open, but refused to let the thought upset him. He jumped out of bed, looking forward to the day's resolution.

Max arrived at the exhibition and approached the main entrance. The deserted grounds were still damp from morning dew; a look that was quite becoming. He realized that, unlike each prior season, he had yet to review the art that made up this year's festival. He had been so consumed with the start of the show, and the tumultuous weeks that followed, he hadn't even glanced at the new exhibits. Veering to the right he passed the gift shop and headed toward the first of many display booths, which lined the festival grounds in a horseshoe pattern.

Stopping at a fifty-inch rectangular canvas, Max studied the brush strokes of a grand beach scene. The swirling blue hues of the waves instantly elevated his spirits. The sky, an icy cerulean, seemed to long for misty clouds. His enjoyment of the piece was as bittersweet as usual; a painful reminder that had his talent not paled in comparison to his appreciation, he would have joined the pantheon of the masters.

Refusing to nourish the concept that his life was in any way unfortunate, he made his way to the children's section. Seeing unfathomable contributions from even kindergarteners, the grasp on his own pride began to wane and he found it difficult to look upon the various entries. From towering graphite landscapes to introspective self-portraits, each piece made it clear that there was no shortage of ability for these rising stars.

He cut short his tour and entered the amphitheater, his eyes searching the empty area. *The swell,* he deduced, walking to the side of the theater and entering the revamped storage room. Inside, Marcia and Katherine busied themselves on laptops as the audiovisual team studied the monitors.

"Where's Jace?" Max asked.

"He and his crew are already up there," Katherine replied, CJ pointing to a screen displaying the team playing cards behind the trees.

"I guess they're not kidding around," said Max as he approached Katherine. "Are you guys going to work in here all day?"

"I've got a meeting in an hour but this one couldn't be pried away," she answered, motioning toward Marcia. Marcia seemed to ignore the comment and continued typing.

"It's awfully early isn't it?" Max asked.

Katherine nodded and folded her laptop closed, glancing toward her partner as if making one final attempt. "You know this is only a theory, right? And even if she is coming, she's not going to sit behind a tree for ten hours. Let's come back closer to eight."

"No thanks, I'm good," Marcia replied.

Katherine and Max exchanged idle looks before leaving the others to their vigils. He followed her out of the room and onto the stage. Katherine surveyed the hillside, her eyes resting on the only entrance to the amphitheater before she turned toward Max. "We'd never hear the end of it if she did come early."

Max lifted his brow in agreement and headed to the back of the stage. "I'll take the chance," he chuckled.

At nearly five o'clock, Max and Katherine had given in and rejoined Marcia inside the swell. Though she seemed as perky as when she started, the loitering was obviously wearing on her boss and partner.

"No, *I* like the idea of adding a vocalist for one number but I think the patrons may not," Katherine said.

Max removed his glasses and wiped the lenses clean. "They enjoy live musicians, so why not give them a live singer it a try?"

Katherine looked at his bare face. "Have you ever tried contacts?"

"I couldn't stand them."

"What about laser surgery?" she pushed.

He gave her a grin that would have made putty out of a straight woman. "Are you trying to say you don't like my glasses?"

"No, I like your glasses, it's just…"

Before she could explain CJ sat up straight in his chair. "I see something." The group hurried to the monitors. CJ pointed to the screen which displayed the bushes lining the sound booth trail. An older woman emerged and made her way toward the clearing.

"Is that her?" Marcia asked.

Katherine's voice reflected her nervousness. "It's got to be."

CJ depressed a button on his walkie-talkie. "We see her. She's making her way toward you, bro," his drone not enough to leach energy from the discovery.

Max ran out of the room and headed up the outermost theater aisle. Marcia attempted to follow but stopped when Katherine grabbed her arm and held her back.

Behind the trees, Jace stiffened as he heard the alert. He covered his ear with his fingers and gestured a warning to his team. Thai quietly readied his camera while Cain struggled to turn his on while maintaining his guard. Jace watched for the woman. Seconds later she appeared, gasping upon seeing the men in wait.

"Okay chill. Now," Jace commanded.

The woman turned to run, only to see Max closing in on her from the sound booth trail.

"Please, wait," she cried.

Max carefully switched his gaze from his terrain to the woman as he ran, quickly catching up with her. He stopped and stared, struck by the familiarity of her face. It was the woman from Claire's gallery; the one that was watching him from behind the window.

"What are you doing here?"

Before she could answer, Jace interjected with heightened bravado. "Are you aware that you're trespassing on private property?"

The woman stuttered as if searching for an excuse. Max analyzed her deliberate features and light olive complexion. Though time had tried, it had failed to take from her what was once an undeniable natural beauty. And while she had no accent and did nothing to tame her bleached- blonde hair that was mixing well with grey, he was certain of her Greek heritage; perhaps second generation. The realization made his already rapid heart-rate increase. "Why are you doing this? Have you been following me?"

"We're going to call the cops," Jace yelled.

"No! I'm sorry. I just wanted to see..." Sobs halted her response and she let her knees fall onto the soft earth below her feet.

Jace pummeled her with a barrage of questions while his teams' cameras captured the inquisition. Jace pointed toward Max. "Are you in love with him? Is that what's going on? Are you the reincarnation of Isaura and angry that the lady in gold has stolen your lover?"

Max felt completely embarrassed for the old woman as he watched confusion come over her dusty face.

"No, of course not," she replied.

"Why did you whisper then? We have the recording." He pulled a digital recorder from his pocket and depressed the play button. The ghostly hiss sounded and Jace mouthed the words, 'stay away; he's mine'. "What were you going to do to her if she didn't stay away? Why are you so angry?" he continued.

Max studied her face which no longer appeared bogged by fear as much as sorrow. She looked down as tears washed streaks of dirt from her face.

"I'm sorry. You won't see me again. Please, just let me go. I won't come back."

Noting her misery, Max found himself unable to remain angry. "Go," he said, holding up his hand before the ghost crew could object. They watched as she ran back down the trail and out of the amphitheater.

Max helped the ghost crew load their equipment into the large van parked outside the exhibition entrance. Katherine approached Jace, Marcia following like a shadow.

"Thank you for everything. I really appreciate it."

Jace hugged her. "Are you kidding? We were happy to do it. And it was tight hanging out again."

Max walked over and shook his hand. "Thanks, man."

"Don't mention it. I still wish you'd let us figure out the identity of the lady in gold," Jace replied.

"I think we'll just give her some time."

"So, when's the show going to air?" Marcia asked with eyes as full as her grin.

"Oh, not for a few months at least. But I promise I'll call you and give you a heads up. It's going to be a good one," he replied.

Thai waved before getting in the van. "Take care, guys."

"You too... bro." Max smiled, his awkward delivery causing the ghost crew to erupt in laughter. Max and his team watched as the van pulled out into traffic. He put his arms around his friends. "Well ladies, if you'll excuse me I have to go shave my legs."

The woman giggled as they headed toward the main entrance, Max parting ways and walking toward the ocean.

Back home Max changed into an outfit he had been considering ever since he heard about Claire's opening. He stood in front of his full-length bedroom mirror, fussing with his collar as he eyed himself. Max hoped that the smoky blazer and grey corduroy pants looked professional yet youthful; he couldn't remember ever having been this nervous about meeting a woman. *Lose the glasses?* Taking them off he realized he wouldn't be able to see Miranda. He repositioned them and headed to the car.

Max spent most of the drive practicing a fetching introduction, intermittently dodging random thoughts of the sad old woman. He pulled the car into a less than roomy space at the bank-by-day, extortionist-by-night parking lot near Claire's gallery. Paying a slovenly parking attendant ten dollars for a mere two hours, Max reminded himself that this was yet another reason to abide by his walking over driving policy. He checked his hair in a local store's main window and straightened his already shipshape blazer before entering Claire's gallery.

Inside, a wealth of impressively dressed patrons browsed the many exhibits. They sipped champagne, discussed the torturous summer traffic, and bonded over their abilities to inflate what they knew, or more often didn't know, about the various paintings. He searched the room for any sign of Claire or her intriguing friend. A server handed him a champagne flute, inadvertently distracting him from seeing Claire duck into her office.

Max found his way to a wall of personal pictures, awards, and framed newspaper clippings. Examining each item, his eyes landed on a dormitory photo. In it Claire stood hugging another then young woman as they modeled their matching college sweatshirts. For

the second time that week Max was struck with a
sense of familiarity. The woman with Claire... he
knew her from somewhere. He searched for the
answer, frustrated with his inability to put a name to
the face.

Claire pulled Miranda into the office and closed
the door before grabbing a short glass from an elegant
cocktail cart. Choosing a flavored vodka she poured
her shaky friend a generous serving. "Now, I want
you to try this. Go ahead. It will help a lot."

Miranda reluctantly accepted, downing the harsh
liquid. She coughed, grimacing against the burn.

"Good. One more," she urged as she reached for
the bottle, compelling Miranda to throw up her hand.

"That's enough," she managed to say despite her
stinging throat.

"How are you feeling?" Claire asked.

Miranda gave a helpless shrug.

"Okay," Claire took Miranda's arm and gently
guided her out of the office. Seeing the space
overflowing with patrons, Miranda assigned her gaze
to the burnished hardwood flooring and focused on
her breathing. Ever the extrovert, Claire smiled
brightly as she looked around the bustling room. She
noted Max in a split second and nudged Miranda, who
immediately attempted to shrink into herself. "That's
him, Rand, that's Max Turner. God, he's gorgeous,"
she whispered.

Miranda's eyes ballooned and she stared at her
feet, her breathing growing labored. From across the
room, Max seemed to sense her presence, and
immediately approached. Miranda scrambled for
some excuse to leave, but it was too late. Max
extended his hand to Claire, though his eyes remained
locked on Miranda as he spoke.

111

"Hello, Miss Simmons."

"Claire," the flirtatious gallery owner corrected. "I'm so glad you could make it."

"Hello Miss Cova. I'm Max," he uttered softly, his eyes burning as if with curiosity.

"Miranda," she eked out, unable to look at him.

"What a pleasure," Max smiled, gently taking her hand.

A strange jolt accompanied his delicate grasp. Miranda shuddered, concentrating on maintaining her balance.

"I must tell you, I don't remember the last time I felt so drawn to an artist's work," he praised.

She refused to look at him though she ardently wanted to. "Thank you."

"You should come to my show sometime. I think you may really enjoy it," Max baited, hoping to illicit a telling reaction. "Both of you."

"We'd love to. Maybe next weekend. Excuse us, Max," Claire smiled.

"Of course. It was very nice to meet you, Miss Cova. I hope to see you again soon."

Miranda peeked up just long enough to take in the amative blaze in Max's eyes. It was the most irresistible expression she had ever seen and this time she found it difficult to look away. She swallowed hard despite the lack of moisture in her mouth. After what seemed like an interminable amount of time, Claire ushered her away. Miranda regained a modicum of control before arriving at a veiled easel. She stared at the velvet drape as her body went numb. Only then did she realize the problem with showing that piece. Her heart rate shot up and she gulped for air.

"Claire, I don't want to show the new piece," she quivered.

Claire laughed. "What are you talking about? It's spectacular."

"Please, I just don't want to."

"Nonsense. Have a little faith in yourself, Rand. I'll be right back." Claire positioned herself alongside the easel and began quieting the crowd. "Hello everyone, good afternoon or I guess evening now. May I have your attention, please? Thank you all for joining us for this special event. I could spend all day raving about our featured artist's work to date, but I wouldn't be telling you anything you don't already know. And so, without making my infatuation for her gift too obvious, I give you Miranda Cova's latest masterpiece, Liebestraum."

Miranda forced her eyes closed as Claire peeled the velvet away from the canvas, revealing a painting of a nude man and woman, not as a statue, but very similar in positioning to that of The Embrace. The guests applauded loudly as Miranda, dizzy with anxiety, struggled to avoid running out of the gallery. Her heart beat pelted her chest wall and drummed against her ears. She stared at the ground, concentrating on her breathing while attempting to force away the sounds of applause.

Max felt his heart stop, his lips parting as he stared at the piece. He couldn't hear a sound; couldn't will a charge over his expression. It was her; his strange beauty had a name. Miranda Cova. He tried to swallow as another reality struck him, one nearly as startling as her identity. Not only had she made their embrace the subject of her latest creation, which in and of itself was an astonishingly good sign, she had given her piece a very profound title. *Liebestraum*. He dissected the word with what little he knew of the German language. *Love's... dream.*

113

Claire, smiling broadly as she let her eyes roam across the room of patrons, appeared confused as she noticed Max. She watched as his expression slowly evolved from one of shock to one of adoration. He gazed at the piece, and then scanned the crowd. Claire turned as if to look for Miranda, and appeared alarmed to find that she was gone.

Max drove toward the exhibition as fast as he could without attracting unwanted attention from Laguna's finest. He spoke into his car's hands-free telecommunication device, gushing as his words raced out of his mouth.

"It's definitely her, Katherine. I'm sure of it."

"I must admit it does seem to be the case." Max heard Katherine reply

"I'm here. Tell Annie two seconds."

Screeching up to the valet curb, Max jammed the vehicle into park before running passed a friendly attendant.

"I'll catch you on the way out, Jason."

"No worries Mr. Turner," the attendant smiled as he watched him run. Max hurried onto the exhibition grounds and made his way to the makeup room. Once inside he saw Annie, who held up his thong with obvious irritation.

"I'm allergic to adrenaline, Max."

He ripped the thong from her, bolting into the changing room and pulling the curtain closed. Smacked by sudden recognition, a slow smile came over his face. He yelled out to her as he changed. "Sorry, Annie. I was just getting the scoop on our mystery lady."

"You figured out who she is?" Annie shouted back, her face far more apprehensive than her tone revealed.

"I did," he announced ominously.

Max walked out of his dressing room wearing a robe. He slinked into a makeup chair as Annie fiddled with his head piece nervously.

"Her name is Miranda Cova. Her best friend Claire was your college roommate," Max peered suspiciously at the paralyzed woman through her reflection in the mirror. She remained fixed in place for a moment before confessing.

"I'm sorry, Max. I wanted to tell you, but she begged me to keep it a secret."

"Claire?"

"No, Miranda."

Max reeled, amazed that the sound of her name could have such an effect on him.

"I'd met her a few times and she knew I worked here. She was with us on the day I tried to convince Claire to become a nude."

"How did you do that exactly?"

Annie looked back at him as if confused by the new line of questioning. "I told her it wasn't what she was thinking. That it was very elegant and that no one would even know it was her with all the makeup."

"That's all?"

"I think I mentioned that it's healthy to push oneself and that you're not really living if you're staying in your comfort zone... why do you ask?"

"And you weren't directing any of that toward Miranda?" he asked in an accusing tone.

"Maybe a little. It's not like I thought she'd actually take it to heart; she was practically a shut in. I kind of always thought Claire coddled her too much and that Miranda might do better if she started fighting her fears instead of giving into them."

Max suddenly realized how instrumental Annie had been in Miranda's decision. "So, Claire broke her arm. Then what happened?"

"It's a long, long story."

"That's okay, you have just under two minutes," he said with a sarcastic grin.

Katherine adjusted the old backstage monitor as Max approached in costume.

"Thank God. You really cut that one close."

"Yeah, in more ways than one." Max indicated to his smoothly shaved leg.

Katherine ignored the pun. "So, how did Annie take it?"

"It's a really great story that I can't wait to tell you, but first I have to expose myself to nearly three-thousand patrons of the arts."

The designer opened the side door and Max followed him up to the hillside platform. Taking his position, Max tried to exile the thoughts which imperiled his undoing. *She knows that I know. She's not coming. She's gone forever. You just had to push the identity issue...* Max's heart sank as the MC's monologue began. The stage lamps would be firing at any moment. *Where are you?* Max closed his eyes, offering a silent prayer.

Seconds before illumination, Max recognized a heavenly fragrance, hopeful that he hadn't just imagined the growing warmth against his chest. He looked down to see the elegant golden frame that he'd come to adore. The couple stood, silent and motionless, as the lights came up and the audience applauded. Max closed his eyes again, totally aware of his growing affection for his bizarre partner.

"Thank you," he whispered though pursed lips.

The lights dimmed as the MC began his Cupid and Psyche monologue. Max swallowed nervously, knowing that he had only ninety seconds before the finale would conclude, ending their time together.

116

"Miranda, I know it's you. I promise I won't tell anyone who you are. You're safe. I just want to talk to you." Searching for the right words, Max's thoughts turned to the diabolical piece he originally fell for in the gallery; the indelible image of a woman with two faces.

"Is the Vie Diaboleque a self-portrait?" he asked, immediately regretting the intrepid decision. For sixty seconds his partner stared in silence over the crowd. A deep sadness came over Max as he processed the gravity of his mistake.

"Yes," Miranda whispered, shocking Max.

"That's good," he said mostly for himself. "I understand... I think you're very brave and so gifted. I don't know why you're helping us, and I promise I won't ask, but thank you for being here tonight. For whatever reason," he rambled.

Her whisper was almost inaudible but somehow stronger than he would have anticipated. "It's helping me."

Max felt dizzy, overwhelmed by the heartfelt yet baffling confession. The lights once again illuminated as the audience cheered and the finale music played.

The hoard of cast and crew members heading toward the talent garden exit, went mostly unnoticed as Max sorted the thoughts swimming about his mind. Katherine, seated at the tree planter, smiled provocatively as she watched her obviously smitten boss pace around her.

"I'm telling you, Katherine, she's breathtaking. You should see her work. I can't even describe it."

"But what was *she* like?"

"At the gallery opening she was quiet, beautiful, fragile. Then I see her on the platform and she's this strong, daring creature."

"Is she going to keep sneaking on and off the platform every night?"

"I kind of think so, yeah."

Katherine glanced down as if in contemplation before peering at her Max. "Are you going to tell her how you feel about her?"

Max shook off a shy smile. "That might be too much for her right now," he said, a boyish smirk playing across his face. "Hey, do you want to grab a bite? I'm starving."

Katherine stood and headed toward the exit, turning left as Max followed. They only had to walk a few yards before arriving at the Terrace, an outdoor eatery dripping with Laguna charm. They climbed the steps to the elevated dining room and helped themselves into a cozy corner table. Situated against the misty hillside, the restaurant looked like an opulent tree house.

The perimeter would have been little more than a wooden frame of trees were it not for the layers of lush plants and flowers which spiraled around the wooden border, creating walls of natural foliage. Hundreds of tiny twinkle lights flickered amongst the leafage, enchanting the space, as did the delicate votive candles which danced against the stark white linens upon each table. The star-streaked sky, graced by the occasional tree branch, served as the only ceiling.

Max had always loved this place but doubted he had ever appreciated it with the avidity he suddenly felt. "Marcia coming?"

"She's on her way." Katherine replied in her usual flat manner.

Max stifled a chuckle as Katherine focused all of her energy on studying the menu she had already managed to acquire. How funny it was that the beauty of the Terrace had such negligible effects on Katherine, especially when she was hungry.

A waiter approached, greeting them cordially. "Good evening and welcome to The Terrace. Can I start you off with something to drink..." he stopped, his eyes warming with recognition. "Mr. Turner? I thought it was you. Hey, I love you as the Greek Nude guy!"

"Oh my God," Max groaned.

Katherine's eyes stretched as she stared at the menu, clearly worried that looking up would only make the moment worse.

"Oh, is that a secret? It's okay, there are still some people who don't know yet."

Max cleared his throat and glanced around the room. To his relief, the waiter seemed the only person interested in him. "Comforting," he quipped. "What are your specials this evening?"

"I have a pear and Gorgonzola soup with a grilled steak salad…"

Max interjected, "I'll have that, please."

"Make it three. And a bottle of wine." Katherine added.

"You're a saint." Max replied. The waiter, as if finally aware of his discomfort, slinked away.

Max unfolded his napkin and laid it across his lap. "Six more weeks and my public indignation will be but a memory."

"You can start enjoying body hair again," Katherine teased.

"The benefits are endless. How do you think the waiter knew?"

Katherine smiled as she looked at Max's arm. "Well, for one thing, you're shimmering."

Max followed her gaze, noting the subtle luminescence a shower had failed to erase from his arm. "Wonderful," he murmured. The waiter returned and began a proper wine service. "I've got to figure out a way to get Miranda to open up to me. Any ideas?"

"I don't know, Max. But what I do know is that even if you can, given your rather impossible time constraints, you'd still have some serious mental health issues to contend with. Are you sure she's worth the trouble?"

"Without a doubt," he answered, images of Miranda pushing all other concerns from his mind. He thought of how delicate she seemed in his arms; how the gold reflected off her elegant neck each night. He imagined how close he'd just been to her, their bare skin nearly touching. Max inhaled sharply.

Marcia approached, breaking his trance. "Hey, how was our mystery lady? Did you figure out who she is?"

Max laughed as he looked at his lively friend.

In the distance, the old woman watched as Max laughed and joked with Katherine. Max felt strange sensation nagging him to look around. He shifted in his seat as he gazed out over the festival grounds. Before she could be spotted she darted into the lush foliage surrounding the restaurant, safe again in the forested hillside.

Chapter 11

The next four weeks were difficult for Max to understand. Though Miranda had responded to him on their first night after the unveiling of Liebestraum, she had been silent ever since. Each night Max would whisper to her, hoping for a response. He spoke of his fascination with her paintings, of his early struggles in art, and eventually of his hope that they could spend time together outside the amphitheater. Still, each finale would end and she would leave him in darkness on the platform. He tried to appreciate why she would bother coming each night if she was not interested in communicating. It had been so long since he had heard her voice he started to doubt that he ever had. Sometimes he fantasized that they had been together in a past life, destined to be together now. Those musings always ended in feelings of foolishness.

Max parked his car and headed toward the talent garden. *What did she need to hear?* He entered the makeup room, happily realizing that his days of ingrown hairs and obscene undergarments were nearing an end. The exhibition would be over in two weeks; a thought that became immediately distressing when he considered Miranda. There was a real possibility that he could lose any chance with her, and that was truly unbearable. He thought about reaching out to Claire but couldn't imagine what he's say. In all likelihood she didn't even know that Miranda had taken her place. He couldn't risk outing her.

Max slipped into the dressing room and changed into his thong. From behind the curtain, Max watched as Annie painted the face of a young man. He had seen him many times before and remembered him to be extremely quiet. Usually Annie talked enough for the both of them so it hadn't been an issue. But tonight was different. Maybe it was Annie's mood, something on her mind, but she was not her chatty self. Pulling his robe over his shoulders, Max walked to a large mirror in the corner of the room. He positioned a headpiece over his wavy hair, and began sponging gold makeup onto his face. His gaze intermittently on the young man, he piqued as the silent college student finally spoke to Annie.

"How's your evening going?" the young man inquired shyly.

"Well, we ran out of burnt peach, and I had two no-show artists who I plan to maim later this week, but other than that I'm great," she replied.

Another long pause went by. Max watched as the young man's whole persona began to change.

"Any plans for what's left of the summer?" Max heard him ask.

"Handful of weddings, then opera season will start." She glanced around the room. "Hey Miguel, can I get a spray down?" she yelled, indicating toward Max.

Max contemplated what he had just seen. Maybe silence was the answer. The thought of forgoing any attempts at communication was not a happy one, though he doubted he had much to lose. Before he could consider the notion any further it was time to make the trek to the platform.

Miranda emerged from the forest and slipped into Max's arms. She was about thirty seconds early, which was a first. It occurred to her that she would have that much more time with Max; the thought was exciting. She leapt into position. Mozart's clarinet concerto began as the MC delivered the Embrace monologue. Any moment now she would feel the warmth of his breath against the back of her head as he whispered to her. The platform lights illuminated as the chorus of the piece played. Miranda stood motionless as the stage lights blocked out her view of the audience. She listened to the music, spellbound as always by its beauty. After a few bars it occurred to her that Max was uncharacteristically quiet. *He's probably sick to death of your issues*, she heard the angry one bark. Ignoring the insult, she waited for the lights to dim. As darkness fell upon them, Max's painful silence tugged at her emotions. She knew she had to speak up. Pushing herself, she kept her lips as still as possible.

"Do you select the music?" she whispered.

Startled, Max stammered. "Ah, no. The music director usually handles that. I did choose this piece though."

"You did," Miranda reiterated.

Max struggled to rationalize the heaviness of her tone. "Yes."

"Wehrlose Liebe," she uttered.

Max searched his mind. "German? I don't know what it means."

"It's a beautiful arrangement. You should hear it with the libretto."

While Max had never known it to be anything more than an instrumental, he was far more interested in the fact that Miranda was finally speaking to him.

After a brief pause she continued. "Why did you choose it? Why this piece?"

Max answered quickly. "Because it sounds like victory... as if love itself reigns triumphantly."

Miranda's eyes welled with tears. "That's right," she said.

To Max's extreme irritation, the stage lights shone upon them, ending the puzzling conversation. He stood in silence trying to make sense of the last two minutes. As the stage lights dimmed, he hoped that his silence would once again encourage Miranda to speak. Instead, he watched her slip out of his arms, fading into the dark foliage of the hillside.

In his office, Max sat at his desk, his back aching from holding the phone against his ear for the last five minutes. While he realized he could simply put the phone on speaker, he didn't want to risk disconnecting the call as relying on his only German friend to get back to him in a timely manner was also out of the question. Franz was a most free-spirited artist; the worst kind. After an eternity a man's voice cut through the stillness.

"Maxy! You don't waste any time, ha? I just got your email."

"Yeah, sorry about that. If there's a fit I'd need to act fast."

"Well okay, here goes. Oh Maxy, do you want the literal translation or figurative?"

"I could get the literal off the web."

The heavily accented man chuckled. "Okay, okay, here we go." Max took notes as Franz translated each line and then made sense of the words. "The first verse is interesting enough; typical metaphor comparing a man and woman to a king and his queen." Franz continued to the chorus, Max's eyes widening as he listened.

"Are you certain?" Max asked, amazed that his interpretation of the piece so closely matched the words.

"It's pretty straightforward. You seem surprised," Franz added.

"The word wehrlose?"

"Defenseless."

"Practically speaking what does that mean, powerless?" Max pressed.

"No, no, not weak. I would liken it to surrender. A love that could not be stopped." Franz explained.

Max held the phone to his chest, unable to move for a moment. Hearing his friend whistle for his attention he thanked Franz and disconnected the call, quickly making another.

Miranda sat across from Dr. Bales, concern bearing down on her smooth face. "No, I wouldn't want that. Of course not," she said.

"But you're running out of time, aren't you? The show will be over in a little more than a week."

"Yeah," Miranda replied sadly. "Pretty backwards isn't it?"

"How so?" Dr. Bales inquired, though Miranda was certain he already knew the answer.

"Most people worry about having to take off their clothes for someone, not about having to put them on," she admitted.

"In this case it makes perfect sense. You've been hiding behind a character. Your nudity was nothing more than a costume. Max has never seen who you really are," the doctor explained.

"He did once. He came to the gallery opening," she reminded.

"That wasn't really you either. That was just a scared child. After all you've said about him, I imagine he'd be much more interested in Miranda the woman."

She resisted the urge to make a smart remark, and wondered if Dr. Bales realized how sappy that sounded. Still, she knew he was right. She thanked him with a timid hug, set up another appointment, and made her way out of the office.

Stepping out onto Main Street, salty air swirling around her, Miranda felt better. As frightening as it was to imagine spending time with Max outside their unusual summer ritual, the thought of losing him filled her with despair. *He'd be more interested in Miranda the woman... No kidding. Why don't you just let me take over?* She heard the angry one suggest. *Because I'm still here,* her mind answered. Miranda stopped walking, tears filling her eyes. The scared child was still a bigger part of her than the woman she yearned to be. *We have to do this together. I have to learn to be like you.*

Miranda walked on, wiping her eyes. "What would brave me do?" she laughed as the words escaped her lips. "Jeez, I sound just as bad as the doc." Suddenly aware that she was walking down the street and talking to herself out loud, Miranda glanced around before allowing her thoughts to return to the plan. As silly as it was, *what would brave me do* actually made sense. The scared child was real and couldn't be retrained. But she would have to commit to a new way of thinking.

That evening Miranda hid in the foliage of the forested hillside, just as she had for the last seven weeks. In a moment she would see Max and her heart would flutter inside her chest. She recalled the first time she'd seen him. Camouflaged in leaves and brush, she had watched as the Galen figure took his spot on the platform and she knew that she only had a few seconds before the lights would shine upon them.

She was about to slip into his arms when she felt a most inexplicable sensation stab through her, one that first presented as a painful blow but quickly escalated to one of affection, stunning her for a moment. She remembered hearing the orchestral music and realizing that her time was up. She had leapt into the Galen figure's arms. Relishing the feeling, she had heard her future-self speak for the first time. *It's him; he's finally here.*

Miranda had forced herself to remain still, though her body felt as if it was a tuning fork which had just been struck. Her insides seemed to vibrate as her mind raced to reconcile the ridiculous sensation. *Who is he? This is not the same man from last week.* For reasons that escaped her, Miranda was aware of every inch of her skin. She forced her eyes away from the gilded, muscular arm that shielded her bare chest from the audience. She could feel herself starting to pant and worked to calm her breathing.

The lights dimmed and the Galen subject began whispering to her. His voice, gentle yet strong, reignited the fever that Miranda was already struggling to contain. She couldn't even process what he was saying. Her eyes throbbed and her skin burned. In nearly three decades of life she had never felt anything like this. The lights ignited over them. Sorrow shot through her as she realized her time with him was coming to an end. Darkness hit the platform and for a moment Miranda considered staying in his arms.

Forcing away the beginning of a sob, she ripped herself from his body. She ducked into the greenery of the lush hillside and wept in her hands as he was guided off the platform. *What just happened?* She searched her mind for an answer as she hurried toward the back of the amphitheater. Snatching a dress she had left on a tree branch, she covered herself before heading down a covert path. On any other night she would have slipped into the back entrance of the shower room and rid herself of the gold before being seen. Instead she ran the six blocks to the beach, doing her best to avoid attention by favoring the backside of the small store fronts which lined the Laguna Canyon Road. She remained detached from herself until the firm concrete gave way to cool sand. Only then did she attempt to make sense of what had transpired.

It was simple, she had reasoned. She had fabricated the electric connection with the new male subject. It was nothing more than her imagination. Her attraction to the love story of Isaura and Galen had done its worst. And now like a great fool, she was standing on the empty beach, covered in gold makeup in the dark of night. Knowing what was sure to follow, she administered her own punishment before the angry one could intervene. Removing the dress she ran into the black water, inhaling briskly as the cold stung her flesh. Illuminated by the moon, the shimmering paint began to mix with the foamy tide, creating a golden pool at the water's surface. Gentle waves caressed her hip. She wanted to give herself over to her tears, but feared the wrath that was sure to follow. Instead she stared out over the ocean, soaking up its strength as her golden cloak was washed away.

Back on the platform Miranda shook off the memories of the first night she'd seen Max, startled to find that she was already in his arms. The platform lights dimmed as she looked out over the crowd, orienting herself to the present.

"Hey, are you okay?" Max whispered. "I thought I lost you there for a moment."

"I was with you," Miranda assured under her breath.

Max hoped he hadn't imagined the tenderness in her response. "September's right around the corner. Our evenings will be ours again. I meant, you'll have yours and I'll have mine," he stumbled. "Perhaps we can arrange to meet for more than a couple of minutes sometime." Max's voice shook slightly, causing Miranda to will away tears. Before she could respond, infuriating platform lights quieted her. The next thirty seconds of illumination felt like an hour. Finally the crescendo of victorious drum beats ushered in darkness across the platform. Tears moistened Miranda's eyes. "Someday," she whispered before hurrying off the platform.

Claire arrived at the gallery before dawn. The summer was nearly over and this was one of the last big tourist weekends. She locked the door behind her and headed toward her office. As she passed the patio, she noticed that the door was ajar. She cautiously approached, relaxing as she noted Miranda seated at the bistro table, staring out over the ocean. She took a seat next to her.

"Miranda, what on earth are you doing?"

"I'm going to lose him."

"What are you talking about? Who..?"

Miranda whimpered, interrupting her. "Max."

Claire looked at her strangely. "Max... Max Turner? I don't understand." Claire studied Miranda as if searching for insight, some of the tension in her face lessoning as she seemed to consider a new possibility. "He was talking about you? You took my place." Claire stood, stunned by the revelation. "But how? You've never even... I don't understand." Seeing her friend's misery she seemed to forgo

129

curiosity and instead leaned forward. She wrapped her arms around Miranda who quickly gave into her tears.

It was the last show of the season. The instrumental arrangement of Mozart's Clarinet Concerto began as the MC cleared his throat in preparation for his monologue. Just as he had for the last fifty-something consecutive nights, Max waited in gilded silence atop the dark hillside platform. Right on time Miranda slid into his arms, forcing him to purse away a smile. "I have a surprise for you," he whispered before burning stage lamps could suspend his words. Miranda held her position though Max thought he could detect a change in her breathing. Together they endured the prison of illumination before the blessed darkness offered its solace. "I thought about what you said… about this music. Since it's our last night I figured it would be nice to hear it with the libretto," he explained.

As the MC's monologue for the Sappho and Phaon piece neared its conclusion, a change in the scripting caused Miranda to tense. Max eyed her taut shoulders, wondering what must be going through her mind.

Over the orchestral version of the song's chorus, the MC continued. "While we realize that very little could make our finale music more spectacular than it already is, here is one of Holland's most celebrated vocalists to sing German lyricist Dagmar Alexander's, Wehrlose Liebe." The chorus repeated, this time accompanied by the powerful voice of the gifted Dutch tenor. Miranda stood in rapture as the glorious sound enveloped the auditorium. The words penetrated her, filling her with an unearthly exhilaration. The chorus repeated again, the singer adorning the harmonious melody with indescribable beauty. As he delivered the lyrics, Miranda whispered their translation to Max.

"This love that has no borders, that knows no boundaries, look... cries my heart, what defenseless love can do."

Finale drums, booming louder than Max had ever recalled, seemed to signal the triumph of love over all adversity. The sentiment was climaxed by the crashing symbols and wild audience applause which followed. Max clenched his teeth, desperate to fight off the agonizing impulse to enfold his arms around Miranda. He instead watched helplessly as she disappeared into the forested hillside, her footsteps fading away. What would he do if tonight was their last together? The thought was more painful than anything he had experienced. As the designer approached he forced himself to turn and follow him.

"Hey bud, did you drop something?" he heard him ask. The designer aimed his flashlight at the ground making Max aware of a small note which now glowed back at him. He snatched it, unfolding it to reveal feminine writing.

The cove tomorrow at noon, it read simply.

A huge grin consumed his face and before he could stop himself he had his arms around the designer, heartily squeezing him. "Was this a great show or what?"

"Yes, Mr. Turner," he laughed uncomfortably.

Still in a state of bliss from the note, Max's mood couldn't be squelched. "How long have you known it was me?" he asked.

"I pretty much figured it out right away, Sir."

Max smiled. "Thanks for not saying anything."

"Katherine said she'd fire me if I did. Am I fired?"

"Not tonight," Max replied. He followed the designer down the trail and prepared himself for a very sleepless night.

Miranda watched Max from the forest. No longer able to contain her amusement over his reaction, she giggled under her breath before receding into the hillside. Hearing her own laugh her mind conjured the image of her future-self. First laugh in fifteen years? Making her way toward the tree branch which served as a hanger for her dress, she imagined her impending date with Max. It would be her first... ever. While fear dominated her senses, a feverish anticipation was making great strides as contender. *He wants to see me tomorrow, not the dithering mess.* Miranda huffed at the angry one's warning, though unable to deny its validity. *Maybe so, but I can't fake you yet*, she reminded. She focused on quieting her mind, dispelling the voices of doubt. Any more reflection over tomorrow's meeting would jeopardize it completely. Arriving at the shower just outside the makeup room, Miranda let the water once again carry away her mask.

Chapter 12

Max sat at the mouth of the cave scooping up handfuls of white sand. He let the fine granules sift through his fingers as he gazed out over the ocean. A few yards away Miranda, hidden behind wide sunglasses, tan cotton gloves, an oversized long-sleeve shirt and billowy pants, watched him. Her hands began to tremble. *I know you can't be fearless, but you must be brave*, she heard her future-self say. *But he won't understand*, she worried back. *He might, but we'll have to explain.* Fraught with trepidation, she slowly approached Max. She looked down at him, her eyes wide with uncertainty. He hadn't seen her yet; she could still run. As if grabbed by the arms and forced down, Miranda turned and slid to the ground, her back against his. Startled, Max jumped before recognizing her sweet fragrance.

"Can we sit like this?" Miranda asked.

Max allowed his rigid back to relax against hers. "Of course, whatever you like," he replied gently. If he noticed the gloves he didn't mention them.

Miranda gave a weak nod as if encouraging herself. Her flushed skin made her feel grateful for the coastal fog layer which offered some resistance against the rising temperatures of the sun. She closed her eyes, granting herself a moment of reflection. Feeling Max's back expand and contract with each breath, his warmth passing to her, she marveled at how safe she felt being with him. The only other man she felt safe with was Dr. Bales and that didn't count.

"I normally don't talk much," she whispered apologetically.

"Perfect, I'm actually quite the chatterbox," he replied, doing his best to match her soft tone. "It was lucky for me that our part this summer was brief or I would have already driven you off with pointless banter."

Miranda smiled, nuzzling her head against his.

Max returned the gesture, encouraged by her affirmation. They continued to sit in silent connectedness. After a few minutes Max opened his eyes, smiling as he saw prisms of movement just beyond the breakers.

"Look... dolphins."

She turned, twisting at the waist for a better view. Tempted as he seemed to look at her face, Max maintained his gaze on the animals. Miranda adjusted her position, sitting alongside him as she looked across the water. Max appeared to force himself to keep his eyes in front of him. A pair, the playful animals bobbed and spun around each other in the waves.

"They look happy," she said with a hint of envy.

Max seemed unsure of how to respond to the melancholy undertone in her delivery, but responded in an upbeat fashion. "They're very social creatures."

"I've heard they feel rubbery," she said.

Max seemed to search for an accurate description. "Have you ever run your fingertips across a marble fountain when the water was running?"

Miranda nodded, her eyes fixed on the dolphins.

"They feel like that; like polished wet stone, so smooth their skin almost creates a resistance against your own."

Miranda grinned, appreciative of the poignant illustration. She looked down before turning her head toward Max, her gaze stuck in the sand. "I'm not... I'm kind of a mess."

As if aware that she was offering all that she could, Max kept his eyes on the water. "This is a beautiful cove. I don't get to the beach enough. It's perfect at noon; not too hot, not too crowded," he remarked as he glanced around the shore. "I think I'd like to make this a routine. I hope you'll consider doing the same." He softly nudged the back of her hand with his knuckles before standing.

Miranda watched him go, refusing to take her eyes off him until he was out of sight.

Max crossed Pacific Coast Highway, practically springing onto Forest Avenue. Exhilaration coursed through him making him tingle all over. She had come and had even confided in him; two solid wins as far as he was concerned. Of course, the relationship would be difficult. But at least they would have one. He had played it cool and was confident that he hadn't seemed as desperate for her as he felt. Max fondly rubbed the part of his hand that had contacted her skin. Such an affect she had on him. His smile widened as he imagined nudging her hand again, this time to feel hers clasp around his.

He continued to walk along the picturesque street, his distance from the beach growing as he passed sea glass shops and imaginative gastro pubs. He thought of what it would be like to be with Miranda; to see her smiling up at him from one of the simple wooden tables of Alessa, his favorite Italian café. He imagined her walking alongside of him, describing the city in the way a true artist could. What a thing it would be to know her; really know her. His visions of happiness were suddenly assailed by the sharp reality of the converse. To understand her he would also have to know her pain. She had a difficult upbringing, the secretary had said. Max fought to avoid speculations, refocusing on the memory of her back against his. *No reason to ruin a lovely first meeting*, he coached himself.

Miranda made it home in less than five minutes, unable to recall the actual path that she had taken and oblivious to the figure that watched her leave the beach. Her consciousness was consumed with reflections of her time with Max. And while she had been taken by him since their first inanimate encounter, she found herself more affected than ever before. Hearing his sweet, gentle invitation for another meeting caused a most dizzying feeling; like she had been spinning in circles and quickly stopped. She imagined Max's enthusiastic smile and wished she had been able to see his face while he was talking to her.

She opened the front door and hurried inside, slamming the door closed before sinking the three bolts deep into their sturdy housing. Glancing around the living room-turned-workshop, her eyes caught several fresh canvases propped against the window. She quickly sorted through them before finding a circular canvas stretched over a timber frame. Placing it on a black and chrome easel in the middle of the room, she clamped the canvas into place and adjusted it into the lowest position, sitting on the floor in front of it. She removed her gloves and ran her fingers along the hardwood below her, knowing that allowing her eyes to analyze the surface at the same moment her fingers palpated it, a deluge of information would follow. The grainy texture created corresponding images and she began to see the wood in her mind. Each groove was unique; peaks and troughs met the occasional blemish just as points blended into smooth areas of erosion. Color began to accompany the texture; brown hues seemed almost black depending on the depth of the crevice, while more superficial fibers appear gold-tinged.

Within seconds every stroke, every layer of color was outlined for her to see, creating an exact blueprint in her mind. With her senses married, Miranda conjured images of her time at the beach with Max. She could hear waves washing out the cries of seagulls. Ocean air filled her nostrils as she remembered turning away from Max only to slide down him, the small of her back gliding down Max's strong frame. His warmth, coupled with that of the velvety sand below her, soothed her restless thoughts. Relaxing into him, the crook of her neck nestled into his. It seemed that no matter what part of her made contact with Max Turner, a cradling sensation was sure to follow. She again felt the expanse of his shoulders with each breath and wondered if he could sense her tremble as it slowed and finally ceased.

Miranda reached up, positioning her fingers around the flat graphite pencil in her right hand, and delivered the first contour line of the rough sketch. At the bottom of the line she created a division, the right branch evolving into the compound curve of her seat in the sand, followed by the upstroke of underside of her leg. Aware that her arm bisected her legs as she held her knees to her chest, she left a gap before outlining the dimensions of her calf. She made a soft indentation to illustrate her sand-dipped heel, a straight line along the bottom of her foot, and a rounded area at the tip of her toes.

Outlining the shin, she again created a gap for her clasped hands and formed her knee, blending it into her upper arm and shoulder. She stopped, allowing her hand to rest as she examined the drawing. She repeated her steps, starting at the division and veering left with a new branch. She outlined Max's dimensions with ease, the contour of his muscles impossible to forget.

Rounding the turn of Max's shoulder, she again stopped, unsure of how to proceed. She hadn't considered which of their faces to illustrate, the nature of the pose dictating that it could only be one. She closed her eyes, her mind going back to the beach. She remembered her own face, a confusing mixture of fear and relief. Was she ready to share that with the world; with anyone for that matter? *You may have been scared but I wasn't; let them see my face,* she heard a familiar voice taunt.

Miranda imagined the fiery, boastful eyes of the angry one staring back at her. For a moment she felt as if Max had been taken from her, conquered by a stronger woman. But shaking the image away and replaying his words to her, she understood that the Max she knew would not be content with someone so impervious. She could almost hear the joy in his voice as he beckoned her to return to the beach. She imagined an envious sun stealing kissing along his smooth face and defined jaw. Positioning her pencil where she had left off, she began to illustrate Max's blissful affect.

Max drudged through evaporating sleepiness as his cell phone rang. Seeing that it was just after five in the morning, he was instantly worried. He answered the call, wincing as his father's voice confirmed his fears.

"Max, I'm at the hospital. You're mother's had a heart attack."

Flinging off the covers and shoving his glasses in place, Max tried to hide the concern in his voice. "Where is she? Is she…"

"Mission Hospital. ICU."

"I'm on my way." Max disconnected the call, threw on his clothes, and raced toward his car. He descended the turns leading away from his home with little regard for his screeching tires. He made it across town in only fifteen minutes. Max arrived at the main lobby and hurried toward the volunteer at the desk. "Cardiac Intensive Care; the patient is Joann Turner. I'm her son."

The volunteer handed him a sticker and pointed toward the elevators. "Second floor, room seventy six," she said.

"Thank you." Max sprinted toward the elevator and selected the second floor. The elevator doors started to close but were interrupted by another visitor. Max ran his hand through his hair as the doors opened back up, then slowly closed. The assent was impossibly slow as Max shut out his worst thoughts. Emerging onto the second floor he found his father waiting outside the double doors of the intensive care unit. "How is she?" his voice cracked.

"She's pretty pale, Son. They have her on oxygen and, well… a lot of monitors."

"Can I see her?"

"She looks awfully different right now," he said, as if studying Max for uncertainty.

Max tried to imagine the reason for his father's apprehension. "I don't care about that."

"She's worried it'll upset you."

Max stared, his eyes welling. "She's worried about me?"

The older man looked down. "She knows how… visual you are."

The insinuation hit hard, causing a tear to roll down Max's cheek. He couldn't believe his own mother thought of him as superficial. He wanted to fight, to defend himself against yet another accusation of being depthless, but stopped himself as he considered the situation. "Can I just see her please?"

"I can't go with you. They only let in one person at a time." He waved a visitor badge in front of a sensor, handing the badge to Max as the doors opened.

Max walked into the unit, scouring the doors for numbers before finding seventy six. He slowly entered the room, steadying himself as he looked upon the sickly woman in the bed. His mother's eyes opened as if feeling his presence. He approached and took a seat on the chair next to her. She looked up, her voice faint. "Hey Max."

"Hi Mom," he whispered.

"Do me a favor... don't get old," she managed to say.

Max grinned against his tears, refusing to burden her with their escape. "I promise. You look good."

"So everyone tells me. You know what that means."

Max laughed, relieved that her sarcasm hadn't died along with a portion of her cardiac tissue. "How bad is it?"

"I only lost a third. I still have more than enough to get me through, I'd say," she smiled. "If I didn't know better I'd swear you're even cuter than the last time I saw you. Is something going on?"

Max instantly thought of Miranda. "There is a girl actually."

She pretended to act surprised. "No."

"Is it that obvious?"

"It's not hard to tell that you've fallen for someone. How long have you been dating?"

Max chuckled. "I can't say that we've had a real date yet."

"Oh boy. You look like this and you haven't even taken her out? She must be pretty flawless."

Max again felt saddened by the implication.

A nurse entered, depressing a button on one of the monitors. "Visiting hours are over now. It's important that Mrs. Turner gets some rest. You can come back after lunch if you'd like."

"Okay. See you in a little while," he said. Max leaned over and kissed his mother's forehead.

The double doors opened as Max walked toward his father. "What happens now?" he asked.

"They've put her on blood thinners. Apparently she had a rhythm problem we didn't know about, so she's on medicine for that too. She'll have to stay a few days," he explained.

"The season is over so I'm totally free. What can I do to help?"

"Tomorrow we'll have a hospital bed delivered. We can set it up in the den so she can watch TV. She can't be going up and down stairs for a few weeks. I don't want to leave her," the old man said.

"No, I'll take care of it. Would you like to grab breakfast?"

"That'd be nice."

Max sat across from his father, doing his best to read him without arousing his attention. Considering that they had been close his entire life, Max now struggled to find words of comfort as the older man sipped at his coffee.

"Seeing anyone special?"

The question surprised Max. Why parents asked such things during times of crises, he didn't understand. He considered how to reply. George

141

Turner had always been a loving, supportive parent; one that Max often confided in until his distaste for complicated relationships earned him an unfair reputation. "Actually, yeah. Just started."

His father seemed relieved to have a pleasant topic available. "What's her name?"

"Miranda. She's an artist."

"Plenty to talk about, then."

Max looked down, unsure of how to respond. The waitress arrived with two plates, serving them both vegetable omelets before excusing herself.

"We'd love to meet her. You should bring her by the house."

"I don't really know how she feels about me just yet."

"Any girl who isn't over the moon for you must be crazy," he said.

Max looked away uncomfortably.

"Something wrong? This is usually the part where you look bashful and say 'stop Dad'. She isn't actually crazy, is she?"

Max looked down, amazed by the unfortunate direction the conversation had taken.

"Max, you're starting to worry me."

"No, of course not. She's great," he said.

His father looked at him, his wise eyes inviting him to go on.

"She's different, that's for sure; brilliant and very special."

Noting his father's cautious silence, Max sighed. "I don't know. Every time I see her or even think of her I'm totally struck by this impulse to be with her. It's overpowering." His father remained quiet as he listened. "Dad, she's got some trust issues. I don't know how severe just yet." He looked over expecting to see disapproval. Instead his gaze was met with a gentle smile.

"The fact that you're even interested in giving it a try is a good sign."

Max shook his head. "Am I really that known for being hypercritical?"

The older man looked as if he was contemplating leveling with his son. "Relationships are so challenging; even the best relationships. You never seemed terribly interested in slogging through the mud, so to speak. It made us a little nervous; made us wonder if you were capable of the kind of effort love takes."

Max felt his eyes moisten as he took in the muted blow. He flashed back to thoughts of Christy and the women before her. Neither were even a fraction as convoluted as Miranda. Still, Max couldn't deny his intolerance of their mild to moderate flaws. "I don't think I really cared before. No one else seemed worth the effort."

George Turner looked at his son lovingly. "That's a real good sign, kid. When do you see her again?"

Max coughed mid coffee sip as he realized his oversight. "Oh God. Sorry Dad, I have to make a call."

The older man humbly waved his permission as Max dialed a contact on his cell. "Katherine, I was wondering if I could persuade you to go to the beach."

Chapter 13

Marcia and Katherine crossed Pacific Coast Highway and headed toward the cove. Their business attire having been replaced by capri pants and graphic tees, they looked unrecognizably youthful and carefree.

"How about The Cliff?"

"The food is so conservative."

"Kat, nobody goes to The Cliff for the food. It's all about the view."

Katherine laughed at her wistful partner. "It's not like we're visiting from Wisconsin, we live at the beach. This view isn't good enough for you?"

"You just want to go to Nick's again."

Katherine shot her a playful smirk. "Tell me you're not craving the asparagus fries."

Marcia glanced around, stopping in the sand. "I think this is it." She pointed to an oversized rock near the cove's north inlet cavern.

"Must be," Katherine replied.

"So, we're just supposed to wait here? What if she doesn't recognize us? She'll think Max stood her up."

"Well, we don't have a phone number so it's a chance we'll have to take. I drew the line at bringing a poster board with her name on it."

Marcia seemed genuinely surprised. "He asked you to do that?"

"I think my tone shortened the life of that scheme."

Marcia laughed hard and took a seat in the sand. "He must be pretty into her if he asked you to do something so lame."

Katherine eased herself down next to Marcia. "Guess so."

"How's his mom doing?"

"She's okay. Max thinks she'll be home by Friday."

"Thank God. Scary isn't it? She seems too healthy for a heart attack."

"I know. I told him we'd like to come see her once she's feeling up to visitors."

Marcia glanced at her partner, clearly touched by her supportive instincts. "Beautiful day, isn't it?"

"Very," Katherine replied lifting their clasped hands and kissing Marcia's wrist.

Twenty feet away Miranda stood, watching the women. Thoughts of self-doubt swirled frantically in her mind. *I'm kind of a mess*, the angry one viciously parroted. *And what a surprise; now he's gone.* Miranda wrenched herself away from the cove, forcing a quick retreat toward her home.

"I was just being honest," she said aloud. *You were just being pathetic as always.*

"Something could have come up. We don't know why he didn't come." *Yeah, maybe a family emergency. Maybe he was hit by a bus*, the voice again mocked.

A tingle down her spine ended the internal argument as quickly as it had begun. Miranda was again taken by the sensation that she was being watched. She stopped as she looked around the city, skimming the crowd. *What's the matter? Are you scared?* "No, I am not," Miranda hissed. She resumed her brisk pace, anger shielding her from fear.

Max and his father waited outside the ICU, standing in unison as the doctor emerged from the double doors and approached.

"She's doing extremely well. The VQ scan showed no additional clots so the worst is definitely over. I presume someone can keep a good eye on her for the next few days?"

"Of course, thank you doctor," Max's father replied.

He and Max shook the doctor's hand, hugging each other once alone.

"I'm going to head over to your place and get the den ready. Could you tell her I'll come by after lunch?"

"I will. Thanks Son."

Max pulled into the empty driveway of his childhood home, smiling as he rediscovered his love for the place. Built in the 1930s, the Cape Cod-styled house was immaculate for its age. The traditional white trim popped against the fresh coat of blue-gray paint. The dormered windows on the right side of the upper story contrasted the large bay window on the left side, salvaging the design from its monotonous predecessors. He made his way up the rock-laden path to the front door and picked up the morning newspaper, the plastic sheath around it still beaded with dew.

Before he could protect himself, a terrible truth pierced his consciousness; one day this house would belong to someone else. New owners would dwell within the walls making it as strange to him as any other in the city. One day he would not be warmed and welcomed by this place. Max was taken aback by the lonely ache that coincided with the morbid reality. Closing his eyes he forced his attention on the task at hand. He unlocked the front door and entered the home, instantly soothed by the heartening smells that existed nowhere else.

Though he visited often enough, he was always surprised by how small the house seemed in comparison to the stately version his younger mind recorded. Looking over the den he was grateful his parents had such good taste. The décor was sparse; sophisticated oceanic accents elevated the room rather than overwhelming the space. Dark hardwoods met with white walls and a light L-shaped sofa for a rich, clean look. Old seemed to pair perfectly with new, Max thought, as he looked over the simple wooden coffee table which sat between the sofa and the white marble fireplace. Though the room could have tolerated a high-end work of art over the hearth, a local painting of a lone surfer along a crystal beach hung instead.

Guess they didn't need any help from the art director, he laughed. Taking one last glance around, Max decided to push the sofa to the corner of the room. He dragged the coffee table to another corner, careful to avoid disrupting the rope-covered sea glass float which sat atop it. A club chair was relocated to the living room. He inspected the impressively open room, certain that there would be plenty of space for a bed and night table. Max reached into his pocket as his cell phone vibrated.

"This is Max... yes, thirty minutes... very good. I'll be here." He disconnected the call as he pondered how to spend a half an hour alone in his parent's home. Heading to the kitchen he found a bottle of French Gewurztraminer breathing on the built-in marble buffet. He imagined his father insisting he have a glass, which undeniably would have happened had the old man been there with him. He poured himself a small portion and walked through the living room, exiting into the backyard. Max took a seat in one of two mahogany Adirondack lounges that lined the petite, lagoon-style swimming pool.

A pool was an extreme rarity for a single family home under the two million dollar mark in Laguna Beach, but his mother had insisted on adding one. Sipping on the sweet, crisp wine and admiring the breathtaking ocean view, Max tried not to worry about Miranda, fully aware that being too preoccupied would distract him from his mother. Joann Turner had been a force his entire life. A self-proclaimed "loser" in high school, she frequently admitted that as a teenager all she had cared about was starting a family. She had managed to get through most of her sophomore year with average grades, but completely failed her junior year, as landing Max's father was her only concern. She married George when she was only seventeen, and immediately became pregnant.

No longer distracted by her nesting urges, she became the model student. Through a secondary program she completed her senior year requirements in record time, and was achieving straight A's for the first time in her life. Once Max was born she enrolled in a trade school. George was in his last of a four year Naval commitment and the two had little money. As soon as George received his honorable discharge from the service, Joann began work as a beautician. Her income, combined with George's GI bill and part time job, helped him get through a four-year degree, making him the first in his family to accomplish such academic success. Once George graduated and began working in the professional sector, Joann returned to school, destroying the curve in each of her classes.

By Max's tenth birthday the couple that should have been awaiting government assistant checks purchased their first home. Now, twenty-five years later, the woman who defied her own odds at every turn was lying in a hospital bed because some chance blood clot cut off the circulation to her otherwise healthy heart. Max wondered how someone so proud and independent would cope with mandatory medical regiments and irrevocable limitations. A knock at the door saved Max from a full blown slippery slope meltdown. He hurried to the door to find two hospital supply delivery men.

"Mister Turner?"

Max offered his hand. "Yes."

The stout man read from a list as his partner raised the door of the moving truck. "We got an adjustable bed, O2 equipment, that's the chemical abbreviation for oxygen...," he continued as if impressed by own his medical acumen. "...bunch of other stuff. Where do you want it?"

Max pointed to the cleared den. "I'm hoping this will work."

The delivery man peered into the room. "Not bad. Is this your place?"

"My parents' actually."

The delivery man went to the back of his vehicle and assisted his partner. "This stuff is for one of them?"

Max wasn't happy about the unnecessary questions but decided to push himself through the small talk. "My mom."

"Huh. I only ask because gender plays an important role in how we set this stuff up."

Max tried to avoid rolling his eyes. "Oh, I see."

"Yeah, ladies prefer everything to flow nicely but be sort of spread out. Men just want it done. The less medical looking the better, you know what I mean?"

Finding the simple man's perspective somewhat affable, Max allowed himself to make eye contact. "That makes sense. Can I give you guys a hand?"

"Oh no, the insurance is very strict about that. Only home health delivery specialists can handle the equipment."

"Got it. Maybe some water, then?"

"That's real nice of you."

Max headed to the kitchen and grabbed two bottles of water from the refrigerator. He returned to the porch to see a bulky hospital bed emerging from the truck via an electric dolly.

"Wow, that's a lot more extensive than I expected. My mom's on the small side," he joked.

"Believe it or not this is standard. Seven hundred pounds give or take. My old man had to have one before he died. Got him a fancy one; the kind that turns you so you don't get bed sores. Didn't do a lick of good. When he went his tailbone looked like something had taken a bite out of it."

Max paled, turning to avoid looking as squeamish as he felt.

"That's horrible."

"Tell me about it. And the smell was unreal."

Max looked away, banning the unwelcome images that followed. "I've got to make a call. I'll be in the back yard if you need me," he said before returning to the sanctity of his Adirondack chair. Sinking back down, he entered his cell phone's passcode and called the most recent number. "Hey, did you see her?"

His hopeful face fell as he heard Katherine's response. "Sorry Max, she didn't show; not that we could tell, anyway."

"You actually looked for her though?"

"Marcia scanned left and I scanned right. But honestly Max, if she saw us from a distance we wouldn't have noticed."

Max rubbed his temple. "Of course; thanks anyway."

Miranda walked fast, her dizzying pace commensurate with the flights of self-doubt soaring through her mind. And while Claire was anything but good company, she knew that being alone was not a great idea given her state. Arriving at the gallery, she slipped in through the front entrance and past the secretary before an objection could be made.

"Miranda?" Claire asked in disbelief as her friend bolted into her office.

"He didn't come," Miranda replied, her voice quaking.

"What are you talking about?"

"Max… to the beach. He asked me to come back and then he wasn't there," she said, her eyes bouncing around the room aimlessly.

Claire approached her friend and gently guided her to a stylish sofa. Sitting beside her she took her hand.

"Did you come straight here? Maybe it's time for a cell phone, you know? He could have left a message on your home machine."

"He doesn't have my number."

"Oh," Claire replied, some of the concern fading from her face. She smoothed a lock of Miranda's hair behind her ear. "Then maybe it's a little premature to worry."

Miranda tried to find comfort in Claire's words despite her looming insecurities.

"What time were you supposed to meet him?"

"Noon," she answered.

"Gosh Rand, what if he was just running late? He could be there now. It's only twelve thirty."

Miranda felt a glimmer of relief as she considered the idea.

Seeing her friend relax, Claire grabbed her purse. "Shall we hoof it or do you want me to drive you back?"

Miranda hesitated, rubbing her fingers together. She hadn't been in a car in years and the thought was not a pleasant one. "You'll put the top down?"

"Whatever you need."

Miranda struggled, aware that not pushing herself would earn her a visit from the angry one. Still, a car was just too much. Compromising with her judgmental inner guardian, she nervously removed her sunglasses and peeled off her hat and sweater.

"What if we walk really fast?"

Having never seen her so unmasked in a public area, Claire stepped back as she eyed her with approval. "Nice, let's go."

The two hurried out of the gallery and headed toward the beach. Claire took Miranda's arm in hers, smiling ear to ear as she glanced out over the street. "This is so weird. I'm proud of you."

"Thanks," Miranda said, instantly aware of Claire's meaning. "It's a work in progress."

"Do you go out a lot?"

"Every day for the last six weeks; mostly to the cove. Sometimes I even buy lunch at a restaurant. But I take it to go."

Claire leaned her head on Miranda's should momentarily. "He must be something."

"It's not just for him," she said, her voice serious.

"Oh no of course not," Claire replied as if guilty for being so presumptuous.

"He does sweeten the deal," she admitted, causing both of them to laugh.

152

Claire released Miranda's arm as they crossed the street. Reaching the sand, Claire reflexively turned left. "The cove?"

"Yeah," said Miranda, uncertainty finding its way back into her voice.

Claire seemed to grow nervous as they neared the large rock just before the cove's inlet. Rounding the corner of the empty beach, they entered the desolate cavern. She hugged Miranda who stood motionless, her affect flat.

"Rand, it doesn't mean…"

Miranda held up her hand, unable to overcome her disappointment.

Max fiddled with the hospital bed's controller, raising and lowering the head of the mattress. All he could think about was Miranda's reaction to his absence. Katherine and Marcia said she never came. The only thing worse than feeling he'd let her down was imagining that she'd never shown up anyway; that she'd rejected his invitation for another meeting. Alone in his parents' living room Max had never felt more helpless. Flashes of memories invaded him; images of Miranda's smile, her golden frame enveloped in his arms, her face as Claire unveiled the Liebestraum piece. *Claire*. "I'm an idiot!" Max cried out as he grabbed his phone from his pocket. Navigating his contacts he dialed Claire's studio. After two rings her answering machine was activated.

"You've reached the gallery of Claire Simmons…"

Max disconnected the call and went to his phone's browser. He typed in a search for the Laguna Beach Yellow Pages.

Exhausted from more walking than she normally did in a week, Claire turned onto Forest Avenue and approached her gallery. Seeing a flower delivery man walking away from her entrance with a gorgeous bouquet, she quickened her pace.

"Can I help you?" she asked.

"I'm from The Flower Stand just a few doors down," he pointed. "I have a delivery for a Miranda Cova care of the Claire Simmons Gallery; a rush order from a Mister Maxwell Turner."

"I'll take them. Thank you very much."

Her secretary arrived just as she signed for the flowers. "Oh they're beautiful! I'll put them in some water."

"No need, they're for Miss Cova. I'll be back in a bit," she replied, taking keys out of her purse.

Miranda sat at the mouth of the cavern, sifting sand through her fingers. Her uncertainty had been replaced with a quiet resignation, causing a loneliness which was compounded by the miles of deserted shore. For a moment she thought she'd imagined hearing her name. When Claire's voice rang out a second time she stood and turned toward the bridge leading from the parking area to the cove's southern inlet. In the distance she saw Claire holding a bouquet of flowers.

"I got you something," Claire yelled.

Miranda bowed her head slightly, embarrassed that she had assumed the flowers were form Max. Expertly reading her body language, Claire rolled her eyes.

"Not these," she yelled. Pretending to read the card with unfamiliarity, she continued. "These are from a Maxwell Turner? I just got you this so that you can call and thank him," she said, holding up a sleek, white smart phone. "You should give him your number. It might make life easier for everyone."

Miranda giggled and hurried over to Claire, her face alive with renewed affection as she took the flowers and the phone.

"You better let me give you a lift," Miranda said as she used her knuckle to caress one of the large, pale-pink blooms with the vibrant fuchsia center.

"Good call," Claire joked as she indicated toward Miranda's strange way of stroking the flower. "Last thing we need right now is for you to actually touch it and get lost in a paint trance." She paused before continuing. "Stargazer lilies?" Claire sported a naïve look as she spoke. "Aren't these supposed to symbolize romance and purity?"

"Maybe," Miranda said bashfully.

"Ah ha. That's what I thought," Claire responded with a complacent grin.

Miranda clutched the bouquet as she walked with her friend. "Okay, you were right. It was premature of me to worry."

"He left his number on the card there," Claire pointed.

"I see it, thank you." Miranda replied, trying not to laugh as she maintained a serious expression. Arriving at Claire's car, Miranda slipped into the passenger seat of the convertible.

"You better call me after you talk to him. It's the least you can do after today's saga."

Miranda beamed as Claire started the engine.

Chapter 14

Max poured his second glass of wine and returned to his seat in his parents' back yard. His cell phone vibrated and he examined the screen, hopeful upon seeing that the Orange County number was not already one of his contacts.

"Hello?"

"Max it's… this is Miranda."

Max smiled as he heard the timid reply. He adjusted his rigid posture, settling into the lounge.

"I'm so glad you called."

"Thank you for the flowers; they're beautiful."

"You're welcome. I'm very sorry I couldn't make it today."

"Make it to what?" she asked.

Max paused, struck by the question.

"I'm kidding," she chuckled. "You did have me worried though."

Max closed his eyes in relief. "Yeah. I didn't have your number obviously and didn't think of calling Claire until it was too late. Katherine and Marcia waited at the cove to let you know I couldn't make it, but they said you didn't come."

"Oh my gosh, that was them? I didn't recognize them. They looked like kids."

"I guess it was a long shot. Anyway, I'm with my folks. My mom had a small heart attack."

Miranda looked at the floor, guilt filling her. "I'm so sorry."

"No, it's okay. She's going to be fine. I'll be back the day after tomorrow. Shall we try the cove again? Noon?"

"Okay," she answered.

Max sat at the mouth of the cave, his back turned toward the north inlet of the cove. Aware that Miranda would enter from that direction, he didn't want to intimidate her by staring; that and he was so anxious about their meeting he feared he'd involuntarily flinch upon seeing her. He imagined her nervous smile, the one she always tried to downplay upon peeking up at him. Feeling instantly enlivened by images of her, he took a deep breath and attempted to fight back the beginning of a blush. After a few restless minutes he heard the subtle compression of sand under light footsteps. The sound increased in volume until the scent of her sweet skin filled him. A tingle went across his shoulders and down his back, deliciously confirming Miranda's presence as she slid against him into the sand.

He's going to think you're sitting this way because you're afraid, she heard the angry one warn. Miranda realized that the observation was likely accurate, though her motivation was not due to fear this time. Rounding the cave her pulse had quickened upon seeing Max. He was wearing a silky teal shirt and white linen shorts, a combination that made him look like a Tommy Bahama model. Streaks of gold shown throughout his hair, and his wavy locks were as glossy as she'd ever seen them. He was intensely beautiful; why he wanted anything to do with her she couldn't understand. She took a deep breath, enjoying the warmth of his back against her own.

"Hey," she whispered.

"Hey," she heard Max answer, the smile on his face audible.

"How's your mom?"

"She's doing great. They put her on medication to help pace her heart. It should keep her safe."

Miranda listened, struggling to balance the strange combination of sympathy for his ordeal with the excitement that being near him compelled. "That's so good," she said, hoping her tone didn't broadcast her overlapping emotions.

"How's the painting going? Are you working on anything special?"

Miranda's thoughts leapt to the image of her latest creation, and she grinned as she remembered outlining his frame. "I think so," she said, pausing for several seconds. "I've been looking forward to something."

Max waited, as if hoping that his silence would encourage elaboration. Instead, Miranda closed her eyes and slowly adjusted herself so that she was facing him. Very slowly Max did the same until they were seated in front of each other. She forced her eyes open, keeping her gaze low.

He looked at her and seemed committed to memorizing the details of her face as she stared as his chest.

"I wish I weren't so afraid," she uttered, surprising herself with her own honesty.

"I think it's a good thing. If you weren't this wouldn't mean anything to you," he reasoned.

"Are you afraid?" she asked, dropping her eyes downward.

"Of you? Terrified," he admitted without a trace of humor in his tone.

Strangely comforted, Miranda allowed her eyes to drift from the ground to his chest, climbing his body until meeting his gaze. Max's breathing became more obvious.

"Why are you afraid of me?" she inquired, her huge eyes strained with confusion.

He hesitated as if contemplating the potential dangers of full disclosure. "Because you could really hurt me."

The answer hit Miranda hard. She reeled, looking at him with disbelief.

"I know I'm supposed to be cool. I'm supposed to act like I have a million things on my mind and hide my feelings for you. But the truth is that ever since I met you... *I'm* kind of a mess," he said, his boyish face melting Miranda with her own words.

She peered into his copper eyes, the vulnerability in his voice still echoing. Willing herself to close the distance between them, she inched toward him. Just as before, he remained still as if keenly aware that any movement could frighten her. Though Miranda ached to feel his lips against hers she could not bring herself to kiss him. A foreign power rose within her, threatening the moment with a ferocity which she was certain she couldn't contain. *No*, she commanded internally. *It has to be me.* Imagining her future-self, confident and whole, she slowly leaned into Max and dabbed her lips against his inquisitively. She brushed her mouth along his cheek, noting the texture of smooth skin under the faintest trace of a potential beard. Her hands came up and she allowed her fingertips to explore the soft angles of his jaw.

Nearly breathless, Max forced himself to keep still despite the frenzy Miranda was provoking. As strenuous as it was to remain motionless, he endured each electric touch while fighting hyperventilation. Miranda's kisses were almost too gentle, each sweep of her lips past his causing a ticklish ripple down his neck. And as certain as he was that he couldn't withstand much more, he desperately hoped it wouldn't end. Feeling her gradually pull away Max dared not open his eyes, certain that they would reveal his fervent thoughts.

As if delighted by his inability to look at her, Miranda appeared unable to conceal a shy smile. Max was conscious of how spent he must look and hoped she would find it flattering. Hearing her giggle he finally allowed himself to open his eyes, suddenly aware of an innocence he hadn't seen in her before. The sunlight made her hair shine almost artificially. And the blush of her skin drew attention to another feature the gold makeup had cloaked during the last few months; traces of honey colored freckles just above her cheekbones. Max couldn't think of anything rational to say.

"You feel so soft," he heard her say.

"I feel soft?" he said, finding it difficult to imagine anything more delicate than her silky features.

"Mm hmm."

"I'm very glad you think so."

She peered up at him. "Have you kissed a lot of girls?"

While the question was one Max would have normally found off-putting, coming from Miranda he took no offense. "I guess... there have been a few."

She looked down and for a moment Max worried that he had upset her. She seemed to struggle as her eyes crept back up to his. "Was that alright?" she practically whispered, exploring his face for a reaction.

"Miranda, it was... unforgettable."

As if convinced of his sincerity she relaxed, allowing her forehead to touch his. "Unforgettable?" she grinned.

"Not an exaggeration, I assure you," he said, gently kissing her temple. Once again he forced his eyes closed as an intense heat arose inside of him, threatening his composure.

Miranda studied him like she was unsure of what she was seeing. "Are you okay?"

"Yes definitely. I'm just not used to being so affected by someone."

"I guess that's a good thing," she said, a confident glow finding her. "Would you like to take a walk?"

Max stood and extended his hand which she happily accepted. She laughed at the ease by which he pulled her to her feet. Realizing that her gloves might be asking too much for anyone to endure, she took her hand back and removed the cotton covering. It would be okay... she would just have to be very careful to avoid combining looking at and touching any one thing at the same time. She slipped her hand back into his; the decision was met by a rush of sensation. She tried not to seem breathless as they walked leisurely along the secluded shore.

"I'm always amazed by how few people come to this cove," he said.

"It's the kelp," she replied, pointing toward several large mounds of soggy ocean plants which lined the sandy embankments. "I heard a marine biologist teaching a group pf kids. The seaweed drifts in from the kelp forests on Catalina Island. The piles attract so many gnats and sand fleas it can be a little distracting. I try not to sit too close."

"Doesn't seem like a good enough reason to avoid such a gorgeous place."

"I wouldn't think so either but who am I to say what should bother someone?"

Max glanced at her, hoping for some insight as to what he could safely discuss. The truth was he knew very little about the woman he was falling for, a fact which he found disconcerting.

As they reached the edge of the inlet, Miranda looked at the rocky tide pools which separated the cove from a popular stretch of the three-mile state beach. As quickly as she entertained the thought of proceeding, she realized that failure to do so would arouse the scorn of the angry one. Inhaling deeply she looked at Max with uncertain eyes.

"Feel like off-roading?"

Max glanced at the jagged rock wall which plunged into the ocean.

"Ah sure," he said, suppressing his surprise.

Miranda climbed onto the perilous formation and carefully made her way over the massive marine terrace. Max looked at his shoes skeptically before following her over the course terrain. Miranda emerged onto the next stretch of beach, relieved to see Max right behind her. Back on soft sand, they strolled toward the cove's historic center, finally coming upon a small wooden fence, its pickets misaligned and dilapidated. Walking past overgrown ragweed interlaced with lanky beach grasses, Max felt as if they had been transported to the East Coast. Following the fence line with his eyes, he noticed the first of nearly a dozen beach cottages that graced the seaboard. The nautical bungalows, each drenched in coastal appeal, were almost a century old and looked like something out of a movie set.

Miranda looked up at Max with spirited curiosity. "Have you ever stayed in one of them?"

"No but I've always wanted to. I've seen pictures of the interiors; they're just as magical on the inside as they are on the outside."

Max forced away fantasies of himself and Miranda sharing a passionate kiss on one of the private balconies.

Miranda strolled along the uneven planks which outlined a modest trail. "They all have names. That one's called the painter's cottage."

"Maybe it's a sign," he replied, his voice taking on a smoky quality which caused Miranda to wrestle with her own poise.

Unaware of his effect on her, Max let his eyes explore the cream-colored bungalow and imagined the view of the ocean from such a vantage point. Surrounded by dramatic bluffs, it was almost too lovely to be real. *We should stay here*, he heard his mind shout. As if struggling with the same thought, Miranda left the trail and headed toward the ocean. Max followed her, allowing the foamy tide to encircle his canvas shoes without the slightest concern. Resisting the urge to wrap his arms around her, he kept a reasonable distance as Miranda kicked off her shoes and waded in the cool water.

"I used to dream of the ocean; refused to throw away old tropical calendars. It was the only landscape I'd draw. If I had seen this cove as a kid..." she trailed off, her voice replete with fondness.

Max nodded empathetically. "I get it. I grew up here and I still can't get enough." He avoided the question that should have naturally followed, delighted to realize that she must have come to the same conclusion.

Her voice was distant when she spoke again. "I grew up in Colorado just outside of Denver."

"So you're used to seasons," Max offered, trying to remain light.

She seemed to appreciate his caution, some of the heaviness leaving her face. "Yeah, I've had my fair share. It used to take me twenty minutes each way to make it to the art museum but I did it every weekend; braving the snow on my pink and green Schwinn."

Max joined her in a chuckle. "Wow, that's dedication."

"I handed out brochures, learned the scripting for every tour by heart, and worked my way up to docent by the time I was twelve. I even had a 'D-A-M good volunteer tee shirt."

Max looked perplexed as he mouthed the letters before decoding the acronym. "D-A-M... Denver Art Museum. Cute," Max grinned. "Do you still have family there?"

Miranda's smile faded despite being prepared for the inquiry. She forced a more pleasant expression back into place before answering. "No."

Seeing that he had hit a nerve Max searched for safer ground. "Well, then I suppose there's no need to subject yourself to any more harsh winters."

Miranda relaxed again, wriggling her toes into the wet sand. Standing there, the sun flattering her flaxen hair and warming her skin, she felt closer to her future-self than she ever had. Allowing her knuckles to brush against Max's wrist she was elated when he took her hand.

"What's your favorite color?" he asked, the random question making her laugh.

"Blue. Definitely. You?"

"Black."

Miranda looked at him judgmentally, causing him to chuckle.

"I'm kidding. Green. Favorite song?" he continued.

Miranda grinned before looking up at him, as if encouraging him to guess.

He pondered the challenge for a few seconds, answering softly. "Wehrlose Liebe?"

Miranda nodded, giving him a smile that begged for a kiss. Locking eyes, Max slipped his hands around her waist and studied her face for any trace of distress. Caution still affecting her movements, Miranda slowly brought her arms up, resting them on Max's shoulders and clasping her hands around his neck. The space between them dwindled as their faces crept closer and closer together. As their noses touched Max softly pressed his lips into hers, the smooth skin of his mouth enveloping her. His cheeks burned and he wondered if Miranda could feel it. A tiny sigh escaped from her throat as his lips massaged hers. And though he hated the idea, Max gave himself only a few sweet seconds before releasing his grasp.

Miranda opened her eyes to see him once again searching her face for a reaction. She forced away a tear, touched by the constancy of his attentiveness. Noting the redness of her cheeks and the more pronounced rise and fall of her chest, Max grinned irresistibly.

"I think we're getting pretty good at this," he uttered.

"I'm feeling a little dizzy," she said as if embarrassed by the confession.

"I'm sure you're just hungry. The Beachcomber is a short walk from here. Any chance I could tempt you into having an early dinner?"

"It's not even five," she said, pretending that her apprehension over the prospect of going to a restaurant had anything to do with time.

"Perfect, then we'll definitely get a table. Besides, there's no better place to watch a sunset."

Chapter 15

Miranda reluctantly slipped her hand into Max's and followed him toward the nearby iconic restaurant. She watched as the wait staff began collapsing the wood-framed umbrellas from the outdoor patio, and did her best to avoid looking directly at their faces.

"See that, we'll have unobstructed views," Max said as they arrived in front of the restaurant. Miranda followed him up the sandy steps leading to the patio, the dining area empty with the exception of one other couple. The host quickly seated them at the most pelagic table, the patio's transparent border affording panoramic resplendence. Miranda looked around in wonder, the mind-blowing ocean views second only to the cloudless sky. Salmon hues mixed with blues and purples as the sun began to dip into the horizon. It was the most amazing sunset that she had ever seen. She hadn't even realized that Max had ordered wine until the waiter placed a glass in front of her and filled it with the honey-colored liquid.

"A late harvest Riesling. Is that okay? I didn't want to distract you from the view."

Miranda nodded, still lost in the beauty of the place; the beauty of the day. Keeping her eyes on Max she reached for the wine and took a sip, delighting in the unexpected flavor.

"It's so sweet. It's really good."

Max studied her face, holding a thousand questions back. A waiter came by and handed them menus. Miranda placed it on her plate and glanced at it briefly before returning her attention to the sunset. Her hand brushed against the smooth wooden table and she was careful to retract her fingers before looking down at the elegant setting for the first time. A maple colored pine, the table was adorned with palm leaves, atop which sat a flickering hurricane candle. Elegant and simple, Miranda couldn't envision a more romantic scenario. She dutifully did a final visual sweep of the table, noting the position of her plate, silverware, and wine before banishing her eyes from the table for the remainder of the night. Without the gloves she would have to be careful.

The waiter approached and added more wine into her already filled glass. "Do you know what you'd like this evening?"

Her best efforts notwithstanding, something in the waiter's voice troubled her. She kept her eyes downward, hoping that Max wouldn't notice her growing anxiety. "Oh, ah…"

Max looked at her, clearly unsure if he should interject. "Would you like to hear the specials?"

"That's okay, do they have anything fried?"

Max covered a smile with the back of his hand as the waiter's face revealed incertitude. "We have calamari," he ventured.

"Okay that would be great, thank you," she replied, sipping her wine nervously at having no concept of what she had ordered.

"I'll have the grilled scallops."

"Very good, Sir."

The waiter hurried away uncomfortably as Miranda fidgeted with her wine, resting the back of her other hand on the table.

"I'm sorry. That probably sounded dumb."

"Not at all. So, you like fried food," he replied, clearly amused.

His voice calmed her in a way she was starting to find indispensable, her rigid shoulders settling.

"Claire says I defy caloric law."

"She's very nice. And she has excellent taste in artists," he smiled.

Miranda looked down, wishing she could take the complement more gracefully. As if sensing her angry inner counterpart's growing frustration, she quickly offered a bold confession.

"I didn't want you to stop kissing me."

Max paused and held back what may have otherwise been a giddy smile. He leaned in, brushing his finger down the palm of her hand. "That's a mistake I can rectify."

She looked away as she heard the playful response, certain that he was the most attractive person she had ever laid eyes on. A gust of wind blew her hair off her shoulders, exposing her long neck. Max gazed at her as if finding it difficult to speak.

The waiter returned and Miranda quickly diverted her attention to the sea. This time Max seemed acutely aware of her reaction. Their plates were positioned in front of them and Max tried to thank the waiter discreetly, though his eyes stayed on his timorous date. He didn't speak until they were alone.

"Do you know him? The waiter I mean," he gently beckoned.

"No, he just... something about him makes me nervous."

Max remained silent, a gesture she recognized as his way of encouraging without being pushy. It was one of many things she was beginning to love about him.

"Unfortunately it happens a lot... usually with men. He didn't do anything wrong. It's very frustrating to be afraid all the time."

"It's commendable that you don't let it keep you more restricted."

A shudder of humiliation forced her eyes away. "I used to. Last year I only left the house four times." She looked up in time to see Max swallow hard.

He studied her as if unable to process the questions spinning around his head.

"I guess you could call this my break out year."

"Without a doubt," he said, bewilderment obviously affecting his tone.

"I will answer them all... in time," she replied. "I get that you must have a list of questions."

"I could think of a few, yeah," he said.

Miranda smiled back before looking down inquisitively at the two dozen fried circles composing her plate. "Little onion rings?" she asked, making her napkin the focal point as she picked up a small circle and placed it in her mouth. Her perplexed face made Max laugh out loud.

"No, it's squid," he chuckled, an intense look of concern suddenly washing over his face. "You're not allergic are you? To shellfish?"

"No," she briskly reassured, still chewing the first piece. "It's a little rubbery though."

Relief seemed to return the smile Max's fear had likely stolen. "Yes, but in a good way I think."

Miranda took another piece despite the texture.

Max tended to his meal and cut a large grilled scallop into quarters. Piercing one of the quarters and dabbing it into the accompanying chanterelle mushroom sauce, Max offered her his fork. "Have you ever had scallops?"

"Definitely not," she giggled before accepting the bite. Her eyes brightened as she took in the creamy flavors. "That's incredible."

"Let me get another plate? We could still snack on the calamari."

While Miranda's first inclination was to object to what she considered an imposition, Max's eager expression promised it was not. "Okay, that'd be great."

Max wasted no time in gesturing for the waiter and ordering a second dish, scooting her calamari out of the way and positioning his scallops in between them. Miranda shook her head discreetly as she watched the seamless exchange, a strange awareness coming over her as a gentle voice spoke inside her mind. *He actually likes taking care of me.* Miranda blinked as she pondered the observation and its origin. Another voice would have been a disastrous thought but there was something comforting about this presence. As soon as it was uttered Miranda knew it to be true.

She had heard the voice before. It encouraged her when she created new pieces and complemented her upon their completion; it cared for her. It was not judgmental or harsh but devoted and cheerful. *He actually likes taking care of me*, Miranda replied the statement. *Me.* It was then that Miranda realized that she was talking to herself; but not with her scared voice, and not with the contemptuousness of the angry one. She smiled brightly, filling her lungs with the littoral breeze as she looked on Max's intrigued face.

"You look a little jubilant all of the sudden," he grinned.

"I just had the nicest thought."

Max crooked his head, inviting her to share. Instead Miranda pierced a section of scallop with her fork and took a hardy bite. Max laughed, following her lead. "Okay, some other time. Favorite film?"

Miranda pressed her lips together, giving Max a light-heartedly guilty look.

"You don't watch movies? What about TV?" he asked.

"No, I don't even have one. It's a voices thing."

"Wow, okay," he said, deciding that sharing his would be lost on someone so unfamiliar with the subject. "Favorite food?"

Miranda almost shouted the answer, her face youthful. "Chili fries."

Max coughed, swallowing a bite of potato gratin before chuckling a response. "Right, the fried food obsession. How did that start?"

"It was Claire actually. The first week I was here... I mean after I left home...I didn't want to come out of my room. She tried everything; cookies, sodas... one time she made three bags of popcorn just to smell up the apartment. Nothing worked. Finally she put this big Styrofoam box of chili fries outside my door. I don't know if it was because I was so hungry or if it was just what called to me, but I took them and went back into my room; finished the whole container. It was the best thing I'd ever eaten. After that I opened my door and she came out of her room and sat across the hall from me. She didn't push me to talk she just let me take my time."

Max's expression was neutral as he considered her candor.

"Sounds like she knew just what you needed."

"Yes, some people seem to be good at that,' she smiled weakly.

Max took the complement, a sympathetic affect momentarily detracting his smile.

The waiter approached with a slice of coconut cake topped with pineapple ice cream, clearing their plates before situating the desert between them. Max couldn't tell if he was imagining it, but Miranda seemed less afraid of him, though she still refused to acknowledge him with her eyes.

171

"Favorite city," Miranda asked as if trying to lighten the mood.

Max snapped out of his heaviness as he answered. "We're in it, or at least bordering it. I don't think I could live outside of Laguna; at least I wouldn't want to try."

Miranda dug into the tart ice cream.

"I grew up here, I think I told you that, and though I've been to every coastal town in the state, my own city can't be beat. Of course it's very convenient to have the exhibition so close. It's the only show of its kind now, which has always made me feel certain that I was meant to be here."

Knowing that any discussions of the past could inadvertently trigger an upsetting thought for his date, Max took a cool mouthful of the buttery cake, hopeful that he hadn't yet done so.

Miranda finished her last sip of wine as the waiter dove in to refill her glass before hurrying away. She looked at it with doubt.

"Please don't worry about it. You certainly don't have to finish."

"I'd be in a coma," she said, as if relieved that he was not offended. "Are you on a break from work?"

"Yes, it's one of the perks of the job. I get two months at the end of every summer, which is great because it's sunny through September. I never feel like I'm missing out."

"How do you do it? Make a whole show every year?"

Max patted his lips with his napkin. "In November Katherine and Marcia, my art researchers, will present a handful of submissions for the next season; maybe five or so. Based on what we select, the next step is picking a theme. With a motif in mind, we then scour the world for another fifteen or more to include. I'm sorry, that's way more detail then you probably needed."

Miranda waved her hand as she swallowed another bite. "Not at all, this is great."

"Next we have a meeting with our set and costume designers, and our lead makeup artist Annie, who I understand you've met," he smiled sportively as he continued, "We also meet with our script writer and our musical director, and we outline the entire show. Pictures of the pieces then go to our set designers so they can start construction. Once that's done we take measurements and pictures of the sets, and those go to the costume designer, Sally. As soon as her team finishes, we send out a casting call over local radio stations and Frankie measures volunteers for costume matches."

"It sounds so exciting."

The waiter returned to the table and Max asked for the bill. "It's funny; even though I'm involved with every aspect of the show's creation I'm still awestruck when I see it all come together. It's like being a kid again and seeing it for the first time."

"What do you do during your break?"

Max was handed a receipt which he signed without inspection.

"Travel mostly, though I usually keep it fairly local. Last year I visited Sonoma and Napa, and spent a few weeks in Santa Barbara; got my fill of wine country. Even my trips are themed, I guess."

Miranda looked slightly nervous as she toyed with her wine glass. "What about this year?"

Max peered at her, completely unsure as to how to proceed.

"You don't have to answer," she quickly replied.

"No, I want to I just don't… forgive me if this seems like I'm moving too fast, but my answer is that I was hoping you'd be a part of that decision."

Miranda felt her pulse quicken.

"I have no intention of rushing things between us but it would be dishonest to say that I'd go away for any real length of time if you weren't potentially interested in joining me. If not, then I'd rather just spend the time here and slowly get to know you. Did I mention the slow part?" he added as he examined her nervous face.

The budding anxiety the conversation had provoked was suddenly dealt a comical blow.

Miranda giggled, her eyes filling with tears that Max prayed were born of laughter. "Yes, you mentioned that a few times, she replied.

Relieved, Max smiled at her, his voice hushed. "Honestly, if today represents the limit of our physical affection for the summer, I'll take it. Gladly."

Miranda nodded as if reassuring herself that his insistence was legitimate.

He looked out over the water. "We could talk about a simple day trip; see what's going on further down the coast."

Miranda shunned her insecurities and attempted a confident tone. "Like I said, this is my break out year. Would tomorrow be too soon?"

Max returned his gaze to her. "I think I can sort something out."

Miranda looked away, unnerved by his boyish grin. "We should get going. We've got a long walk back."

The two stood and Miranda was startled to find that the restaurant was now congested with happy diners; she hadn't noticed them packing in around her. It was another first. The couple headed toward the patio stairs, descending them and stepping out onto the now cool sand.

"Are you cold?" Max asked, setting a relaxing pace.

"No, I'm great. Thanks."

Max stared at the ocean, the black sky lit only by a bright moon. "I love the beach at night. My dad used to take me on grunion runs here."

"What is that?"

"When the season is right and the tide is high, these skinny little fish, Grunions, make their way to the shore for mating. The moonlight over their scales makes them practically glow. It's kind of eerie and cool to see them lining the shore. We would set up a fire in one of the pits, drink hot chocolate and wait till the tide was high enough; sometimes not until midnight."

"Would you catch them?"

"No, so I guess it's technically not a grunion run if you don't catch any, but we just liked the ritual of it all. You can catch them with your hand but you have to have a fishing license."

"You have to take a class?"

Max looked confused.

"To get a fishing license?"

"Oh no, you just have to pay."

"What's the point of paying for a license if there's no class?"

Max smiled at the innocuous question. "Just the way it goes, I guess. Think of it as a donation to the Department of Fish and Wildlife for their preservation efforts."

Miranda appeared uncharacteristically matter-of-fact when she spoke again. "I never knew my dad. He left when I was little."

"I'm sorry to hear that."

"It's okay."

Reaching the jagged outcropping of the rocky barrier, Max offered Miranda his hand. She took it as they carefully stepped over the rugged wall of earth and emerged onto the cove side of the beach. Max waited for her to release his hand but was pleased when she didn't. They made their way back to the mouth of the cave and up the trail toward the street.

"Max, this has been... today was my favorite day."

"It was pretty great. Can I drive you home?"

"I'd like to walk if you don't mind."

Max had to fight to avoid objecting, reminding himself that she was used to walking home in darkness.

"Can we meet here tomorrow morning?"

Max resisted a frown. "Whatever you like. Is nine alright? The traffic should have died down by then."

"Okay. See you," Miranda said turning and heading to the nearby crosswalk.

Max sank a bit as he saw her go. Comforting himself with the enormity of the day's successes, he slowly walked toward his car. The faint sounds of footsteps made him turn back around to find Miranda hurrying toward him. She took his face in her hands and kissed him softly, making his pulse race. He carefully placed his hands over hers as the kiss continued.

Max could barely contain his excitement as he managed the five minute drive from his house to the cove. Miranda had come so far is such a short time. He thought it was too good to be true but tried to manage his expectations. He was still dealing with a very fragile soul; one that was inherently afraid of most men and battling significant social anxiety to say the least. Still, she wasn't afraid of him. *I didn't want you to stop kissing me*, he remembered her say, a warm tingle accompanying the memory. As he arrived at the street adjacent to the cove, he looked at the digital clock on his console which read nine am sharp. A moment later he saw Miranda emerge from a tree-lined street and cross Pacific Coast Highway. Her long hair flowed over a denim jacket and stylish pink scarf, the color consistent with her full length skirt. He thought the white shirt underneath the jacket may have been a tank but couldn't be sure.

His happiness over seeing her took a turn as they approached the car, a worried expression coming over Miranda's face. He hurried out of the driver's seat and opened the passenger door for her.

"Good morning," he said, making himself available for a kiss without instigating one.

"Hi," she whispered.

Instead of getting in the car she seemed to be assessing the vehicle uncomfortably. At first Max couldn't understand what she was doing but seeing the fear in her eyes, he made a guess. He pressed a button near his hand break and the lid of the trunk opened from the wrong direction. The car's hard top separated from its once undivided frame and folded into the trunk, the lid closing it tightly into place. He watched in delight as Miranda's anxious expression was replaced with a smile as she witnessed the transformation.

"It's a convertible?"

"A regional imperative if you ask me."

"How did you know to put it down?"

Max stood over her with a sweet smile. "Just a hunch."

Miranda gratefully stroked her lips against his before taking a seat. Max closed her door and returned to the driver's seat, proud of his efficacious assessment.

Chapter 16

Miranda untied her scarf and positioned it over her hair as Max headed down the highway. "Where are we going?"

"Naples," Max replied.

Miranda tipped her head. "I know I don't get out much but isn't that a little ambitious for a day trip?"

Max laughed, doing his best Hugh Grant impersonation. "Milady, surely you don't think that I deliberately kept my answer vague in order to arouse your suspicion."

Miranda laughed, trying to mimic his aristocratic delivery. "No, never," she joked back.

"Oh good, then I presume you've yet to experience the delightful part of Long Beach with the distinguished yet misleading title."

"You would be correct, I have not," she continued.

"I'm confident that you will no doubt take great delectation upon discovering the many splendors of our first destination."

"Please Sir, do tell," she said, unable to resist playing along.

"Not a chance. You shall have to see it for yourself. Would you care to find us an amusing radio station for our travels or would you rather select a specific piece from my phone's musical library?"

Max unlocked then handed her his cell phone.

Miranda looked at the screen and found the icon indicating music. She touched it, her eyes widening upon seeing the huge assortment of music. Noticing a black and white picture of a good looking younger man, Miranda tapped his face, which opened another screen with the same picture and the title "Symphonies." She again tapped the picture with no result. Clicking the title itself she seemed surprised when a music video began playing. Max smiled as he heard one of his favorite songs by Dan Black begin, and wondered if Miranda would take interest in the lyrics.

She watched the phone's small screen, amused by the vintage look of the video and the song's stirring melody. Hearing the chorus she looked over at Max.

"This is really nice. I didn't imagine this would be your taste."

"I'm kind of all over the place musically."

Miranda found an album labeled 'awesome singles' which contained no album artwork. She clicked on it, reading the first song title. "Hit Me Baby One More Time?" she looked at Max judgmentally, causing him to chuckle.

"It's not what you think."

She selected the song and an acoustic version of the popular hit began. After a few instrumental bars a man's voice was heard, singing slowly with a string guitar as his only accompaniment. "This is somehow worse than I was thinking."

Max laughed as he anticipated the next part of the song. As the chorus played, more male singers joined the lead, their voices almost deliberately awful. Laughter from a live but obviously small audience was audible in the background of the recording.

Miranda looked to Max, his smile spreading to her. "What is this?"

"Fran Healy. His band is called Travis. Despite being one of the most talented pop artists of our generation he also has a hilarious sense of humor."

Miranda continued to listen, coming around to the comedic nature of the performance. "You really are all over the place."

"Is there anything in the line-up you're familiar with?" Max asked, hoping the question didn't seem like an obvious inquiry as to their musical compatibility.

Miranda clumsily scrolled down the albums. "I've done this on Claire's phone," she said as if aware of her amateur handling of the device. Finding a particular title she clicked the album cover and scoured the listings for one song. A sweeping melody began, followed by an angelic female voice. Max instantly recognized the piece as O Mio Bambino Caro, and wondered if Miranda had chosen it accidentally. Peeking at her while he drove, her closed eyes and sincere smile made it clear the selection was deliberate.

Miranda seemed to sense the question Max longed to ask. "When I was little I couldn't understand why anyone would want to listen to something they didn't understand. My grandmother would read me these stories from her childhood; they made no sense, so I just pretended to listen. Then I heard this song. I was watching a Peanuts episode of all things," she laughed as she recalled the day, unaware that Max, his expression wrought with astonishment, seemed to know exactly what she was going to say next.

"Peppermint Patty was about to compete in a figure-skating competition and her accompaniment tape ate itself in the machine. There she was, posing on the ice while the kids all stared, ready to die of embarrassment."

"Until Woodstock saved the day by whistling this melody," Max said.

Miranda's eyes spoke of how close she was starting to feel toward Max. "So we both became opera lovers thanks to a cartoon."

"Well Bugs Bunny kind of cinched the deal with the Wagnerian stuff but yeah, I'll always blame Charles Schultz."

Miranda laughed through misty eyes. "I heard the song again a few years later, that time complete with vocals. Even though I didn't understand the words I knew what they meant. I was hooked. I even started paying attention to my grandmother's stories."

Max glanced over, careful to devote most of his visual attention to the bending highway. "I can't imagine a stranger thing to have in common with someone. Perhaps we were meant to be."

Miranda swallowed hard, the thought having crossed her mind so many times over the last two months. She looked out over the ocean, amazed by the view from the road. "This is unbelievable."

"Five-hundred miles stretching from Baja to Washington State; it's not your average highway."

Another enticing melody began, making Miranda jump. "Oh my gosh, can you turn this up?"

A delicate flute solo gave way to a husky male voice and rich minor chords. Max listened, frowning skeptically. "You're a Salvatore Adamo fan?"

"Parlami D'Amore, Mariu," Miranda boasted with an impeccable Italian Accent.

Max's jaw dropped, his eyes sparkling with interest. "I guess you are."

Hearing the chorus Miranda began softly singing along, Max listening with his mouth agape. "And you speak French?"

"Well this is actually Italian but oui," she laughed.

181

Max shook his head as he smiled at his mysterious date. "Why on earth did you learn French?"

"I was listening to so much Bizet and Debussy it sort of started sinking in, I guess. When Claire found out she bought me language lessons on CD. It only took a couple of years for each one."

Max appeared confused. "Each CD?"

"Each language. I did the three most common in opera; German, French and Italian."

"You are kidding, right?"

Miranda shook her head, unable to read Max's expression.

"You must be some kind of genius," he whispered.

She looked down, the joy having left her face. "No, I just had a lot of time on my hands which is something I'm not proud of. I've spent the last eight years alone in that house."

"It's still an amazing accomplishment. You could be very useful," he said, his voice taking on a playful quality.

The change in inflection brought a small smile to her lips. "How so?"

"Well, for starters you can tell me what the hell the Ninety-Nine Red Balloons song is about."

Miranda laughed hard. "It's an anti-nuclear protest song."

Max stopped chuckling and looked at her, his smile still intact. "Seriously?"

"Yeah."

"You're sure?"

"Positive."

"That kind of ruins it," Max joked, causing Miranda to giggle. She studied him as he navigated past the Huntington Beach pier, the adoration in her eyes clear.

Max pulled in front of a small coffee house, one of a dozen or so boutiques lining the main street of a region of Long Beach known as Belmont Shore. Miranda stepped out of the car and looked around at the charming community before her. An eclectic area of town, rugged Irish pubs sat shoulder to shoulder with creperies and spirited home décor shops. Each business was uniquely owned; there wasn't a chain or franchise in sight. The city's occupants were equally spirited, walking down the streets with everything from pampered pets to sandy surfboards. A young woman with blue hair and a matching bikini skated past them just as two men in their sixties shared an ice cream. It was incredibly refreshing.

Max escorted her into the coffee shop. She continued to take in her surroundings as he spoke. "We need a good strolling drink."

"A strolling drink?" Miranda relied.

"Absolutely. An iced coffee or tea; something you can sip on while you walk. I assume you're okay with a long walk?"

"Of course. A mocha?"

Max approached the barista as she waited for his order.

"Two blended café mochas please."

The barista rang him up then went about making the two drinks herself.

Miranda glanced at the loud yet well-thought-out interior colors, each wall featuring a different hue. "Cute place," she said as she examined the prominently displayed local artwork.

"Midnight Espresso. As the name implies it has a great night life as well as a decent lunch crowd."

Max took their coffees, handing one to Miranda as they exited the establishment. "We're almost there;

it's only a few streets down but we should take the car. Parking is kind of a commodity along the storefronts."

Miranda slipped back into the passenger seat as Max started the car. Making a U-turn they passed several more blocks of eccentric shops before Max turned the car down a very narrow street just past a flower shop. Tiny beach bungalows, many of them quite reminiscent of those found in Laguna neighborhoods, grew logarithmically larger the closer they came to the ocean. Charismatic two-bedroom homes were replaced by spacious European-inspired houses, and finally by coastal mansions. Max parked at the end of a cul-de-sac and got out of the car. While Miranda didn't understand she followed as he took her hand and walked to a staircase to the right of the cul-de-sac's edge.

Her faith paid off as they reached the top of the stairs and emerged onto a ten-foot bridge, their view of the unusual neighborhood unhindered. In every direction gorgeous homes lined sweeping canals. And if the glimmering waters of the Alamitos Bay weren't inviting enough against the opulent dwellings, the row of moored boats at each private dock certainly made an impact. Miranda stared out over the canals in awe; the place was something out of a fairytale.

"This is insane," she finally whispered, slowly reaching the end of the bridge. Max helped her down another small flight of stairs which led to a winding street. Taking her first few steps Miranda couldn't absorb the beauty of the city fast enough. The homes, like their smaller predecessors, were of mixed styles. She studied the first house on the street, which possessed a clean, contemporary design. Brushed metallic wall panels composed the front of the home and though there was no break in the metal, the size of the panels indicated that the house was at least two stories. Miranda let her eyes follow the trickling pond which took up the entire front lawn space. She noted a gap at the bottom of the wall and watched as pond water passed underneath.

"The foundation is raised... the pond goes into the house?" she asked rhetorically.

"Not too shabby, huh?" Max replied.

Coming upon the next home Miranda shook her head. A Medieval tutor revival; its massive chimneys and bold timber framework implored her to have a closer look, which wasn't difficult. Miranda realized that each home was conspicuously devoid of any curtains; from the street anyone could see right in, making it clear that the owners of these lavish properties were as ostentatious as they were affluent. Exotic plants adorned decorous gardens; no two designs alike.

"What do these people do for a living?" Miranda speculated as she gazed at a carefree cat napping in the open mouth of a sculpted shark.

"I know. I almost wish they would post their resumes on the door."

Max stretched his arms in an effort to glance at his watch without being noticed. He set a quicker pace, Miranda naturally adjusting as well. They passed an Italianate Victorian, a mini Southern plantation, a handful of Mediterranean revivals, and a house that looked exactly like a Parisian Chateau.

Miranda looked up at Max. "I just can't believe how beautiful it is here."

"It's definitely one of a kind. Are you getting hungry?"

"I'd say yes but I never want to leave this place," she half joked.

Max covertly peeked at his watch again then headed to one of the docks and glanced around the canals. Miranda stood at his side, something in the distant waters catching her attention.

She squinted, her hand ineffectively shielding her eyes from the sun. "Is that? Is that a Gondola?"

A stripling grin came over Max, a look that would have made Miranda sigh had she noticed it. "It sure looks like one." Despite his best efforts the ignorant tone was less than believable, and earned him a suspicious look from his date.

As the vessel approached a strapping Gondolier became visible. Seeing the strange man, an uneasiness began to work its way into Miranda's consciousness. She took a few breaths and imagined her future-self, hoping it would bring about her calming presence. Fear and frustration boiled in her as the boat came closer, and she forced her gaze downward.

Max looked at her, alarmed to see her trembling. "Miranda? Are you okay? What happened?"

"I don't know... I just don't know if I can do this," she said, her voice quacking.

The jovial Gondolier used his oar to expertly position his boat alongside the dock and loudly called out to the couple, completely unaware of their issues.

"Ciao bella gente," he exclaimed happily, his booming voice heavily accented.

Miranda's breathing began to normalize and she stopped rolling her fingers.

He waved his hands around as if in love with life. "Cio che un giorno perfecto!"

Max watched Miranda as the tension seemed to evaporate and a tiny smile found her lips.

"What did he say?" Max asked, hoping the question would push away the last of her distress.

"Hello beautiful people, what a perfect day," she said as she afforded herself a quick glance at the Gondolier.

"Oh, you speak Italian! Benissimo!" he extolled, breaking into song.

Miranda smiled and took Max's hand as he helped her into the boat and took a seat by her side.

The gondolier handed them two wine glasses and filled them quickly. He brought out a linen-draped basket and uncovered the contents; an assortment of breads, olives, cheeses and grapes awaited them.

"Buon divertimento," he cried out before entertaining them with an impressive operatic solo. As if he had never been happier, he sang and steered through the canals.

Miranda nestled up to Max and put her head on his shoulder. "Sorry about earlier," she said.

Max kissed her forehead. "Please don't be sorry. What was it that… got you out of it?"

"His accent. The more foreign the better. No chance it'll sound familiar," she replied, hoping that he would understand despite the limited explanation.

Max seemed to think for a moment. "You know we could always move to Italy. I'm not that crazy about Laguna."

Miranda laughed at the obvious joke. "Yeah right, I've never seen someone so in love with a city. But thanks anyway. If there was only one trigger it might actually be a good idea but I'm not that lucky."

Max felt heavy with sadness as he realized how cognizant she was to her own condition. He looked into her eyes with a deep sincerity. "I'm pretty lucky," he whispered, causing Miranda's eyes to well with tears.

The gondolier turned around. Seeing her eyes he gasped dramatically.

"Non è possibile. Non è possible piangere. Questo posto è troppo bello. Alcuni formaggi. Essa contribuirá," he insisted before continuing the serenade.

Miranda laughed hard.

"What was that all about?" Max chuckled.

"He said it's impossible for me to cry because it's too beautiful and that I should eat some cheese because that would help."

Max laughed and dug into the basket. "It sounds like the man knows what he's talking about." He pulled out a variety of the snacks and made a plate for them to share. "I would have thought the wine would have more healing properties but I'm no expert."

Miranda took a bite of a cream-colored cheese wedge, its nutty flavor making her mouth come alive. "He's not wrong; the cheese is pretty sublime," she said, covering her mouth with her fingers.

Max pretended to be serious. "Yes, but healing?"

"I'm not crying anymore," she teased.

Max gave her a gentle kiss before stroking her hair affectionately. "No, you're not," he smiled.

As they navigated through the canals, the sun pulsing off the rippling water and the wine warming her skin, Miranda heard a familiar voice. *He's too precious to lose. Whatever it takes; that's what will have to be done.* It was her future-self, the gentle tone was unmistakable. And though she wanted to lash out, to ask why she hadn't been there during such a time of need, she knew better. Her future-self had never been able to break through true dread. Nerves yes, but never deep fear. Should that ever change, Miranda realized, it would mean the end of her imprisonment.

She separated a grape from the bunch and wrinkled her lips as the flavor contrasted with the wine. Max must have known she was now staring up at him, but he didn't seem to mind. She studied his profile, his defined features that somehow managed to seem soft. The sun was illuminating his eyes in a way that made her long for a kiss. She looked down at his hand and imagined being held by him as she had on

188

so many summer nights. Nothing in her life had ever been more satisfying then standing there, completely exposed, yet protected in his arms. The sensation was almost spiritual. She remembered the night she asked him about the finale music. *It sounded like victory*, he had said. Miranda brushed her cheek against his strong shoulder. That's what being with him felt like. Victory.

Before another tear could be conjured she felt the gondola turn, its master maneuvering it against the dock with incredible ease.

Max leaned down. "Did you have a good time?"

Miranda giggled, in part due to wine, and in part the question.

"Max, it was unforgettable," she repeated the words he had used to describe their first kiss.

She smiled as his lips dabbed hers, his hand caressing her cheek and making her thoughts spin. The gondolier helped them out of the boat before pushing away from the dock, blowing them kisses and yelling, "Arrivederci, grazie!"

The two began to walk back toward the car.

"And now it's time for a very important question. What to have for lunch after exploring the canals of Naples?" Max asked, putting his arm around her.

"Tacos?" she said, making his expression fall. "I'm kidding. Italian of course," she laughed.

"Good answer. You really had me going. I'm pretty big on appropriate pairings so just give me a minute to recover. Okay, we want quality of food combined with historic Belmont charm; it has to be Dominico's."

Chapter 17

It took less than five minutes to arrive at the understated Italian restaurant with its green and red awnings and its outdated interior. The two were immediately seated at one of the unlit tables at the back of the rustic establishment. Miranda was instantly taken with the place and welcomed the dark retreat after a day out in the open. After returning from a quick trip to the ladies room, she picked up her menu and slid her seat in closer to Max.

"What do you usually get here?"

He pointed to the second page of her menu. "The pizza; it's pretty special. The crust has a great crunch and is thick enough to hold the massive amount of toppings without being overpowering."

"The word pizza is really all I needed," she said with an adorable grin.

"That's right, my junk food girl."

Miranda giggled as she took his hand. "Not that your description wasn't convincing."

"I'm sure. Any topping preferences?"

"Heavens no. I'm surprisingly uncomplicated whereas it pertains to food," she replied, her aristocratic accent having returned.

"Jolly good," Max matched.

The waiter approached and Max ordered without using the menu.

"We'll start with a classic Italian salad and move onto the supreme ten inch. We're sharing everything."

The waiter scribbled onto a notepad. "And to drink?"

"Coke," Miranda interjected.

Max smiled as if delighted by her eager tone. "Two please."

The waiter hurried off, allowing Miranda to return her attention to the smooth fingers which gingerly toyed with her own.

"Would you tell me something honestly?"

Max clasped his hand around hers. "I would."

"You have six weeks left of your break. What would you be doing if you could do anything you wanted?"

"This, Miranda. Without a doubt. We'd spend every day in some new city along the coast; get you all caught up. Once the season begins I'll be pretty tied to the process. We'll still have plenty of time together, just not this much of course. Tomorrow we could visit San Pedro; it's only a few miles down the highway. Whatever makes sense."

"If I wasn't such a problem we wouldn't have to drive back and forth every night. We could just spend the night somewhere and move on to the next spot. That's what people do, right?"

"Some people, yeah. But you're not a problem. Look at how far you've come. You only left your house four times last year? You are truly courageous. I'm convinced that if you want something bad enough you will get it."

"Max, I had one meltdown and two near misses today and it's only lunch time."

"And here we are, still having lunch. You didn't give up, which is the only thing that could stop us today or any other day. I'm sure not disappointed, but I can see that you are. I wish you wouldn't be so hard in yourself."

191

The waiter approached with their drinks and salad, serving them quickly.

Miranda stayed locked on Max, his words giving her strength. "I want to do an overnight trip."

Max dropped the fork he had just picked up, and stammered a response. "Let's work up to that, okay? I wasn't kidding when I said I didn't want to rush things."

"I don't mean… that. We can get two rooms or beds or whatever people get."

Max smiled and rubbed her upturned palm with his thumb. "Let's give it a week. We can still see a new city each day; a two hour round trip is nothing."

"Okay, but next week for sure. I want to try it."

The urgency in her face made Max feel both hopeful and strangely sad at the same time. What was so easy for others was so hard for the woman he had already fallen in love with. But the opposite was also true, a fact he couldn't deny as his thoughts went to her paintings and sketches. Her gifts were unparalleled.

"I'm going wherever you are so just let me know," Max said.

His dedication to her made the back of her throat feel full and she knew that she was close to tears.

The pizza arrived before they had touched the salad, savory steam swirling above the substantial yet modestly-sized pie. Max freed a slice from the metal pan and served it to her.

"Why aren't you already taken?" she asked as she watched him.

Max looked at her as he tried to think of the right words. "Can I answer that in time? I'm afraid I wouldn't make any sense if I tried to explain it right now."

Noting his pained expression Miranda offered a caring smile. "Take your time. I'm not going anywhere."

Hours passed like minutes as Max and Miranda explored Belmont Shore. Instead of having desert at Dominico's they savored the creamiest, most flavorful post-lunch tiramisu in the county by visiting Angelo's Deli; an establishment that seemed to hide behind an agrestic storefront just so that it may remain authentic. Angelo, a proud Italian transplant, only made one tray of his award-winning desert each day and had no qualms about routinely declaring that fact in disjointed English. Angelo's customers loved him almost as much as his cooking.

An unconventional jewelry shop paired Day of the Dead figurines with exaggerated handbags in the same display case; a disparity that somehow worked after seeing their collection of avant-garde wall clocks.

Max and Miranda found a home and garden store which featured artistic folk spins on modern inventions, and made an enticing case for considering Eastern religions. Chancing upon a display toward the back of the store, they noted a small object that looked like an easel. A thin paintbrush and water dish sat beside it.

A young clerk seemed to notice their interest in the novelty and approached them. "It's called a Buddha Board; it's super cool," she smiled. "You just wet the brush, paint your design on the surface of the board, and whatever you painted will show up like black ink. When the water evaporates the painting fades. It's great if you're just staring out; no need to waste paper. Would you like to try it?"

Miranda took the brush from the excited girl and looked at her face for several seconds. She dabbed the brush in the water and created a round streak against the board. Delivering several smaller strokes and curves, she finished her trial in less than a minute. Max could hardly contain his amusement upon seeing a shockingly accurate representation of the girl's face, its stunned subject's mouth wide open as she stared.

The couple left the store hand in hand, Max unable to remove a stubborn grin from his face. Once out of the clerk's earshot he allowed himself a much needed laugh.

Sharing a pint of Guinness was the only rational decision after peeking into a brooding Irish ale house; the impervious wooden enclosures around each table making it seem as if they were the only two souls in a bygone refuge.

Max took Miranda's hand as they arrived at Michael's, a modern looking restaurant about four blocks east of the city's center. Opening the heavy door it looked as though they'd entered a posh living room, complete with an adjoining wine cellar.

"Whoa," Miranda whispered under her breath.

When approached by the host, Max simply pointed his index finger upward rather than disrupting the serenity of the dimly lit dining area. His gesture quickly interpreted, the two were escorted up a winding staircase. A slight chill questioned Miranda's assumption that they would soon nestle into a dark booth, and an ocean breeze dispelled the misconception entirely. Her eyes bulged as she stepped out onto the roof of the restaurant and the host seated them at a cozy table overlooking Second Street. She waited for the host to scoot in her chair and drape her lap with a linen napkin, before erupting into a childlike laugh.

"Are you kidding me?"

Max grinned. "Go big or go home, I believe they say?"

"You're spoiling me completely, I hope you realize," she said.

"Hey, I've explored these cities alone plenty of times. It's nice having someone who appreciates my little finds."

"I never imagined anything like this."

Studying her face Max felt safe in digging a bit deeper. "What did you imagine?"

She shifted in her seat as she answered. "Just being happy I guess. Not being afraid, that's the most important thing. But don't let my lack of creativity hinder your knack for planning an amazing day."

As Max tenderly ran his fingers across the top of her palm, she realized that for the first day in months she hadn't felt as if she was being watched. She looked into his eyes and felt a warmth wrap around her body. Miranda couldn't tell if the cause was her first sip of the champagne the waiter had just served, or the affection in Max's smile that made her feel so flushed despite the chilly night. Either way it was clear that the man sitting across from her was a gift; perhaps cosmic compensation for all that she had endured. Before her mind could find its way to the frightening images and haunting sounds of her past, she distracted herself by leaning in to Max. Her fears weakened and buckled under his kiss until they were whisked away completely.

Weary from the day's treasures, Max and Miranda walked the quarter mile to Ocean Street. They passed scores of homes which, after all they'd seen, now seemed pedestrian in their charms. They crossed Ocean's expansive road and touched down on soft sand, dispatching their overworked shoes before welcoming the cool swirl of the tide around their feet. Putting his arms around her, Max brushed his lips against Miranda's.

"What do you think?"

"I think if we were kicked out of Laguna we'd have to come here."

"You're easy."

"We went on a gondola," she threw up her hands as she giggled. "We had dinner on the top of a restaurant."

Max laughed as she continued.

"This day…" she seemed to struggle to find the right words. "And I thought yesterday couldn't be beat."

Hearing her heartfelt tone Max drew her to him, wrapping his arms around her. He looked deeply into her eyes. "No amount of delight or wonder I could bring you could ever compete with all that you are."

Miranda shook her head as if unable to believe what he was saying. Rather than pointlessly countering, she accepted an endearing kiss.

"What time can I pick you up tomorrow?" he asked in a low voice.

"Tomorrow is… I have to see my therapist in the morning but I could be back to my house at ten thirty," she answered, searching his face for disappointment but finding none.

"Ten thirty would be great. I should probably drive you home tonight though. I'm very bad with directions and I wouldn't want to get lost in the morning."

Miranda laughed as she noted his smirk. "Okay, I guess I can't argue with that."

Max turned, initiating their walk back to the car. "I'm sorry I didn't bring a blanket. It's so beautiful tonight."

"I don't believe the day could have been improved upon."

"That just sounds like a challenge," he said, his voice taking on the husky tone that made Miranda nervous and excited at the same time.

Pretending to be unaffected, Miranda donned a cheery tone. "You know, just seeing these places with you is enough. It's not like every day needs to be this spectacular."

"Oh don't worry. Tomorrow's going to be a snoozer."

Miranda laughed hard at the dry delivery.

"I realize you're not the demanding type but that just makes this all the much more enjoyable."

They walked slowly as they made their way back to Second Street. Max took her hand. "If you could have any of these homes which one would you pick?" he asked as they walked past a house with a traditional Greek design.

"On this street?"

"Sure."

Miranda looked around, her eyes finding a contemporary coastal home with more windows then walls.

"That one."

"It's beautiful," he replied as he gazed at her selection.

"It's ironic."

Max frowned. "In what way?"

"I've always hated windows... hated the idea of being seen. My house was so full of them; it took Claire and me two days to put up all the curtains. They were huge and so heavy. Of course I wouldn't let anyone come in and do them for us."

"You wouldn't be afraid now? To live in a house like that?"

"Oh I would, but someday I won't be."

Max pressed his lips together, his heart aching for her.

They reached the car and Max opened the passenger door for Miranda. He handed her his phone and gave her a wink. "Hook us up," he said before closing her door and getting in on the driver's side.

Miranda scrolled through the albums, shaking her head as she noted the assortment. "You have Algerian Rai," she said clearly impressed.

"You know what Algerian Rai is," he contrasted playfully.

Miranda smiled as she poured over the collection and selected an album featuring some of Bizet's most notable pieces. The famous duet from the Pearl Fisher Opera filled the car with exquisite sound.

"Au Font Du Temple Saint," he remarked in a sophomoric French accent, causing Miranda to giggle.

Repeating the song's title she corrected him, her delivery remarkably precise.

Max took a covert breath and hoped that his cheeks were not as red as they felt after hearing her alluring recitation. "Okay, you're slightly better than me," he joked in an effort to calm his thoughts.

"Vous êtes beau lorsque vous rougir," she said seductively.

"You have to stop now," Max uttered as he ran his hand through his hair and adjusted his position, clearly unraveled by the lustful delivery. "What did you say though?"

"I said you're cute when you blush," she replied with a girlish smile.

Max chuckled with embarrassment. "I'm normally not much of a blusher, I must say."

Miranda looked out over the dark coast. "I love this song. It's one of the most amazing male duets in history."

"Without question. I know they're talking about a woman but my French is a little rusty," he said as he gave her a curious glance.

Miranda quickly obliged, obviously very familiar with the story. "A man and his friend see a beautiful woman; a goddess looming up in shadow and extending her arms. She has a veil which parts slightly. She is a vision. She makes her way through the crowd; so charming and lovely. They both fall in love with her but fear the toll on their friendship and vow to not let it destroy them. They will stay true to each other."

They continued listening to the piece, Max's expression collapsing somewhat. "I can't say I'd be so gracious if someone else wanted you."

"You'd give up your friendship and fight for me?"

"In an instant," he replied, his face tense with sincerity.

"You wouldn't have to, you know. I would never want anyone else. I have never wanted anyone else," she realized.

Max's face bloomed initially yet withered as he started on the road ahead. His expression became forlorn and his grip on the steering wheel caused the leather to wrinkle. Several seconds elapsed before he spoke again. "I want to know what happened to you but I'm afraid once I find out I'll kill the person responsible, and go to jail for the rest of my life."

Seeing the anger in his eyes, his clenched jaw and tight muscles, Miranda was surprised by her lack of fear. Leaving the beach she couldn't imagine feeling safer, but the fire she now witnessed made her feel indestructible, proving that she had once again underestimated Maxwell Turner. She wrapped her arms around his right bicep, calming him instantly.

"I'm so sorry," he whispered. "The last thing you need to be worried about is my upset."

Miranda closed her eyes. "It's nice worrying about someone else for a change."

At nine am Miranda was ushered inside Dr. Bale's office by his apologetic receptionist who seemed unable to take her eyes off Miranda.

"I'm so sorry, Miss Cova. He's only two minutes away. Please make yourself comfortable. Can I get you any water or coffee?"

She watched Miranda, studying her as if she was an alien.

"No, thanks anyway," Miranda replied, oblivious to the woman's befuddled expression as she sat on the Italian sofa across from Dr. Bales' armchair. The door opened and she turned to see the older man as he entered the office, dropping his briefcase as if in shock.

Miranda looked puzzled as the doctor stared at her.

"Miranda. Forgive me, you're just so…" He pulled a laptop from the briefcase and straightened his suit jacket as he attempted to regain full composure. Taking a seat he adjusted his glasses and opened the laptop before briefly assessing her appearance.

"You've changed your style quite a bit."

Miranda looked at her attire, confusion giving way to pride. "I guess I have," she said.

"I noticed that while I was away you didn't make any appointments with my replacement."

"No, I figured I could wait until you got back."

He continued to eye her as if unable to rationalize the metamorphosis. "When we last spoke you were contemplating a date at the beach."

Miranda laughed, the doctor dropping his pen as if startled by her untroubled mannerisms. Fortunately his patient hadn't noticed.

Miranda's smile was huge as she recalled the details of the last few weeks. "Yeah, well we had some trouble. His mom was hospitalized and he didn't show and I freaked out of course, but I had Claire. She calmed me down as always and encouraged me not to worry. Then he sent flowers and told me what happened and we finally had our date."

The doctor looked down at his laptop, his eyes wide. He cleared his throat and continued in a passive tone. "And this was when?"

"Ah, a week ago. We've been together a lot since then. Yesterday we went to Belmont Shore and today... I don't know where we're going today but I'm sure it will be wonderful."

"At the risk of sounding sub-therapeutic I can safely attest that the change in you over the last month is nothing short of astonishing. When I left you were speaking in fragments, your clothes more akin to armor than garments; now you're bubbling over and in need of sun block."

Miranda glanced at her tank top and capri pants. "Is this wrong?"

"No, definitely not. I'm just shocked; and so very happy for you. You're obviously having significant feelings for him."

Miranda imagined Max's smiling face as their lips joined. "Yes. I'm falling in love with him. I think... I actually think I already have."

Dr. Bales paused long enough to recover from the revelation before typing feverishly. "Incredible. Alright, what of the nightmares?"

"I haven't had one in several weeks."

"And the angry voice?"

"Dormant, I guess? Not gone, though. I feel like she's just there waiting for me to mess up."

"How would you do that?" he asked as he pecked at the keys.

"By losing ground. If I do something weak when I could have been strong; that's when she starts. Then I have to make up for it, you know."

"Like joining the show or pulling down the curtains."

"Right," she said as he continued writing. Miranda looked at her lap like a child reluctant to deliver bad news to a parent, and then forced a brave expression. "I want to go on a trip with him."

The doctor looked up, his face clearly concerned. "I think it's too soon."

"We can get separate rooms. I need to keep my momentum. If I don't she'll come back or worse, he'll leave. I know he thinks he won't but he will."

"You wouldn't want to jeopardize your progress. Have you had anxiety attacks?"

"A few but they were manageable."

"And the sensation that you're being watched?"

"Not one time yesterday," she said with a faint smile. "Not once," she pressured.

The doctor gazed at her and appeared to change his position. "I think you should wait but the decision is yours. Is there anything that I can do to assist you?"

Miranda looked up with a sorrowful glance. "Will you tell him for me? When the time is right... I don't think I can tell him."

The doctor hesitated as if saddened by the thought. "We can talk about that at a later date. In the meantime why don't you tell me all about him."

Chapter 18

Miranda rounded the corner in time to see Max pulling into her driveway, his punctuality causing her to grin. He stepped out of the car and opened the door for her.

"Hello Milady. Shall we push off?" he asked in his aristocratic voice.

"Why yes, of course My Lord. What lands await us this fine day?" she replied, slipping into the passenger seat.

"The lovely isle of Catalina, if you please."

"Well, that is a surprise."

Max hopped in the driver's seat and put the car in reverse, disbanding the haughty accent.

"You okay with boats?" he said, the glimmer in his eyes making her feel warm.

"Yeah, I think so," she smiled back.

"Let's do it."

Max and Miranda arrived at Balboa Village in Newport Beach less than twenty minutes later. Miranda's smile took up her entire face as she explored the sights of the waterfront pavilion and the residential island across the water. Nautical rides and glutinous snack booths lined either side of the transportation terminal, flavoring the air with delicious scents.

Max put his arm around her as they walked through the village, his white pants and navy polo unspeakably flattering. Mirada caught a glimpse of her own reflection in his sunglasses; the woman smiling back at her had never looked better.

"The Express doesn't depart for another half hour. Can I interest you in a deep fried funnel cake?"

"What's that?" she asked, her voice full of intrigue.

Max approached the funnel cake stand and handed the attendant five dollars. "Just powdered sugar please."

After shaking a generous dusting of confection atop the nest-like pastry, the attendant handed it to Max who carefully offered it to Miranda.

"They're usually pretty hot; just tear off a piece."

Miranda bit down through the crunchy dough to find a chewy center, the sugars melting against the hot exterior and creating a sinfully scrumptious glaze. "Oh my God, it's like doughnuts and french fries had a baby. I'm in love."

Max laughed as he broke off a piece. "That's the perfect description. Cute place, isn't it?"

"It reminds me of something lost in time." Miranda watched as cars and pedestrians were situated onto a ferry and transported to the nearby island.

"People actually live there?"

"They do. It's pretty packed though, something like three-thousand residents on less than a quarter of a mile."

"Wow," she said before noticing a large, oncoming vessel. "Can't we just take the little boat?" Miranda asked as she pointed to the ferry.

Max shaded his eyes from the sun and looked out over the water. "Oh that's not Catalina, that's Balboa.

We're going way over there," he replied and pointed toward the horizon. We should arrive by noon."

"It takes an hour?"

"Yeah, Catalina's about twenty-six miles away, so we'll have to take the Express boat."

Miranda looked uneasy as she discarded the funnel cake's remains in the trash. Sensing her distress, Max put his hand on her shoulder.

"We don't have to go, Rand. We never have to do anything that makes you nervous."

Hearing him use the nickname for the first time, Miranda felt a sudden endearment which settled her disquietude. She wrapped her arms around his neck and hugged him tight, her skin tingling as he rubbed her back.

"I'm used to things making me nervous. I'm just not used to having something to temper that. You know I'd be lost without you, right?"

Max fought to hold back his emotions as he stroked her long hair.

"Then you'll never be lost."

A horn sounded in the distance and Miranda wiped her eyes. Max glanced at her with uncertainty, smiling as she grabbed his hand and hurried onto the boat. They followed a group of people into the large cabin and took a seat at a small booth, the windows encircling the cabin allowing for ample views despite being indoors.

"They have a bar?" she laughed.

"Of course," Max replied as he glanced at the centrally positioned bistro. "What can I get you?"

Wishing she had a better understanding of cocktails, she shrugged her shoulders. "Something sweet?"

Max headed to the bar and ordered each of them a Riesling. He returned to the table and handed Miranda a glass. "I would have gone with something a bit more daring but they seemed to have limited ingredients; not the best scenario if one is interested in branching out."

Miranda sipped at the glass, recognizing the drink right away. Images of their first dinner together filled her mind. "It reminds me of the Beachcomber."

"As well it should."

Miranda braced her drink as mild turbulence invaded the cabin.

"It can get a little bumpy but it shouldn't be bad. Let me know if you need some air."

"I'm fine, thanks," she replied, noting that once again his fingers were gently brushing her palm. "You're so patient. It's like my problems don't even bother you. I just don't understand how you're free."

Max easily found the irony. "It's funny you should say that."

Before he could finish the sentence Miranda recoiled, pulling her arm away like she'd been betrayed.

"No, I didn't mean that… I'm taken now but only because you're in my life."

Miranda relaxed, peering at him as she struggled to comprehend his answer.

"Funny you should say that because I wasn't always the most understanding guy. Problems, as you call them, were not something I was interested in dealing with."

Miranda's confusion was obvious. "Then why me of all people?"

"Because picturing life without you is agonizing. And because every priority just lost its place at the table. I knew it before I'd ever spoken to you; before I'd seen your real face. It started with The Embrace."

Miranda exhaled and looked away; it was as if he was reading her mind.

"I'll never forget sitting in the conference room totally unaware that my life was about to change. Marcia and Katherine were pitching new pieces. They advanced a slide and I saw the statue for the first time. I didn't breathe for a full minute. Marcia explained the story and I was hooked. Next thing I knew, I lost the two people casted for the piece. Then I find you. I swear if I weren't so pragmatic I'd wonder if we were them in another life; Galen and Isaura," he said with a quiet laugh.

Miranda appeared uncomfortable and took several sips of wine before laughing nervously.

Max took back the theory with a wave. "Ignore me... funnel cake and wine doesn't mix."

The ship pulled into the central marine dock, its passengers quickly disembarking. Max lead Miranda to Crescent Drive where they began their tour down the boardwalk of Avalon, the island's foremost city. Miranda surveyed the area with the animation of an eager child, soaking up each precious shop and dipping her fingers into art deco-tiled fountains. She followed him onto the Green Pleasure Pier, a nautical playground which overlooked Crescent Beach and the plethoric shops framing the bay.

Miranda looked positively giddy as she watched Max scoot up to one of the undersized tables outside the sandy food shack known as Eric's.

"We're eating here?" she asked, aware that the restaurant was a true dive compared to that which Max was accustomed.

Max smiled, unbothered by the shirtless teenagers who devoured cheeseburgers a few feet away, their wet swim trunks dripping sea water onto the french fries below their feet.

"What? Can't a food aficionado take a break once in a while?"

"Don't move… I've so got this," she said as she hurried to the shack's ordering window. A few minutes later she returned with a tray filled with guilty pleasures.

"That's quite a hot dog," Max said as she cut the monstrous tube in half, carefully repositioning the overflowing toppings.

"I figured we'd just share everything," she replied as she divided a cheeseburger, grabbed a handful of fries and onion rings, and placed them all on a plate with half of the hotdog.

"Did that come with a side of Lipitor?" he chuckled, his content girlfriend already sinking her teeth into her burger.

Blissfully ignoring the comment she doused her plate with ketchup. "Oh my gosh this is heaven," she said as she rested the back of her hand against the table, dutifully keeping her palm up.

"I do not understand where you put it, Rand," he grinned, shaking his head.

He looked down as he contemplated the greasy assortment, thoroughly tempted to get up for a fork and knife. Glancing at Miranda, ketchup marring the corner of her smile, he resisted his fastidious urges he took a hefty bite of the messy hotdog. Miranda giggled as he wiped mustard off his upper lip.

A few feet away a school-aged boy and his little sister fished over the side of the peer. The boy watched in envy as the girl jerked her pole out of the water, shrieking with happiness as a petite mackerel thrashed on the line.

"That just made her day," Max said to Miranda as they watched the kids.

Letting out another shriek the girl lost control of the newly freed mackerel which slid on the ground before flopping toward their table.

Feeling the cold wetness against her feet, Miranda scooped up the fish and handed to the girl. The child yelled again as the fish thrashed and slapped its tail against her cheek. Without thinking, Miranda touched her fingertips against the child's face. A dazed look overtook Miranda's expression as she stared at the child. The little girl thanked her and ran off, Miranda's gaze still frozen.

"Rand, You okay?" he asked. "Miranda?" he yelled with increasing concern.

She nodded her okay, though her eyes stared blindly. Max grabbed his cell phone.

"Hang on, I'm calling 9-1-1..." he stammered before noticing Miranda shaking her head and patting his arm.

"No, please. Sorry," she replied, her attention back on him. "I didn't mean to scare you. I'm sorry; it happens. I was just caught in the strokes."

"How do you mean?"

"Her face... the steps to build it. Claire calls it my paint trance."

Max frowned as an unbelievable theory entered his mind. "You don't... are you actually visualizing how you'd paint her?"

"It's involuntary. I used to hate it because sometimes I'd be stuck for several minutes. I'm used to it now."

He studied her in disbelief. "How long has this been going on?"

"Ever since I can remember. This time it happened because I looked at her smile while I touched her skin. I try not to do that; touch things while looking at them. It causes a kind of sync and then I'm stuck for a while."

"That's why you always keep your palms up…" Max felt dizzy as he attempted to imagine the enormity of her talents. "But you can still paint things that aren't in front of you. Do you imagine the strokes in those cases?"

"Yes, but if it's meant to be a serious effort I have to meld my hand with my eyes. It's kind of weird; I don't know if I can explain it properly."

Max looked at her with fascination. "Can you try?"

Miranda flattened her lips together as she looked around. "You see that net hanging by the fish and chips stand?"

Max searched until his eyes found the target. "Yes."

"I find something coarse and distinctive and stare at it while I touch it. Then close my eyes while I feel the nuances," she replied, closing her eyes and rolling her fingers together. For the net, I would explore the frayed hair-like projections, the twisted sinews making up the checkerboard pattern, the strength of the rope against my palm. Soon I can see the colors; each score, and every distinction of the object. Then I know I'm… connected," she paused before opening her eyes to find Max gazing at her, his admiration clear.

"I've never felt like this," he whispered, causing her eyes to water. Images of his lucent arms shielding her from an astounded crowd entered her thoughts.

"For you… I feel like I always have, if that makes any sense."

Max took her hand and kissed her delicate fingers. "I think so. And I'm pretty sure the wine and funnel cake have worn off by now."

Miranda laughed and wiped her eyes.

Max extended his hand as he stood. "Come on, I want to show you something."

The two headed back to Crescent Drive and walked for another twenty minutes before seeing the circular Art Deco structure at the other end of the boardwalk. Stepping inside the massive building, Max guided her to the theater. As he opened the door Miranda's jaw dropped. The domed ceiling was blanketed in seafaring murals, their elaborate design evoking fantasies of mermaids and mythological monsters. Miranda slowly turned herself around, taking in every angle of the incomparable creation.

She seemed unable to separate her eyes from the masterpiece. "Are you serious?" she covered her mouth in surprise, the acclaimed acoustics of the theater having amplified her voice.

Max led Miranda down the ornate carpet of the center aisle and took a seat in one of the chairs, Miranda sitting beside him.

"Guess they didn't need speakers. Late twenties?"

Max smiled. "Very good."

"Do they still play films here?"

"Every Friday night," he replied.

"I always dreamed of being a mermaid... with a glittery green tail and hair that stayed curly even underwater." Letting her eyes wander over the walls, she noted how the red theater chairs and pink undertones of the murals cast a crimson glow all around. She felt her stomach react to the colors, her smile fading.

Max laughed at the thought. "I could see that kind of image getting you through a harsh winter."

A painful flashback of a crying girl invaded Miranda's consciousness.

Max jumped as he felt her shudder.

"Sorry, I'm okay." Miranda turned her attention to the mural and tried to control her breathing. Another flash assaulted her, and she could see an impressive drawing of a mermaid tacked to a little girl's bedroom wall. She flinched against the memory and hurried to her feet.

Max could see the fear in her eyes, his own breathing growing rapid as well. "What's going on?"

"I have to get out of here," she panted, backing out of the theater.

Max followed, extending his hand as her pace increased. "Rand, wait. You're safe with me."

Miranda burst out of the theater and ran to the exit of the building, the powerful sunlight forcing her back to reality as Max caught up with her. The fear slowly left her face as she took several deep breaths, finally looking up at Max. Her eyes welled with embarrassment. "I'm so sorry."

"No please. There's no need for you to be sorry."

"You shouldn't have to go through this," she turned, her face taking on a distant look.

"Stop, okay? Don't say that. I can take it, believe me. Just don't give up. That's the only thing I couldn't take that."

Miranda nodded and took his hand.

"Let's go home, alright? We'll go back to our beach."

They made the somber walk back to the Express in silence.

Boarding the vessel Miranda took a seat on the outer deck at the bow, arousing Max's concern.

"We might get a little wet here; we can go back to the enclosed seating area if you'd prefer."

"Actually I think I'd like to stay if that's okay."

"Of course," he said as he took a seat next to her.

It didn't take long before the ship was in motion, and perfumed air blew through their hair. The expansive ocean all around her, Miranda felt compelled to talk to Max. It was as if energy was seeping into to her from every direction, and she felt powerful and whole. She tried to speak but her voice was indiscernible over the tenacious winds and the cracking of the waves as they pounded the vessel. Max leaned in but couldn't make out her words. He gestured toward the inside but Miranda was insistent on staying.

A pair of dolphins raced alongside the boat, breaching repeatedly as they fought to match the ship's speed. Miranda smiled as she watched them, her heart racing along with them. Her hair was getting wet from the ocean's spray and Max positioned himself in front of her. Watching his protective stance and his determination to keep her sheltered, her thoughts went to their platform. Her mind replayed her memories; the first time she saw him, her gold paint swirling in the dark water after she ran into the ocean. She remembered the incredible peace she could only find in his arms. Cutting through the images, she heard a child's voice as it called out in a foreign tongue. "My only love; never leave me."

Max sat in shock as Miranda covered her mouth, horrified by the realization that the audible voice had escaped her own lips.

Max studied her expression as if struggling with himself.

The boat teetering, Miranda carefully stood and Max held her arm as she made her way to the inside. They found a table and sat. Mortified, Miranda kept her gaze on the wood.

Max took her hand and whispered poignantly. "What did you say?"

"I didn't…" she hadn't realized how cold she was until her teeth started to chatter. She blew warm air into her hands.

Max kept his tone soft. "I've heard that before; in the forest. I know what the words mean, Miranda. I just don't know why you're saying them in Greek."

She stayed silent, uncertainty making her thoughts race.

"I'm not angry. Would you please talk to me?"

Miranda swallowed hard. "My grandmother Althea; she left Greece and moved in with us when I was a baby. She would read me a story every night. It was the only one I wanted to hear. Galen and Isaura."

Max squeezed the edge of the table as if steadying himself.

"I was so taken by their love I think I wanted to be her. Of course I didn't know what I had wished on myself. My grandmother would always whisper the last line of the book in Greek," she recalled, a pained smile revealing her passion for the old story. "She died when I was ten. That's when everything…" her voice faltered as a tear ran down her face. "I took the book with me when I left home. Every once in a while I would read it and finish the last line just like she did. You can't imagine my surprise when I got a visit from Claire last April. She had always wanted to be a part of the exhibition and couldn't wait to tell me that she had been chosen for a nude of all things. She didn't remember the name of the piece but I knew. As soon as she explained the pose I knew she was going to be Isaura."

Max nodded as if finally starting to understand. "And when she broke her arm you jumped at the chance to take her place."

"Basically, yeah," she admitted before looking down again.

Max took her face in his hands and stared into her eyes. "Rand, I know this isn't easy. I know that you hate being afraid and you feel like you're letting me down. But I want you to understand something very important. I believe completely that you and I were meant to be together. I have no doubt. And I will *never* leave you," he stressed the words, his eyes bright with affection. He took her into his arms and kissed her until she was warm.

The Catalina Expressed coasted into the Balboa Harbor as the sun set over the water. The two made their way off the vessel and down the pier, their stroll ending at the historic Harborside Restaurant. String lights elegantly hugged the outline of the grand structure, sending golden reflections onto the waterfront. Miranda marveled as she studied the restaurant, shaking her head with a smile.

"I think you missed your calling as a travel planner."

Max chuckled as he opened the door for her and followed her inside. Again, Miranda was taken by limitless views of the harbor as she was escorted to their table.

"I could get used to this," she smiled as he took her hand.

"I certainly hope so," he grinned, whispering to the waiter as Miranda studied the menu.

"Okay, I took care of the wine. Why don't you choose the entrées?"

Miranda closed her eyes and put her index fingers on two areas of the menu. Opening her eyes she heard Max laugh. "Cioppino and Macadamia Nut Opakapaka," she said in a commanding voice. "I have no idea what any of that means but I'm sure whatever we're having will be delicious."

"You're certainly growing more confident."

Miranda peered at him with a gamesome look. "If we were going to try out a longer trip where do think we might go?"

"Oh, I have some ideas."

Miranda giggled as he kissed the side of her hand.

"You won't tell me?"

"What can I say? I love watching your face light up when you see something new and unexpected."

She looked down briefly, a signal Max now realized as indicative of an approaching server. He placed their order and waited for her eyes to return to his.

"Sorry," she said as if perceiving that her habits had become banal.

"It doesn't bother me at all," he answered, a comforting conviction in his tone.

"This would be a great place for a wedding," she said, startling herself with the comment. She blushed when she heard Max's triumphant laugh. "Well, you have come a long way."

Her cheeks burned with a cherry hue. "I wasn't... I mean I'm not trying to insinuate anything."

"That's too bad," he replied softly. "You sure had me excited there for a minute."

Miranda's heart rate quickened as he stroked the underside of her forearm. His seductive smile, the first of its kind, liquefied her insides. She felt the burn return to her cheeks, her arm tingling from his touch. Seeing her reaction Max looked away as if troubled by lascivious thoughts.

Exhaling, he took a large sip of wine. "Favorite holiday?"

Miranda laughed nervously, thankful for the distraction.

"Fourth of July; well it used to be. I love fireworks and never really did anything on the other holidays."

"You say that as if you're expecting it to change."

She grinned as she clasped her fingers around his. "I guess I am. Maybe it's because I'm starting to believe you; that we were meant to be."

Max closed his eyes, clearly affected by the confession. "I'm very glad to hear you say that," he said before seeing the waiter heading toward them. "Seafood stew or pink snapper?"

Miranda gave him a puzzled glance. "Huh? Oh," she said as she saw the large soup bowl and the plated fish fillet in the waiter's hands. "Seafood stew."

The waiter served their entrées and left them to enjoy the rest of their evening.

Chapter 19

Another sumptuous dinner behind them, Max pulled his car in front of Miranda's house and hurried to open her passenger door. When she stood she found herself face to face with Max. Making no effort to adjust their spacing, she straightened the collar of his jacket.

"I'm feeling things I'm not used to," she said, her face serious but content.

"You're definitely not alone, Miss Cova," he replied, his tone deep and carnal. The sound reignited the warmth in her cheeks and made her take an unusually large breath.

"Would you like to come inside?"

Max sighed, smiling at her with longing eyes. "More than anything else on the planet, but I think I should let you get some sleep. Pick you up at nine for another adventure?"

"Okay," she whispered, kissing him softly.

Max waited by his car until she unlocked her front door and turned on the lights of her entryway. Miranda watched from the door frame as he reluctantly sank down into the driver's seat and turned on the ignition. She touched her lips, savoring the memory of his kiss. Her senses preoccupied, she didn't feel the eyes that stayed locked on her from the shadows of the side yard.

The next morning Miranda woke to the crash of rolling waves. Her eyes still closed, she smiled as she buried her face into her pillow and hugged it happily. Thoughts of the prior day filled her with excitement, making any further rest impossible. She slipped out of bed and stretched against the cacophony of fighting seagulls which filled her room. The color drained from her face as she became aware of the vibrant nature of the sounds, which were normally muted. Scanning the room she saw the cause; the window of her adjoining bathroom was open. Her heart felt like it might punch through her chest wall.

Her hands shook as she grabbed her phone off the night stand and wrapped her robe over her shoulders. *Someone was here. They could still be here,* a terrified voice whimpered inside her mind. She crept out of her room and hurried out of the front door before dialing 911. A dispatcher answered quickly and asked her the nature of her emergency.

"Someone was in my house and I don't know if they're gone. Please come," she begged in a shrill tone. She hung up the phone and called Max, her consciousness skipping in and out as she leaned against the large oak tree in her yard. Though she couldn't recall what she had said to him, it wasn't long before his black convertible screeched to a halt in front of her house. She felt his arms wrap around her, and could feel him tremble as he held her. The police arrived a few moments later and, after hearing Max's understanding of what had happened, entered the house.

The frightened child inside of Miranda whimpered against sounds of a police radio, questions from unfamiliar people, and Max's responses to them. It was more than she could process, her flat expression and dull eyes making her appear inanimate. At some point the police had explained that no one was found but that she should stay somewhere else for the night. They had escorted her into the home so that she and Max could gather her belongings. Miranda walked through the house as if it was someone else's; the noises in her head drowning out any familiar sounds.

After filling her suitcase, Max walked her to his car and helped her sit. Miranda jerked as he reached for the convertible button, a sign which he assumed meant she didn't want to be exposed. Her consciousness continued to come in fragments. She blinked and they were on PCH. Another blink and they were at a house she didn't recognize.

Max hurried out of the car, opened her door, and guided her to his front porch. She stared blankly as they entered the home. She walked with him, through rooms she couldn't remember seeing even seconds after leaving them, until they finally entered his bedroom. Taking small, uniform steps she headed past the foot of his bed and peered out over the city. His immense were windows so clear, it seemed there was nothing preventing her from walking off the cliff upon which the house sat.

She heard Max say something and was vaguely aware of his movements about the room. Her eyes remained fixed on the tiny populous below and she understood why God hadn't saved her; why the very thought of his concern was absurd. Max was speaking again. The tiny people ambled about. She felt a hand take hers and realized that they were walking again. Leaving the bedroom she saw the metal portrait that Max had purchased from the street artist; the painting of the woman engulfed in flames. She stopped and stared at the piece, Max keenly aware that it was her first purposeful movement since he had found her in her yard.

She breathed hard as she studied the illustration, tears pouring out of her eyes. "Why is this happening to me?"

Max dropped his suitcase and held her against his chest, his eyes filling as well. "I don't know baby. I don't understand."

"Now I'm afraid to go back to the only place I felt safe. What am I going to do?"

"You're going to go away with me. The police will be watching your house for the next few nights and we are getting out of here." Max picked up his suitcase and guided her out to the car.

They sat in silence as Max drove down the mountain, occasionally glancing over in time to see a tear roll down her face.

"You know it was probably just a random break in. It happens all the time."

"I always feel like I'm being watched," she said, sorrow abundant in her tone. "It's been going on for years. I thought it was just in my head but now I don't think so."

Max studied her as he tried to think. He blinked repeatedly as if getting an idea. "We'll hire a private investigator. There's no limit to what these guys can figure out nowadays. You can stay with me. I'll put in the best alarm system available," he replied, his excitement growing. "I'll have movers collect your things. You never have to go back again. If someone is watching you they certainly won't know where you've gone."

"Unless they're watching you too," she said in a weak voice.

"Don't worry Rand, nobody's watching me," he replied before the image of the old lady from the forest entered his thoughts. Her face seemed to stare back at him in defiance as he imagined her. Another flash assaulted him, this time the video of the old lady screaming from behind Miranda. Max felt cold as he remembered the surveillance footage.

Clearly drained from the terrifying morning, Miranda closed her eyes. It wasn't long before she fell asleep. Max grabbed his jacket from the back seat and laid it across her chest and legs. He scrolled through the music library on his phone, selecting a compilation from Maurice Ravel. The placid melody drifted from the speakers, clearing his mind.

Miranda woke as the car exited the freeway and headed toward the ocean.

"Where are we?"

"San Diego. There's a little place I think you'll like."

Max made a left turn and the urban streets began to take on a nautical vibe. Miranda looked around the 1950's architecture, noting the Polynesian theme running through every building. They passed maritime restaurants, yacht lettering businesses, and a Tiki liquor store.

"What is this place?" Miranda asked, her face vivid for the first time since waking.

"Shelter Island; it's doesn't necessarily look like an island but it's still really great."

He turned into a palm tree-lined driveway and drove past a handsome fountain which announced that they were entering Humphries Half Moon Inn and Suites. The lush esthetics of the property were distinctly tropical; it was a heavenly oasis and exactly what Miranda needed to restore her spirit. She felt a warmth return to her cheeks as she took in the flourishing gardens and inhaled the coastal air.

Max seemed to sense the change. "Feeling better?"

"Yeah, much better actually," she said with an appreciative smile.

He put the car in park and gave her hand a squeeze before getting out and opening her door. "I'm going to go get us checked in. There's a gorgeous pool past the tropical gardens down that path if you'd like to take a look."

"Okay," she replied, slowly heading down the green walkway.

Following a winding trail she came upon the gardens that Max spoke of, and was surprised to see full-grown parrots flapping in the trees. Below them dramatic Koi ponds rippled with activity. Children splashed in the substantial pool, enjoying the verdurous island planter which seemed to be blooming from underneath the water like a little island in and of itself. Hearing footsteps, Miranda smiled when she saw Max approaching. She wrapped her arm around his as they walked further down the path.

"I don't know how you do it. Just when I think it can't get any better you find another paradise for us."

"That's the look I love," he said as he brushed his lips against hers. He turned and pointed across the greens on the opposite side of the property. "The ocean is just beyond that clearing. We'll be able to hear it from our room. Would you like to unpack?"

Miranda nodded and followed Max past the greens and up a small staircase. Reaching the top of the three-story structure, he opened the door to their corner suite. She took a deep breath before following him inside. Her eyes finding the cozy bedroom to the right, she noted the only bed and swallowed hard. As if reading her mind, Max pointed to the sofa in the adjoining living room.

"It's a pull out. Look, I even get my own flat screen TV and a view of the ocean. I know you're jealous."

She closed her eyes, her shoulders settling back into her frame. Max opened the sliding glass window and settled onto the sofa, pointing a remote controller toward the television set. Finding an incidental music channel and selecting a new age station, he gave Miranda a serene smile. It was enough to coax her into taking a seat beside him though she maintained a neutral distance. Her meek posture pained Max. He looked down, his eyes weighted by a nebulous frown.

You're unbelievable, a toxic voice rang out causing Miranda to stiffen. Dashing her hopes that the recently dormant angry one had left her, the attack continued. *He has done everything to make you happy and you still don't trust him. You don't deserve him. He's going to leave you and I'm going to laugh when he goes*, the voice screamed. As she fought back tears she felt a warm hand take hers, followed by the sensation of soft lips caressing the back of her fingers.

"I'm sorry you have to keep fighting this way. It must be exhausting. Thanks for not giving up on me," he said as he stroked her cheek.

She peered at him, her injected eyes mystified. "You're worried about me giving up on you?"

"I'm sure it would be easier than struggling this way. I don't know that I'm worth so much effort, but I'm certainly glad you seem to think so."

An unfamiliar feeling came over Miranda; it was as if the angry one was being ripped away. The hostile enemy, her criticisms and judgments linked to every facet, every fiber of Miranda's being, was palpably crumbling under Max's loving affirmations. A formidable gleam lightened her smile while the angry one dwindled into nonexistence. Max examined her face, a grin playing across his own.

"What was that?" he asked in a galvanized tone.

"That was…" she shook her head, searching for words she couldn't find. "You are the most important thing that has ever happened to me. And I will not stop fighting until the fear is gone and I can be yours completely."

Max bit his lip, the strength in her voice touching him. Miranda leaned in, consuming him with a powerful kiss. Her lips moved around his as she let her chest relax against his solid frame, her tongue exploring the inside of his mouth. Stunned by the intensity of her passion, Max remained motionless with the exception of his eager mouth. His breathing became labored and he suppressed a moan, his neck tingling as her lips messaged his skin. As thrilling as the moment was, the thought of provoking her fear kept him from giving into to his fervent desires. A small part of him was relieved when she slowly sat up, a content look in her eyes. He touched her lips with his fingertips, the redness lining her mouth reminding him of the erotic exchange that had him lost only moments before.

"We should swim… or do something else cold," he said as he shook his head.

Miranda didn't understand the remark but considered it nonetheless. "I didn't pack a bathing suit."

"You didn't pack anything, Rand. You were a little shaken so I took the liberties. I was actually surprised you even had one."

"Claire. She does that lot; buys me things for my future. I always thought it was so silly."

"She's quite a friend."

Miranda nodded and walked over to her suitcase. She quickly unpacked, then ducked into the bathroom with her bathing suit. She held up the conservative black one-piece, thanking Claire in her mind for the modest choice. She looked at the garment, wondering if she could muster the confidence to wear so little in front of Max, let alone other people. *You've already beaten this little obstacle, remember?* Her future-self encouraged warmly.

Imagining the platform, Miranda laughed and slipped into the suit. She stepped out of the bathroom to find Max wrapped in a waffled robe and holding up a matching one along with Miranda's sunglasses.

"The robes were in the closet."

"Thank you," she smiled as she fastened it around her waist and pulled her hair over her shoulder.

They headed down the stairs and made the short walk back to the pool. Finding two lounge chairs, Miranda took a seat while Max removed his robe and hung it over the back of the chair. A waitress in khaki shorts and a navy polo approached and welcomed them to the hotel.

"Can we get two mojitos please?"

"Raspberry mojitos okay?"

"Sounds wonderful."

Miranda stretched her legs over the lounge and relaxed into the supportive back. "What is a mojito?"

"You'll love it. It's light rum mixed with sugar, lime juice, muddled mint leaves, and club soda. And in this case some raspberries for color."

Miranda let her eyes wander over the other hotel guests. Parents unwound with exotic drinks and chatted with each other, while their kids performed cannon balls and pretended to be pirates. Lean palm trees arched over the pool area, enclosing it from the rest of the world. Hummingbirds flew from one flower to the next, their oscillating bodies popping against the vivacious backdrop of flora.

Miranda accepted her drink from the waitress, the mingling of lime and mint tickling her tongue on the first sip. The liquor worked fast and she felt warm on the inside, the bright sun taking care of her skin. Her mind was as uncluttered as it had ever been. Thick steam rose from the brick-lined spa behind them, bubbling and spinning its hot contents. She extended her hand toward Max which he accepted without delay. An island rhythm escaped unpresumptuous speakers all around the area, completing the experience.

"It's like we're in Eden."

Max chuckled. "I'm not going to argue that one."

She took a long sip of the mojito and closed her eyes, a fuzzy feeling stripping away every trace of concern. "You know what would be a really cool theme for your show next year?"

"Hmm?"

"Second chances. Art is full of them you know."

Max turned to look at her, his intrigue clear. "I like it. It's a nice broad motif, isn't it?"

"Yeah. You could have it be from many perspectives. The career of the artist, a specific piece that seemed fated to be forgotten or incomplete, a returning love interest… could be beautiful."

Max reached out and tucked her hair behind her ear. "It's a great idea. Thanks Rand."

"Sure," she said before taking another sip. "I think it would be fun to work with you."

"Really? I mean, I would truly love that," he replied.

She met his gaze, the copper in his eyes standing out in unabashed brilliance. "Sometimes you don't seem real."

He pulled down his sunglasses, placing them on the end of his nose. "What can I do to show you how real I am?"

The suggestive whisper made her shiver. Locked on his eyes, she imagined their golden bodies atop the platform, his right arm draped across her bare chest and his left shielding the crown of her thighs. She could hear her heart pound as his arms began to drift over her vulnerable skin, fondling her. She gasped as the fantasy shook her, and she turned away, gulping down a mouthful of mojito.

"Are you okay?"

"I'm fine," she lied, keeping her eyes down as she regained her control.

"If you're too cold we could try the hot tub."

Miranda glanced down at her robe, wondering if its presence was responsible for the question. "Sure."

She took off the robe and followed him to the spa, easing herself into the bubbling bath. Her muscles tensed as the torrid water momentarily burned her skin. Adjusting to the temperature, she reclined against the smooth concrete making up the humid basin. Max inched closer until their shoulders touched. Looking out over the pool area, Miranda could tell that they were relatively shielded from the other guests. She turned so that her back was facing Max's chest. As if sensing her motive he leaned in, cradling her in between his shoulders. She let her head dip back and rest against his neck, her apprehension thwarted by her longing for him.

He placed his hands on her shoulders, his fingertips gently grazing her skin in orbicular movements. Scintillating sensations swept over her and she felt as if her internal temperature was now competing with the heat of the water. His fingertips traveled down her arms, up to her shoulders, and back down again in an agonizingly provocative way. She could feel Max's lips against her neck and ached for them to move. Her thoughts, as they so often did, returned to the platform and to Max's protective embrace.

Inside the fantasy, his strong arms did not remain motionless. She could hear him breathing and could feel the intensity of his hunger. His arms slowly unfurled revealing her vulnerable frame, her body totally uncovered save the thin gold veil of paint. A rush of pleasure coursed through her as his hands took full advantage of her exposed flesh. Relentlessly curious, his fingertips explored her aching skin. She heard herself whimper, abruptly ending the fantasy.

Max turned his head, his eyes closed tight as if wrestling with desire.

He ran his wet hands through his hair. "We should get back to the pool. I think we're overheating."

Miranda nodded, wishing he wasn't right. She took his hand as they made their way to the inviting blue water of the pool. Descending the first step, her toes tingled against the opposing temperature. She glanced at Max, giggling upon seeing his grimace.

"I guess we could have waited a second."

"Maybe you could have but I was definitely running out of time," she said with a sly smile.

Shaking his head he picked her up and carried her into the water, ignoring her playful screams.

"You are pushing it, you know that?"

She held her breath as he bent his knees, the cold overtaking her for a few seconds before her body adjusted to being underwater. Max stood quickly, laughing as she splashed him.

"I realize that I've been the perfect gentleman but don't let my restraint give you some false sense of impunity," he said, pulling her into him. "My thoughts are anything but pure."

Miranda felt jittery as she took in his devilish grin. As much as she wanted to continue the game she knew it wouldn't be fair. "Okay, I'll watch my step.

229

But one day you're going to make that face and find yourself in a compromising position."

He kissed her hand, watching the water's reflection as it danced across her eyes. "I'm very much looking forward to it."

A waitress knelt down and offered a friendly smile.

"Can I get you anything? We serve lunch poolside and have a full bar. Jerry over there makes the best Blue Hawaiians in town," she said as she pointed to a handsome young bartender who waved back.

"That sounds wonderful," Max replied. He glanced at Miranda inquisitively. "Two?"

Miranda nodded. "Please."

"Great, I'll be right back."

Chapter 20

Miranda looked up to see a pair of chartreuse wild parrots flying overhead, skillfully dodging palm trees as they disappeared into the plethoric atrium. At the other end of the pool, a group of kids engaged in a belly flop competition.

Miranda watched them with a wistful expression. "I would have killed to be them as a kid. The thought of trading my snow boots for flip flops…"

Max turned and folded his arms over the edge of the pool's deck, resting his chin on his hands. "I'd tell you I know what you mean but I kind of *was* them as a kid."

"Rub it in."

"Sorry, babe. It's a California native thing."

Miranda splashed him again just as the waitress returned with two hurricane glasses filled with the electric blue concoction. Bending down she handed each of them a glass.

"Would you like to charge it to your room?"

"Yes, Turner in 209."

"Great. My name's Mandy. If you'd like anything else just give me a shout."

"It's so cool that they let you drink in the pool," Miranda said, her eyes widening upon taking her first sip of the slushy drink. "Does this even have alcohol in it?"

Max lifted his eyebrows in agreement. "Dangerous, aren't they?"

"All I taste is pineapple, coconut and something… tropical."

"Curacao; kind of a sweet yet bitter citrus-flavored liqueur. It's what gives it the blue color."

"It's wonderful," she said before taking another sip, tiny balls of ice giving the beverage a sparkling character. Miranda began to feel the soothing effects of the undetectable alcohol, her cheeks growing warm. Surveying all that was before her, she leaned into Max who happily put his arm around her. "*This* is wonderful. All of it."

Max touched his lips against hers. "Not bad considering the morning you had."

Miranda squinted as she recalled the recent events that now felt like they were a decade old. "I completely forgot about that. Somehow you made it all go away," she said, searching his eyes for some explanation.

"I had help," he joked as he lifted his glass.

"Really, what happened this morning would have taken weeks… months to recover from normally, and that's if I upped my appointments to three times a week."

Max seemed to consider whether or not to speak.

Miranda crooked her neck. "You have that look."

"What look is that?"

"The one where you want to say something but you're worried it will upset me," she answered softly. "Go ahead, please."

"Okay. If you'd done the therapy route for this; just for the break-in I mean… what would that have entailed?"

Miranda shook her head as she tried to appreciate where he was going. "We would talk about it."

Max took a gamble. "About what happened, all the fears racing through your mind, how the whole thing made you feel."

232

"Yes."

"And after a few weeks of that, thinking about it every day, replaying it in your mind, it would be fairly lodged in there. Don't you think?"

Miranda nodded.

"But just now it was so far behind you the memory was faint."

"You don't think therapy is helpful?" she asked.

"No, I do. If there's something you can't shake, something that's damaged you that you truly can't do anything about… that I get. But for the things that you can do something about, like taking a little trip before moving in with somebody who's crazy about you; maybe I'd just let that kind of thing become a distant memory."

The logic behind the sentiment was undeniable. Miranda fought back tears as she relaxed her face into Max's chest, closing her eyes as his arms enveloped her.

A warm bath in the Jacuzzi tub, combined with the remnants of an insanely delicious blue drink and a remarkably smart new perspective on emotional healing, left Miranda feeling almost too good. Emerging into the living area, her hair wrapped in a towel that matched her white robe, she found Max asleep on the sofa. Warm coastal breezes drifted into the room, making Max's wavy hair bounce gently against his forehead. She carefully eased herself next to him, taking the opportunity to study his winsome features. The natural blush of his cheeks against his light skin and masculine bone structure made him look so youthful and sweet. She resisted the urge to smooth a lock of hair away from his face.

Gazing down at him she was painfully aware of her mounting desires, all of them as exciting as they were unfamiliar. She imagined being loved by him and focused on the immersive pleasure that his touch, however innocent, always delivered. She could feel her body mounting a glorious response to the tantalizing fantasy when all at once a brutal image severed the connection. She jerked her head to the right, shutting out the image. As much as she wanted to believe she could be intimate with Max, she realized it would not happen with her current therapeutic course.

Quietly making her way into her room, she closed the door and took her cell phone from her purse. She selected Dr. Bales from one of three entries in the meager contact list. She listened as the phone rang and frowned when she heard the older man answer.

"Dr. Bales? It's Miranda. Why are you answering the phone?"

"Miranda, hello. My secretary went out for lunch and I was expecting a call."

"I'm sorry to bother you but it's important. I'd like to make an appointment," she said.

"I can have Rosie call you in a few minutes; she has my schedule," he replied, confusion tainting his tone.

Miranda shook her head and swallowed hard. "Not with you. I need to see a sex therapist."

"This is… we need to discuss this. I'll make room for you at the end of the day."

"I'm not in town. I won't be back for another day or so," she replied as she tried to listen for stirring from the living room.

"I'll have Rosie call you the moment she returns. Obviously we need some time together before jumping to something of that magnitude."

Miranda wanted to object but knew better than to insist. "Okay, I'll see you soon," she said, disconnecting the call.

Returning to Max she saw his eyelids flicker and part, the corners of his lips elevating into a bountiful smile. "Don't you look like an angel," he whispered, stroking her flushed cheeks with the back of his fingers.

"I was just thinking the same thing," she grinned. Leaning down she kissed him tenderly, hoping he wouldn't notice that she was starting to tremble.

She went to their special platform in her mind's eye as the kiss continued. Nothing in the world made her feel as strong as that memory could; not even the enormity of the sea, a source of power that she had gradually replaced with gold curves against a black sky. As the momentum of their kiss increased she felt Max pull away.

"Was that wrong?"

Max turned his head to one side, taking a deep breath as he stood. "Nothing, that was extremely right but you're not really dressed and I'm a little too aware of that." He glanced at the cable box atop the television screen across the room. "Oh Gosh, we have dinner reservations in thirty minutes. Should I see if they have anything later?"

Miranda followed his eyes to her robe, smiling as she understood that he worried she would need a time to primp.

"Max, I'm definitely not that kind of girl. I'll be ready in ten," she said as she headed to her room, her cell phone vibrating in her pocket as she closed the door. Guiding it to her ear she whispered.

"Hello, Rosie?"

Five minutes later the door of her bedroom opened. Max gulped as he saw her bronze skin glowing against a white linen dress, her towel-dried hair cascading down her back.

"You got some sun," he said.

Miranda looked down at her tan shoulder just as an image of her future-self popped into her mind, the similarity between the two making her smile.

"Ready?"

Max walked over to her, kissing her cheek. "I thought I was."

Miranda thanked him with her eyes before opening the front door and heading down the stairs. She slipped her hand into Max's and turned toward the parking area, feeling resistance.

Seeing that Max had stopped walking, she turned. "Are we going to call a cab or something?"

Max pointed to the octagonal Polynesian structure across the way. "What do you think?"

"I think I'm having another Blue Hawaiian," she laughed as she dragged him toward the unique restaurant.

"Oh no, tonight we Hurricane."

"What's that?"

"A step down from a Zombie."

"Huh?"

Max chuckled as he tried to keep up with his enthusiastic girlfriend's speedy pace.

After a two minute walk which should have taken five, they arrived at the historic restaurant. Opening the heavy wooden door, Miranda glanced around the audacious interior, the three-hundred-and-sixty degree views nothing short of ambient.

"This is nuts," she laughed as she studied the circular architecture.

The host, not at all offended by her boisterous declaration, smiled as he looked at Max.

"Turner, table for two," Max said with a grin.

"Right this way," the host offered calmly as if doing his best to avoid succumbing to Miranda's infectious elation.

He showed them to their booth, the crystal clear panoramic window making it look as though the ocean could be touched by merely extending a finger.

"Can we get a Hurricane?" Miranda asked before Max could stifle a giggle.

"I'll let your waiter know you're ready to order," he said, the last of his professionalism replaced by a muted smile as he scurried away.

"I think he likes you."

"Who?"

"The kid. He seemed quite taken."

"I'm quite taken," she said, her eyes sparkling back at him.

Max steadied himself upon hearing her words, his look hard to read.

Miranda appeared disconcerted as she studied his face. "Am I being too presumptuous?"

"Oh Rand, after all this you're still not sure how I feel?"

She gave him a coy smile. "I think I do."

The waiter approached and Max hastily ordered before the perfunctory introductions could be made.

"Good evening, could we start with two Hurricanes and the shishito peppers?"

"Right away," the waiter responded before heading toward the kitchen.

When Max looked back Miranda was already considering the menu. "What are all of these? The Rum Runner, Sailor's Grog? Is it a joke?"

"Come with me," he said as he stood.

Miranda followed him to the host's area where a bevy of curious cups behind a glass cabinet caught her eye.

"They're funny," she said as she looked over the collection.

"They're tiki mugs."

"Like the little carvings? I saw one on the Brady Bunch when I was a kid."

"Right, but... well it's rather involved. Tiki culture became popular in the late thirties, started to die down in the sixties, and experienced a revival in the nineties."

Miranda followed him back to the table where their beverages awaited them. "All the crazy names were popular drinks created during the inception. Lots of folks actually collect the mugs."

Miranda took a sip of her coral colored drink. "Do you?"

"No, but I'm a sucker for people who do."

The waiter returned with a plate of small green peppers.

Max looked up at him. "Would you mind selecting your two favorite dishes for us? We're easy to please," he added, handing him their menus.

"My pleasure," the waiter nodded before departing.

Miranda looked down at the appetizer with obvious hesitation.

"They're mild and savory for the most part, though you could happen upon one that's unexpectedly spicy. Luckily you're properly armed," he said tipping his head toward her icy drink.

"I think you're incredibly fun," she cooed.

"Maybe you bring it out of me."

"I spent the last fourteen years hiding from the outside."

"That was then," he smiled as he rubbed the palm of her hand. Looking down he noted that her other hand was, as he'd come to expect, also turned upward in a cupping position.

He looked up, banishing a pang of self-pity in time to offer a docile smile.

"Is something wrong?"

"No, I'm sorry. I wanted to be an artist so badly; I just envy your talent."

"You wanted to be famous? Considered a great master?"

"No, nothing like that," he said. "I wanted to be able to show others the beauty of a landscape or the immortality of unconditional love; to express myself through my work."

A small crease appeared between Miranda's eyebrows. "Don't you do that now... exactly that?"

"I don't create anything."

"But you recreate everything. Your show brings art to life or at least back to life. So instead of being a master of one generation you're a father to hundreds of them. Very disappointing," she smiled, leaning in and kissing him.

The pain in Max's eyes dissolved as her words repaired him.

Max took Miranda's hand as they emerged from the restaurant's entrance and walked toward the inn. Gracing their stroll, a cloudless night boldly displayed its celestial treasures and lit the dark water of the San Diego Bay. Max watched as Miranda carefully tiptoed along the outer curve of the sidewalk; an impulse typically lost by the end of childhood.

Moments later they arrived at the foot of the steps leading to their room. Max stopped, turning to glance toward the pool area. He took a step forward, Miranda clumsily adjusting her gait as she followed Max down the tropical path.

"It's a little cool for a swim, don't you think?"

"I just need to see something," he replied.

The light from the pool casting a blue glow over them, Miranda frowned as Max plucked several Plumeria blossoms from a shrub and headed to the spa. He dropped the flowers into the swirling waters of the hot tub.

"What are you doing?"

"Touch it," he cajoled. "You've got to let me experience this at least once."

"Experience it?"

"Tell me what you see; I want to hear every detail."

Miranda took a step back. "Max, I…"

"Please. You're the only way I'll ever see it."

Looking into his sad eyes Miranda was unable to deprive him of the humble request.

"I've never tried to narrate this but I'll do my best."

She knelt down and let her fingertips palpate the surface of the water, graze over the floating Plumeria, and finally outline the red bricks making up the round border of the spa. She closed her eyes, the description escaping her lips as fast as they could form the words.

"Landscape orientation oil on canvas; aerial point of view. Elementary outline in chalk starting with the arena followed by the brick border and lunar image, ending with circlets indicating floral positioning and reflective orbit of foliage covered brick. Phthalo Blue foundation across basin area, avoiding areas of mirroring as well as floating blooms. Cobalt green light streaked over Phthalo again avoiding structures. The moon's cast and glimmers on the water's edges in King's Blue Extra Pale, with distortions in Manganese. Plumeria blossoms begin as Brilliant Yellow Extra Pale, diffuse into Cadmium Yellow and are finished by the next hue down the spectrum. Onto the foremost brick in Payne's Grey and Mars with highlights of Bice. Piece is completed with Viridian for foliage and flecks of Cinnabar and Chromium Oxide for depth."

Taking a few breaths Miranda stood and opened her eyes to find Max staring at her, unable to speak. Gazing into her eyes as if trying to possess them, he took her face into his hands.

"So, this is how the Gods have their fun," he whispered, his voice quivering.

"I'd trade it all, you know."

"Don't say that," he begged, holding her chest against his. "You're gifts are beyond my comprehension."

"So are my demons."

He released his grip and looked at her deeply. "They don't have to be. I love you Miranda."

She closed her eyes as he dabbed kisses over her cheeks. "Would you sleep next to me tonight? Lie with me?"

"If I must," he said, throwing his head back and placing his hand on his chest. Miranda giggled at the melodramatic gesture of obligation. Max put his arm around her waist and guided her back to their suite.

Chapter 21

They brushed their teeth in silence, Miranda staring at her pupils in the mirror in an effort to avoid the worries which clamored for her attention. She removed her scant makeup and applied lotion to her face.

"I'm just going to change," she said nervously.

"Yeah, me too; do you want to open the door when you're all set?" Max asked, stumbling over his words.

"Sure."

Miranda hurried out of the bathroom and into her room, sealing herself inside. Resting her back against the door she closed her eyes. *This was my idea*, she reminded herself. *Get it together*. Seeing a lamp on the night stand she twisted the knob until it clicked on, a creamy glow emanating. She returned to the door, switching off the main light and opening the door before crawling in bed. She pulled the covers tightly over her shoulders and turned on her side. The room was silent for what seemed an eternity, and she wondered if Max had forgotten about her invitation. Her heart rate jumped ten beats per minutes when faint footsteps let her know he hadn't. She heard the door close and soon felt the mattress depress, the bedding over her skin moving around before becoming fixed.

Another several minutes of silence passed, Miranda's big eyes straining to see any motion in the periphery.

"Max," she whispered. "What would you do if I were normal?"

"Keep looking, I guess," he joked.

"No, I mean tonight."

Max turned toward her, seeing her back to him. "Are you asking me what we'd be doing if you weren't afraid? I don't think I should even try to imagine."

"What about after that?"

Max looked up as if searching for what she hoped to hear. He smiled as the idea seemed to come to him, and pressed his chest against her back as he wrapped his arms around her.

Miranda closed her eyes, a gratified smile finding her. She felt Max brush her hair away from her shoulders, clearing a path along her neck. The smoothness of his skin made her face hot again as he let his cheek rest against the angle of her nape.

"I love you, Max."

She took his hand and tucked it into her chest as she drifted to sleep.

Despite three carefree days in San Diego, Miranda found it difficult to return their city. As she and Max crossed the Laguna Beach city limits, her thoughts returned her to what had driven them from the cozy town in the first place, her mind flashing with images of her open window and displaced belongings. She glanced at Max, deciding to heed his advice and avoid reflecting on her fears. Her worried face grew strong as she committed to disavowing the negative memories.

Max looked over as if intrigued by her confident expression. "What are you thinking about?"

"You must mean, what am I *not* thinking about."

Seeing her smug smile Max laughed out loud. "I like it. It's definitely a step in the right direction."

Making a right turn off Pacific Coast Highway, Miranda peered out of her window in confusion before remembering that he wasn't taking her home. Not to her home anyway. She closed her eyes as they made another turn, the car now making its way up a steep hill. She could feel her heart rate increase, though not with the foreboding accompaniment she was used to experiencing. The car pulled up to a large, modern home that sat alone atop a cliff. Smart lines met with natural elements to create a luxurious amalgamation. The exterior colors were masculine and tasteful, a combination rather appropriate considering the home's owner. Though she had seen it before, she had no memory of the house and was happy to be examining it with less distracted eyes.

Max unlocked the front door and opened it widely, inviting her inside. Were it not for an impressive chef's kitchen, the house would have been indistinguishable from a large downtown gallery. Comfortable chairs sat below prized paintings. Pedestals with Greco-Roman busts flanked the severe fireplace. The walls were neutral in tone, allowing the colors in the diverse and extensive collection to do the eye-catching. And every light fixture was a unique work of art.

"This must have taken years," she said as she studied each piece. "As different as it is, it all works together beautifully. It's going to be weird being the one with relatively bad taste."

"I've seen your living room. You should definitely be used to it by now," he said, grinning as Miranda laughed hard.

"I guess I deserve that."

Max took her hand and led her down the hallway and into the doorway of a guest room. "Will this be okay?"

Miranda let her eyes explore the elegant space, surprised by a view only slightly less grand than the one in the master bedroom. Her suitcase sat at the bottom of a comfortable looking bed. She fought back tears as she noticed her supplies, from her easel to her paints and canvases, all neatly organized around the window.

"I supposed it'll be a good enough place to keep my things."

Max narrowed the gap between them. "Miss Cova, what are you implying?"

"Just that last night was pretty great," she said as she thought of the prior evening; lying in bed with Max, warm and safe in his arms.

"Yeah," he whispered. "I could get used to nights like that." He leaned in, kissing her softly.

A reddish hue in her periphery made her glance at the wall on the other end of the hallway and she again regarded the compelling piece across from Max's bedroom. She walked over to it, staring at it for several seconds.

Max came up behind her, letting his chest support her back. "I bought it off a street peddler."

"It's sheet metal," she replied, a troubled look fanning over her face.

"That's right." Max ran his fingers along the high-glossed surface, unaware of her expression. "Ingenious medium, not to mention one of the most beautifully distressing images I've seen."

Miranda looked across the hall to see the fragile arm of a very familiar houseplant peeking out from the living room.

Max noted her gaze. "It's from your apartment. It seemed like the only thing you had that was just for decoration. I figured it must be important."

The thriving plant was fern-like in appearance. Given its sizable pot, it was several years old. Miranda took Max's hand before he could reach out to touch one of the branches.

"Thanks, it is," she said before kissing him. "I'd unpack but as you know there wouldn't be much to that," she smiled, doing her best to seem light.

"You certainly live by the 'less is more' maxim. Would you like anything? Tea?"

Miranda groaned. "That sounds so good."

"Great, then come make us some," he winked. "It's your kitchen too."

They walked into the living room and Max took a seat at a kitchen bar stool as Miranda went about exploring drawers and cabinets.

Seeing LBPD flash across his vibrating cell phone screen, he hurriedly answered the call.

"Maxwell Turner," he said, not noticing Miranda's smile upon hearing his formal introduction. He listened to the caller as Miranda grabbed the tea kettle. His face dour, he held up his hand for her to see and shook his head. Miranda's smile vanished, suddenly aware of his expression.

"I see. We'll be right there."

Max disconnected the call and stood abruptly. "That was the police. They'd like us to come down."

"They found something?"

Max seemed to fight to avoid sounding alarmed. "I don't know. You should grab a coat."

Miranda ran to the spare room. She returned, pulling on a sweater before following Max outside.

Max and Miranda sat in front of the detective's desk as he reviewed his paperwork.

"Drive by surveillance and nightly perimeter checks for two days yielded nothing. I must say it wasn't easy given the overgrowth along the property."

Miranda looked away, her cheeks reddening.

"We were about to call it quits when neighbors reported a banging sound coming from the back yard. We dispatched a unit to find someone running from the property. The suspect took off on foot and disappeared into a large park. Our officer was not able to chase down the suspect but returned to the residence to find the bathroom window forced open."

Miranda closed her eyes as Max put his arm around her.

"We found a few prints but nothing that matched our database."

Max shook his head. "Well, that's it. You can't go back, Rand. We might as well sell the place."

"Yeah," she managed as she held back tears.

"What kind of options do we have to consider?" Max asked the detective.

"Not a lot to be honest. You could set up a few cameras. I can't allocate any more resources to this but if I were you, I'd want to know who had an interest in Miss Cova. We'd be happy to investigate if you uncover anything."

Max shook the man's hand and thanked him for his help, then escorted Miranda out of the building. They made the drive back up the hill in silence, Max resting his hand on Miranda's seat as a quiet offering which she never accepted. Once back in the living room, Miranda returned her attention to making tea as Max slowly lowered himself onto a bar stool.

"I'll get the cameras first thing in the morning. We'll figure this out, you know," he promised, his face filled with concern as he watched her.

"Yeah. Sorry, I'm just a little freaked out but I'll be fine," she said as she ignited a burner and found two tea cups.

"Maybe somebody's after the art," he said.

"That's probably all it is," she agreed. "I think I should cook."

Max looked at her strangely. "Ah, Sure. Can you?"

"I don't know. Do you have a book?"

Max pointed to the small computer screen in the corner of the kitchen. "I usually look up recipes online. Saves keeping an oily, dust-covered library. Would you like me to do the honors?"

"No, I'm good. It'll keep my mind off things."

"Fair enough," he smiled meekly.

Miranda found the search bar before realizing she had no idea what was available to her. Walking to the refrigerator she examined the contents and then checked out the freezer. Seeing several neatly stacked plastic containers, she sighed and dropped her shoulders. The sound of a growing scream made her jump and before she could make sense of it she felt Max put one arm around her while extinguishing the flame with the other. His movements were so fluid and comforting.

"Just the tea kettle baby," he whispered.

Turning into him she put her head on his shoulder and tried not to cry as he rubbed her arm.

"Okay," he said in a low tone. "We have a couple of problems here." He walked her to his bar stool and helped her take a seat. "First, you need to relax while I make us something nice."

"Second," he hesitated as he scooped up the tea glasses and placed them back in the cabinets, exchanging them for wine glasses. "Since it is break-in number two I think we can skip the tea." Removing the lid of a carafe he poured two small portions, passing a glass to Miranda. She managed a defeated smile as she took a hefty sip.

"You don't seem scared at all," she said, her eyes thirsty for a good cry.

"I'm not. You're here. And Miranda, you couldn't be safer."

His certainty soothed her, giving her strength in spite of her weakened state. He nodded as if reaffirming his statement, then sipped at his wine glass and opened the freezer.

"What is all of that?" she asked.

"This is going to sound a little pathetic but I always cook for two. Not because I'm lonely, it's more for efficiency. There's always a decent leftover available. That said I only have one of everything so we'll have to pretend we're in a restaurant. Our specials tonight include linguini and clams, mushroom-stuffed chicken breast, a Dijon pork tenderloin, or jambalaya."

"Jambalaya sounds good."

"If you choose that we'll have to watch Interview with a Vampire or Hard Target. I'm a sucker for matching the meal with the entertainment whenever possible. What about for entre number two?"

Miranda giggled as she finished her wine. "Gosh, okay how about the chicken."

"Exactly what I was thinking," he said as he grabbed the containers and pulled out two skillets.

Dinner and a movie behind them, Max and Miranda sat on the sofa and cuddled while watching demure flames pulsating off glass pieces which lined the inside of the fireplace.

"You're a very good cook," she said, curling a lock of his wavy bangs around her fingers.

He rubbed his cheek against her hand. "I get by. What are you looking for?" he asked as he noticed her glancing around the coffee table.

"My water," she said.

Seeing it on the sofa table behind them he lifted up and leaned to reach the glass, his upper body looming over her momentarily. She stiffened under him, making him instantly aware of her discomfort. He slowly sat back down looking straight ahead as he handed her the glass.

The hint of irritation on his face made him feel ashamed. "Just grabbing the water; next time I'll stand," he said in an attempt to empathize.

Miranda covered her face in remorse. "I'm so sorry. I didn't mean anything by it; I swear. You've never made me feel afraid."

"That's okay," he offered as he relaxed again into the couch, Miranda putting her head on his shoulder.

"Favorite plant?" she asked.

Max did nothing to conceal his confusion. Though he had no interest in playing their little game at the moment, he considered the question.

"Bamboo, I guess. Yours?"

Miranda looked up at him with sadness, then glanced across the living room, her eyes stopping on the fern-like plant he had brought from her home.

"It's called a Mimosa."

Noting her tortured expression Max whispered, torn between wanting insight and fearing too much. "Why is it your favorite?"

Miranda hung her head before looking away and instead focused on the fireplace. "Touch it," she replied as if unable to watch.

Max stood and walked toward the plant, waiting for her to look at him. When she did not, he extended his hand and let his finger brush the tip of the branch.

The branch crumpled downward and almost seemed to pull away. Max's lips parted upon seeing the dramatic reaction. Lifting his hand he delivered the faintest touch to another branch. It too collapsed abruptly.

"It can't help it," he heard Miranda say, tears affecting her throat. "It's not even that it doesn't want to be touched. It's just a reflex."

Hearing her voice crack he hurried over, taking her in his arms and cradling her as she sobbed. Feeling her heaving back and hearing her agonized whimpering, he wiped his own tears away while maintaining his grasp around her trembling frame.

Max woke to find his arms around Miranda as they lay on the couch, her eyes puffy from the prior night. He looked back at the plant, tempted to throw it out of his bedroom window. This beautiful creature, clearly one of her maker's most cherished possessions, lived such a painful existence. He had never been more in love or more powerless; an abysmal combination. Miranda's eyelids twitched open and she looked at him, her blue irises all the more intense from the redness encircling them.

"Having second thoughts yet?"

"Not a chance," he said, sincerity marking him. "Let's go get some cameras." Max hopped up and pulled her to her feet. "We can do something about this so let's do it."

"Okay. I'll brush my teeth and throw something on. See you in ten minutes."

As she hurried out the bedroom Max smiled, wondering if she would again pop out of her room in only half the stated time, looking like she was ready for a photo shoot.

Chapter 22

Six minutes later they were in the car, Miranda making his convertible even more chic by wearing her wide sunglasses and fashionable scarf. They headed down the hill and into town, finding the local hardware store which looked like a tackle shop; its turquoise walls and cartoonish sign anything but typical. Miranda's phone chimed. Seeing a calendar warning she stiffened, her eyes wide.

"Oh no, Dr. Bales. I completely forgot."

"Right now? How far away is his office?"

"Three blocks from my house," she said nervously.

Max turned the car around without hesitation. "We can be there in five. I'll just drop you off, take care of the camera thing and come right back for you. Okay?"

Miranda nodded, her breathing returning to normal as they headed toward the office. Before the song on the radio could end Miranda gave the final direction, her destination in sight. The car pulled up to the office and Miranda gave Max a grateful kiss on the cheek, hurrying out of the car.

"Just come out when you're ready. I'll be here," he smiled.

Miranda entered the suite and, after receiving a wave from the secretary, headed into Dr. Bales office. "Sorry I'm a little late."

"Not enough to be sorry over." He opened his laptop and secured reading glasses over his nose. "A week ago you decided to go away with Max. Two days ago you called with a rather surprising request. Why don't you explain what's been going on in your life?"

Miranda thought of waking to her open window; she felt fear return as if it had been waiting for the chance to creep back into existence. She cleared her throat and smiled, disallowing the sensation and any thoughts which may give it purpose.

"I'm in love with the most wonderful person I've ever met. He makes me feel safe and warm and excited. I'm actually excited for him physically. I was hoping I could do this on my own; be with him. But when I imagined it I saw *him*," she said, her eyes glistening against the painful admission. "It was just a flash but it was enough. I read online that a sex therapist can help you disassociate negative memories with intimacy. That's what I need."

"Is he pressuring you to have intercourse?"

"No, not at all. He's such a gentlemen I sometimes wonder if he even wants me."

Images of Max's smile ranging from shy to lustful filled her mind. She imagined the hot tub, remembering how her skin reacted to his touch. She recalled the platform fantasy and how his protective arms had uncovered her, exploring her eager frame. She thought of the hotel room in San Diego; how his cheeks flushed against her kiss when he awoke on the couch. A bashful smile toyed with her mouth.

"But I know he does."

"Miranda, I would be remiss if I didn't remind you that your progress…"

"Please, I understand your concern but I'm tired of hearing about how great my progress has been. It doesn't mean anything if I can't be with him."

"If he's not pressuring you I don't see why you can't give it some time."

"I've been coming to you for almost ten years. I tried it your way and only started getting better when I pushed myself."

Dr. Bales looked down, clearly hurt by the comment.

"That wasn't fair; I do remember you trying to get me to venture out," she said, regretting the accusation.

Dr. Bales looked at her with a father's eyes.

"I don't know why it took so long but I'm out. And I'm thriving. And I'm in love. I just feel like it's the last step; the last challenge. If I can make love to him I'll be free."

"Miranda, sex does not heal wounds."

"Well, maybe it will for me. Anyway, I'm going to pursue the therapy. I would hate to have to do so without you but will if that's the only way."

Dr. Bales looked at her, his face a homogeny of sadness and pride.

"It seems you've made your decision. I will have Rosie call you with a referral later this afternoon."

Miranda nodded.

"Miranda, you know how much I care about you."

"I know," she whispered, wiping her eyes before continuing with the session.

Miranda left the suite and made her way to Max's car, slipping into the passenger seat.

"How was therapy?"

"Helpful. How was the hardware store?"

"I got three cameras. They were cheap and should be easy to install according to the clerk."

"Great."

254

Max looked over, aware that Miranda was quieter than usual. He seemed to consider asking her more about the visit but kept his eyes on the road instead. They made it to her house a few moments later. Seeing it after being away for so many days Miranda hardly recognized the place. It truly looked like the home of a shut-in and she wondered for the one millionth time what Max saw in her.

"Do you have a ladder?" Max asked as he opened her car door.

"I think there's one in the backyard."

She got out of the car and slowly approached the porch as Max rounded the corner. Miranda couldn't believe how deserted the home looked despite being uninhabited for such a short time. It was dusty and riddled with cobwebs. Volunteer plants and weeds shot out of the walkway in every direction. Uncollected envelopes fell from her packed mailbox, a pile starting on the ground. Max came back with the ladder under his arm and got to work securing the cameras into place. Each time he positioned another device he stapled the cord along the trim of the house neatly.

"I had no idea you're so good at this kind of thing," she said as she looked up from the lawn.

"I'm absolutely not good at this kind of thing but the instructions were simple." Max stopped as if thinking better of his honesty. "I missed an opportunity to impress you just now, didn't I?"

"Nope, still impressed."

"Nice. Okay, that's the last one," he proclaimed as he climbed down the ladder. Standing next to her he whipped out his cell phone and entered a passcode followed by a pairing code. In short order the camera feeds appeared on his phone. Miranda looked in amazement.

"I can't believe you can watch my house from your phone."

"Neither can I. Would have been stalking you long ago had I known," he chuckled before apparently reconsidering the joke. "Sorry."

Miranda's giggle confirmed she didn't mind.

"Ready to go? I was thinking lunch on the beach. It's been a while."

Miranda followed him to the car and didn't look back as they sped away, heading toward the ocean. After a few blocks Max turned into a narrow driveway and squeezed into an even narrower numbered space. Leaving the car on the rooftop parking lot, the two walked down the winding steps leading to the Watermarc restaurant and its adjoining plaza. French architecture gelled with the plant-rich courtyard making the area look like it was straight out of New Orleans. Max ordered four fish tacos, a bag of shoestring fries, and a large soda to share. Taking the order to go, they crossed the coastal highway and headed toward their cove. Max sat in the sand and began dishing out lunch while Miranda enjoyed the sea air and familiar sounds.

"When was the last time you spoke to Claire?"

"I texted her while you were putting up the cameras. She thinks the cops are just being lazy."

"I understand her concern. She loves you. You should probably have lunch with her soon; it'll make her worry less."

"Maybe once you go back to work."

"Don't remind me," he groaned. "Wow, for the record I have never done that before. I'm usually dying to go back."

Miranda leaned over and kissed him. "I'll take that as a compliment."

"You should as it most definitely is," he smiled and handed her a taco.

"By the way how are Katherine and Marcia?"

"Hopefully fine but since I'm the worst friend ever I wouldn't actually know. But to be fair I'll see them soon enough. Two weeks will feel like two days. I know from experience."

Miranda took a bite of the most succulent fish taco of her life. She looked at Max's phone as it made an unfamiliar chime. Max pulled it from his pocket and entered the passcode.

"What was that?"

"I'm not sure," he said as he studied the device. "Camera one has picked up movement."

"What is it?" she asked moving close enough to see the small screen.

Max closed his eyes and let out a relieved laugh as he handed her the phone. "A cat."

She clutched the corner of her tank top as she saw the animal walk across the lawn. "Maybe this wasn't such a good idea."

"I know it's not fun but we'll feel better once we know what's going on."

"That's the theory anyway," she said, her smile uneasy. She took a sip of soda and tucked her hair behind her ear before taking another bite of the taco. As if feeling her heart stop Miranda was suddenly filled with dread. She looked out over beach seeing nothing that should have triggered the sensation.

"What's the matter?"

"I'm not sure," she said as she glanced up the cliff at the lookout deck and scanned the crowd milling around a telescope. Seeing one figure looking down from the cliff an inexplicable familiarity came over her. The feeling lingered even after the figure was washed away by a new group of visitors.

Max seemed to notice the change in her expression.

"Miranda, what is it?"

"I got that feeling again; like someone was watching."

"You haven't felt like than in weeks."

"No, I haven't. It's probably just being back. I've been known to be a bit paranoid."

Max studied her face. "You'd tell me if you had any suspicions as to what was going on, right?"

"Of course," she answered, her gaze darting toward the opposite end of the beach. "I'm sure it was nothing though. The day's not complete unless I make us a little nuts, right?"

"You've been making ridiculous strides; stop being so hard on yourself."

"Yeah," she said, doing her best to appear relaxed.

The phone chimed again, this time causing Miranda to jump. Max rubbed her back with his left hand while navigating phone screens with his right. "Bird," he said before muting the phone and shoving it back into his pocket.

"I'll review the alerts later. It records episodes of movement anyway. There's no sense in letting every neighborhood animal give us a coronary." He finished a taco and crumpled up the wrapper, grinning at her. "So, did you talk about me to your therapist?"

"Maybe," Miranda said, teasing him with an aloof look.

"Regale him with stories of our adventures?"

Miranda turned away, continuing the game. "My lips are sealed."

"Let me see what I can do about that," he boasted, hugging her while guiding her back to rest against the sand.

"No, what are you doing?" she laughed as he ran kisses up and down her face and neck.

"Did you tell him how fabulous I am; cultured and charming not to mention a sensational cook?" he joked, each kiss making her laugh harder.

"Stop, I can't breathe," she cackled, sitting back up once he released his grasp.

"Fine, I guess I'll just have to wonder," he said, grabbing another taco from the bag.

Miranda watched as he turned the other way and took a bite, feigning disinterest in her. The act made her giggle again.

"Okay, I talked about you."

Max ignored her even when she scooted closer to him.

She grinned and looked up innocently. "I might have mentioned the adventures though I left out the cooking."

"That's okay, you don't have to share," he said dramatically.

Holding back laughter she scooted her chest against his shoulder. "I didn't really have time to praise your cooking since I was busy explaining that I'd fallen in love with you," she said as she twirled her fingers in his hair.

"You said that?" he asked, turning to face her.

"I did."

Max brushed his fingers along her cheek. "You meant it?"

"Yes."

He pressed his lips against her soft mouth. "That's very good. But I still think you could have made room for a culinary compliment or two."

Miranda laughed hard as she felt her back once again guided into the sand, her face assailed by another blanket of kisses.

"You love me?" he said before kissing her again.

"Yes," she squealed.

"Are you sure?" he asked, planting kiss after kiss about her face.

"Yes!" she screamed, chuckling as she pushed his face away and took several deep breaths.

Max looked down at her, smiling sweetly as he watched her chest rise and fall. He gazed at her ruby cheeks and wondered if the longing in her eyes was as real as it seemed.

He ignored the vibration in his pocket and kissed her passionately. Miranda wrapped her arms around his back and pulled him closer, giving herself to his affection. The next time he kissed her neck he did so in a way that made her moan, and she lifted her head back as if asking for more. Though the rolling waves drowned out the sound of his heart beat, he could feel it in his chest as his mouth caressed her face. Consumed by desire, he had forgotten that they were in public until an opportunistic seagull landed a foot away and grabbed the bag of food with his beak, flying off before Max could stop it. The two sat in a fit of hysterics as the determined bird escaped into the air, the respectively large bag dangling out of his mouth as he glided over the shoreline.

Chapter 23

The Santa Monica pier pulsed with life, looking more like a carnival than a wharf. The strip was packed with rides, terribly unhealthy snacks, and various artistic creations from hand-knitted bags to bamboo wind chimes. Miranda beamed as a vendor handed her a hot dog on a stick which had been wrapped in a potato spiral, and deep fried. Max chuckled as he watched Miranda examine the treat as if strategically deciding on the best course of action. She took a cautious nibble of the top of the dog, steam warning her not to continue.

"Jeez, that's hot."

"Now that you mention it," Max laughed.

Understanding his double meaning she punched his shoulder lightly.

"Perve," she uttered as he reached around her waist and drew her closer. Momentarily giving up on the blistering snack she noticed a middle-aged Asian man deftly molding a ball of soft plaster into the image of a three-year-old's face. Within five minutes the child's undeniable likeness was hardening, the parents happily parting with twenty dollars in exchange for the creation.

Miranda turned to Max, her face filled with excitement. "We have to get one done of both of us."

Max obliged her, approaching the man. "Can you do us?" he asked as if unsure of the man's fluency.

"Two at the same time; very hard," he replied in broken English.

Max pulled out his wallet and offered the man a fifty-dollar bill. The convinced man called out to his partner who had just finished a transaction with another customer. The two discussed it briefly then each grabbed a ball of plaster. They instructed the couple to stand side by side with their heads touching. The men worked quickly; one focused on Max, the other on Miranda.

"This is so cool," Miranda muttered while trying to keep her lips still.

Max crooked his neck. "I can't believe how fast they are."

"It's crazy," she agreed, her eyes looking up. "You haven't mentioned the surveillance in a while. Anything interesting in the last two days?"

"There was a floating plastic bag that just about scared the crap out of me last night and a stray dog yesterday; nothing worthy of mention."

Finishing the job one of the men grabbed a plaster slab and affixed the delicate sculptures to it. Max studied the piece, shaking his head as he handed them the money and took the sculpture.

"It's incredible. Thank you very much," he said as Miranda accepted the piece. The men thanked them in return before looking for their next customers.

A trill from Miranda's pocket made her look down, then glance at Max for assistance. He took he sculpture from her and she removed her phone.

"Hello? Oh, hi Rosie. No, this is a good time. Okay… tomorrow? I'll be there. Thanks," she said. She put the phone back in her pocket and took a bite of the cooled hot dog.

"Rosie?"

"My therapist's office; she's the receptionist."

"You're going back so soon?" he asked, hoping his tone didn't come across as judgmental.

"Yeah, I was kind of thinking that maybe we could go together."

Max seemed surprised by the request. "Yes, of course. Is there anything special I should do... or know?"

Miranda looked nervous as she thought about the question.

"It's okay, I'm totally good just playing it by ear," he said, giving the back of her neck a reassuring squeeze.

She smiled though her expression seemed worn. Glancing at the hot dog she took the next opportunity to drop it in the trash.

Max noticed the unusual change in appetite and stopped, taking her face in his free hand.

"I'm not worried, Rand. The truth is I'm touched that you would let me into this part of your life. It's a big step."

"Yeah, maybe bigger than you think," she replied, her worried eyes jetting around randomly. "Would it be terrible if we went home?"

"No, it's fine. Let's go," he kissed her forehead as they walked back toward the city. Making it to the car Max unlocked the doors and opened Miranda's.

"Top up or down?"

"Up," she replied, her face still bothered.

Max started the car and offered her his phone. Miranda shook her head. "I'm not in the mood," she said apologetically, placing it on the middle console.

"Not a problem," he smiled, looking at his dashboard in response to a bell. "I need to fill up."

Seeing a gas station he pulled in and shut off the engine. He stepped out of the car, not noticing the vibration of his phone as he shut his door. Miranda looked down and picked up the phone. A motion detection message flashed across the screen – "2:36 pm Camera 1." Entering Max's passcode she hit the play button. On the screen she watched as a lazy cat crossed her front lawn.

"Stupid cat," she whispered. She switched to a view of the second camera as the cat breached the side lawn and turned to meander into the back yard, camera three showing the animal's final destination atop a plastic chair. She clicked the phone off as Max opened the car door and took his seat.

They were home by five o'clock, a fact that made a long bath and a glass of wine seem like the perfect plan to Miranda. She ducked into the kitchen and grabbed a decanter.

"I'm going to take a soak. Would you like a glass of wine?"

"No thanks. I have a bit of a headache," he said as he relaxed into the sofa.

"Should you take something for it?"

"I'll wait. It'll probably go away on its own."

Miranda walked over, giving him a quick kiss before heading into her room. The tub filled fast, the scent of sea salt and coconut filling the space. She selected an oceanic soundscape from her phone's music library and settled into the warm bath; bubbles popping all around her.

She tried hard to quiet her mind and avoid the nagging fears surrounding the next day. So many insecurities quarreled with so many unknowns. She had lied to Dr. Bales when she'd said she had researched sex therapy online. In truth Claire had given her the idea weeks ago. And though Miranda had intended to look into it, she thought it better to dive in; the less information, the less there was to ponder. She took a sip from her glass. The wine warmed her insides while the frothy water heated her skin. *Whatever it takes, no matter how uncomfortable, it must be tolerated. You know it's the only way,* she heard a long quieted voice whisper. *You must do it for Max. He is not Galen and his love is not unconditional,* the firm but gentle voice offered.

Miranda pressed her lips together, her eyes brimming as her subconscious lodged the painful observations. *Cry all you want but you must get through tomorrow.* "I know that," she said out loud. "Don't you think I know that?" Her chin quivered as she finished her wine. She sat in silence for a long while, time doing little to settle her thoughts. She looked at her palm, her wrinkled fingers indicating that it was time to get out of the water. She dried off and changed, the darkness in her room catching her off guard. Was it that late? She walked into the living room to find Max asleep on the couch. She smiled, comforted by his peaceful expression.

Max's phone vibrated on the coffee table and she rushed to grab it before it could wake him. "Camera 3 – 6:42 pm" the screen displayed. She entered the passcode and pressed play. Seeing movement in the black yard, she stayed fixated on the screen. A chill crawled up her back as the movement, though vague, continued. She watched in horror as a white figure entered the frame. Miranda gasped, seeing the spindly woman with long, unkempt hair creeping toward her bedroom window. Miranda covered her mouth, stifling a scream inside her throat. An angry voice hissed inside her mind. *Oh, don't act so surprised. You felt her; you've been feeling her for years.* The voice taunted. *Say hello to Mommy.*

Miranda's stomach pitched and she involuntarily disabled the surveillance feature. A message confirmed the end of surveillance prompting a yes or no. Her mind was spinning as she tried to imagine what would happen if Max saw the footage. Miranda knew she didn't have the strength to explain, nor the skill to play it off. Tomorrow he would know everything; the timing was absurd. She depressed the yes button, suspending the surveillance before her shaking fingers lost control of the phone.

The thud woke Max who strained to see her more clearly as she grabbed the phone off the floor and placed it back on the coffee table.

"Hey Rand, you okay?"

Growing more conscious he frowned as he noted her trembling body.

"Fine," she replied.

Max stood, sleep no longer clouding his awareness. "What happened? What's going on?"

"Nothing, I just thought you were sick or something," she said, her voice shaking.

"Oh, no. I'm fine," he said as he pulled her to him and enveloped her in a hug. "Jeez, you were that scared?" he asked, her quaking body troubling him.

"I'm okay now," she whispered as Max rubbed her back.

"Let's get you something to eat."

He took her hand and guided her to a bar stool before opening the freezer. "Hey you're in luck. Homemade mac and cheese with truffle oil. It's positively addictive."

"Sounds great," she said, willing her voice to remain steady.

"Are you still worried about tomorrow?" he guessed, waking over and taking her hands.

"A little," she said, hoping the admission would keep her new secret safe.

"Maybe we should wait. If it's going to upset you this much I can go another time."

Don't you do it, the angry voice again rang out, startling Miranda.

"No, it's the wine. I haven't eaten and it was dark and I saw you lying there… I just got freaked out. I want you to come tomorrow."

"Okay," he said as he kissed her hands. He returned to the kitchen and placed the frozen macaroni in a microwave-safe bowl.

"Can I get some more wine?"

"On an empty stomach?" he asked.

She forced a smile. "I'm a big girl."

Max poured two glasses and handed her one. She took a healthy sip, followed by another.

Slipping into bed Miranda curled her back against Max's chest. He pulled the covers over her before wrapping his arm around her grateful frame. She found sleep fast, though it was anything but peaceful. The nightmare started in her childhood home. In her tiny bedroom she could see the drawing of the ocean her mother had taped to her closet door. The room was cast in a pink hue to the red Victorian lamp which eerily illuminated the wretched space. Her dolls seemed to watch from the chest on the opposite wall. Would they close their eyes if he came? Maybe they would just watch.

Miranda's eyes snapped open and she was back in Max's bedroom, his arm still draped around her waist. She was so tired; so desperate for sleep. She tried to think of the sea, her heart racing as her mind dragged her back to the little house in Colorado. Her bedroom door opened and she pressed her eyelids closed, pinching off tears which rolled across her temples and made her hair wet. If the dolls were watching they wouldn't help her any more than her mother who slept soundly in the next room. She could always hear her snoring while he hurt her. But tonight something was different; there was no sound other than her own pounding chest and the squeak of her doorknob turning… no snoring form the next room. Maybe it meant that her mother was awake; maybe she would hear him and come to save her.

Miranda woke to find her hair wet from the sweat that beaded along her forehead. She ran her fingers under her eyes. She had been crying in her sleep, which was something that hadn't happened in years. Her eyes filled and she fought away sobs, knowing that if she gave into them Max would surely wake and forbid the next day's therapy. She imagined the platform and his protective arms. She thought of how they must have looked from the audience's point of view; the black sky their backdrop, twinkling stars surrounding them.

Drifting back to sleep the fantasy changed; she and Max had transcended their platform and were now part of the heavens. Weightless among a sea of stars, his gilded arms resembled bands of light around her luminescent body. She was celestial… impenetrable… and much too far away to be hurt. Even if she weren't, the golden bands of light shielded her from all harm. The image changed again and she was no longer human, she was light itself… they both were; a dazzling astral phenomenon intertwined for eternity.

Miranda woke to the feeling of Laguna sun shining in from the massive window. The horrible nightmares replaced by fantastic images of golden steaks of light, she felt strong again. She rubbed

Max's arm, smiling as he moaned and tightened his grip around her waist.

"Morning, Rand," he said in a muffled tone, his face partially buried in his pillow.

"Good morning," she replied. Her eyes bulged as she heard the hum of Max's phone against his nightstand. It couldn't be the house; she had turned off the surveillance feature.

"Do you want me to get that?" she asked, hoping the faint tremble in her tone was not as noticeable as it seemed.

Max sat up and grabbed the phone. "I got it." He glanced at the screen, noting a calendar reminder. "It's my dad's birthday tomorrow. I'm so glad I gave myself a whole day's notice," he said sarcastically.

Miranda closed her eyes as the tension in her face subsided.

"Let me whip up a little breakfast and then we can see about doing some shopping if you don't mind."

Miranda cleared her throat. "I was hoping I could make breakfast."

He looked at her quizzically.

"I have to start somewhere. Why don't you shower and I'll take care of the food."

Max rolled out of bed and bent down to kiss her forehead. "I'm not going to argue with an offer like that," he smiled, whistling as he stood and walked to the bathroom.

Miranda stared at the ceiling as she heard the shower door click open. Suddenly she was back in her dark bedroom, the thud of her bedroom door marking the departure of her stepfather. She had cried in silence through the assault, straining to hear any sounds from her mother's room. There were none. She sobbed into her hands as she realized what that meant. Her mother hadn't been asleep. It could only mean that she knew. She knew what he was doing and she didn't come to stop him. Young Miranda lied awake for the rest of the night. Dawn couldn't come fast enough. As morning light changed the sky from black to dark grey she threw on warm clothes, grabbed her backpack and her volunteer badge for the museum, and hurried out the front door. The dreary winter sun seemed to refuse any offer of condolence.

She maintained a brisk pace, refusing to cry as she heard the snap of her footsteps crushing the untouched snow against the ground. The last time she cried while walking to school she had icicles in her hair, so it was important that she resist the urge to sob. She made it to her classroom and tucked her backpack under her chair, then bit the tip of her glove and pulled it off her freezing hand. A friend took a seat at the desk next to her and said good morning. She didn't respond. The hours forged ahead until the bell rang. Her teacher called her name before she could leave. She stopped, feeling as if it was the first time she had heard her teacher speak all day.

"Miranda, are you feeling alright?"

The pale child nodded.

"Your mother called. She said you can go to Shelly's house. I guess you're going to be spending the night there."

"Okay. Thank you." Miranda forced herself to smile at the concerned woman.

"Have a good weekend, sweetie."

Miranda left quickly, wrapped her scarf around her neck as the brutal outside air chilled her face. She ran up to another sixth-grader.

"Shelly, wait up."

Chapter 24

Having survived another long, cold walk, she followed Shelly into her backyard. The two worked at kicking off their snow boots and hanging their outerwear over a bench under the home's covered patio. Shelly hadn't stopped talking the entire time though Miranda had no ideas what she had said. Tomorrow she would be at the museum all day which meant she wouldn't have to see him for at least twenty-four hours. She wondered if the museum would ever hire a twelve-year-old. She knew just as much about the art as the senior docents did and people seemed to like it when she spoke. At least they had until he started hurting her; she hadn't spoken much sense.

She endured three hours of mindless television, and a painful meal with Shelly, her kid brother and her mother. Apparently their gift of gab was genetic as they rarely came up for air, talking over each other with incredible stamina. The constant banter made her silence even more noticeable and when she saw Shelly's mother regarding her with concern she flipped on a fake smile and filled the next thirty minutes with as many museum facts that she could recall. When she ran out of things to say she switched to how early she would have to wake up to make it to the museum by seven, and rambled on about not minding because she loved walking and early morning was her favorite time of day. It worked very well, Shelly's mother happily returning to her own babbling.

Once everyone had retired to their rooms she slipped into the bathroom. Standing in front of the mirror she looked at her face. Her shiny blonde hair cascaded over her shoulders like waves of gold, a beautiful contrast to her blue-green eyes. *Such a pretty girl*, she heard an angry voice whisper inside her mind. *No wonder he does those things to you.* Miranda looked down in shame. She had heard the voice before and though harsh, the words often made sense. *You must like it. I already told you what you need to do.* Miranda's eyes filled with tears but she pulled them back, refusing to give into them now.

She opened one of the vanity drawers, searching through it before closing it and opening another. Finding what she was looking for, she grabbed a pair of scissors and stared into her own eyes through the mirror's reflection. Taking a large lock of hair in her left hand, she brought the scissors up, hacking off the lock at ear level and throwing it into the toilet bowl. She looked at the unsightly result, the corners of her mouth twisting into a disturbing smile. She hastily carved off the remaining locks and flushed the toilet. Slipping into Shelly's room she was thankful to find the hyper-verbal girl fast asleep. As exhausted as she was from the prior night she knew she would be out in no time.

She crawled into the sleeping bag on Shelly's floor. It had been weeks since she had slept without fear and she welcomed the luxury of a safe rest. As she closed her eyes she imagined the ocean; not the drawing on her closet door but the real ocean, surging with power. California had too many beaches to count. The whole state was practically one big shore, she imagined. One day she would go there, she decided. She would leave the frozen hell that she called home and disappear into a sandy cave on a deserted cove. Maybe even change her name; it would have to be something nautical.

Max's vibrating phone brought her back to his bedroom, the shower still running. Miranda jumped out of bed, pulling her hair into a ponytail and hurrying toward the kitchen. She opened the refrigerator and grabbed a carton of eggs, a bag of shredded cheese, and a pint of heavy cream. She cracked the eggs into a bowl and mixed in some cream and shreds of cheddar. Sprinkling the mixture with salt and pepper she sloshed the contents into a nonstick pan and turned on the burner. Whipping around she found a loaf of bread in the pantry and removed two slices, popping them into the toaster.

Max stood in the shower, lifting his head and allowing the water to splash against his face and run down his body. Mixing with his shower gel, the water was reborn as Eucalyptus steam which rose around him. His thoughts went to Miranda and the beach; on how she had pulled him onto her, her kisses growing stronger and more certain each day. The fragile creature that had joined his show was now a distant memory, and he smiled as he contemplated her transformation. He wondered when he could introduce her to his parents, hopeful that he would somehow know when the time was right.

He turned off the water and stepped out, wrapping himself in a towel. He walked into the bedroom, blotting his hair with a towel as he grabbed a cotton t-shirt and jeans from his dresser. His cell phone vibrated against the nightstand, reminding him of the long-forgotten surveillance. Another calendar alert distracted him from the thought of the cameras. "Miranda's appointment -0900." He dressed quickly and returned to the bathroom, running a dollop of gel through his hair. He heard Miranda call his name and tucked his phone in his pocket before heading into the living room. Seeing her in the kitchen, her lean frame swimming in his oversized apron as she worked on breakfast, he tried to appear pleased without looking like a love-struck school boy. She handed him a glass of orange juice and offered him a peck on the mouth.

"Scrambled eggs and toast?"

"C'est magnifique," he replied, kissing his fingertips.

"Ah, très bon," she smiled, "Vous êtes un naturel."

Max pressed his fist against his mouth, having forgotten about her multilingual abilities.

"By the way what time is the appointment? I did a generic reminder on my calendar but forgot to ask."

"Four o'clock."

"Oh gosh, then we have plenty of time to find something for my dad."

Miranda scooped some eggs onto a plate, added a buttered slice of toast, and passed the plate to Max.

"I was thinking of painting. I'm not really feeling the shopping thing. You don't mind, do you?" she asked, making herself a plate.

"No, not at all; it'll just motivate me to finish faster," he winked.

Miranda smiled back and took a seat next to him. "What's on the short list?"

Max swallowed a bite of eggs and sipped his juice. "Hmm, the guy has everything. I used to be more experimental but after a few flops and the certainty of an expanding lame-gift collection in his garage, I learned to keep it simple. I'll probably go with a nice bottle of wine and a complementary cheese."

"That shouldn't take long," she said, her tone making Max wonder if she was hoping for more time alone.

"No more than an hour. I'm not sure if I should give it to him today... he might be out with mom tomorrow. Of course if I go over there I won't be allowed to leave for several hours," he laughed, finishing his toast.

"You should totally go. I wouldn't want him to think you've dropped off the face of the planet. They probably miss you."

"I'm sure you're right. I'll be back by three. You'll call me if you need anything?"

"You know I will," she grinned, watching him take the last bite of eggs. "Well?"

He dabbed his mouth with a napkin and kissed her. "That was actually really nice, thanks Rand."

"You're welcome." Her eyes followed him as he headed to the bedroom and grabbed his phone and keys.

Once Max was gone Miranda went to her room and flipped through a selection of blank canvases. Finding a three-by-five she pulled it from the others and chose a charcoal pencil. She made her first line as she allowed herself to process the many thoughts raging inside her tired brain. Why was her mother breaking into her home? How long had she been watching her? What did she want?

Miranda had always assumed that her mother would remarry and start over. She had Miranda when she was twenty, so having more children was certainly possible. Claire still had family in the Denver area. Miranda remembered the day her friend came home from the gallery with news of Miranda's stepfather's death. She had said it as if it was a bad thing. Miranda later learned it was only because Claire worried that it would mean the young girl

275

would wish to leave Laguna and return to her mother, as if she could forgive her for letting him hurt her.

She continued to sketch, her mind totally engrossed in her thoughts. Maybe her mother was crazy too. She would almost have to be if she spent her days stalking her grown daughter. Maybe she wanted money, or worse, absolution. She would get neither. She was awake on Miranda's last night at home. People don't just stop snoring one day. The house was so small... two bedrooms, a closet-sized bathroom, a living room and a kitchen. She knew and she didn't stop him. She had lied to her too. Miranda found out he wasn't her real father just before her grandmother died. The older woman had been honest because she loved her in a way her mother couldn't have. About a year after she was gone, the visits began.

Miranda picked up a narrow pencil and continued drawing. Perhaps her mother let him hurt her because she was jealous. The young girl had been so close with her grandma. Her mother probably hated them both for it. And now she was back to torture Miranda for getting away and making a new life. She should have changed her whole name. That must be how she found her. It didn't really matter how she found her; she was not going to jeopardize her new life. After today Max would know everything and he would protect her. The new therapy would be successful and she would be whole... the future-self she dreamed about becoming.

Everything rested on getting through the day. Once she was complete she would confront her mother with all that she'd put her through. It hadn't been part of the original plan; she would have preferred never seeing the evil woman again. But things change. She was here for whatever reason and she deserved to feel her daughter's wrath. Drained,

Miranda looked at the canvas and was appalled by the hideous creation born of her fury. A small child lay in her bed trapped under a male figure while a young woman listened from behind an invisible door, a fiendish smile contorting her garish face. Miranda screamed, picking up a palette knife and slashing the canvas before backing away.

Sitting in his parents' backyard Max was as distracted as he'd ever been. He tried to focus on the visit but his thoughts lingered with Miranda; she seemed different somehow. It was a big day for her; for the both of them. He hoped that was the reason for his restlessness, and checked his watch for the tenth time. Two thirty. He would leave in fifteen minutes; that would give him plenty of time. He wondered if he would be ready to hear whatever she wanted to tell him. A part of him was sad she felt the need to do so in the presence of another as if he wouldn't be supportive enough. Maybe the therapist was for him… could her story be so vile that he would need help coping? The thought sickened him.

He kissed his mother and hugged his father before hurrying to his car. The grip on his steering wheel made his knuckles blanch as he zoomed through the busy Laguna streets toward his home. Whatever it was… no matter what had happened to her, he must not allow himself to fall apart. Miranda had been dealing with it her entire adult life. The last thing she needed to was to have to comfort him as well. He would listen to her story and be there for her; he would be brave. Refusing to mull over the infernal 'what if's' he turned on the radio, twisting the volume to an almost uncomfortable level.

He maneuvered up the hill and into his driveway to find Miranda standing outside in wait. He swallowed saliva he didn't have and studied her as she eased herself in the passenger seat. With a quick kiss she said hello, her face unreadable but not unpleasant.

"Same office as before?" he said with what seemed to be a forced lightheartedness.

"Um hm," she replied softly.

Max wanted to tell her everything would be alright; that he would be there for her regardless of what he would learn and that he would always protect her... that above all. Looking over and seeing her stoic stance he decided to keep it to himself. When the time came he wouldn't have to tell her; his actions would be sufficient. Besides, he sensed that while her demeanor was calm enough, her nerves may be fragile and he didn't want to contribute to weakening them further.

They pulled into the parking lot and entered the office together. Miranda headed to the reception desk and wrote Max's name on the log. Rosie looked up at her with sympathetic eyes and glanced toward Max.

"Mister Turner, the doctor is ready for you."

"What?" Max whipped his head toward Miranda, his confusion evident.

"Please, just go. I'll join you soon. It will all make sense later, I promise."

Though every fiber resisted the idea, Max stepped into the office and watched her close the door behind him. He turned to see Dr. Bales who offered his hand. It took a moment for Max to accept it, his distress palpable.

"Max, I'm Dr. Bales. Thank you for coming."

Miranda took a deep breath as she arrived at Suite 310. A thin man in a muted suit opened the door.

"Miranda," he waited to see her nod. "I'm Dr. Jenner. Please come in."

She followed him into the office, unnerved to see no patients in the lobby and no secretary manning the reception desk.

"I've just set up shop and haven't found a good secretary yet. Dr. Bales tells me you're eager to begin therapy."

She timidly followed him down the hall and into a small study. He offered her a seat on a cheap sofa, positioning himself in a chair several feet away.

"Yes, that's true." She thought of Max and wondered if he had already been told. She tried not to focus on the idea as Dr. Jenner continued to speak.

"He also told me of his reluctance to provide a referral."

Miranda glanced at the floor. "He doesn't think I'm ready."

"But you feel that you are."

She looked at him, her gaze strong. "I know that I am."

"That's good. Let me tell me how I typically conduct these sessions." He stood and walked to his desk, removing a bottle of pills from a drawer. To the right of the desk sat a mini refrigerator. He opened it and removed a bottle of water, then returned to his seat.

"I find that my PTSD patients are able to make strides far more rapidly and successfully if they take an anxiolytic prior to their time with me." He held up the bottle of pills as Miranda shifted in her seat. "This is Valium; it will help relax you so that you can focus on progress rather than being delayed by unnecessary fear. I'd like you to take one. It should begin to work in as little as fifteen minutes which will give us time to talk."

Miranda felt her heart pound as she looked at the bottle. *That's okay. Just say no. In fact why don't you just leave? You'll never get better anyway*, she heard a bitter voice say from inside her mind.

She extended her hand. Dr. Jenner shook the open bottle allowing one pill to drop into her palm. He then offered the water, smiling as she swallowed the medication.

"Why don't you tell me where you see yourself in five years?"

Max shook his head, unable to look at the older man. "I thought we were doing this together. Why isn't Miranda here?"

"She asked me to share her story with you."

"She couldn't tell me herself?"

"Not just yet. Given her remarkable progress I am certain there will be a time when she'll be strong enough to discuss it with you but right now she is only interested in developing her future rather than focusing on the past."

"Then why not just wait and tell me when she's ready?"

"Miranda has chosen to expand her therapy. She worried that you would not approve unless you understood what happened to her. Please, make yourself comfortable," he instructed, patting the back of the sofa.

Max took a seat, though totally disinclined.

"There's no easy way to tell you this so I'll be direct. Miranda spent her first eleven years being raised by her mother, stepfather and maternal grandmother. When her grandmother died her mother went through a bout of depression and withdrew from the family. Her stepfather, who had raised Miranda as his own, began sexually assaulting her. She was twelve."

Max lowered his head, covering his face with his hands as the doctor continued.

"A docent at the local museum of art, a young woman only six years her senior, had become her only real friend. She was supportive and nurturing, and thoroughly taken by the girl's artistic talents. She began to recognize that Miranda was growing more and more despondent, so she confronted her. Miranda admitted to being repeatedly raped and shared that she was certain her mother was aware of it. The young woman, who was preparing to relocate for college, took Miranda with her."

"Claire," Max whispered, his eyes filling with tears.

"Miranda never saw her parents again. Claire obtained a small apartment and raised her alone. She was lucky enough to have substantial financial support from her wealthy parents. She would go to school, then come home and teach Miranda everything that she had learned. Miranda's only therapy was her art which she tirelessly created. Claire tried to get her to go out. She read so many psychology books she probably could have minored in post-traumatic-stress-disorders. After a few years she realized that Miranda was not getting any better. That's when she found me."

Max wiped his red eyes, his lip shaking when he finally spoke. "How could anyone do that to a child?"

Dr. Bales shook his head, his silence making it clear that the idea was completely inconceivable.

Max's voice cracked. "Her mother knew and didn't stop him?"

"That is what Miranda believes. I don't know that it's fair to say since she left without speaking to her

281

about any of it. I must tell you it's not uncommon for abused children to vilify the non-violent parent."

Looking blindly about the room Max seemed overwhelmed with thoughts. "Did you tell the police? Aren't you required to?" he said, growing agitated.

"By the time I came into Miranda's life her father had passed and her mother was gone. I did report the abuse at once but the mother had relocated and the authorities were unable to find her."

Max hugged his knees as he listened. "Where is Miranda?"

"I mentioned that she has chosen to expand her therapeutic regimen. I'd be dishonest if I said that it was something I would have suggested, but she was adamant."

"I don't understand. Where is she?"

"At her behest I have made arrangements for to see a sex therapist."

Max jumped to his feet, his body tense with anger. "What?! After all she's been through?"

"Max, I know it seems absurd, especially having just learned of her ordeal but you must remember the choice was hers. This is new to you but to her... it was fifteen years ago. She wants to move on."

Max twisted around, running his hand through his hair as he paced aimlessly. "This is wrong. It's too soon. Why would she do this? I don't want this. I don't want her pushing herself. Does she think I want this?" he stammered, and felt himself losing control.

Dr. Bales bowed his head as if affected by Max's pain, though his voice maintained a steady tone. "No, she wants this. She wants to be with you and longs to do so without reservation or fear."

Max sat back onto the couch, his hand holding up his forehead. "Why didn't she tell me?" he asked despite knowing the answer.

"She knew you'd say no, just as I did when she first brought it to me."

Max stared at the man, his eyes burning with sadness. "Then why did you give in? You could have stopped her."

"Max, I have been seeing Miranda for over ten years. There were times I wondered if I was a complete failure. We didn't know if her agoraphobia was related to trauma alone or if her unusual talent had brought with it an artist's eccentricities."

Through watery eyes Max seemed to consider the theory.

"Multiple factors were involved. Many times I contemplated asking a colleague to take over in hopes they would be able to help her where I couldn't. But there were risks in that. We had a strong relationship of trust. I didn't want to push her. Then one day she woke up and decided she wanted to change. It was a monumental step; the first of its kind. Not long after that she met you and her evolution become unprecedented. Of course I wanted to say no. I love her like a daughter. But I realized I couldn't hold her back. This is what she wants, Max."

"What does a sex therapist do? I mean they don't..." he trailed unable to finish the question.

Dr. Bales seemed to understand his concern. "It's purely verbal in nature. Such a specialty involves exploring feelings and fears related to being intimate with another person. This will likely span several months. We were lucky that Dr. Jenner, one of the better specialists in the field, just moved into town. She'll be fine, Max."

Chapter 25

The medication had clouded Miranda's mind and she felt as if she'd drunk a half-bottle of wine. She glanced at the side table noting a beautiful glass orb with a brilliant blue center. It looked like a sky encasing a circular ocean. A content smile found her and she relaxed into the sofa. She explained the life she envisioned with Max and told Dr. Jenner of her future-self. She could almost feel Max's love her for as if he were sitting right beside her.

"It sounds wonderful. Seems you've found a great guy. I can understand why you don't want to lose him and I can definitely help you with that. PTSD patients have a negative association with sex in every regard save one: they typically realize how important it is for having and sustaining successful relationships. Sadly though, their awareness is often trumped by fears associated with the sensory aspects of sex; sights, sounds, and physical sensations, however pleasant can, be distorted by the affliction."

Miranda nodded, her mind recalling the awful images that sabotaged some of her most treasured moments with Max.

"The only way to rid the victim of these negative associations is by creating new, positive ones. We're going to begin by watching a clip of a man and woman making love. Seeing it for the beautiful, natural phenomenon that it is will assist you in reconstructing your views toward sex."

Miranda watched the screen, her heart pounding as she heard the moans of the woman in the clip as the man moved on top of her. She tried to focus on the pretty glass orb in the periphery.

"You see, this is a pleasurable experience. Not at all like what you went through. You're doing very well. Now I'm going to put my hand on your knee. It may be frightening at first but we must desensitize you."

Miranda's breathing grew rapid as she felt his hand on her skin.

"Keep watching the clip and take nice, easy breaths."

Miranda's eyes scanned the room, her pulse climbing commensurate to her breathing. Her fingertips began to tingle.

"Easy Miranda, you don't want to hyperventilate. Take slow, steady breaths. The clip is almost over. See how his hand strokes her upper leg? I want you to imagine that it's Max touching you."

Miranda gasped as he slid his hand upward and rested it at the top of her thigh. He moved his hand back and forth along her skin as the first few teardrops wet her eyes.

"See how his hand caresses her breast? How she reacts to his touch? What he's doing is bringing her pleasure. It's normal for a man to touch a woman this way. I want you to imagine that it's Max. You're doing so well," he said in a low voice, his hand running up her arm and across her chest.

"No, please, I can't do this," she whimpered as tears poured down her face.

His hand explored the curves over her shirt before unbuttoning the top three buttons. He slipped his fingers under the fabric and underneath the cup of her bra, ignoring the shrill cry that rose from her throat.

"Just relax, Miranda. You'll never be the woman you want to be if you can't be intimate with Max. You must get used to being touched. I'm only doing this to help you," he insisted, one hand groping her breast as the other slowly ascended her leg.

"Stop!" she screamed repeatedly. She felt his fingers slip under her skirt and tug at her panties. Her mind succumbed to the hysteria brewing within and she took the glass orb from the side table, bashing it against the side of his face. The blow forced his head back and he fell to the ground. Across the room she saw her dolls, their dead eyes staring back as she sobbed and buttoned her shirt. They wouldn't help and mother wasn't snoring. She knew. She knew and she didn't care. She looked down to see her father's unresponsive face. She kicked it hard, knowing that she would be in trouble for doing so. She had to leave and never come back. Miranda ran out of the office and slammed the door before running out of the suite. She raced across the plaza and headed toward the beach.

The door to Dr. Bales' office opened and he and Max looked up to see Rosie, her anxious expression reigniting Max's nausea.

"Doctor I have a detective from Sacramento on the line. It's regarding Dr. Jenner."

Max glanced at Dr. Bales, the color instantly leaving his face. He rushed to his desk and snatched the phone. Max followed, hitting the speaker button and docking the phone back in the cradle. The older man tried to object but remained silent upon receiving a look of warning from Max.

"Dr. Bales this is detective Marson. I've been investigating a Dr. Jenner and understand that he's recently set up a practice in your building."

"He has. Why is he under investigation?"

"That's all you need to know right now. We will be sending a unit to obtain him. There was no answer at his office. Do you happen to know if he's there now?

"Yes, he is. He's with one of my patients. Please, why is he being investigated?"

Dr. Bales grabbed Max's arm before he could lunge toward the door.

A muffled sound came over the line as if a hand was cupping the phone. "Dispatch two units to 310 Argyle Street, Laguna Beach. Tell unit command there is a potential for a hostage situation."

"Please detective," Dr. Bales screamed into the phone as Max paced.

The muffled sound was replaced with clarity and they heard the man's voice, his speech rapid and urgent. "We've received a number of complaints regarding his methods; some of his patients claimed to have been touched inappropriately. We contacted the board and confirmed that the type of touch described was not in accordance with acceptable therapeutic tactics. They suspended his license while we looked into criminal charges. Last week another patient came forward. Her description of a recent session was much darker. He raped her, doctor."

Max ran out of the office with Dr. Bales close behind. Max turned right as he emerged from the office, stopping hard and reversing direction as Dr. Bales yelled for him to follow. Max scanned the suite numbers as he ran. 308…309… Max kicked in the door of suite 310.

"Miranda!" he screamed.

Seeing the empty lobby he ran to the closed door at the end of the hall and bashed it in with all of his strength. Dr. Bales caught up with him as he entered the room to find a man in his early forties lying on the floor, his face and suit bloodied. He ran to the man and grabbed him by his shirt.

"Where is she?! What have you done with her?!"

The man only gurgled in response.

"Did you touch her?!" he yelled, his eyes blazing against tears.

Dr. Jenner did not respond. Enraged, Max beat his face repeatedly before Dr. Bales could pull him off the now fully unconscious man.

"We have to find her," he pleaded, saliva flying from his mouth.

"The police will be here any minute," he said, looking down at Max's bloodied hands. "I'll stay and tell them how I found him. You were never here," he urged.

Taking his advice Max backed away before running out of the office and into the parking lot. He flung his car door open and pressed the key into the ignition as tears obscured his vision. Screeching out of the parking area he sped to her home, hoping to God she had gone there. He pulled the car up to the home and ran to the front door screaming her name. His hands shook hard as he searched his keys for the right one, plunging it into the keyhole and twisting. He nearly fell into the entry way and ran from room to empty room. He bolted out the kitchen door and scoured the backyard with his eyes, again calling for her.

Inside Dr. Jenner's office the police took Dr. Bales' statement as paramedics secured Dr. Jenner onto a gurney.

"I was with another client when detective Marson called."

Just as he uttered the name, a man in a well-worn suit and sunglasses extended his hand.

"I'm detective Marson. The name of the client you were seeing?"

"Confidential, of course," he said apologetically.

"Why did you attempt to confront Dr. Jenner if you knew the police were coming?"

"I had no interest in confronting him, I assure you. I was only interested in making sure my patient that he was seeing was unharmed."

"Your patient's name? Confidentiality no longer applies."

"Yes, I understand. Miranda Cova."

The detective glanced at him with a suspicious glint. "You're saying a female did this much damage?"

Another officer approached and began collecting fingernail samples from Dr. Bales. He used a blue light to examine his palms, fingers, and then the top of his hands while the conversation continued.

"Considering what she's being treated for and what he likely did to her, I'd say he got off easy."

Seeing Dr. Bales' eyes pool the detective softened.

"And he never said anything to you?"

"I found him like this. He never said a word."

The officer examining Dr. Bale's hands shook his head at the detective.

"Should we take him in for processing?"

"No, he's clean," the detective replied. "I'll need Miss Cova's information as well as any emergency contacts. It's important that we assess her for injuries and get a statement. Did she have a cell phone?"

"Yes, follow me," Dr. Bales said as he made his way back toward his suite.

Under the sofa, Miranda's cell phone vibrated.

Darkness had fallen and Max had been to every meeting area he and Miranda had ever shared within the city. He called her cell more than fifty times, though he always hung up before triggering her message. He knew that hearing her voice would be too much. Max drove for hours, unaware that his rapid heart rate and weak feeling had grown more to do with dehydration than with grief. Claire was a basket case when he told her. She too was searching for Miranda though doing so separately.

The next day's search was as emotionally devastating as the night before. Max had called the police station every hour since the incident, finally receiving an invitation to wait patiently for them to call him. After his third trip to her house he realized the surveillance system hadn't sent him any alerts in two days. He grabbed his phone and went into the application, perplexed to see that it was off. He turned it back on and headed back to the cove. The detective called with news that they had found her phone inside Jenner's office. It was a devastating discovery; one that made Max physically ill upon hearing it. He made flyers with her picture and took them to the Beachcomber, 230 Forrest, Alessa, and all their other favorites.

Tomorrow he would search each city they had visited; Claire would stay in Laguna in case she turned up at any of their homes. Katherine and Marcia had agreed to cover beach patrol, promising to check the cove and all surrounding areas regularly. Each time he thought of stopping for the night he imagined the futility of doing anything other than searching. Was he supposed to try to get some sleep? Miranda was out there. Somewhere in the city she was cold and scared, maybe even injured. The tears would dry for a time but always returned with the image of her smile or the memory of her laugh.

At three in the morning he pulled up to his house, praying as he did each time that he would see her on the porch. He had never even thought to give her a key, a realization which conjured more tears than he thought he had left. He unlocked the front door and entered the dark home. Standing inside the house of his dreams, nestled in the hills of the city he couldn't imagine living without, he felt ill; like an outsider that had no connection to the place. In such a short time she had made herself an irrevocable part of his existence and each minute without her was misery.

He went into his room and looked out over Laguna. All of the awe, the magic… it was gone. He glanced over at his bed. It was so easy to see her there. *Please don't let her be hurt. Just let her come home.* He walked to her room though she never stayed there. Seeing her supplies he approached the window and knelt to the floor. One of the canvases was face-down on the carpet. He lifted it back up, gasping as he saw the terrible sketch telling the story of her last night at her childhood home. Knowing that the drawing hadn't been there before, he realized that she had to have created it while he was visiting his parents. *I never should have left her alone.* Choking sobs overtook him.

The next two weeks were a brutal haze. Max received word that Dr. Jenner had died at the hospital as a result of his injured. The detective also explained that Miranda had withdrawn five-thousand dollars from her back account just twenty minutes after fleeing the office. There had been no further activity with any of her accounts. A search of the local transit systems proved useless, and the airlines had no record of her ever having flown. Max continued his own search; every day a new city, every place haunting him with memories of their love. He could see her so clearly in the hot tub at Humphries Half Moon Inn.

He could hear her voice; how it sparkled each time she tried a new food or laid eyes on an unfamiliar haven.

He imagined lying in bed with her at night and telling her of how he missed her. She would respond by kissing him and saying something steamy in French. It began to feel as if the whole thing had been a dream. If it wasn't for the team searching for her he would have believed the entire romance was a fabrication; his imagination having run wild upon seeing the golden beauty on the hillside platform. It made sense. After all, she had joined the show in a way that was fairly unbelievable. No one could validate her or prove her existence in that regard.

Perhaps he had assigned her the injured artist's identity so that she could be more real. Claire had said that it couldn't be her, he just wouldn't listen. It really made sense. It was all in his head. A statuesque Goddess who had savant-like artistic skills and spoke several languages? How ludicrous he had been. *Why else would she leave and never come back? She wasn't real. She'd never been real.* He couldn't fall in love because no woman was as perfect as art. So, he made up a fantasy; a woman that was his own living work of art.

Only she hadn't been perfect at all; far from it. She was broken and tragic and dreamed of being someone else. He remembered her fear; how she hated it and wished to be free. He couldn't have imagined her; she must have been real. But if that was true then she left him. He had accepted her and loved her unconditionally and she had left him. For that he hated her. He didn't deserve to be cast aside as if they were nothing to each other. She was heartless and cruel. Why else would she leave? Unless she was… she couldn't be dead. She had gotten away. If Jenner

292

had killed her she wouldn't have been able to pull out money.

What if he hurt her so badly she couldn't remember any of it? Maybe she was lost and didn't even know who she was or that she belonged to him; that she was his world. The tears returned as the pain of her absence crippled him. The cycle continued over and over again; she was his creation, she was his enemy, she was his lost love. He spent half of each day begging the Gods to bring her back and the other half wondering if he could even look at her if she did come back. He had returned to work to see sympathetic faces all around. Though he had told his friends he was okay and just needed to move on, he could tell they didn't believe him.

In truth they were right not to believe him as he still spent each weekend searching the city; her house, their restaurants, Claire's gallery, the cove. After a few months of feeling as though he couldn't live in a world where she didn't exist he realized the opposite was true; he couldn't remain in a fantasy where she potentially did. He gave up the searches and shared his decision with his friends and family, asking them to refrain from bringing her up again. It was time to forget about Miranda and face the reality of his life before he invented her. He had paid the price for his great dream and was no longer willing to endure the resulting nightmare.

He walked to work, not out of love for his city, but because driving would seem different and more than anything he wanted the disparity to stop. Entering the festival grounds he made his way to the theater. There he saw his team busy on the stage, the new season's creations taking shape. He remembered how the theme was chosen, but didn't recall choosing any of the pieces for it. He had been sitting in the conference room with Marcia and Katherine. Miranda had only been missing for three weeks. Marcia had asked about the theme. Second chances popped into his mind as a possible motif, tears filling his eyes as he reasoned why. It was Miranda's idea. She had said it while they were at the pool in San Diego. He couldn't bring himself to say it.

He had wiped his eyes, doing a terrible job of faking a smile as his friends looked at him sadly. "Do you have any ideas?" he had asked.

"Well it's your show but we had a few," Marcia had responded, putting on glasses before reading the electronic document on her laptop. "Good versus evil, the human form, sweeping landscapes, the world of fantasy, sacred art…"

"Sacred art… we could do that. Why don't you get some pieces ready and we'll start on the lineup."

Katherine cleared her throat and spoke softly. "We actually have quite a few right now if you're up for it."

"Sure, why not," he had said, his tone flat.

The women seemed to fight their own tears as they sat with their shell of a friend.

Max remembered Marcia's morbid expression as she turned on the large monitor. Selecting a slide she began her pitch. "Adam and Eve…"

Max heard her say before tuning her out completely. For the next hour he had agreed to most every piece; the new season's selections having been dispassionately decided upon in record time.

A wave from Marcia ended the memory and Max was back in the amphitheater. She beckoned him to join her on the stage. Standing in front of a giant recreation of the Garden of Eden from Ruben's Adam and Eve, Marcia lifted her chin and gazed at the piece.

"Exquisite isn't it?"

Max glanced at it briefly before turning away. "It's fine. I've got to go make some calls," he said as he headed toward the exhibition offices. Katherine emerged from the wings and gently approached her partner.

"How's he holding up?"

"He's not," she replied, her eyes tearing.

Katherine hugged her as Marcia whispered into her shoulder. "What are we going to do?"

Katherine shook her head.

That weekend Max opened his front door, looking grimly at Katherine and Marcia as they stood on the porch.

"Can we come in?" Katherine asked.

Max backed away from the door and took a seat on the couch. "Please don't tell me this is another intervention. Because between you two, my folks and every other person I've ever known or have ever even met, I just can't take one more."

The women sat across from him, their concern clear.

Katherine folded her hands. "Max, it's been nearly six months."

"Yes, it has. Thanks so much for that."

Marcia wiped tears from her eyes, her voice trembling as she stood. "Max stop. This is crazy. You can't go on like this."

"Unfortunately I can. I'm sorry if my lack of zeal is putting you out Marcia, but I'm afraid I've never been great at faking anything. She taught me many things but that wasn't one of them."

"So you're angry now? Well, that's good. At least that's something," Katherine replied, her own anger coming through.

"Is that what this is about? I haven't been open enough about my feelings so you don't think I have any?" his voice shook as his pitch escalated. "She's all I can think about and I can't stand it. I go from being sick thinking that she's dead to feeling like she had better be because I'll never forgive her if she isn't. Do you have any idea what that's like?"

"Max you need help. You're not well. There are antidepressants that…"

Max ripped two bottles of pills from the pockets of his robe, holding them up with a grief-stricken scowl.

"You think? Now what? Do you have another solution? Maybe you should tell me I'm going to meet somebody or that I'm better off without her."

He threw the pills across the room and hurled Miranda's plant off its stand, tears pouring down his face.

"I can't do this, Katherine. I can't even look at this stupid fucking plant. She changed the way I see everything and then she left. If I can't find her I can't protect her. Why did she leave me, Katherine? If I could understand I think I could get through it but I don't understand!"

Max fell to his knees, his friends running to his side. Katherine knelt down put her arms around him, Marcia doing the same.

"I don't understand either Max. I know there's nothing I can say to make this go away. But we love you. You're not alone; you just feel like you are."

Katherine looked up, seeing that the mantle art had been replaced by the fiery metal piece of the woman in flames.

"You've got to let us help you, Max," she said, standing and walking to the mantle. "This isn't healthy. You're torturing yourself." She took the piece off the mantle and rested it against the hearth.

"No," Max tried to object.

"We'll keep it at our house. Our lesbian friends will like it," she said bluntly, causing Max to laugh, though through tears, for the first time in months. "You need some distance. You know I'm right. What else can I take?"

Max stood and walked into Miranda's room, the women following. He pointed to the art supplies.

"Okay. Anything else?"

Max held up his cell phone.

"I know we're not ready to delete. Just upload them to your computer and get them off your phone. Deal?"

He nodded, his face visibly less taxed.

"Throw on some jeans. We're going for a drink. And don't worry about getting too pretty. You don't have what I need," she winked.

Max chuckled as he complied, shutting his bedroom door.

Chapter 26

Max waited at the table with Marcia, trying to adjust to what was the loudest music he had ever endured at a bar. Two men walked by holding hands, followed by a second couple.

"You say this place is called Bounce?" he yelled out of necessity.

"Yep, it's one of our favorites," Marcia shouted over the music.

Katherine returned with their drinks and took a seat next to Max. She leaned over to yell into his ear. "Maybe it's too soon but if you decide to swear off women at some point the bartender seems very interested."

The three erupted in laughter. "Tempting, believe me," he said.

"Cool place, right?" Katherine asked.

Max nodded and sipped his drink. "Yeah, it's fun. Do you only go to gay bars?"

"Mostly. Two women at a straight bar looks like an invite. When we come here they know we're together and we can just hang. How do you like the drink?"

"It's really good. What's it called?"

Katherine looked at him like a kid unsure of their parent's coolness factor.

"An adios," she fibbed poorly.

As Max took second sip, another gay couple walked by, yelling in unison.

"Adios motherfucker!" they laughed.

Marcia cackled as she looked at Max's bewildered face.

"Katherine what have you done?" he asked.

"Pay no attention, they're just playing."

"This isn't going to kill me, is it?"

"Not by itself, no."

A second couple walked by, yelling the same phrase.

"What gives?" Max asked Marcia.

"Okay technically that's the drink's full name. It's kind of a ritual to say it to whoever orders one; like a funny warning."

Max shot Katherine a comical sneer. "Hilarious."

The drink worked fast and Max smiled as Marcia danced horribly in her chair.

"She's white and she's gay. What chance could she possibly have?" Katherine said dryly making Max laugh out loud.

Max leaned over, smiling at her. "Thanks for this, Kat. I know I haven't been a friend…"

Katherine put up her hand. "No, we're not doing this. You're out of the house for a purpose other than work, you've got a hell of a drink, and you're smiling. We're not going to ruin this with any apologies, self-disparaging thank-yous or anything else that may dampen the mood. Got it, Turner?"

"Yes Ma'am," he said, kissing her ear.

"Good, now finish your drink. We're not done with you."

Max slurped down the potent cocktail and followed the women across the street. They entered a colorful folk art shop and Katherine headed to the back of the store. As if all part of the plan she grabbed a thirty-by-forty art mosaic piece decorated in decoupage, its vibrant colors and fanciful images the opposite of something Max would like.

"What is that?"

"This is going over your mantle."

Max read the quote strewn across the top of the piece. "The other day I ran into my ex, so I put the car in reverse and ran over her again," he laughed as he crooked his neck at Katherine. "That's terrible."

"That's funny," she said, taking a picture of him with Marcia who reflexively gave him bunny ears.

Katherine paid for the piece then guided them into a bizarre candy shop filled with old music posters and silly maxims on wooden planks.

She selected a few items while Marcia and Max waited outside. Joining them she made her way to a nearby liquor store and grabbed a bottle of vodka. "Do you have any orange or cranberry juice at home?" she yelled to Max.

"Yeah, both I think."

She emerged from the store and led the group back to her car.

"Are you sure you're okay? Cause I'm pretty fuzzy."

"I had seltzer water, Max. Get in."

She quickly drove up the winding hill. Parking the car, she unloaded her purchases and distributed them to her friends. Max opened this front door and Katherine hurried inside, opening the vodka and heading to the kitchen. She grabbed three glasses and filled them with a mixture of alcohol and juice from the fridge.

"Gather round; let's go people."

Marcia and Max joined her, each taking a glass.

"To me and Marcia for being super awesome friends; you're a lucky guy, Max. That's all I've got," she said without a hint of a smile.

Max cracked up and they each took a sip, grimacing uniformly.

"I think it's too strong," Marcia choked.

"It's perfect. Let's redecorate."

"Huh?" Max uttered.

She placed the colorful mosaic on the mantle and grabbed one end of the sofa. "Give me a hand," she called out to Marcia who quickly obliged.

"Up against that wall," she turned her head to indicate the area. "Good. Let's move those chairs over to the window."

Max watched, obviously not a fan of the makeover. "We didn't really... ouch!" he said as Katherine punched his shoulder.

"Don't say "we." You say "we" you have to drink. That's the rule tonight."

"Okay, I get it," he said, rubbing his shoulder before taking a hairsplitting gulp of the foul concoction.

"Where's the TV?"

"We... Ouch!" Max hid behind Marcia as he accepted another blow from Katherine. He took another punishing drink. "I," he emphasized, "don't own a TV."

"I hate that. So, you think you're better than everyone because you're too intellectual for normal pleasures?"

"No, I just never got into it."

"Get your laptop. We'll have to make do."

Max grabbed his laptop from a closet in the hallway and brought it to Katherine. "What are we watching?" he asked as Katherine punched his shoulder for the third time.

"Hey!" he laughed, "That one shouldn't count."

"Okay but watch it," she warned as she set up the device. "You still have to drink though."

Max woke the next morning to find Katherine and Marcia asleep next to him on the floor. He looked across the room to see a nearly empty bottle of vodka and it occurred to him that he was queasy. Glancing around the living area a smile elevated his face; everything looked different. It felt good to see something different. He lifted himself off the floor and stretched as he headed into the kitchen. His eyes locked on the refrigerator as his lips parted in surprise.

Dozens of pictures decorated the appliance, most of which he didn't realize had been taken. There was one of the three of them at Bounce. Katherine's extended arm revealed that she had taken the shot; it captured Marcia's laughter as Max took his first sip of his nefarious cocktail. Next to it he saw a picture of himself asleep on the floor, Katherine and Marcia smiling as they lay next to him grinning. The image made him chuckle. Scattered throughout the photos were shots of various works of art and Max distantly recognized them as the pieces comprising the new season.

It was startling how disconnected he had been over the last several months, an oversight he would remedy come Monday. As for today, he had two amazing friends to treat to a greasy hangover breakfast. He made a pot of coffee then headed to his room and changed. He laughed when he saw his disheveled desk and the nearly finished glass of vodka-cranberry juice which sat atop a pile of photo paper. How much fun they must have had creating the fridge collage, and how lucky he was to have them in his life. Looking out his bedroom window he scanned the city below. He had always loved his home and he was beginning to see a way by which he could love it again.

Max arrived at the exhibition holding a large carryout container filled with smoothies which he brought to the stage. And while crew members and set artists poured out of the wings to cheerfully receive his gift, they seemed even happier to see the obvious change in Max.

"The girls from the shop are bringing several more containers so don't be shy," he said.

He went around the side of the theater and climbed the steps, emerging onto the stage to join his team. They seemed eager to show him their progress as if having been all too aware of his prior disinterest. He felt a familiar excitement building inside his gut; it was just about time to send out a casting call.

"Has anyone seen Sal?"

The ever-frenetic woman hurried toward him as if thoroughly insulted by question.

"Has anyone seen Sal?" she mimicked. "Has anyone seen Max? Because I know I sure haven't. We were starting to wonder if you'd cleaned out your office. But please, now that you're ready to play director again what can I do for you and don't you dare ask me where we are with costumes because I've been leaving you messages for days!" she said, trying to catch her breath after the colossal lambasting.

Max grinned like a kid caught doing something too cute to get punished over. His eyes twinkling as he carefully constructed a question. "And the messages implied that we were…"

"Oh my God, you didn't even listen to them!" she yelled, trying to demonstrate extreme irritation as she spun around and dramatically stormed away.

"I love you… I'm very sorry," he giggled. "Can I run the ad? Please?"

From the opposite end of the theater he heard an exasperated sigh. "Yes, you can run the ad. Ugh! You're just impossible," the distant voice complained.

Max shook his head as he made his way into the wings and down the steps leading to the design rooms. He passed the makeup area and waved at Annie who looked stunned to see him. Breaching the final door he entered the talent garden and surveyed the beautiful space with renewed wonder. It was prettier than he remembered. He took a deep breath and headed to the exit, stopping at the little office inside the doorway. Frankie looked up and gave him a huge smile before wrapping her arms around his neck.

"Maxy! Oh, you're looking great, kid."

He hugged her back, closing his eyes. "Not as good as you. Gosh I missed you. I feel like I haven't seen you in ages."

"I'm pretty sure you haven't seen any of us in ages. But I'm very glad you're back. Just here visiting or is there something I can do for you?" she said with a spirited expression.

"I was hoping you could put out a call for me. We're right on schedule," he replied.

The older woman clapped her hands together and picked up the phone. "Woohoo, this is going to be a great show. I can feel it," she made a triumphant fist before dialing a number. "We're in the business of making art come to life, Maxy. Every season is special; every summer filled with the promise of a new story. That's what keeps me going. It's the magic of this place."

Max listened, his eyes becoming glossy as he processed the sentiment. As she began giving instructions to the person she had called, Max blew her a kiss and exited the garden.

Within a few weeks all of the volunteers had been sized and selected, the festival grounds having gone from desolate to bombastic. Max watched as gigantic backdrops were rolled onto stage and set designers assisted cast members into position. The show he couldn't remember assembling had quickly become one of his all-time favorites. He watched with proud eyes as the magnificent reproduction of Adam and Eve was completed.

Max felt a gentle tap on his shoulder and turned to see a tall, slender woman in period dress, her hair and makeup momentarily hiding her identity. His heart raced as he studied her, his hopeful expression disintegrating once she spoke.

"Max, I don't know if you recognize me…"

His eyes fell to the ground. "Of course I do. Hello Claire; you're looking well."

"Thank you," she replied, an uncomfortable silence following. "I've wanted to call you so many times."

"It's okay. I wouldn't have been worth talking to anyway."

"The police still haven't…" her voice cracked, Max interjecting.

"Not yet," he heard his own dispassionate voice answer.

Claire began to cry, Max making a weak attempt at comforting her as he patted her back. "I'm sorry Max. I just can't believe she's gone."

Max looked up, his resilience crumbling. Katherine approached and took Claire's hand, whisking her away as Max attempted to hold back tears. The rest of the day was little more than a grueling effort to concentrate on anything other than the painful memories Claire had awakened within him. It was as if the shields he had assembled over the last four weeks no longer existed. Everything reminded him of the woman he lost. The music which magnified the glory of each piece now chipped at his soul, breaking him down. A thirty-second conversation had stripped him of all happiness, leaving him the skeleton he had been before Katherine and Marcia had intercepted.

The platform lights flickered and Max felt his stomach churn, sweat moistening his forehead. Before the finale music could wield a terminal offense, he found Katherine and explained that she would have to finish the rehearsal. He promised that he would be fine; that he just needed some time alone.

Driving home he sincerely hoped she would grant him that wish, as he hadn't the strength for another pep talk no matter how helpful. He arrived at his home and turned on his shower, stepping in before the water was fully hot. His cool, wet skin glistened as he worked up a soapy lather. Without warning he was back in the tepid shower of the makeup room, sheets of gold rolling off his body. He brought his arm around his chest, images of his gilded muscles entering his thoughts. Suddenly he was on the platform with Miranda, their combined temperature making him oblivious to the chilly Laguna night. He saw her slender frame, how fragile she seemed inside his formidable grasp. He could smell the sweetness she imparted in the air around them.

Max turned off the water and dried himself before throwing on jeans and a cotton tee. He blotted his wet hair with the towel and took a wine glass from the kitchen cabinet, sitting on the floor of the living room. He studied the overly chromatic mosaic piece that Katherine had placed above the mantle, doing his best to think of his friends. They had tried so hard to bring him back from the depths of depression; it would be unfair to let Claire ruin that. Not that it was Claire's fault, he reasoned. She had no way of knowing how destructive her words would be. *I just can't believe she's gone*, she had said, breaking his heart all over again. He had wanted to cry with her; to sob in her arms and never stop. But he had to let go.

The knock at the door brought a frown to his face, knowing that his friends just couldn't respect his request for time alone after a horrible day. He closed his eyes, practicing the nicest *leave me alone* speech he could manage as he opened the door.

"Listen guys, I…" Max stood in shock, holding the door as a wave of dizziness rocked through him. Joy and anger collided as he gazed at the face he both hoped and feared he'd see again one day. His heart thrashed against his rib cage making him breathe faster, which he tried to hide.

He opened the door wider and watched Miranda walk into the living room. Her gait was different, though he couldn't discern how. She lifted her sunglass up and rested them on her head, clutching a purse as they stared at one another. Max stood motionless, unable to decide if he wanted her to speak. Would her voice be different too? Would he be able to hear it with without crying or burning with rage or both? He was able to will his hand to nudge the door closed.

The waves had been blown out of her hair. It was shorter and she wore it in an elegant ponytail. Her clothes were fitted; she looked professional and older somehow. Though fear still occupied her eyes it wasn't in the way that he remembered. She cleared her throat and cautiously peered at him.

"Obviously I owe you a huge apology," she uttered as if testing her own voice.

The admission made his cheeks hot with anger. He steadied himself as he felt his body tremble. "You think?" he said, tempted to unleash months of agony while desperate to hold her.

"I don't know if you can forgive me but I'd like to tell you what happened."

"Please," he said, his sarcastic tone clearly affecting her as she looked down.

"Should we sit?"

"You can if you like. I'm fine here."

She dabbed the corner of her eye with her index finger before taking a seat in the armchair. "As you know the last day we were together I asked you to join me at therapy."

"Which was more than a little misleading," he couldn't help but say.

Miranda closed her eyes and Max wished he could take back the sardonic comment, hoping though not certain it would be the last.

"I guess that's fair. I knew I couldn't tell you all that had happened. But I also knew my time was running out; you had to know. And Dr. Bales agreed to explain everything so that I could focus on my next goal."

"Sleeping with me, right? Because I gave you some indication that I couldn't wait and that I was for one moment interested in risking what we had?"

Miranda stopped speaking and closed her eyes, her chin quivering. Max dredged his hand through his hair, frustrated with himself for being so hostile.

"I'm sorry. Go ahead," he whispered as he leaned against the door and folded his arms at the waist.

"I knew it would take a while but didn't know how long. It was getting hard… the more time I spent with you the more I wanted to be with you. I would have these images of us together and you would touch me. Then I would see *him* and it would ruin everything. I couldn't stand the idea of associating you with him. It made me sick; that I could be afraid of you… I couldn't take it. I decided that the therapy had to change. I told Dr. Bales I wanted to see a sex therapist. That's where I went after I left you with him."

"So he explained. Then we got the call from the police and realized how much danger you were in. Imagine that; hearing what had happened to you and then finding out you were in the clutches of a rapist." Tears filled his eyes as he stared at her. "Then we got to that office and found him the way we did... and you were nowhere to be found. I couldn't stop imagining what might have happened to you. Claire and I searched for weeks, Miranda. Were you really so screwed up you couldn't think about us?" he said, his voice cracking as he wiped his eyes.

She pulled a tissue from her purse and pressed it underneath her lower eyelashes. "Yeah, I was. Remember the night you fell asleep on the couch? I saw your phone vibrating; it was a motion alarm. But not from a cat. An older woman was trying to get into my house. Her clothes were tattered; she was very thin and she had long, frizzy blonde-grey hair."

Max's body tensed and his eyes grew wide as he thought of the woman from the forested hillside behind the platform.

"My mother," she softly confessed.

Chapter 27

"You're mother?" Max's legs wobbled and he slid his back down the length of the door. Sitting on the floor, holding his knees to his chest, he tried to comprehend what she had said.

"She'd been searching for me for …," she paused as she looked down. "…a long time. For so many years I lived with this unmistakable feeling that someone was watching me. And I was sure I was crazy. I was so sure. But I wasn't crazy. It was her all along. She was with me everywhere I went. Makes sense now, doesn't it? The only time I didn't feel her was when you and I went on our out-of-town adventures," she smiled as if remembering better times. "She even came to the exhibition."

"She was on the platform with us. I kept hearing sounds; we even put up cameras. I saw her whispering in the dark. We thought she was trying to get to me, but…" Feeling foolish and confused, Max started putting the possibilities together in his mind. "…you turned off the surveillance," he realized, a trace of betrayal momentarily coming across his face.

"I was so upset when I saw her on the motion alert; I didn't know what to do. I just kept thinking that if I didn't get through the next day, I would never get better and I'd lose you. I should mention that I wasn't always alone up here," she said as she tapped her temple. "It could get loud. I knew I had to get through the session no matter how uncomfortable.

Then he started touching me. I don't remember what happened after that but there was blood on my hands and it wasn't mine. I had hurt him without even being aware of it. I wasn't safe."

"You didn't think I could protect you?"

"I didn't think *I* could protect *you*. I wasn't safe to be around. What if you touched me and I hurt you? I decided the best thing to do was go home and never come back."

"I checked your house a million times."

"Not that home," she said with a remote look.

Miranda's mind flashed to entering a bank and withdrawing her savings. Finding two teenage girls, she offered them two-thousand dollars for a ride. After a long journey she got out of their car and looked at her childhood home for the first time in fifteen years. Entering the abandoned house she saw that the pictures of her stepfather had all been smashed and she wondered if she had somehow destroyed them. She went to her room and closed the door.

"The home I never should have left. I was crazy and a danger to others. If I died there I wouldn't have to worry about going to hell. I laid in my bed for just over a week and waited for death. After the first three days I wasn't hungry or thirsty anymore." Miranda's mind returned to her tiny bedroom wherein she wasted away on her dusty bed, the picture of the ocean still taped to the closet. She glanced over at the dolls; their lifeless eyes black and fixed. "Then one day mother came home. I thought she might."

From the other end of the room Max listened in disbelief, wiping his face as she spoke.

"She came into my room and knelt by the bed. She was crying. She asked if I was okay but I couldn't talk. She told me how much she loved me and how she'd been searching for so long. I hated her and hoped I'd die soon… I wanted her to see me die. She left my room and came back in with a wet rag. She washed my face. A little of the water got into my mouth and I started to move my tongue. It was hard opening my mouth but I did it."

Miranda envisioned herself in the bed not as an ailing woman but as a dying child as she finally spoke to her mother. "Why did you let him hurt me?" she asked, her voice barely audible. "I know you heard him. You weren't snoring."

Her mother's eyes brimmed with tears as she looked at her daughter. Her heavy face, worn from years of heartache and exposure to the elements, seemed to toil with how best to explain.

"I'd been sick ever since Ya Ya died. I thought it was grief; I was always tired and nauseous. Every morning I woke up and felt like I hadn't moved all night. My muscles were sore from the pressure of my body against the bed. You hadn't spoken or even smiled in days. I just assumed your pain was from missing her; I had no idea it wasn't that. One morning I woke with a terrible stomach ache. I went to get some water and I saw a white residue in my teacup from the night before. That evening I ran a bath but hid in the kitchen. I saw him putting a powder in my tea. I pretended to drink it and went to bed. A half an hour later I heard him stirring. He checked to make sure I was asleep and then crept into your room," she explained as a sob broke her concentration.

"I heard what he was doing to you," she whimpered as tears assaulted her. "I went to look for the gun but couldn't find it. Then he stopped. I climbed into bed before he came back into our room. I had to lay next to him in silence all night, knowing what he had done. I sent you to your friend's house for the night and made his favorite stew just to make sure the bastard would eat enough. It was all I could do to keep from smashing his face into it," she continued, the grief in her tone undeniable. "I had stolen the poison from the animal hospital. As it started to work I told him how he was going to die. I just stood there, laughing and crying. I watched him writhe and gag. And I felt better."

The child on the bed was replaced with Miranda's adult frame, her face no longer ripe with betrayal. She looked down at her mother with sorrowful gratitude.

"But it was too late... I lost you. I dreamed of finding you and telling you but what would I have said? I killed your father."

"He wasn't my father."

Her mother shook as another sob ripped through her.

"I didn't know you knew that. God I wish I had. That was almost the worst part; thinking that you didn't know that your real father would never have hurt you. He was a good man and I was wrong for not telling you. I'm so sorry baby. I'm so very sorry," she pleaded.

Miranda reached out and put her hand on her mother's head. The older woman rose to her knees and put her arms around her, Miranda's dehydration making a tear impossible.

Back in the living room, Max hurried over and held her as she cried.

"It took a couple of weeks to regain my strength but she took care of me; it was like she'd always wanted to... like she'd been waiting for the chance. We talked and talked. There was so much to say. I told her about you and how I could never see you again. She cried with me. She told me about her visits to the exhibition."

In an instant Max was back on the platform, his skin taught from fear as he heard the snap of a branch followed by the hiss of the old woman's voice. He analyzed the threatening whisper with new ears, finally understanding what she had really said that night. It wasn't "Stay away, *he's* mine"… it was "Stay away, *she's* mine."

His heart pounded as he took in how wrong he had been about the old woman. She had been protecting Miranda all along. Suddenly everything made sense. Max looked down to see Miranda in his arms, her uncertain smile buffering the intensity of the moment.

"You thought she was stalking you?" Miranda let out a faint laugh as Max chuckled against his own tears.

"Yeah, I feel awesome for thinking that."

"I figured we'd stay together in the house forever. I didn't feel like there was any other choice and I knew she'd be happy. But one day she said she'd gone to the library and found something that could help. She'd researched electroshock therapy and the results were extremely promising. She went with me when I chose a facility."

Max lifted his hand, caressing her temple and head. New tears filled his eyes. "You let them shock you? How could they… are you okay?" he asked, his voice tattered from pain. "Did they hurt you baby?"

Miranda gave him a hopeful grin though her voice shook. She again tapped her temple.

"No. They took him away. He's mostly gone now," she whispered, a genuine smile forming. "I'm finally whole. At least I think I am; as long as you're still with me. Are you?"

Max hugged her legs and pressed his eyes together, hoping her words weren't something he'd imagined.

"Are you kidding me? I am nothing without you. Even on my best day."

The doorbell rang and Max's eye bulged. "Oh no."

"What is it?"

"Angry lesbian therapists."

"Angry what?"

Max opened the door to see Marcia and Katherine in their best Bounce wear.

"Get in the car," Katherine ordered.

"Now's not such a good time," he said weakly.

"Get your ass in the car, Turner," she repeated.

Max opened the door all the way to reveal Miranda. His friends gasped as they looked at each other.

"Is that?" Katherine asked.

Marcia whispered to her partner. "She looks different."

"Can you give us a little time?" Max asked, his red eyes wild with happiness as he regarded his dumbfounded friends.

"No," Katherine insisted. "Is she back?" she insisted, staring at Max as if unable to comprehend his consideration.

He stared at the ground, refusing to entertain a fight.

"Cause if she's back she must be a whole lot better and I need to see it for myself. Let's go," she said in an uncharacteristically playful tone.

Miranda peered at Max, pulling out a driver's license and giving him an adventurous look. "Want me to drive?"

Max stared at her, speechless once again.

Bounce was even louder than Max had remembered, a fact that was instantly forgotten as he took Miranda's hand and helped her make her way through the packed crowd. Seeing her face, so familiar and yet so different, he had to remind himself not to stare.

"This is great!" she yelled to him as they found a small table and quickly sat down.

Max could hardly believe she was praising a place that, only a year ago, would have left her paralyzed with fear.

"It's not bad," he shouted back and pointed toward Marcia and Katherine who stood at the bar. "We actually come here a lot."

"Really? I wouldn't have guessed you'd be interested in a place like this."

He chuckled as he rubbed the back of her hand. "Right, well… I'm just full of surprises," he offered along with a look that made her breathe in and avert her gaze.

Katherine returned with four short glasses of beer and four shots glasses while Marcia carried a tray of cocktails. The women disbursed the drinks as Max frowned.

"Ladies, I just got her back. I'd like to live through the night if you don't mind," he yelled.

Katherine pushed a glass of beer and a shot toward him. "Oh Max, there's no need to panic."

"Three drinks?"

"But these two are really only one," Marcia explained as she indicated toward her beer and the shot glass. "It's called a Shoot-the-Root. The shot goes in the beer like an Irish Car Bomb."

"Huh?" Max looked at his lively friend.

"You grab the shot with one hand and the beer with the other, drop the shot glass into the beer without spilling it, and drink the whole thing as fast as you can. It's easy. Ready?" she lifted her glasses.

Max and Miranda looked at each other with uncertainty as they picked up their glasses.

"Ready?" Katherine grabbed her drinks. "One, two, three."

The group dropped their shots into the beers which immediately fizzed in objection. Max coughed as he tried to chug it down, foam from the beer going up his nose. His reaction made Miranda giggle as she swallowed the last of her concoction.

"Nicely done," Katherine praised.

"It tastes like root beer," she shouted, her big smile warming Max as he wiped foam off the tip of her nose.

"Max you've got some work to do," Marcia joked.

Max laughed and dabbed his mouth with a cocktail napkin. "Yes, I'll get right on that."

"Onto the main event," Katherine said as she reached for a hurricane glass filled with a tea-colored beverage.

"Why are we doing this again?" Max asked Katherine.

"For fun, silly. So Miranda, what have you been up to for the last half a year?" she inquired without a trace of judgment in her tone.

"It's rather personal, Kat," Max interjected.

"It's okay," Miranda replied. "I don't mind sharing... maybe in a place where I wouldn't have to scream it though."

Marcia laughed, causing her partner to smile.

"Of course, I wasn't thinking," she said, her cheeks blushing.

Miranda took a sip of her cocktail and coughed, covering her mouth. "Oh my gosh, this is super strong."

"What did you give her?" Max said as he eyed Katherine.

317

"She's got the Hanky Panky, yours is the Incredible Hulk, Marcia has the Singapore Sling and I am having the Culture Shock."

Miranda picked up her glass. "Okay then, to great friends."

The others followed her lead, picking up their glasses. "Thanks for being there for him when I couldn't," she said, her eyes glistening.

As they tapped their glasses together Max gave a grateful nod to the women who seemed touched by Miranda's toast.

"What do you say we finish these fast and hurry back to Max's for some laptop TV time?"

Max stared at her in irritation.

"I'm totally kidding," she laughed. "I'm sure you two have a lot to sort out. We'll grab a cab home."

Max thanked her with his eyes as Miranda took several sips of her drink.

"Wow. You're putting quite the hurt on that thing."

Miranda leaned in, doing her best to be heard without being loud. "I'm just eager to be alone with you."

Max smiled, closing his eyes before taking down half of his drink.

Katherine watched them, the last of her concern melting from her face. She picked up her phone and ordered a taxi service via her phone app as Max and Miranda hurried to finish their drinks.

"A car should be here in ten minutes. It's yours if you want to take it," Katherine offered to Miranda.

"That's okay, you take it," Miranda replied. "I was hoping we could go for a walk." She looked at Max as if trying to read his expression.

Max stood and took her hand as she rose from her seat. "Ladies, thank you for this. We'll all have to go out again."

"Soon, please. It was so fun," Miranda added. She hugged the women and thanked them. Max reeled as he watched the effortless interaction; the way she carried herself was unrecognizable.

Emerging from the bar the two linked hands again and began walking toward the ocean.

"I noticed your hands... you don't keep your palms up anymore."

"I have far greater control over my own thoughts since the procedures."

"Can you still do the download?"

"Not after the drinks but yeah, I didn't lose anything good."

As if aware of what he must be thinking, Miranda stopped and looked into his eyes. "It's not like in the movies. With modern ECT they use anesthesia and muscle relaxants. I didn't have to bite down on a stick or anything."

"It's amazing. I'm so glad you're better. I just... I wish I could have been there."

They continued walking. "I couldn't let you see me like that."

"But it wasn't uncomfortable?" Max said, trying to understand her last comment.

"No, I meant I couldn't let you see me how I was before the treatment. It wasn't good. I had to take so many pills just to begin therapy again. I found a psychiatrist who specialized in psychological conditions brought on by trauma. She utilized a variety of treatments with the most invasive saved for last. We did exposure therapy, eye movement desensitization and reprocessing, group counseling with me and my mom, and finally the shock therapy. The whole thing took five months. I didn't stay away any longer than I had to. Believe me, I was holding onto you the entire time."

"Why didn't you call? You could have at least told me that you were okay."

"I thought you'd come. I didn't want to see you until I knew for sure that I could be back in your life. And not as some scared little kid who always needs to be taken care of; as a real woman who could take care of you back. I knew I was getting better but until the last ECT, I didn't know if I would be better enough."

They arrived at the end of the road and took a seat on a stone bench, staring out over the massive black sea.

"So your mom's better too?

"She is. She's back in the city now. She has some money but a lot of her savings went to my therapy. I thought I'd just let her stay at my old place. I'm going to bring some of her work to Claire; I think it will be really successful."

"She paints?"

Miranda nodded, watching him closely as she answered. "It's incredible. Her technique results in pieces that look as if their moving. She specializes in recreating the motion of the elements. People are always drawn to her work."

"I'd love to see it sometime."

Miranda turned and kicked her legs over his lap, cozying up against his chest.

"You already have. She was worried when you bought it; thought you might figure out that it was me."

"The woman in flames," he whispered, tears returning to his eyes. "It always reminded me of you but ... Did you know?"

"The thought occurred to me but it seemed like too big of a stretch."

Max wiped his face, peering at her intently. "If you knew how many nights I sat just staring at that piece. Do you have any idea of the hell I went through without you?"

Her watery eyes remained locked on his. "I honestly do," her voice trembled. "I'm so sorry, Max. Do you think you can forgive me?"

His lips found hers as a final tear rolled down his face. He felt his cheeks becoming increasingly warm as he savored the delicate kiss.

"Perhaps I could in time," he whispered happily, giving himself back to her supple mouth.

"That's such good news," she uttered before brushing her lips along his face, smiling as if aware of her effect on him.

Max felt dizzy as she took his face in her hands, kissing him gently. She let her mouth wander to his neck, brushing her nose and mouth against his skin.

"You have to promise you'll never leave again no matter what happens," he said with diminishing restraint.

"I swear it, Max. You're stuck with me," she replied, giving him a provocative smile that made him audibly sigh.

He fumbled with his phone and placed an order for a cab. "We should get home."

"That's probably wise," she giggled as she ran her lips across his ear.

Pulling away he took several deep breaths. "Okay, I know I've been pretty conservative with you but the booze and the ear thing don't really mix."

"What the matter, Darling? You seem out of breath," she teased.

Max tried to remind himself that while she may be enjoying flirtation she didn't necessarily mean for it to end the way he hoped it would. The cab couldn't come fast enough and he tried not to look directly at her.

"Nope, I'm good. We should call Claire and let her know you're alright."

"Not tonight, Max. I'll call her first thing in the morning."

"Are you sure? What's the harm in one quick phone call?"

"Because she'll want to see me and that's not what I want to do tonight," she said as she leaned toward him.

Max accepted her lips again, wincing against the thrill that followed.

"Please, no more kissing," he said, pulling his face back. "Not until we get home, and then only cautiously if you don't mind."

"That doesn't sound very fun," she pouted.

"It's for your own good, believe me. You're normally so big on safety I would think you'd be more careful with someone who's disastrously in love with you and verging on carnivorous," he said, his shy smile making her appear intoxicated.

The cab pulled up before she could respond and Max thanked the cosmos for the interruption. The ride home was excruciating. Every time her skin contacted his he felt like his nerves were humming. Miranda seemed all too aware of his vulnerable state and made it clear that each accidental touch was anything but accidental. *Easy Turner,* he would tell himself. *She only seems like she knows what she's doing.*

Chapter 28

They arrived at the house and Max hastily overpaid the driver before wrestling with the latch on the front door. Miranda whispered in his ear as the cab's lights faded away.

"I've never seen you like this."

He turned the key and opened the stubborn door. "No, you definitely haven't," he replied, kissing her hard as they breached the threshold.

"I'm going to go take a quick bath," she said softly. "Would you like to join me?"

Max closed his eyes and struggled to appear calm. "Um, sure. Why not?"

The nonchalant display made Miranda giggle and she kissed him again. "Why don't you give me ten minutes."

"You got it," he said as he watched her disappear down the hall and into the bathroom. Once inside she turned on the faucet and poured a generous amount of bubble bath into the stream of water. The fragrant smell of a beach in summertime filled the room. She lit the many candles which lined the tub and turned on a sound machine, selecting crashing waves. She brushed her teeth as the tub filled with sudsy water. Slipping out of her clothes she dimmed the bathroom lights and stepped into the tub. She wet a washcloth and placed it over her eyes as she relaxed her back against the porcelain and waited for Max to arrive.

The door opened a short time later and Max smiled as he entered the sensual space. Approaching the bath he let his towel drop to the floor and sank into the tub opposite Miranda. She stirred and removed the wash cloth.

"Mister Turner," she said with a sexy smile.

"Miss Cova," he returned. "Love what you've done with the place."

"I was just trying to impress the most attractive man I've ever known and lure him into a night of forbidden passion. Do you suppose it will work?"

"I'd say your chances are exceedingly good. Of course you may have to take the lead. I'm sure your gentleman wouldn't want to make any assumptions with a creature as gorgeous as yourself."

Miranda bent her had back and laughed. "Well I suppose if I must."

She sat up and leaned toward him, a move he emulated until their lips were touching.

"Nice job with the bubbles," he smiled, noting that they were nearly overflowing onto the floor. He didn't stop kissing her as they spoke.

"I can't imagine why I'd be feeling overzealous. It's not at all like me; well, at least not the old me."

A wave of dizziness came over Max again and he realized her lips had traveled to his neck. He ran his fingertips up and down her shoulders, searching for any negative reaction to his touch. Sensing none he let his hands find her back, softly ascended and descended her silky frame. The intensity of her kisses grew as he caressed her skin and he yearned to explore the body he had spent a summer dutifully protecting. *Easy Turner*, he again warned.

Max felt her hands drift down his back and rest along his hips, micro explosions of electricity following. He slid his fingers from her back to her sides, deliberately avoiding escalating the moment without her clear desire for him to do so.

"Okay, I'm getting too hot," she whispered and he immediately backed away.

"I'm so sorry, Rand."

She smiled as if grateful for his concern. "That's not what I meant. The water was getting to me."

He grinned and bowed his head as she stood and wrapped herself in a towel.

"Are you coming to bed?"

Max nodded, relieved beyond reason that he had not upset her. As she left the room he stood and dried himself. Heading into his bedroom he steadied himself upon seeing her curvy outline in his bed. He slipped under the satin sheet that protected her skin from his gaze. She immediately turned and began kissing him, not even stopping long enough to allow him to reposition himself. Max turned onto his side. Miranda pulled her chest up to his, the feel of her skin against his making him suppress a moan.

"You okay?" she whispered.

Max chuckled, his lips still occupied by hers. "Yeah. Thanks for checking," he said.

"I want you so much. Please don't be afraid of me, Max."

"I'm trying."

Max found the curve of her back and restricted his fingertips to the distance between it and her shoulders. Her kisses seemed hungry and though he was sure she wanted more he couldn't bring himself to be so bold. Pushing his back against the bed Miranda leaned over him and took his hand out from behind her, forcing his palm against her breasts. He felt her skin tighten and grow more defined under his touch, and took the invitation to let his fingertips expand their search. Her breath was hot against his neck and the rate was increasing. Stroking the peaks of her chest he heard a pleasurable cry escape her lips.

He felt her hand glide under the sheet and graze his upper thighs. Miranda lifted up off the bed and slid herself onto him, his body stiffening against the overwhelming sensations now sweeping through him. He pressed his eyes closed as she rocked back and forth, his skin buzzing with the exquisite torment of her gentle movements. Every inch of his body was tingling and he had to force himself to remain still.

"Please don't be afraid of me," she begged as she turned to her side and rested her back against the bed.

Understanding her desire he positioned himself over her and entered her carefully. Moving as slowly as his body would permit he rocked his hips, showering her face in kisses. She lifted her head back, her breath becoming more of a pant. She allowed the cadence of his hips to grow faster and heard her respond with an excited sigh. His body tensed as he felt a swell of sexual energy and fought to avoid pitching forward as the climax shook through him. A trickle of sweat ran down his back and Miranda smiled as she ran her hands through his hair.

When he looked up he saw that a pool of tears had collected in her eyes.

"Did I hurt you?" he asked, his voice trembling.

"Not at all; I'm just a little overwhelmed. First time, you know...voluntarily anyway."

Her words hit him hard and tears found his eyes as he wrapped his arms around her.

"Sorry Max, I didn't mean to make it all sad at the end," she said sniffling. "It was pretty great though."

"Yeah, I thought so."

"But next time you'd better not go so easy on me," she said making him erupt into laughter as he rolled onto his back.

"Okay... I love you Miranda."

She reached over and brushed his cheek with her hand. "I love you more."

Miranda finished garnishing two plates as Max walked into the living room. Though he'd had her back for nearly six weeks he still wasn't used to seeing her in the kitchen with flour on her cheek and a worried look in her eye.

"Looks amazing," he said as she pulled a roasted chicken from the oven.

"You know what they say about looks, right?"

He headed into the kitchen and put his arms around her; kissing her tenderly.

"I'm sure it will be great."

"Are you ready for opening night?"

"I will never be ready for any opening night. But I am looking forward to it. We'll do the dress tomorrow night, open the night after, then fifty-nine short evenings later and I'll be yours again."

"I'm going to miss you."

"I know, Rand...me too. Sometime next week you'll have to come see the show."

"I can't wait. I'm just painting while you're gone so any night would work."

"Are you still working on the one you won't let me see?"

"I finished it this afternoon," she said as she regarded him nervously.

"Well, can I see it?"

Max followed Miranda into the spare bedroom and watched as she grabbed a canvas from an easel that was turned toward the window.

"It's still a little wet and quite a departure from what I normally do." She turned it to face Max and he

327

examined the piece, a smile slowly forming as he took it in.

The piece appeared to be a swirl of light, almost resembling the outline of a man holding a woman, set against a starry sky. The luminescence of the golden light against the dark night moved Max and he gazed at it fondly.

"It's absolutely beautiful."

"Are you sure?"

He cupped her face with his hand, his veneration clear.

"Completely sure," he insisted as he kissed her.

The two arrived at the exhibition, Max striving to keep a straight face as he escorted Miranda onto the stage. Crew members and designers popped out of the wings as if eager to meet with the woman who had captured their boss.

"Miranda this is Sally. She does all of our costumes."

"So nice to meet you," Miranda smiled.

"Likewise, I never got to work with you last year since you were… "

"Naked, no I remember," Miranda giggled as she shook Sally's hand and Max held back laughter.

Max guided her to another group and introduced her to the rest of the crew. Walking down the backstage steps they emerged in front of the makeup room, Miranda's eyes widening as she saw Annie.

"Oh my gosh, hi."

"Hey lady, good to see you again. You look different with clothes but then so does this one," she indicated toward Max.

"See, a joke that never gets old," Max replied.

"Okay, I get it. Have a great night, you two."

"Thanks Annie," Max said before walking her into the talent garden where Marcia and Katherine waited. They offered welcoming hugs.

"Welcome to the show, Miranda."

"Thanks, I can't wait to see it."

Katherine seemed anxious as she looked at them. "We should probably get you to your seats now."

Max glanced at his watch. "It starts in ten minutes. It'll only take three to get to the loge section."

"That's not exactly where your seats are. Marcia and I took the liberty of making you a private viewing area. We'll have your old friend escort you," she said gesturing toward the Embrace designer who waved at both of them.

"Again I find myself with so much to thank you for," he said as he kissed Katherine's cheek and hugged Marcia.

"Have a great night," she said as she watched them follow the designer out of the stage door.

The three walked up the uneven hillside steps, Max steadying Miranda with this hand. They followed the designer to a small clearing in the hills overlooking the theater. There they saw a blanket, a basket of food and wine, and a pair of binoculars.

"This is just fantastic, thank you," Max said to the designer who had taken him to the Embrace platform so many times the prior summer. He shook his hand earnestly.

"My pleasure. I'll let you too position yourselves tonight," he laughed before descending the stairs and disappearing into the dark hillside.

The auditorium lights began to flicker as the audience members found their seats. Max opened the bottle of wine and poured Miranda a glass. They heard the Master of Ceremonies' voice boom over the speakers as the stage lights faded to black.

"Many of us are familiar with the story of Christ's birth, life and death. But few of us know much of the young woman who accepted the divine opportunity to bear the son of God. Italian painter Raffaello Sanzi may best be famous for his Madonnas and various cherubic inclinations, but it is his Spozalizio which reveals his intrigue for Mary's personal life. Here in all of its grandeur is Raffaello's breathtaking interpretation of The Engagement of Virgin Mary."

The stage lights illuminated to showcase a life-sized version of the piece as its viewers reacted with gasps. Max smiled as he listened to the reactions while Miranda studied the piece through binoculars.

"I can't believe it looks so real."

"Yeah, I have a pretty fantastic job," Max admitted, unaware of Miranda's silent concentration on the piece. "If you think about it, I get to breathe in artistic contributions that span centuries, cross continents, and defy even time itself. And they pay me."

"Oh, I think that kid just sneezed," Miranda said as she pressed her eyes against the binoculars.

Max looked down and smiled as his girlfriend watched for more movement, clearly having ignored his speech.

The show ended with a dazzling recreation of Da Vinci's Last Supper and was accompanied by Meditation, from Massenet's opera Thais. The combination of sight and sound was unspeakably beautiful.

As audience members streamed out of the amphitheater Max helped Miranda down the steps where they joined the sea of patrons. Wrapping her arm around his, she snuggled close as they headed toward the exit.

"Which one was your favorite?" she asked.

"The appearance of Christ to Mary," he replied. "I love Ivanov's work. Too bad you have to go all the way to Russia to see it in person. What about you?"

"Innocence Choosing Love Over Wealth; it gave me chills."

"Was that due to the ambiguity of Wealth's Gender or because of the inadequacy of the fabric covering Love's package?"

Miranda roared with laughter and opened her program, re-examining a picture of the piece. "Wow, it's just a little ribbon, isn't it?"

As they continued toward the exit a man greatly resembling Dr. Jenner hurried toward them. Miranda gasped, panic overwhelming her as she tried to run. Max quickly grabbed her, tucking her into his overcoat as she struggled.

"It's not him, Miranda. He's dead. It's not him."

She continued to fight and twist in his arms as if unable to hear his words.

"Please, Miranda," his voice cracked in desperation. "It's not him. You're safe with me. I'll always protect you."

Instead of allowing herself to be swept up in a storm of dark memories, Miranda's thoughts went to Max. She saw their platform... his smile... her own body enveloped by his in bed... their celestial transcendence among the stars...Max putting his arm out when braking the car...Max steadying her as they walked on the uneven path. She stopped struggling and gave herself over to his protective grasp, trembling in his arms. Holding her through her fear for the first time, his eyes filled with relief.

Not a word was said on the drive home. They arrived at the house and Miranda took a quick bath before joining Max in the bedroom. She entered the dark space, her wet hair dripping onto her robe. She stood in front of the expansive window with a vacant expression. Max slowly approached, a plush robe hugging his body.

"Quite the remarkable evening, huh? There's nothing like art, fine wine, and a bit of terror to make you feel alive," he said, the light from the window the only thing making him visible.

Miranda stared out the window, her eyes red from crying. "I guess I was wrong. I've failed, Max. I'm still afraid. I think I'll always be afraid," she admitted as tears streaked down her face.

"Maybe you will but you'll always be loved and you'll never be alone."

"I wanted to be done... free. I wanted to be strong and well and whole for you," her voice shook.

Max leaned in, touching his chest against the back of her head.

"What if you and I were never intended to be separated from one another? It used to be so important to me; knowing that I didn't need anyone else to be happy. But I can't feel anything when you're not with me. You've shown me what it is to be whole; it's something that I never want to be without again. You make me feel perfect even though I know I'm not. When I'm holding you and loving you and protecting you I feel perfect. What makes you feel perfect Miranda? If you'll tell me I'll do whatever it takes for the rest of my life to give it to you."

Her mind went back to all of the images from before. So many pictures flashed in her eyes telling her the story of his love. In the jeweled night she saw them as spirals of gold light, safe from all harm. *What makes me feel perfect?* She thought about the question for a moment before realizing that she didn't need to think about it at all. Rolling back her shoulders she slipped off the robe and let it slide to the ground.

Completely aware of the meaning behind the gesture Max let his own robe fall to the floor. He wrapped his arms around Miranda, covering her just as he had on so many nights while they stood on their platform. And as the downtown city lights flickered far below them, love's faithful protector offered his injured beauty a promise of undying constancy and his eternal… embrace.

The End